Starfire

MIMI STRONG

BOOKS BY MIMI STRONG

For a current listing of books and
series, visit www.mimistrong.com

CHAPTER 1

Adrian Storm's lips tasted like beer, and I wanted to know if his tongue was the same flavor. I kissed him harder.

It wasn't easy to kiss Adrian.

First of all, we had a major height difference. I'm a curvy blonde, and I'm not exactly short, but I had to stand on my tiptoes just to reach his tasty lips.

Secondly, he was the last person in the world I should have been kissing. Even as I felt a thrill of excitement through my body because this gorgeous, smart, athletic man was kissing me back, I also got the urge to run away.

Something banged over by the dumpster. Did I mention we were standing in the alley behind a bar?

I chose to ignore the noise. Adrian's lips were so soft and enticing, and everything about him was appealing. His hard, muscular chest was just waiting to be discovered. I slipped one hand up between us, under his shirt, enjoying the heat under my palm. His skin was smoother than I expected, with no chest hair.

He kept kissing me, unable to resist my charms. I didn't used to be so popular with guys, but as of that summer, I'd become irresistible to them. Even the hottest guys, who you'd think would be way out of my league, were chasing me around.

Something banged again over by the dumpster.

Adrian pulled away from me, his blue eyes wide with concern. Even in the harsh light of the alley, his high cheekbones and angular face looked perfect and handsome.

"Peaches," he said. "What was that noise?"

I poked him on the nose with one finger. "It's just the sound of you, throwing yourself at my feet, big boy."

He chuckled. "So that's how it is, huh? I only came out here to check on you, because you stormed off in a big huff over a little harmless teasing from your friends."

"I'm fine, Adrian. Sure, I've had a few drinks, and I might fall over, but I feel AMAZING!"

He gave me a sidelong look. "You do *look* amazing, I'll admit that much." His eyes moved, roving up and down over my body. "That dress. Your body. It just doesn't quit. Can you please stop being so sexy around me? I'm going to have to kiss you again."

I blinked up at him. "Why did you stop?"

He grabbed me in his arms, turned me around so my back was against the building, and leaned down to kiss me again. His mouth was hot and exciting.

I looped my arm around his neck, trying to get rid of any space between us.

He reached down to my hips, then secured his hands under my buttocks and hoisted me up. I wrapped my legs around him as he pinned me against the wall.

"Wow," I said, breathless. Nobody had ever picked me up like that before, but Adrian was strong. He had the muscles to handle my curves, and I liked it.

We kissed some more, my pulse pounding with excitement. If kissing Adrian was wrong, I didn't want to ever be right.

Something banged again over by the dumpster.

Adrian grunted an apology and set me down on the ground. We both turned to investigate the noise.

When I'd first come out to the alley, I thought the shapes over by the dumpster belonged to people. Looking more carefully now, I could see the shapes weren't human.

"Oh, it's just raccoons," Adrian said, then he turned to kiss me again.

I pulled away from him. "*Just* raccoons?"

If there's one thing that gives me the willies even worse than dragonflies, it's raccoons. They scare me even more than cougars and bears.

Adrian called out to the raccoons, "C'mere, little guys. Come say hi."

I turned and watched in horror as one raccoon ambled toward us, followed by two more.

My reflexes were slow from drinking, but I sure as hell wasn't sticking around to get mauled by raccoons.

I took off running down the alley, away from danger.

"Bye, Adrian!" I yelled over my shoulder. "See you around!"

I hit the end of the alley, and instead of turning left and going back into the club to join my friends, I turned right and headed for home at a brisk walking pace.

Adrian jogged up behind me, laughing. "You're a chicken," he said.

"Kissing leads to trouble," I said. "I shouldn't have kissed you."

He laughed again. "I meant about the raccoons. Don't worry about the kissing. What's the worst that can happen? You like me. I like you."

He put his arm around my shoulders and gave me a lighthearted squeeze.

I bit my lower lip and kept walking, trying not to think about the worst that could happen. Or what his naked body would feel like on top of mine. Or how quickly we could get back to my house and into my bed, now that we were headed in the right direction.

"We were both too shy in high school," he said. "One of us should have made a move."

"That was a long time ago, Adrian. I don't feel the same way about you now."

He stopped walking and grabbed me confidently as he kissed me again. I melted in his arms, powerless at the touch of his lips and hands.

"You're wrong," he said, pulling away. "You still feel the same way about me. You're wrong about this, like you were wrong about so many things with the yearbook. Remember how you wanted to include a page with everyone's signatures scanned in?"

I scowled up at him, but didn't pull out of his embrace. "That was a great idea. That way people wouldn't have to get their books marked up if they didn't want to."

3

He held me tight against his lean, hard body, which made his words seem more convincing. "Peaches Monroe. I think you're missing the whole point."

"Shut up and kiss me."

He flashed a grin, then leaned down and used his lips for something better than talking.

~

The walk back to my house took over an hour, because we kept stopping to kiss and put our hands all over each other. By the time we reached my front door, I was so hot, I was practically in a lather.

"You do like me," he said as we stood on the porch while I fumbled around for my house keys. "I knew for sure when you sent me that photo of your nipple."

"That was a joke. You're the one who sent me a blurry picture of Mr. Happy."

He laughed. "I sent you a picture of me giving you the thumbs-up gesture. Like this." He put his thumb up close to my face, where my eyes couldn't focus on it properly. "Get it? Thumbs up because I wanted more photos of your goodies!"

"You tricked me with a blurry photo."

"I'd *never* send a dick pic to a girl. She'd send it around to all her friends."

I bit my lower lip. "I'd never do that," I lied.

"If you want to see what I have, the offer is for in-person viewing only."

I pushed the door open. Ahead of us lay the stairs up to my bedroom. "Show time," I said.

"You're drunk," he replied.

I stepped in through the door, but he hesitated.

"You're afraid of raccoons," he said, chuckling.

"Yes, I am. And you're afraid of what I might do to you in my bedroom."

"No, I'm not."

"Then why are you standing out there on the porch? Get in here so I can climb you like a tree again. I liked that." I grabbed his hand and rested it on my hip. "I know you liked it, too. I could *feel* how much you liked it."

4

He grinned, looking sheepish. "You don't actually want me, Peaches. You just want a warm body to soften your fall."

I backed away, further into the house.

"Of course I want you."

Adrian stepped inside and leaned in toward me. I expected him to kiss me, but he just dragged his tongue up the side of my neck. I shivered and tilted my chin up so he could do it again. He did, this time stopping to suck on my pulse point.

Close to me, he murmured, "You want to use me like a drug, to change how you feel. But you said it yourself tonight—you don't feel the same way as you used to."

"Adrian." My voice was pleading.

He pulled away. His blue eyes were cold. "I should get going. It's a long walk to my parents' house."

"Adrian, if you walk out that door tonight and leave me, you'll never walk back in."

He took an audible breath in, then he turned and let himself out. The door clicked shut.

In the silence, I sensed him standing there on the porch, just on the other side of the door.

He'd kissed me so passionately the whole walk home. His hands had been all over me, and I knew he wanted to be with me. Was he just teasing?

I pulled open the door, expecting to see him there with a big grin on his face. The porch was empty, though. Adrian was long gone.

MIMI STRONG

CHAPTER 2

Saturday morning, my brain featured a double matinée showing of that movie nobody wants to see: *Embarrassing Highlights From Last Night.*

We could call this horror film EHLN for short.

When I first woke up, EHLN was at the part where I told my friends they were being jerks for making fun of me.

That night at the bar, I realized they must have been talking about me behind my back. Maybe it was innocent enough, and just friendly teasing, but I wasn't in on the joke, so it wasn't funny to me.

I'd just returned to Washington State from LA, where I'd modeled for a plus-size lingerie photo shoot, and my friends were obviously jealous. Remembering that part of the previous night, I didn't feel so bad, because they had it coming. Also, storming out is badass, so long as you don't forget your purse and have to go back for it.

With a groan, I crawled out of bed while EHLN continued to play in my head.

As I was brushing the fuzz out of my mouth, I revisited another classic moment: drunken kisses.

If my life really was playing on the big screen, and not just in my head, I think most people would agree that Adrian had totally asked for those drunken kisses. He'd been flirting with me on and off all summer, and then he *had* come out to the alley just to check on me. (Ah, the sexy aphrodisiac of concern on a man's face.)

Next, we had walked to my house, kissed some more, argued over yearbook stuff from high school, and talked about me sending him a picture of my nipple. Okay, that was all embarrassing, but not too horrible.

7

The horrible part came next, when he stood in my doorway and flat-out rejected me. Never mind that he had a valid point about why hooking up was a bad idea.

What was that excuse he used?

Something about cushions and falling?

Suddenly and clearly, I saw his face and heard him say, "You want to use me like a drug, to change how you feel."

I spat out the toothpaste in my mouth and moved over to the toilet, feeling like a volcano about to purge.

The movie playing in my head paused and rewound to play the scene again in perfect focus.

Adrian had said, "You don't even want me. You just want a warm body to soften your fall."

As much as it hurt, I had to admit he wasn't wrong.

I was a lousy person who used other people. Looking back, I'd used Keith Raven in LA to cushion my fall. Keith had promised our fling was mutual, but was it? Really?

Keith let me stay at his apartment, treated me with so much kindness, and drove me all around town in his van, and what had he gotten in return? Some sex and a pep talk?

There was something wrong with me. I needed to stop hurting people, and stop being such a mess.

When you're naked and kneeling on the tiles in front of your toilet, choking on regrets, can you ever forgive yourself for your weakness?

~

Someone knocked gently on the bathroom door, which was odd, because Shayla rarely knocked, let alone gently.

I pulled open the door, brushing my teeth for the second time. In came a petite blonde, our friend Golden, who grunted at me on her way to the toilet.

I moved my arms to cover my breasts, though she didn't seem awake enough to notice I was naked. I grabbed a big bath towel from the back of the door and wrapped it around myself.

She said, "Sorry for barging in, but I've been obsessed for hours with getting up to pee, and I couldn't wait another minute."

"No problem," I replied.

"After you left the bar last night, Shayla made me do body shots. Tequila."

"Another fun night at Cougar Town, huh?"

"Did you sleep with Adrian?"

She asked the question over the sound of her tinkling.

Two points to Golden for being direct! I knew she had a crush on him, and they'd been hanging out recently, but just as friends.

Did I sleep with Adrian? No. He turned me down.

"Nope." I rinsed out my mouth and took an assortment of pill bottles from the medicine cabinet. "Vitamins?" I offered.

She was wearing one of Shayla's workout T-shirts, which looked like a dress on Golden's petite frame. Her eyes were rimmed in red, but I couldn't guess if she'd been crying, or if that was just her morning face.

"Do you even care about Adrian?" she asked. "I don't know why you'd bother with him when you have a rich movie star."

I backed toward the door. Even though Golden was being calm and strangely detached, I still felt uncomfortable. Was this a confrontation?

"Of course I care about Adrian."

"Since when?"

"We've been friends for a long time. Like, since high school. We're totally friends, and that's it."

"Plus you work together."

"Not really. He works on the days I'm not there."

"What happened last night?"

"Nothing," I said hurriedly.

"Why did you get mad at everyone and leave the table? We were just teasing you. That's what friends do."

I adjusted the fit of my towel. I wanted to take a shower, but not if Golden was going to keep interrogating me.

"My feelings were hurt," I said. "You guys could try a little harder to pretend you're happy for me. I don't think I was talking about LA that much."

"Beaverdale is small."

"Yes. Your point being...?"

"Some people don't appreciate having their noses rubbed in the fact they haven't left here for anything."

"Are you kidding? I love this town."

"You'd be out of here in a heartbeat if you got the chance."

"Oh, please, Golden. You're just mad at me because things aren't working out in your life how you planned. Don't try to play it like I did something awful. I've done terrible things, but I haven't done them to you, okay?"

She put her face in her hands and made a choked sound.

Oh, flaming bag of poo, she was crying, wasn't she? I pulled the bathroom door open and peered around for Shayla. She was the one who brought Golden home, so that made her responsible for the girl. I adjusted my towel again and tried to think my way out of this problem.

I'm not the kind of girl who instinctively comforts a crying girl. I recently helped out a pregnant girl who was sitting next to me on an airplane, but that was different from this. That girl had a legitimate reason for being upset.

I called down the hallway, "Shayla, we have a situation!"

No response.

I looked back at Golden, who still had her face in her hands.

What would cheer me up if I were in her position?

"Golden. Hey, listen. I'm an asshole, okay? You're really nice, and you're super pretty. I'm sorry about everything, and I'm definitely not into Adrian. He's actually gross. He's too tall and he has weirdly long legs like a giraffe."

She blew her nose on some toilet paper and looked up at me with her giant, baby blue eyes, her adorable face framed by her curls. Her golden hair had been streaked with colors ranging from pumpkin to platinum, and even with messy bedhead, she was cute. I had to wonder: *why wouldn't Adrian make a move on her?*

"He does have skinny legs," she said, nodding in agreement.

"The next time I talk to him, I'll punch him right in the nuts and ask him why he isn't taking you out on romantic dates."

She winced. "Maybe don't punch him."

My cheering-up was working. Golden was almost smiling at my jokes. Now I just needed one more great idea.

"Let's go eat some bacon and pancakes," I said.

She nodded. "Okay."

I heard a shuffling down the hall, and my roommate (and cousin, and best friend) Shayla appeared at her doorway, rubbing her eyes. Her black, wavy hair was fluffy on one side and flat on the other. Her golden brown eyes were barely open.

"Did someone say bacon?" she asked.

"Yes. Five-minute showers and then we saddle up. I promise not to talk about LA."

Shayla shuffled her way into the bathroom, a guilty look on her face. "You can talk about LA if you want. I'm sorry we went too far last night. You know we only razz you because we love you."

"And because you're jealous bitches."

She smirked, one eyebrow quirking up with amusement. "Yes. And because we're jealous bitches. But we're YOUR jealous bitches, and you're stuck with us."

I shrugged. "I'd much rather have you guys than some other jealous bitches."

"Damn straight." She gave me a fist bump, then she dove at the tub and called dibs for the first shower.

I went back to my bedroom, got under the covers, and pulled my laptop off the night stand. Instead of checking email and Facebook, I pulled up google and typed in *Dalton Deangelo*.

The weird thing is, my fingers just did that on their own. I swear I hadn't even been thinking about the guy—not consciously, at least.

I cried out in surprise and horror when the google autocomplete function suggested I was searching for "Dalton Deangelo porn."

With sick curiosity, I clicked the search button.

I knew I shouldn't go looking for the stuff, but knowing it was wrong only made me more interested. It's like… deciding you're going on a diet, and then suddenly all you can think about is eating an entire birthday cake to yourself, and not even a tasty one, but the cheap grocery store cake that makes you hate yourself as you shovel pale, under-flavored lard into your mouth by the fistful.*

*Or so I've heard.

As the search results came in, my jaw literally dropped.

11

MIMI STRONG

CHAPTER 3

I stared at the search results for "Dalton Deangelo porn."

First, the name.

In his adult film, he was billed as Chandler Boink.

When you heard that, you probably laughed, right? I did, too.

And then my google hijinx took a turn for the regrettable. I clicked on an article that had school photos of a young Dalton. My heart broke.

Before his adult film role, and long before he became a famous TV-series actor, he was just a big-eyed kid with dark hair sticking up from his cowlick.

He was born David Blake, and if the article on the gossip website was to be believed, he was four years older than me—twenty-six.

The liar had said he was twenty-four. Or had he? He'd said he was "officially" twenty-four, and then been evasive.

Who was he?

I closed my eyes and imagined his face. David? No, he was a Dalton. No offense to the Davids of the world, but Davids manage grocery stores and fix furnaces. They don't play brooding vampires and sweep small-town bookstore managers up in a tornado of fame and emotional dysfunction.

Touching his school photo on the screen, I felt the emptiness of missing him. He was still in LA, probably hiding from the prying paparazzi in that big house of his, and here I was in Beaverdale, hungover and getting fingerprints of sadness all over my laptop screen.

Shayla popped into my room, one towel around her body and another one around her showered hair. She jumped on the bed next to me.

"Whatcha shopping for?"

I tried to shut the laptop, but she was fast.

"You caught me," I said with a sigh. "But we can't talk about it, because I swore I wouldn't bore everyone with the LA stuff."

She glowered at the screen and chided me, "I hope you didn't find the you-know-what, because he was under eighteen, and that makes it child-you-know-what and very illegal."

"Gross! I wasn't looking for the actual film."

"That's too bad, because here it is."

I screamed. "Delete it! Gross, gross, gross. Get it off my computer!"

"Calm down. They don't have the video, just stills. Like those blurry screen-caps. Hmm." She chuckled. "Chandler Boink."

"That's not funny."

"Hmm." She kept clicking, riveted to the screen.

"Shay, how do you feel about Dalton right now? Like if we didn't know him, and you were just a regular girl again, watching the show with your friends? Do you think his career is ruined because of this?"

"He plays a moody vampire, Peaches. He's not Meryl Streep."

"So, you don't think it matters?"

"Oh, it matters. I don't care how fast you run, you never outrun something like Chandler Boink, starring in *Pizza Delivery Sluts Love Anal.*"

I fell back on the bed and grabbed a pillow to cover my face as I screamed.

Shayla said, "I know, right? Why did it have to be anal? I mean... it's porn, so there's always anal, but why did it have to be in the title? Poor Dalton."

From under the pillow, I asked, "How many girls did he screw?"

Shayla patted my foot. "Just one, baby. Just one in this movie, and I'm sure that's it. You were definitely the second girl he slept with, ever."

I yanked the pillow off my face and blinked at her in disbelief. "Really?"

14

Shayla smirked and shook her head. "No, not really. For a girl genius you sure are dumb sometimes." She laughed. "Really, Peaches, he's probably slept with more girls than a year has days. You're better off without him."

I hugged my arms around my body. "What about him, though? Is he better off without me?"

Shayla raised her eyebrows and gave me a serious stare.

"He's coming to Beaverdale," I said. "There's no Keith here to protect me from Dalton's charms."

"His charms?"

"And his penis."

"And his bumpy chest."

"But mostly his charms," I said, stifling a giggle.

"Right. Because it was his *charms* you were blowing when you guys trespassed onto the Weston Estate."

This time, my giggle would not be stifled. Dalton had taken me to the hot spring of local legend, and I'd played mermaid for him. Just thinking about how good it felt to be naked outdoors with him, touching each other in the dappled sunlight… it put a smile on my face. Even running naked through the woods with some shotgun-wielding maniac on our heels was making me grin, now that some time had passed.

Shayla asked, "What would Keith say if he found out you went back to Dalton?"

"I don't know what he'd say, but I can picture the hurt look on his face."

"Would he consider it cheating? Are you guys dating long distance?"

"No, Shay. I told you. We never were dating. We were just doing a mutual rebound thing, to *unbreak our hearts.*"

She made a popping sound with her mouth.

"You're right," I said. "Unbreak our hearts sounds ridiculous out loud."

"Maybe Keith is the guy for you. I've never heard one bad thing about him."

"He puts parsley in smoothies, and he made me go to the gym."

15

She shook her head. "In that case, you ought to press charges for cruel and unusual treatment."

I glanced over at the heart-shaped mylar balloon tethered to my night stand. It had been a gift from my family, but looking at it made me think of Keith, and how he'd phoned me the night I returned home from LA, exactly when I'd needed him. That was just so like Keith, to do the sweet, sensitive thing to show he was thinking about you.

"I miss Keith," I said. "He's in Italy now, doing something with his life."

"And you're here with me. Poor you."

"He's riding around cobblestone streets on a little scooter, I just know it. Ugh, the Italian girls are going to be all over him. He'll have to beat them away with a breadstick."

"Breadsticks," Shayla said, rubbing her stomach. "I'm so hungry, I could eat tofu wieners."

Just then, Golden called out that she was done in the shower, and I could take my turn.

Shayla looked down at my laptop, frowning. She clicked, then typed furiously for a moment, then frowned some more.

"What is it?" I asked. "More bad stuff about Dalton?"

"Yeah."

"Was there a Pizza Sluts sequel?"

"No." Her voice was high and strained, almost like she was asking a question.

I tried to grab the laptop from her to see, but she yanked it away and clicked the button at the bottom to pop out the battery.

"You're killing me!" I wailed. "Now I need to know what you read! I'm burning with the heat of a thousand suns to know what it was!"

"Too bad. I'm hungry for pancakes and bacon, and… it was nothing at all. I just took the battery out so you'd have your shower and we can all go eat."

I got up and started toward the bathroom, giving her a squinty-eyed look to let her know I didn't believe her.

"Fine," I said. "Murder my laptop. I'll just ask Dalton when I see him."

"Maybe you should give him some space."

"We're friends now. Friends help each other in crisis."

"Yes, but…" She stood up and flicked at the heart-shaped balloon, which had lost some helium and now floated three inches below the ceiling. "Get in the shower before I go Low Blood Sugar Godzilla on you."

Heeding her warning, I rushed off to do as I was told. (You don't mess with Low Blood Sugar Godzilla.) The other girls had gone over the five-minute limit, and my shower was on the chilly side, but the cold water woke me up, and I've always liked how goosebumps make your skin feel tight.

After showering, as I was drying off with a big towel, I noticed that the small hand towel was missing from the rod next to the sink. Golden must have used it to dry off her petite body after her shower.

The realization made me scowl at myself in the mirror. The thing about accepting your own fabulous size is it's not a one-time thing. You have to accept your body over and over again, every time some little thing happens to remind you that life isn't fair, and other people don't walk around with the same curves and creases you have. Some people can dry their little bodies off with a little hand towel. And what do you do when that reality hits you in the face? You smile at your beautiful face in the mirror and tell that girl you love her, big bath towel and all.

~

The three of us went to brunch at Pancake International. It's a little like the International House of Pancakes chain of restaurants, but all the furniture was sourced from yard sales, none of the dishes match, and they only have six laminated menus, so each table has to share one. Actually, they're nothing like IHOP, except for serving pancakes.

I ordered the Elvis in Paris, which is crepes with peanut butter, bananas, and honey; bacon on the side, and… heaven help me but just talking about it now makes my stomach rumble for more. I'm not even going to tell you what the other girls had, because you'll go insane. Let's just say that while the restaurant lacks in menus and decoration, all is forgiven when they wheel over the bubbling chocolate fountain.

We were done with our plates and I'd ordered a mocha refill when Shayla pulled out her phone. Golden and I laughed and pointed at her.

"Screw you guys, it's a stupid rule," she said.

I shrugged and pulled out my phone, since there was no need now to keep ignoring the message alerts.

Shayla had broken our little dining etiquette rule first, so she would be covering the tip portion of the whole meal, and now I was free to check Instagram and the other Usual Suspects.

A message from Adrian popped up first.

Adrian: *There aren't enough five-dollar bills in the float, so I need you to come over and do a run to the bank while it's still open.*

Me: *I think not.*

Adrian: *Then come take over for me and I'll go to the bank.*

Me: *Just put the "Back in Ten Minutes" sign up.*

Adrian: *But people won't clear out of the store! They have takeout coffees and they're all comfortable. We should get rid of the chairs.*

Me: *If we don't have chairs, they just sit on the floor and lean on things. Trust me, chairs are better.*

Adrian: *I'm trapped. Trapped by customers.*

Me: *Pick the most trustworthy one and tell them they're in charge for ten minutes.*

Adrian: *That's no way to run a business.*

Me: *A business makes profits. Peachtree Books is more like a cultural institution.*

Adrian: *Come help me. You owe me.*

Me: *Owe you for what?! For ditching me last night? I only wanted you to come upstairs and talk.*

Adrian: *Your hands were not interested in talking.*

Me: *Oh, please. I barely touched you. Not like when you were playing Hide-n-Seek at my parents' house and you pulled me down onto the bed on top of you.*

Adrian: *That was an accident.*

Me: *Last night was an accident, too.*

Adrian: *You regret kissing me?*

Me: *I don't like labeling things.*

Adrian: *I enjoyed kissing you. No regrets. You have really soft lips.*

Me: *Stop thinking about my lips, because you had your chance and you blew it.*

Adrian: *You mean last night? I told you. I don't want to be with a drunk girl unless she's my girlfriend. I'm not that kind of guy. Don't say I blew my chance, because that's not fair.*

Me: *I meant you had your chance in high school. Back when I was in love with you and you were in love with Chantalle Hart.*

Adrian: *I'm not in love with Chantalle Hart. She's pretty, but she doesn't have a lot of character.*

Me: *You're weird.*

Adrian: *Come visit me. I need five-dollar bills. And I want to see how hungover you are.*

Me: *I'm really busy. I've got a lot of stuff to do at my house.*

Adrian: *I know you're at Pancake International. That's three blocks over. Just come by when you girls are done demolishing the chocolate fountain.*

I looked up from my phone and glanced furtively around the small restaurant. Who told him I was there?

Paparazzi, I thought with horror. They'd followed me here from LA, and now they were taking pictures of me with food crumbs on my chin, and uploading the images from the restaurant. Within minutes, "hilarious" trolls would be using their limited intellect to cobble together misspelled words, making memes of me for Tumblr.

Across the table from me, Golden laughed, her gaze down on her phone. Was she blushing? And twirling one of her pretty blond ringlets with her little hand? Yes, she was. And lately she'd been doing that whenever she flirted with Adrian Storm, which meant... there was no paparazzi stalking me after all. Adrian was two-timing me on the text messages.

I was both relieved and disappointed. I had my privacy, but only because I was just a regular girl.

"Sounds like a plan," Shayla said to Golden, in response to a text Golden must have sent her from two feet away. That's the danger of texting at a restaurant—it's hard to stop once you start.

To me, Shayla explained, "Adrian needs a favor, so we're going to swing by Peachtree Books after here."

"Sure," I said, pretending I hadn't been talking to him myself.

Both of the girls stared at my hand, which was twirling my own blonde hair. My face burned with embarrassment.

"Who were you talking to?" Shayla asked.

"Keith Raven."

"Isn't it the middle of the night in Italy?"

I quickly pulled up his Instagram page on my phone and showed it to them. "We weren't talking. I was just stalking his photos. Like a stalker. Feel free to make fun of me."

"Who's that chick?" Golden asked.

I glanced down at the photo. "That's Tabitha," I said calmly.

"One of the bag-of-hair girls? His sister or his ex?" she asked.

My mouth went dry, but I tried not to let on my surprise. "His girlfriend," I said, my words sounding strained as they came out of my tight throat. "I totally predicted they were getting back together, which is why I wouldn't go to Milan with him. I didn't think it would happen so quickly, but she's a model, too, so… it's only natural… and stuff…"

Shayla reached across the table and patted my hand. "I'm sorry, P."

"Don't look at me like that. Nobody died, okay?"

Golden said, "If you don't mind me asking, why were you sleeping with that Keith guy when you were in LA?"

To answer her question, I scrolled back through a few of Keith Raven's photographs and showed Golden one of him wearing nothing but a pair of tattered jeans, his chiseled torso catching the light and shadows like a sculpture.

"Oh," she said, nodding.

"His personality is just as nice," I said.

Her face scrunched up. "Didn't that feel weird, being naked with a real model? I know you did the underwear thing, which makes you a real model, too, but…?"

I sighed. "Keith dragged me to the gym once, but he never made me feel fat. He said he used to be shallow, but I don't know if I believe it. Whenever he looked at me, I felt like he was seeing my soul."

Golden's eyes widened. "Scary."

Shayla leaned across the table and socked Golden on the arm. (I totally forget what a tomboy Shayla is until we're out with smaller girls and she goes around punching them, like a dude.)

"Why scary?" Shayla asked. "Is your soul all crusty and foul?"

Golden laughed, but the smile didn't reach her eyes. "We don't want guys to know what we're really like. Not until it's too late for them to escape."

Shayla tried to punch her arm again, but Golden jumped up from the chair and excused herself to the washroom.

"That girl has a dark side," I said to Shayla once we were alone. "She practically told me to stay away from Adrian or she'd murder me in my sleep."

"Did he do more than walk you home last night?"

"We're just friends."

"Blowjob friends or handjob friends?"

I pulled out some money for my portion of the bill and pushed the tray over to Shayla. "None of the above, which means I'll be swept up in Hurricane Dalton. And I'm kinda looking forward to it."

"But we hate him, right?"

"I'm willing to admit I may have overreacted just a bit to his movie script and those cheesy lines he fed me."

"Peaches, I hate to break it to you, but…"

"What?"

Golden returned from the washroom, and the waiter came by to clear more dishes.

"I'll tell you later," Shayla said. "It's probably nothing."

As we gathered our purses and left the restaurant, I did wonder why she was being so cryptic, and if it had something to do with her removing my laptop battery, but then we walked outside and my attention was caught by a stylish woman slowly approaching in a convertible.

I recognized her as Dottie Simpkins, a seventy-two-year-old woman who gives charm workshops at the Beaverdale Community Center. She dyes her hair pink, and I'd like to say she doesn't look a day over sixty, but my eyes work too well.

Dottie wore big sunglasses and a bigger grin. In the seat next to her was a rust-colored dog the size of a standard poodle.

21

"Hellooooooooo!" Dottie called out as she drove by slowly, waving at the three of us. We waved back and stood motionless on the sidewalk, as though we'd showed up in that spot, at that time, just to watch the very small parade of Dottie in her car.

"I want to be like that when I'm old," Golden said.

"I want to be like that right now," Shayla said. "But younger, and with a hot guy next to me."

"You could do worse than a Labradoodle," Golden joked. "They're intelligent, devoted, and hypo-allergenic."

"Those are the exact qualities I want in my next boyfriend," Shayla said. "Also, I'd like for my next one to be gay. I think I could really commit to someone who won't sleep with me."

"Labradoodles are good for cuddling."

"Golden, do you have puppies you're trying to unload?"

"Did you know they were originally bred as guide dogs, but people really took to them as pets?"

I turned and gave Golden an appreciative look. You gotta love it when the topic turns to your friend's field of experience, and they get to show off a little, but in a cool, understated way.

Golden worked as a veterinarian's assistant, and was utterly happy with her career. She didn't make vastly more money than me, but I envied the "realness" of her job. Unlike being a bookstore manager, people didn't ask her what she was planning to do next.

We walked the four blocks to Peachtree Books, and I couldn't help but gloat that Adrian had said it was three blocks, not four, and he was so, so, so wrong about that. I was right and he was wrong.

He was helping a customer when we walked in, so Shayla and Golden started browsing the new arrivals, and I grabbed some large bills from the register and crossed over to the bank.

When I arrived back at the bookstore with fives and rolls of coins, Adrian was entertaining the girls with a story about some idiot running through the forest in the dark.

He continued, "And then Peaches tripped over a tree branch and went splat on the path. She tried to blame poor, nearly-toothless Cujo for her clumsiness."

Apparently, the idiot being discussed was me.

"Your dog attacked me!" I injected.

22

"Old Cujo can barely attack mushed-up dog food from a can."

"He's such a sweetheart," Golden said. "I always enjoyed his checkups, and seeing your mom, but now you get to bring him to see me."

"Right." Adrian turned and gave me a funny look.

Golden noticed him making extended eye contact with me and shot me a hurt look.

"Your change is in the drawer," I said, backing away toward the door. My armpits began to sweat as memories of the previous night came back unwanted. Me, kissing Adrian. Adrian, kissing me back, but then leaving me. All those moments back in high school, when I would have just melted if he'd given me the slightest interest. And now... seeing him invading *my* bookstore, the place that used to be my domain.

As I stared at Adrian's lips, pink and surrounded by blond facial hair stubble that glinted like raw, brown sugar, I felt a powerful desire to kiss him again. I'd been drunk enough the night before that I couldn't remember exactly how he kissed, but I did recall how it made me feel.

I shuffled closer to the door, wanting to leave, but also wanting to stay in his company. Why was Golden looking at me with so much suspicion? Could she read my mind? Did she know I was thinking about Adrian's hot mouth around my nipple? My face flushed.

Peaches, don't think about anyone licking your sweater puppies. Don't think about them cupping your flesh and hungrily dragging their tongue across your flesh, your nipple hardening and straining toward their hot, open mouth.

The door behind me jingled merrily with a customer walking into the bookstore, and I jumped.

"Not so fast," Adrian said, pointing an accusatory finger at me.

I caught the open door and backed away, toward the sunny sidewalk. "Dude, today's my day off. You're working, not me."

"Staff meeting," he said.

"News flash: we don't do staff meetings."

Adrian crossed his arms, his sinewy forearms drawing my eye. The guy really had filled out since high school, when he was so skinny and tall, like a string bean. I'd crushed on him pretty hard back then, and now that he'd filled out, he was even hotter—not just because muscles are hot, but because he looked strong enough to handle a curvy woman.

Adrian shrugged and rolled his shoulders back, his round bicep muscles straining against his black Led Zeppelin T-shirt, which was from his high school wardrobe and on the small side.

Oh, yes. Adrian had the strength to handle some dangerous curves. He could probably pick me up and hold my back to the wall, as I wrapped my legs around his waist, and...

"Seven o'clock," he said. "I'll just swing home and grab my mom's car, then I'll come pick you up at your house."

"For a staff meeting?"

He glanced over at Golden, who was now pretending to peruse the magazines with Shayla. "Yeah. For bookstore business. I have some ideas."

"Is Gordon Junior coming?" (Gordon is the reluctant owner of Peachtree Books. He inherited the business with the building, and he spends most of his time next door with his true love, the wine store.)

Adrian smirked and said sarcastically, "Of course Gordie's coming. He's *very*concerned about all the details." He smirked some more. "I have some information about Black Sheep Books."

"Those sheep-lovers?" I quickly covered my mouth in embarrassment, since there were customers all around. My filters weren't working well, due to the hangover.*

*Sure, we'll blame the hangover.

"Seven," he said with authority, then he dashed off to help a vertically-challenged customer pull down a book from the top shelf. With his height, he could actually reach everything in the store without needing a stepladder. He was really good at the job, and he seemed so comfortable and friendly with the customers, too. And now he wanted to call a staff meeting? Was he trying to take over my job as manager?

I didn't like any of these new developments, but that didn't mean I wasn't excited about seven o'clock.

CHAPTER 4

We left the bookstore and walked Golden over to her car, still parked at Cougar Town from the night before. She didn't seem to want to say goodbye to us, so we let her drive us back to the house.

At the house, she seemed like she wanted to talk to me some more about Adrian. Naturally, I bolted from the vehicle like it was on fire, without looking back.

Back at home, I started looking through my closet for something perfect to wear to my first-ever staff meeting.

A few times, I did get the tugging sense I was forgetting something important. I'd forgotten all about the Dalton stuff on the internet, and whatever Shayla had uncovered.

By the time I remembered to ask Shayla for my laptop battery back, she'd already left for her shift at the restaurant, and I didn't dare search her room for it. The last thing I wanted was to reach under her mattress or open a drawer and come face to face with her vibrator, currently named The Assassin.*

*Possible marketing slogans for a vibrator named The Assassin:

1. The Assassin. Because he gets in and does the job.

2. The Assassin doesn't ask questions before, and he doesn't demand cuddles after.

3. When you need to slay a dangerous ladyboner, call in The Assassin.

4. Service with a smile. Just kidding. The Assassin never smiles.

5. The only bridal shower "gag gift" that will have her gagging for more.

6. Deluxe personal massager. Dishwasher safe, top rack only.

7. Fifty shades of... that's all we can say, due to trademark laws regarding copyright infringement, but you know what we mean, wink wink.

8. Girlfriend, this is a vibrator. Put it on your sweet spot. If you don't know where that is, you're about to find out.

9. Every night is Date Night. Vibrating bow-tie and tuxedo accessories sold separately.

10. Your curves look so good in those sweatpants. Girl, you're making me crazy horny. Now step away from that rum raisin ice cream you inexplicably like so much, put on some Justin Timberlake, and get ready to have your sweetness annihilated by The Assassin.

(That last one may have been a little specific, but you get the idea.)

~

My clingy wrap dress, Creamsicle orange, made me look delicious.

I stared at myself in the mirror, turning from side to side, letting the fabric swing out then fall back down to graze my thighs. The dress was one of my scores from my trip to LA. It came from a designer boutique, and the cut and quality was so good, I didn't even consider wrestling on a pair of Spanx underneath. Tight undergarments would ruin the sensory experience of such a gorgeous dress.

What point is there to beautiful, soft fabric, if you can't feel it against your skin? Skin is for more than holding your spleen inside your body and all that stuff your learn in science class. Skin is a canvas for personal art, a medium for piercing, and a damn handy place to keep your body glitter. It's also nice for licking, sucking, and spanking.

At 7:05, Adrian knocked on the front door.

My cheeks reddened at my naughty thoughts while I ran to answer.

I passed one more mirror along the way and thought of that quote by style icon Coco Chanel: "Before you leave the house, look in the mirror and remove one accessory."

My bracelet with the turquoise beads was one of my favorite pieces, but I probably didn't need sparkling clip-on earrings *and* a necklace, did I?

The shadow of Adrian on the other side of the privacy glass shifted, and a butterfly flitted around my belly. He knocked again, louder, and I grinned deviously over keeping him waiting. Hands shaking, I took off the pendant necklace and dropped it in the bowl next to the spare keys.

I opened the door to find Adrian's back to me. He looked even taller from behind, and he wore grown-up clothing rather than his usual jeans and black T-shirt. Gray trousers made his legs look long, but not too skinny, and his butt looked (dare I say it?) perky. Completing his date outfit was a fitted dress shirt, black with gray pinstripes, rolled up at to the elbows for a casual look. His blond hair looked crisp and recently-trimmed.

A summer breeze shifted, and a fresh scent with a hint of citrus hit me just as he turned around.

"Wow," he said, staring down at my dress, his blue eyes open wide. "You look like a girl."

"I am a girl."

"So people keep telling me."

"What people?"

"My mother, for one."

"How is your mother?" I asked.

He stared down at my peaches, mouth slightly open.

I held my hand in front of my cleavage and moved my fingers like a hand puppet. In a silly voice, I said, "Tell your mother my sweater puppies say *hello*."

He stepped backward on the porch and looked down at his feet, shuffling them as he stuffed his hands in his pockets.

"You look nice, too," I said in the ensuing awkward silence. "Is that how you used to dress when you were a high-powered real estate mogul?"

He coughed. "Mogul?"

"That's the right word, isn't it? Mogul. Or am I thinking of those ski bumps? *Mogul*. Mogul?"

"Mogul." He looked up thoughtfully, avoiding my eyes.

"Mogul. Hmm. Now it just sounds made up."

Adrian pulled out his phone. "We can solve this dilemma in two shakes."

After a few seconds, he glanced up at me, tilted his head to the side, and put the phone back in his pocket. "Interesting," he said.

"Are you going to tell me?"

27

"Are you going to invite me in off your porch? Or did you mean what you said last night? That if I walked out, I wouldn't walk back in again, or something to that effect."

To avoid answering him and talking about my humiliation the night before, I pulled my phone out of my purse and looked up the word. FYI, mogul can describe an influential person, and it also can be a bump on a ski hill, or a member of the dynasty that ruled India until 1857.

As I put away my phone, I said, "We were pretty drunk last night. I'm sorry for trying to take advantage of you, but you're just SO handsome and desirable. Honestly, you'd better stay out on that porch, because heaven help you if you set foot inside my lair again."

"I knew I should have brought my bear spray."

He made a show of coming right up to the door frame, resting his forearms high on the frame, and looking around but not coming in. For an instant, I was reminded of the first time Dalton Deangelo came to visit, and how he'd lurked on the porch before trying to scare me with his vampire character's fangs.

"You're not invited in," I said coldly.

"Why not? Where's Shayla?"

"It's Saturday night, and I'm wearing a designer dress from a boutique in LA. Look at my toes, peeking out from my dressy sandals. That's a fresh pedicure, and fresh pedicures always need to go out, so, no, you're not invited in to eat potato chips and feel me up on my secondhand sofa."

Grinning, he said, "That's good, because I have reservations for us at DeNirro's."

I pulled my purse strap up my shoulder and grabbed my keys. "Now we're talking."

~

On the short drive to the restaurant, I tried to pry out of him whatever information he had on Black Sheep Books, but he refused to give it up so easily. *Typical Adrian, playing hard to get.*

He really did have restaurant reservations, which was a good thing, because the little Italian restaurant with the red-checked tablecloths was full of people. The air was rich with that gorgeous Saturday night aroma of perfume, wine, and fresh bread. Absolute heaven. And the gorgeous man sitting across from me didn't hurt, either.

"You shaved," I said once we were seated.

He leaned in across the table and patted his cheek. "Feel."

I reached across the table tentatively and stroked his cheek. "Smooth as a freshly-powdered baby's bottom."

He took my hand, and—to my surprise—popped my thumb into his mouth. He made eye contact with me as he sucked my thumb in his hot mouth. My nipples went BA-WANG. He licked the tip of his tongue along my thumb. All the other parts of me also went BA-WANG.

Chuckling, he withdrew my thumb and gave me a wink. "Couldn't resist," he said.

My cheeks flushed with heat as I looked around the crowded restaurant. It didn't seem like anyone had noticed, but ever since I'd become an Internet-Famous Person, I'd gotten a touch paranoid about photographers and evil reporters—not that they're typically found in a small town like Beaverdale, Washington.

I grimaced and pretended to be disgusted by Adrian's saliva on my thumb. I rubbed off my thumb with a cloth napkin. I whisper-yelled, "How dare you fellate my thumb in public."

"You don't enjoy a little pre-dinner thumb fellatio?" he asked, feigning innocence.

The waitress, who thankfully wasn't anyone I knew, came up to take our drinks order. She gave me a knowing smile and said, "Pitcher of sangria again?"

Adrian laughed. I didn't know the waitress, but she sure knew me. I kicked him under the table, then ordered a Diet Coke. He ordered a root beer float.

"That was my favorite drink in high school," he explained. "I'd rather have beer, but I'm not drinking if you aren't. You already outsmart and outwit me too easily when I'm sober. You always did."

I laughed, shaking my head at his attempt to flatter me.

Did I outsmart him all the time? Of course I did. I knew that.

His flattery washed over me repeatedly, and I did feel myself glowing from the compliment. I always have been a smart girl, even though I've done insanely stupid things (like not realize I was pregnant, until I was giving birth at fifteen, alone and unprepared).

He said a few more flattering things, but I didn't catch all the words. Instead of hearing him, I shuddered at the memory of nearly dying alone because of my stupidity. Why could I never just enjoy someone saying something good about me without torturing myself with my mistakes?

Perhaps it was an internal fail-safe to keep me from getting a big ego. For the last few days, acquaintances had been coming out of the woodwork, complimenting me on scoring an underwear line endorsement and being the model for the ad campaign. To most of those people, I'd blurted out, "Yeah, but it's a plus-size line, so they wanted a regular girl, not a model." Even though I *was* a model, part of me still rejected the notion.

The waitress brought our drinks, and we ordered dinner. I sipped my Diet Coke as I eyed Adrian's root beer float, which was foaming over like a science fair volcano.

He offered me a taste, but I demurred.

"Shouldn't we start the staff meeting?" I asked.

"Totally. It begins with thumb fellatio. I already did yours, so it's your turn."

I snorted, but he held his thumb out to me in a very flirty manner.

I snorted again. "You're messing with me. Why can't you just be normal? Why do you have to look things up on your phone and not tell me? Why the teasing?"

"Anticipation is the best part. When I was a real estate—" he grinned "—*mogul*... the most fun I had on any project was the startup. Pushing hard to get a piece of land rezoned. Tearing the architectural drawings in half and telling the team we could do better." His blue eyes glinted with a ferocity I'd never seen before.

"You sound excited."

"I used to get so keyed up, I couldn't sleep. I was like a degenerate gambler, except the socially acceptable kind."

"What the hell are you doing here, working entry-level part-time jobs?"

"I could ask you the same thing. You were the smartest girl in school, and you would have been valedictorian, if Brie Harrison hadn't... *you know*."

"Know what?" My heart started to race. Even after five years, it still nauseated me to think of Brie Harrison smugly taking the stage for the valedictorian address. She gave a terrible speech, too. She started off by quoting lyrics from a Britney Spears song. I think she meant to be ironic, but it was just insincere.

Adrian explained, "Well, you do know her dad paid off some people with a generous donation to the school's expansion fund, right?"

I gasped. "No!"

"Anywhere there's power and money, there's corruption."

"How do you know this?"

"I have no hard evidence, but most of the students actually voted for you. Samples don't lie."

"I didn't think people liked me that much."

He grinned. "People liked you a lot more than you thought, but more importantly, they knew you were the smartest girl—or boy—in the class."

"I'm reeling, Adrian. I'm totally sober, but the restaurant is spinning around me. I'm literally reeling from this information! I should have been the valedictorian." I patted my cheeks with both hands, making a light slapping sound. "My whole life could have been different."

"As cruddy as it seems, she may have done you a favor. Brie went off to New York with all these expectations hanging over her. I bet every time she stumbled, she got that Impostor Syndrome thing. Where you feel like a fraud, and they're going to catch on to you."

Our pasta hadn't arrived yet, but the bread had. Adrian unfolded the burgundy cloth and set a warm bun on my plate without asking, before serving himself.

"Did you have that Impostor Syndrome?" I asked.

"Nope. I guess that makes me a monster, because I thought I deserved every bit of success."

"Was there a girlfriend? You said you had a big house and you felt lonely."

31

He looked away. "There was one or two. Mainly one."

"And?"

"There's nothing fun about getting your heart ripped out, and it's not that special of a story. You've heard it before. Boy meets girl, boy becomes successful man, girl likes shopping, man goes broke and gets dumped."

"Any girl who dumped you over money isn't worth having. I mean, you do have terrible taste in music, but you have other great qualities."

He laughed. "I never did convert you to being a Led Zeppelin fan, did I?"

"I tried to like the bands from your shirts. Boy, that sounds really immature now that I hear myself saying it."

He finished gobbling down his first bun and reached for another for each of us. He certainly wasn't afraid of carbohydrates, though his lean frame would say otherwise.

"Why Led Zeppelin?" I asked.

He laughed. "Honestly, I listened to the same music as everyone else, you know? I mostly wore those shirts because nobody else did, and I thought it made me seem interesting. The shirts and the lip ring were a disguise. A kid's gotta do something to distract everyone and distance himself from his dad, the cop. My plan didn't work that well, though."

"I never thought of you as a cop's kid. You were just Adrian. With your spider legs and your floppy hair, always reading Stephen King books at lunch."

"Ouch."

"You were cute."

He nodded, smiling at the memory. "The up side to being a loner is you don't get much peer pressure. I never even smoked so much as a cigarette, let alone anything more interesting. A lot of cop's kids are way more rebellious."

"Do you think people expected you'd snitch to your dad?"

He smirked. "The irony is that thanks to my dad, I knew who all the dealers were and where the bootleggers operated. I had it all, but didn't know what to do with it."

"You could have been the most popular guy in school."

He nodded, his expression wistful. "And you could have been valedictorian, except for some bribe money."

As I let these revelations wash over me, Adrian flicked at his lower lip with his tongue, which took me back in time, to watching him flick that piercing he used to wear in his lower lip.

"When did you take the lip ring out?" I asked.

"The first day I started working after school. I arrived in Seattle, by bus, and saw a bunch of skinny kids with piercings hanging out on the sidewalk outside the bus station. When I walked by, they nodded at me like I was one of them."

"Street kids?"

"Yes. But I *wasn't* one of them, because I had an internship and an apartment lined up. I slipped the lip ring out about two blocks later."

"Did the hole completely close up?"

He took a drink of his root beer using the straw, then said, "I'm not dribbling, am I?" He patted his chin, pretending he wasn't sure himself. "It closed up after two weeks."

"I wish I could have kissed you back when you had the piercing." I gave him a flirty look. "Just to satisfy my curiosity."

He squared up his shoulders and gave me a smoldering look, his blue eyes blazing with interest. "We're adults now, Peaches. You don't need an excuse like curiosity. If you want to kiss me, just kiss me. No labels, no restrictions."

We were interrupted by our dinner arriving, hot and fragrant with fresh parmesan cheese. My cheeks were flushing from all the talk about kissing, and I felt nervous about what might happen after dinner.

I pushed away my half-empty glass of Diet Coke. "I'll get a vodka and soda," I told the waitress.

"Make it a double and I'll have the same," Adrian said.

We silently dug into our food, eating and exchanging goofy looks. The drinks arrived, and we stared into each other's eyes as we started to drink.

His eyes crinkled, and he didn't set the glass down, so I didn't set mine down either. I won the drinking contest, setting down the glass, empty except for ice, first.

"Liquid courage," he joked.

"Courage for what? Are we going on a crime spree after this?"

"Thanks to some recent intel from my dad's cop buddies, I've got a few ideas."

I shook my head, a perma-grin plastered on my face. "What am I getting myself into?"

"A bunch of trouble we should have gotten into five years ago. You know, I didn't even have fun at prom."

The vodka sent delightful swirls of relaxation through my body. "You never came to prom."

He made a funny face. "Oh, I was there. For all of ten minutes. You were having such a good time with your friends, and Jett Spencer." He frowned. "I had this whole speech figured out, and I was going to tell you about Brie rigging the vote, too. But you looked so happy, and I wanted you to be happy, even if it was with Jett Spencer."

"You need to stop dropping these bombshells on me, Adrian."

"Black Sheep Books is closing down."

My jaw dropped open.

Adrian grinned.

My jaw remained in the ajar position.

He explained, "The owners have been in the red for two years, and they're calling it quits. On behalf of Gordon, I'm negotiating taking over their inventory, rather than having them liquidate and glut the local market."

I whispered, "I hate those sheep-lovers."

He nodded, looking sly. "I know you do. That's why I wanted to tell you the good news myself." He rubbed his hands together. "Negotiations are going well."

My head was buzzing with vodka and the intoxication of Adrian's attention, plus this delicious news.

"I hope you stick it to them," I said.

"Oh, they're going to spread wide for all the things they've done, like poaching employees."

"You're going to bend them over that negotiation table, aren't you?"

"I'm going to spank that exposed ass. And after we've had our way with them, we'll be back on top."

I licked my lips. "My panties are so wet right now."

Adrian pretended to gulp-swallow with nervousness. "Negotiating makes me hard, too."

"You're a dirty boy."

He gave me a devious look. "You don't know the half of it. We could move Peachtree into their space and take over a fifteen-year lease at below-market rent."

I groaned. "How big is it?"

"Oh, Peaches. It's big. So big. Think of the things we could do with all that space."

"In-store readings. More staff picks. A modest used books section."

His eyelashes fluttered. "Three thousand square feet, plus a below-grade stock room that isn't counted toward the triple net."

"Sweep these dishes off the table and take me now!"

He laughed, then growled at me, "Don't think I won't."

As we stared into each other's eyes, I grabbed his hand and brought it to my mouth.

Starting at the tip of his thumb, I swirled my tongue one around his digit, then plunged it halfway into my mouth.

Adrian's eyelids widened, and he sat up straight in his chair. I gently sucked his thumb as he held completely still, his breath frozen.

His thumb tasted salty and fleshy, and my mouth watered around it as I took him deeper.

He let some breath out, muttering swear words softly. I grazed my teeth over his fleshy thumb, then bobbed my head and took him in to the hilt. I wrapped my lips tightly around him and gave a powerful suck.

He tilted his chin up with respect and gave me a nod.

I withdrew his thumb slowly, dragging my lips tightly along the surface, then gave the tip a soft kiss.

"Yum," I said.

"Good staff meeting. Should we get the rest of our pasta plates to go?"

"To go where?"

"Somewhere we should have gone five years ago."

MIMI STRONG

CHAPTER 5

Rollerskating.

Adrian Storm took me to the Beaverdale Rink so we could go rollerskating.

"I haven't been here in years," I said as I laced up the rented skates, white with four blue wheels on each one. The arena scheduled times where people could rollerblade, but Saturday night was for the old-fashioned style of skating only.

"They're actually busy tonight," Adrian said, peering through the plexiglass shield from where we sat in the bleachers, putting on our gear. I had bare legs due to my pretty orange dress, so I opted for the kneepads, just to be careful.

As I pulled on the kneepads, I shot Adrian a lusty look and said, "These might come in handy later."

"They dim the lights in the bleachers after nine, and they send the little kids away."

"Yes, I know. You act like I'm the one who lived in big cities the past five years."

He chuckled. "Of course. Then you've probably heard that sometimes people go for a romantic skate and take a little detour into the bleachers to... catch their breath."

"I bet they do."

He stood up and took my hand. "Let's skate. I can't wait to see that fancy dress swirl around your beautiful legs."

As we walked down the bleacher steps carefully, I looked at Adrian's legs and tried to think of a compliment to give him, but the black roller skates made his long legs look even longer, and all I could do was giggle at his spider legs.

37

"What are you giggling at?" he asked. "You're drunk." He pointed up to the posted regulations. "Look at that: *Inebriated patrons will be escorted out.*"

We reached the rink surface. Adrian proceeded to windmill his arms and, from a dead standstill, wipe out on his ass.

People kept rollerskating in a circuit, paying us little attention. I helped him back up carefully. "You're the drunk one," I teased, slinging his arm over my shoulder.

The music changed to an Abba song, and a few people skating the circuit cheered. Adrian considered this busy for the rink? We weren't alone, but the place wasn't exactly crowded, either. A dozen little kids were racing around as fast as their parents would let them, and another forty people were skating around at a more leisurely pace. A good portion were white-haired seniors, with big smiles on their faces.

Adrian and I started skating, both of us a little rough at first, but getting into the flow. Soon we were skating along smoothly, holding hands like most of the other couples, and Adrian got confident enough to drop my hand and skate ahead to do a spin for me. He actually pulled it off, causing me to say, "Not bad, Mr. Storm."

He came back to my side, put his arm across my shoulder, and used his free hand to tilt my chin toward him. He kissed me as we skated past the speakers. I kept my eyes open for balance, but he closed his, getting that dopey, sweet look guys get when they can't believe they're kissing someone.

The lights dimmed, the music changed to a romantic folk rock song, and the small kids filed off the rink. Adrian kept kissing me, and our skating speed slowed and slowed.

I noticed a very grown-up feeling I was having between my legs. Miss Kitty was purring.

We came to a standstill near the gate we'd come in through. My purse was checked into a storage cubby back at the skate rental counter, but our shoes and leftover pasta boxes were sitting up in the bleachers.

I pulled away from Adrian's succulent lips and glanced up toward our pile of stuff, halfway up the bleachers and barely visible. "We could take a break and finish our dinner," I said.

He reached up and touched my ear. I'd forgotten I was wearing earrings. My earlobe pinched as he fiddled around with the earring, probably looking for the backing and not realizing they were clip-ons. The first one fell off into his hand, and he'd barely touched the other one when it did the same.

"What are you doing?" I asked.

"We're recreating lost teen experiences, aren't we? Let's go up into the dark bleachers for some good, old-fashioned necking."

"Necking! You sound so old-timey."

He tucked a strand of hair behind my ear and ran his fingers down my neck, then along my throat to my collarbone.

He murmured, "Your heart's beating fast."

"From all the rollerskating," I lied.

"Nobody's looking. Quick, let's get on up there."

I pushed open the hip-height wooden door, freshly painted but dented from decades of hockey games. In the winter, rollerskating switched to ice skating and hockey games, and the arena would be packed every Saturday night with hockey fans and parents.

We climbed up, stepping sideways so we didn't murder ourselves on our roller skates. We grabbed our things and proceeded up higher and higher, until we were in darkness. I could barely see Adrian's face, but I found his lips easily.

We kissed, sitting next to each other on the flat wooden bleacher step. I took his lower lip in my mouth and felt carefully with my tongue for the tiny scar from his lip ring.

He pressed his tongue hungrily into my mouth as one hand came across and landed on my bare knee.

He moved his lips away from mine, and over to my ear. He took my earlobe in my mouth and gently sucked it, the way he had my thumb. My skin prickled all over, and I felt myself begin to glow with sweat.

Moving down my neck, he licked and sucked and gently bit my skin until I was moaning. I could hear the crackle of his saliva as he sucked my neck, let go, and held it again with gentle pressure.

At the same time, his hand moved slowly up my leg with trepidation, like the hand of a young guy trying to get to third base for the first time.

39

I whispered, "Adrian, are you trying to get to third base?"

He pulled his hot mouth away from my neck, the saliva evaporating and cooling my neck suddenly. To accentuate this, he blew air gently on my neck. I shuddered with pleasure at the sensation.

In the shadows, I saw him lick his lips, then say, "It would be a crime for me to skip second base." His gaze was directly on my peaches, looking luscious and heaving from my rapid breathing.

"May I?" he asked, holding out both hands, inches from my sweater puppies.

I grabbed his hands by the wrists and brought his hands firmly to me, squeezing over his hands to get him started.

"This is heaven," he said, squeezing them together and lowering his face to the crease, breathing deeply.

I entwined my fingers in his hair and held him tightly to me—not smothering-tightly, but firm enough to let him know I liked him touching me.

"You smell unbelievable," he said, his voice muffled.

My elbow over his head, I reached around to my back and unzipped my dress several inches. I shrugged the wrap dress down, and it fell to my waist. The cool, musty air of the rink hit my moist skin and brought the moment into crystal clarity. I unlatched my bra and let it fall away.

I braced my hands on the flat surface behind me, and leaned back, my torso at an angle and my hard nipples pointing at Adrian as an invitation. Oh, how I wanted his smart-talking mouth on my breast, his tongue circling my nipple.

He took a deep breath, got up from his seated position, and came around to kneel before me. Without a word or glance at my bare chest, he unlaced one of my roller skates and pulled it off my foot, and then the other. He grasped my knee pads and also removed them.

When I saw him slip my folded-up knee pads under his own knees, I realized what he was doing, and laughed nervously. He was planning to be on his knees for a while. I shivered at the thought, and then we were kissing again, his hand on the back of my neck to bring me down to reach him.

He left my lips and kissed a trail along my cheek, and then down the neck, on the side where he hadn't been yet. As he sucked my earlobe, my whole body squirmed, as if all of me was trying to get into his beautiful, wet mouth via my earlobe.

Adrian shifted back, placed both hands against the small of my bare back, and moved his face down my chest. His smooth, freshly-shaved chin slid easily across my skin, and he rubbed the sides of his cheeks along the outer edge of each breast and around the bottom with his chin. Finally, he targeted my nipple, taking it in with a wide open mouth, slurping as much margin of flesh as he could.

He sucked, the sound of his mouth crackling again in the dark, relative quiet of the upper bleachers. The speakers were miles away, and the music was good, but I was barely aware of the song playing. With Adrian's hands on my back and his mouth on my breast, I was contained only within his touch, and nothing else in the world mattered.

One song blended into the next, and people continued to roller skate far below us. The announcer called out over the music for everyone to change direction, to counter-clockwise.

Adrian pulled away and said, "Change direction."

He kissed my lips, his tongue touching mine. I moaned with pleasure against his mouth.

He pulled away and moved back down, his tongue swirling around one nipple, then the other, in what I imagined was counter-clockwise.

I let my legs move apart.

He didn't make a move, but continued to handle and taste my peaches.

I leaned back and parted my legs enough so I could hook one foot around his back and pull him closer for more contact. He shifted in to kiss my lips again, and I hugged him tightly, pressing my tongue-damp breasts against his dress shirt.

His hands moved to my thighs and stroked up and down my smooth, moisturized, bare legs. Was he going to try for third base? He didn't seem that eager, which was a shame, because Miss Kitty really wanted a pat. I could feel my pulse throbbing down inside, and all these soft, sweet kisses were driving me crazy.

Adrian kissed my earlobe, breathing in deeply with his nose nestled in my hair. "I'm really digging your tits," he said. "I mean breasts. Sorry."

I giggled and licked the side of his neck, finishing by catching his earlobe between my teeth. "You can call them tits," I whispered. "Or peaches, melons, or anything fruit-related."

He held my melons with both hands. "I want to take them home with me. What do you think? Can I borrow them for a few days?"

"You're funny."

He squeezed, supporting them up, then letting them drop, still nestled in his hands.

"You didn't have these in high school," he said.

I walked my fingers up his arms and squeezed his upper arms. "And you didn't have these muscles."

"We both filled out for the better."

"Did you really mean what you said at dinner, about prom? Were you really disappointed I went with Jett?"

"I would have never asked you. It wasn't until Jett asked you in the cafeteria that day, that I even figured out how much I liked you."

I playfully pushed him away. "Too bad. I would have rocked your world after prom."

He frowned and dropped his hands down to my knees. "Like you rocked Jett's world?"

I frowned back instead of answering. Were we really doing this? Getting jealous over past lovers, real and imagined?

My voice flat, I said, "Jett got himself a few inches away from my taco stand, if you know what I mean, but he didn't sample the taco delights."

He shook his head. "I don't know what that means."

"Jett lost his couch-cushion virginity that night. But don't worry. The couch didn't get pregnant. He used a condom."

"I can't tell if you're being serious or messing with me."

"Both. I'm a woman."

He looked around, seemingly distracted by the sounds of the roller skaters. My nakedness began to feel incongruous. Here we were in musty old bleachers, where people stamp their feet and cheer on the local hockey league.

Fumbling around in the dark, I located my bra and slipped it on quickly, followed by my dress.

Adrian blinked at me. "What did I do?"

"Nothing, I just…" I shrugged. My emotions were confusing, especially the way they were mixed with my body sensations. Adrian and I were on the edge of something, and depending on what happened next, we could either be climbing each other to ecstasy, or picking up our leftover pasta to leave.

I blinked up at Adrian. He could decide what happened next, because I didn't trust myself anymore.

"Golden," he said.

I smoothed down my hair and busied myself zipping up my dress while avoiding eye contact.

"We should tell her," he said.

"You tell her."

"But she's your friend."

"This morning, I swore to her I wasn't interested in you."

"Why would you say something like that?"

"Because you made me feel bad. When you left last night. You didn't want me."

He was still kneeling on the step below me, his face just slightly lower than mine. He slipped his arms around my back, grasped my buttocks, and pulled me toward him. My legs parted to accommodate his body, and I felt his crotch make contact with mine. Through my dress and through his clothes, I felt something firm and rod-like.

His face close to mine, his blue eyes pale and silver in the dim light, he growled, "You think I didn't want you?"

"Oh my lord, is that…"

He ground his hips forward, mashing his rod against my engorged flesh. Sparks shot through my body. Contrary to what I'd joked about to Golden a few weeks ago, there was absolutely nothing wrong with his equipment. Except, maybe, that his equipment required a minimum of two people to operate, once engaged.

"Peaches, I do want you. More than you know."

I sighed and arched my back so I could get better contact where I wanted it. Why did we have so many clothes on?

"Mercy!" I bit him on the neck, where it met his shoulder, and wrapped my legs tightly around him.

He slapped his hands down on the step just behind me and leaned forward, rubbing rhythmically back and forth.

The clothes were still between us, but that didn't even matter. I just wanted him… to keep…

He rocked his hips against mine and groaned. "I want you."

"Oh no," I said. My neck and ears burned, my heart racing. I groaned, and my voice caught in my throat. I was coming, or I would be, if…

I grabbed his hips and forced him against me, harder.

"Peaches," he murmured. "I want you."

My whole body shook as the long-delayed orgasm rolled through me. My hands didn't know where to go, moving up Adrian's muscular back to his shoulders, then back to his ass.

I let out a long sigh when it tapered off, then said, "Oh, no."

I leaned back to catch my breath.

Adrian winced and pulled back. "Did you just come?"

I pushed my butt back on the step, bringing my legs together. "Maybe."

He started to laugh, then tipped his head to the side. "I guess we really are living out our missed high school opportunities. Dry humping and all."

"Let's not tell Golden about that. Or anyone."

He untucked his dress shirt and let it loosely fall over his crotch, hiding his still-impressive tower of man-meat. I may have peaked, but he hadn't.

"Buzz kill," he said. "I'll call her. Don't worry, I'll take care of everything."

"You could just date us both at the same time."

Why did I say that? The orgasm must have loosened me up to a very strange place.

He frowned. "Should I date other people because you're still seeing that actor?"

My eyes widened in horror. "It was just a joke," I said. Damn it, I always got so weird after a sexual encounter. If I wasn't grabbing my clothes and fleeing the scene, I was saying something stupid, or impersonating a cleaning lady.

"I guess we are adults," he said. "We just need to have some rules."

Um, what? Was he serious?

He scrunched his face and adjusted the front of his pants again. "I'm not thinking clearly, am I?"

"Want me to chop that tree down for you?" I flashed my eyes at his crotch.

He cleared his throat and got to his feet, then sat next to me. "Chop down my tree?" He sounded alarmed.

"Bad metaphor. It's just that you have a lot of wood in there." I held up my hands next to my mouth and stuck out my front teeth like a beaver.

He chuckled. "Is that... your beaver face?"

I felt my cheeks flushing with embarrassment. Jokes are supposed to diffuse tension, not make it worse!

He leaned over and nibbled my neck. "I am looking forward to seeing your lips around my package."

MEOW! BA-WANG!

The lights flicked on, bringing our stark surroundings into reality.

Nodding, he said, "But our time's up."

I blinked up at the fluorescent lights, high overhead, as they buzzed and flickered to life.

Adrian unlaced and slipped off his roller skates. He flexed his socked feet, which were quite large—not that I should have been surprised.

I scooped up my roller skates and knee pads, and pointed with my chin to our shoes, several steps down the bleachers. "Are you able to walk straight with that bouncy castle in your boxers, or do you want a piggyback ride?"

He squeezed my hand and started stepping down, his untucked shirt covering his stiffness. "I have a bouncy castle in my shorts? Please. *You're* the bouncy castle," he said slyly.

"I'm more like a water park."

"If you're the water park, what does that make me? The family of four with a coupon for all-day fun?"

45

"That depends on how much you like water slides."

We stopped to pick up our shoes, then made our way out to the rental desk, joking the whole way about height restrictions on rides and other innuendo-laden metaphors.

CHAPTER 6

Before I knew it, we were pulled up in front of my house, sitting in Adrian's mother's nice car. It had a sweet leather interior, and still smelled new over the mild scent of Cujo's dog blanket on the back seat.

"What kind of mileage do you get in this thing?" I asked.

Adrian raised his eyebrow. "Didn't your father ask my mother the same thing over dinner a few weeks ago?"

"Hmm. I think he did."

The engine was still running, and Adrian didn't seem to be preparing to get out and walk me to the door. *What the hell, Adrian?* It wasn't even ten-thirty.

"Great staff meeting," Adrian said.

"Full of surprises."

"Listen, Peaches, about the thing I said earlier, about us dating other people, I shouldn't have gone there. Just because I'm afraid of commitment, that's no excuse to jerk you around."

I waved my hand. "Pfft. Commitment? Nobody's getting married, okay? Honesty is way more important to me than commitment. I don't think I'm in a place where I want to get locked down either, you know?"

He gave me a sidelong look. "Are you saying we should keep it casual, and date other people?"

Squirming in my seat, I said, "I don't know what I'm saying. My teeth feel loose from those drinks we had. I think my double was a triple."

"Your teeth are loose? I can't say I'm familiar with that expression."

My hand went to the latch and pushed the door open. My legs were jumpy all of a sudden, like I wanted to run away from Adrian and this conversation.

"What's next?" he asked.

"What's with all the questions?" I asked. "This date was much easier when you had my boobs in your mouth."

He licked his lips and smiled, speechless.

I edged my way off the seat, pushing open the door.

Adrian turned off the engine and got out of the vehicle, rushing around to my side like a gentleman. I kept walking toward the lighted porch of my house. The night air was cool enough on my bare legs that I didn't want to linger outside without a jacket.

As we walked to the house and up the steps, I made up my mind about what I wanted. I liked Adrian, but I couldn't be sure things were over with Dalton. There was something about the sexy actor that couldn't be pushed out of my heart by another guy. The more I thought about Adrian's suggestion to date other people, the more it seemed like having your zero-calorie cake and eating it, too.

"You should take Golden out tomorrow night," I said matter-of-factly, as we walked up the porch steps.

"Is this a trap?"

I poked him in the chest. "I'm serious. She's a sweet girl, and she really likes you. But you have to be completely honest. And then on Monday, I'll make you dinner, and we can have another staff meeting. We have a lot of bookstore business to discuss."

He gazed down at me affectionately, then tucked my hair behind my ear. "Discussing… your perfect, gorgeous, raspberry-shaped nipples in my mouth?"

I clamped my hand over his mouth. "I have nosy neighbors," I whispered.

He glanced suggestively at the door. "Here we are again."

In a flash, I remembered us being there, not twenty-four hours before. As I thought of him leaving me, my body heated with indignation.

"Not tonight, loverboy," I said.

He made a face, shrugging my words off. "Fine. I didn't want to come in anyway. I have to work in the morning." He fake-yawned, watching me out of the side of his eye.

"I'll see you back here Monday. Make it seven-thirty, since I have to work at the bookstore all day and straighten out whatever disaster my incompetent co-worker has made over the weekend."

"He's not incompetent, just inexperienced."

"Then I guess I'll have to teach him a thing or—"

I was cut off by Adrian's lips on my mouth. His long arms encircled me, his kiss electric and charging my whole body. When he let me go, every inch of my skin was tingling, from my scalp to my toes.

And then he turned and walked away, a bounce in his step.

I opened the door, slipped in, and kept the interior lights off as I stood in the dark living room and watched the car's red tail lights streak away in the night.

Alone in the dark, I asked myself out loud, "Peaches, what do you think you're doing?"

~

On Sunday, I had a ton of energy, and I not only cleaned my room and did my laundry, but I also put all the laundry away instead of giving up partway and leaving the clean stuff in the basket. It wasn't even my week to clean the bathroom, but I did it anyway, grinning with satisfaction as I scrubbed the antique claw-foot tub to a sparkling shine. Whenever I started to think about something I didn't want to think about, I just found a new zone to clean!

Ladies, if you want to get your house into tip-top shape, I recommend you send the guy you're dating out on a date with another girl. Yes, you'll get some conflicting feelings, ranging from curiosity to outrage, but your house will ultimately benefit.

And, remember, it was all your idea! So when you fluff up all the pillows and start punching them, that's all you, baby.

At six-thirty, my father came by to pick me up for dinner at their house. I'd only seen him once since my trip to LA, and he had a million questions for me about the underwear photo shoot and the commercial filming. I filled him in as best I could in the car, summarizing the awkward details regarding my love life.

"And your boyfriend Mitchell is modeling underwear in France?" he asked, getting all the details jumbled.

"No, Mitchell's just a friend. Keith was my, um, boyfriend while I was in California, and he's in Milan now."

"But Mitchell took you to Disneyland, right?"

"No, that was Keith."

"Disneyland can be very romantic."

"Dad, are you feeling okay?"

We pulled into the driveway of the house, and he tapped on the car's odometer. "The mileage on this thing is terrible. I like to buy American, but this is ridiculous, and when is the movie star coming back to town?"

(I swear, that's exactly how he asked me about Dalton Deangelo—as though his car's fuel economy and the actor's visit were obviously tied together.)

"He's more of a TV star than a movie star, and I don't know when. His butler was here on Friday getting a cabin or something set up. I haven't talked to Dalton since I left LA."

We got out of the car and walked up to the house. My father's gaze was straight ahead as he said, "You're more than good enough for anyone, Petra. Never forget that."

My mother swung open the door to greet us. Kyle ran through the house behind her, chasing another little boy with a big, plastic shark raised high over his head.

"The famous model is here!" my mother exclaimed.

The boys' yelling diminished slightly as they clambered up the stairs and down the hall toward Kyle's room. My mother's cheeks were rosy, and her blond hair looked dark, as though it hadn't been washed in a while.

I gave her a big hug, still puzzling over what my father had said.

"Is everything okay?" I asked.

She squeezed me, hard. "Nothing a little girl talk with my favorite supermodel can't cure."

Dad stopped for a moment to straighten the lid on the cut-crystal candy dish where we keep the spare keys, then he disappeared back out the door muttering about having left some lights on in the workshop.

"Really, Mom, what's going on? Dad just tried to talk to me about boys, sort of."

She led me into the kitchen and handed me a bottle of white wine, cold from the fridge, and the corkscrew.

"Kyle's been acting out lately," she said.

"Do you want me to talk with him?"

She smiled wanly as she set out two wine glasses. "When did I get to be so old? What do you think of those no-surgery facelifts?"

"What did Dad do now?"

"It's not your father."

I poured the wine, and she switched the subject to me, asking questions about my time in LA, and nodding at the answers while staring off into the distance.

We put together the salad and got all the food out onto the table.

Dad came in and we sat down to eat.

Kyle's friend had shockingly bad table manners, but his behavior seemed to improve when we stopped paying any attention. The boys wolfed down their food, and when they asked to be excused, my mother seemed relieved.

She finished her third glass of wine, and finally she spit out what was bothering her. "A woman at the summer camp meeting thought I was Kyle's grandmother."

The three of us were alone.

My father calmly and quietly said, "But you *are*."

I turned and patted my father's hand. "You may be excused."

"There's nothing wrong with the age that brings wisdom," he said.

I nodded. "Okay. Bye. Have fun in the workshop."

He stalled for a moment, gathering up a few dishes and putting the lids on the pickles.

After he walked away and left us in the dining room, I said, "Tell me who it was, and I'll punch her some new freckles."

"One of those yummy mommy types."

"Gross. I hate her. Does she drive a Range Rover and wear tiny little designer jeans?"

My mother grinned. "Yoga pants. The designer kind, though."

"Yoga pants. Uh-huh. With perfect hair and full makeup?"

"Plus diamond earrings."

I shook my head. "Don't you worry about her. Those chicks have it the worst. I see them at the bookstore. Do you know how many self-help books they buy?"

She sighed. "It was just the way she looked at me, you know? She invited me to some party she's having, obviously out of pity."

I glanced up at the antique grandfather clock standing in the corner of the dining room. Was Adrian on a date with Golden?

As my mind wandered, my mother kept talking about the way the yummy mommy had looked at her.

A gentle presence settled over me, and I thought of Keith Raven, my sweet LA rebound boy. We'd talked about our days a few times, and agreed that what most people desire more than anything, more than money or fame or stuff, is someone to complain to for thirty minutes a day.*

*Not talk to. *Complain to.* Let's be honest here, it's not a conversation we're after, not always.

My mother had stopped talking.

"You said Kyle was acting out lately?" I prompted.

"Boys are not like girls," she said, and launched into a tirade about the weird things he'd been doing. When she got to the part about him not doing a great job wiping his bum and leaving streaks in his underwear, I had to stifle my laughter.

Describing the lengths she went to sanitizing the laundry did seem to give my mother satisfaction. I patiently listened without interrupting.

We moved out of the dining room and cleaned the kitchen. When it was bedtime for Kyle, we pulled out the trundle bed for his friend, and I helped her get both boys settled in.

I don't know how much I feel differently toward Kyle than I would if he was actually my brother, and not the child I gave birth to at fifteen. I never had a brother, so how would I know to compare? I do love the little guy. I love every hair on his head, but he's a sweetheart, and who wouldn't?

He never nursed from me. Despite understanding the health benefits, and understanding that it would be the right thing to do, I hadn't been emotionally able to do it. Honestly, that probably made it easier for my parents to bond with him as their own.

Still, there were times like that night, when I was around both him and another boy his age, and I would compare. Was the other boy taller and stronger? Did he seem smarter, having benefited from pre-natal care? Comparison is the thief of joy, but we all do it with our children, or our appearances.

After we closed the door to Kyle's room, my mother began to cry, smiling through the tears. "I'm so blessed," she whispered. "So what if I have some wrinkles? I have two beautiful children who make me happy."

"And one of us knows how to wipe properly."

She held onto my arm as we walked down the stairs. "He'll figure it out. None of us is born knowing all the answers."

"Except Dad."

"Hah! Your father is exceptional, of course."

"Of course," I agreed, both of us giggling.

~

Monday.

Contrary to what I expected, the bookstore was not a disaster on Monday morning. Adrian had been distracted by the negotiations with Black Sheep Books, and hadn't moved any of the fixtures around.

Gordon Oliver came over from next door, and we had a heart-to-heart about the future of the store.

"Change is hard," he said, his elbows on the counter.

Gordon has black hair and almond-shaped brown eyes. One of his parents is Thai and the other is Eastern European. He's a handsome man for a guy in his forties, but he's never been married, as far as I know. He enjoys his fine wines and his trips around the world, and dating a new divorcee every year or so.

His latest girlfriend had allergies to a number of common wine additives, so he had thrown himself into sourcing organic wine they could enjoy together.

When he said that change was hard, I wasn't sure if it was about the bookstore or avoiding allergens. The woman was vegan, too, which explained why he'd been coming over to the bookstore side to wolf down takeout from Burt's Burger Barn. As we talked about plans for moving the store to the bigger location, the scent of his recently-devoured burger with feta-cheese dressing hung around us in the air.

53

"I'll miss having you right next door," he said.

"But you'll be able to expand the wine store."

He got a mischievous look. "Oh, right. I guess I will."

"You love the wine more than the books."

He poked around at the pens in the tin can pen-holder on the counter. Kyle had made the cup for the grand re-opening of Peachtree Books after the Big Split, when Gordon had divided the space to open the wine store.

"The lease negotiations are pretty much final. We're moving. Do you think Dalton Deangelo will come to a grand opening party?" he asked.

"That won't be for another month or two, will it?"

"I imagine he'll be back and forth all the time," Gordon said.

"We're not actually a couple."

"Sure, but he'll have ties to the town. He bought the Veiner cottage."

"He did what?" The Veiner cabin was a historical site at the edge of town, between Beaverdale and Dragonfly Lake. It had belonged to the town's founding father, Leonodis Veiner. Our main street had been named after him until 1942, when my great-grandfather accidentally renamed it Leonardo Street. This all caused a bit of a scandal that resulted in several properties being zoned historical sites, including the cabin.

Gordon explained that his girlfriend was the real estate agent who'd brokered the deal with Dalton to buy the cabin.

I stammered, "But that cabin is falling apart. Does it even have running water?"

Gordon waggled his eyebrows. "You'll see. I hear it's very romantic."

"We're not together. We're just friends."

"Friends with benefits?"

"Gross, Gordon. You're my boss. I'm not discussing it with you. We have a highly professional relationship."

He laughed, because over the years, we'd enjoyed a number of lengthy chats about... well, everything. After a bottle of ice wine, I'd given him oral sex pointers, complete with a diagram drawn on a napkin. For years, the poor guy had been trying to use his tongue for

54

STARFIRE – Peaches Monroe #3

penetration only. After that talk, he'd expanded the store's selection of sexuality books. "See, books open new worlds, and knowledge is power," I'd teased him when he'd reported back to me that his divorcee at the time was a satisfied customer.

But enough about Gordon's sex life.

I had a date that night with Adrian.

The day passed quickly, and I locked up right on time. I was buzzing with excitement as I picked up groceries after work and hurried home to start cooking.

Shayla swung by the house on a break from her job to help me get everything ready.

"I'm ashamed of how much I'm enjoying this," she admitted as she set the table. She knew all about Adrian dating both me and Golden, having heard from both girls. "This is like one of those dating shows, but in real life, and I have an all-access pass."

"Remember the rules," I said. "No telling the other contestant."

When I'd informed her about Adrian's plans to date both me and Golden, I thought she'd try to talk me out of it, but she was too fascinated. As friend to all three of us, she was in the unique position of getting to know everything. Like some omniscient being. She actually rubbed her hands together in excitement. I asked if she wanted to book herself into the rotation, but she declined. (Not that Shayla would go after a guy I was interested in, anyway. Her loyalty to me overrode any lust, which is one of the many reasons I love her and would give her a kidney without hesitation, whether she needed one or not.)

I asked her, "Speaking of kissing and telling, who or what did you have in your bed that night I heard you singing the O song?"

"Don't burn the lemon sauce," she said, changing the topic.

"You'd better not be zooming your boss again."

She smirked. "Oh, I'm not."

We tidied up the kitchen as best we could, since our only table was also in that room.

The doorbell rang, and I got so nervous all of a sudden, my legs actually quaked.

55

Shayla ran out the door, car keys in hand, telling Adrian not to do anything she wouldn't do. She disappeared, leaving the two of us alone for our date.

Adrian whipped out some flowers from behind his back and handed them to me. The tag showed them as being from Gabriella's, the fancy florist, and the bouquet was a small but exotic blend of flowers that weren't orchids.

"Please, come in," I said. "I'm glad these aren't cut orchids or both of our mothers would be mad."

He chuckled. "Those orchid nuts."

Adrian stepped over the threshold, a drip of sweat running off the side of his brow. Was he feeling guilty about our open arrangement, nervous to see me, or had he rushed to get there? I started to ask, but he gave me an awkward kiss immediately, his lips brushing my nose and landing on my chin as I turned.

"You look beautiful," he said.

I pulled out my phone to take a photo of the pretty flowers. "For my mother," I explained.

He grinned. "I already sent a picture to my mom."

"Hey! We're Bodwives* buddies."

*Bodwives is a modified version of the acronym for the Beaverdale Orchid and Dandelion Wine Society, which both of our mothers were part of.

The ladies love growing orchids, and abhor seeing them used as cut flowers in arrangements.

I put the flowers in a tall water glass of water and set them on the table.

"How's Golden?" I asked. "Did she have a bunch of exciting news and scandalous gossip that turned out to be nothing but the neighbor's mail-order catalog arriving at her house by accident?"

"I'm here with you," he said firmly, his pale blue eyes momentarily as stormy as his last name.

"One time she took twenty minutes to tell me that her single guy neighbor gets Victoria's Secret catalogs. Big shocker, right? How about you, Adrian? Do you get anything in the mail you want to tell me about?"

"Not yet." He looked up and down my body appreciatively. "But I'm on the mailing list for one of Victoria's Secret's strongest competitors. I hear their models are extra hot."

"One of them is."

"I can hardly wait to see your pictures."

"I guess I'll have to autograph your catalog for you," I said with a sigh.

"If you can pry it out of my hands."

"Why slobber over a photograph when you can have the real thing?"

He shrugged. "A photograph doesn't talk, and doesn't make you feel sixteen and totally freaked out again."

I put one hand on my hip. "You'd like me better if I was silent?"

He pointed a finger at me. "Nope. Not taking the bait. We did nothing but argue back in school, and look where that got us."

We stood in the kitchen, and I moved away from him, putting the peninsula section of the counter between us.

MIMI STRONG

CHAPTER 7

I had all the preparations for gin and tonic drinks, including cucumber slices, set out between us. Without asking, I poured us one each. We clinked glasses, and quickly downed the drinks, the same way we had at DeNirro's on Saturday. Combined with the two shots I'd had with Shayla while getting ready, the drink made my body hum at a pleasant frequency.

Adrian seemed to relax, tilting his head from side to side and rolling his shoulders back.

"Candy is dandy, but liquor is quicker," I said.

He looked down at my fidgeting hands, then grabbed one of my wrists gently and brought my hand up to his face. He stared deeply into my eyes as he rubbed the tip of my thumb across his swollen lower lip. Still giving the sexy eyes, he slipped my thumb into his mouth and started sucking. My legs quaked again as an electric current shot down my spine and beyond.

"You like sucking on things," I murmured.

"Take off your shirt and find out."

With my free hand, I squeezed my sweater puppies together from the side. The top button of my blouse popped open as though I'd planned it. "You want a taste of these, big boy?"

He gave my thumb another suck and grazed it with his teeth, making me shudder. I could feel all of my lips swelling and watering. So much for my plans to keep things casual until he picked a girl. I'd lusted after Adrian for so long, and it was time to find out how my fantasies compared to the real thing. He released my thumb and dared me with his eyes to make the next move.

"Hmm?" I trailed my wet thumb across my collarbone and down the crease of my chest.

"Mmm," he growled, his gaze moving down to my breasts. "You know I want a taste, but I don't want to be rude, and you've made all this dinner for us."

"It's just a deli chicken staying warm in the oven. The chicken won't mind if we start with an appetizer."

"I did have a late lunch, so I can't say I'm all that hungry... for dinner."

I slowly unbuttoned my blouse, eager to get his mouth on me again.

"Is that a Peaches Monroe bra?" he asked, his eyes lighting up at the sight of the midnight-blue underwire bra.

For a second, I was confused by the question. I'd not fully adjusted to the idea of being a brand name.

"They're still in production, but this is a sample. Funny story, actually. They test-marketed some of the designs, and this is going to be purple, but they'll just shift the color on the photographs rather than re-shoot. Apparently, clothing lines do that all the time, and— oh. Mercy. Oh, mercy."

He'd leaned across the counter and buried his face in my bosom, his big, warm hand slipping under my loose blouse and landing on my back to keep me in place. He inhaled deeply and audibly, making every part of me shudder in anticipation.

When he came up for air, his eyes heavily lidded, he said, "What's that sauce on the stove?"

The burner was turned off, but the warm lemon sauce was still fragrant. "Lemon butter."

He pulled away from me, turned to the stove, and returned back to the peninsula counter between us, setting the sauce pan down before hunting around in the drawer for a spoon.

"We're alone in the house?" he asked.

"Yes. Shayla's at work until late."

"You have a new refrigerator."

I stammered and turned to look at the fridge. "The landlord replaced it when I was—"

Adrian moved swiftly around to my side of the counter, grabbed me under the arms, and hoisted me up to sit on the counter. There were only a few inches of overhang on that side, so it was safe enough to sit there, though I never did. Sitting on counters was something tiny girls did. I liked the view up there, though.

Adrian slipped off my blouse and unfastened my bra.

Can you guess what he did next?

Yeah.

That long-legged sex maniac used a wooden spoon to dribble warm lemon butter sauce on my breasts and then licked them clean.

Repeatedly.

I moaned and squirmed around, the bits between my legs becoming slippery inside my panties and jeans.

More lemon sauce.

Heavy breathing.

Kissing.

Licking.

Sucking.

When I couldn't take it anymore, and long before we ran out of sauce, I got hold of Adrian's jeans and sprung him from the fabric.

He leaned back from me and stretched up to pull his shirt off over his head. Wow, it was a long way up there to the other end of his body. From where I sat on the counter, it looked like his fingertips grazed the ceiling of the kitchen.

Holding his bare chest to mine, he said, "Sticky."

I grabbed him by the thunderstick.

He stopped talking as I squeezed his firm rod in one hand, palming the head with my other hand. "Two-hander," I murmured.

He groaned what seemed like a question, but leaned down and started kissing my mouth and neck. He knew he was packing a two-hander, and didn't need me to tell him.

The change in his pockets jingled as his jeans slipped to the kitchen floor along with his boxers. He got harder and harder in my hands.

I pushed him back so I could hop off the counter.

He shook his head. "I'm sorry. I didn't bring a condom."

I bit my lower lip, thinking about the stash I usually had upstairs. The stash had recently run out, though, and had I picked up more? No, I had not. Every time I'd been to the drugstore recently, someone I knew from high school had been working the checkout, and I'd delayed the purchase.

Adrian's manhood pulsed in my hand, inviting me to take a ride. I dropped to my knees and gave it a long lick, from base to tip. After all the lemon butter sauce in my mouth from Adrian, his skin had almost no taste. I cupped his balls in one hand and buried my nose in his trimmed pubic hair. I breathed in deeply, his musk triggering the memory of my high school crush. While other boys' hormones and diets made them smell disgusting, Adrian had always smelled good to me. I'd stand behind him when he was on the computer lining up photographs for the yearbook, and I'd lean in close enough to smell the crown of his head.

Oh, but we'd both grown up, and now we would make up for lost time.

He shifted around to lean back against the counter, his palms braced on the edge for what was to come next.

My mouth watered as I opened wide and took hold of him with force.

His breath whistled in through clenched teeth, and his thigh muscles flexed. As I coaxed him in and out of my mouth, my lips making faint popping sounds as I negotiated the head and its contours, his breathing became ragged. I listened and slowed down my breaths to be in time with his.

He got so hard, about to blow, and grunted a warning. "Easy, or else," he said.

"Or else what?" I asked, pulling away to speak.

He raised his eyebrows and looked down at me knowingly.

I licked the head, swirling my tongue around while giving him a sidelong look up. "Come in my mouth, big boy."

He just closed his eyes and smiled.

I took him back in my mouth, savoring the musky scent of his skin, so familiar and intoxicating. His balls pulled up under my touch, and his breath caught in his throat.

I started moaning like a porno princess, like I just couldn't get enough of his big, huge wonderfulness. He put one hand on the back of my head, entwining his fingers in my hair.

"Slowly," he moaned.

I glanced up. His eyes were still closed, and the whole front of his gorgeous chest was glistening as he tensed and released his muscles repeatedly.

I slowed right down to half speed.

His fingers rubbed the back of my head, as though impatient. "Not that slow," he moaned.

I pulled him out of my mouth, grabbed his hand and put it on the back of my head with the other one. Something had gotten hold of me, and I felt dirty. I had that hot, juicy, desperate feeling. I didn't know what I wanted, but I wanted it now.

He stared down at me, a look of concern on his face. "What now?"

"You're such a big boy." I kissed the engorged red head before me and grasped my right hand firmly around the base. "I've got a hold of you so you won't choke me."

"Okay." His hands were both still loosely embedded in my hair at the back of my head.

"Now grab hold my hair like you mean it, and go for it. Don't close your eyes the whole time. Look at me when you come in my mouth."

He nodded and tilted his hips as I took him back in through my lips. My jaw clicked as I opened wider. Blinking, but still making eye contact, he filled my watering mouth and began to pump, his hands firm on the back of my head as he moved faster and slower.

My hand held him firmly, adding to the limited reach of my mouth.

I slipped my other, free hand down the front of my own jeans without thinking, and rubbed away at the throbbing tension.

After a moment, Adrian's body tensed and shook, releasing his hot climax down my throat. Four pulses, then one more. And another. I moaned in pleasure, softening my friction to be gentle. I hadn't come, but I felt so damn good, like all of my skin was an extension of that one sensitive area.

With a sigh, he leaned over and eased himself down to the floor next to me, his gaze on the moving lump that was my hand inside my own pants.

I pulled my hand out, embarrassed.

"Don't stop," he said. "That's beautiful."

"So much for dinner." I looked around sheepishly.

"Do you like oral sex?" he asked.

I gave him a sidelong look. Was he kidding? "No, I just asked you to do it as a joke, Adrian."

He reached down and grabbed my crotch through my jeans, holding me firmly between his long thumb and fingers. "Smartass. I mean receiving."

"I dunno. Do you like giving it?"

His hand started to squeeze and rub me, sending waves of pleasure through my body. Since encouraging him to be forceful, Adrian certainly did have a more aggressive vibe, and I liked it.

He growled, "Tell me how much you like to have this licked."

I glanced up in a panic that the kitchen window was open and my neighbor could hear everything. Thankfully, the window was closed.

"I like it," I whispered.

He squeezed me with more force. "Indulge my fantasies," he said. "Tell me to lick it."

My body writhing, sitting next to him on the kitchen floor, I felt ridiculous. I put my hand over top of his face, forcing his eyelids down with my fingertips. "Adrian!"

He shook his face free of my hand. "Either command me or beg me. Your choice."

"You filthy boy."

His face lit up with a grin.

Well, I wasn't going to beg, so… "I command you to lick me. Make me come, Adrian. Do it."

He gave me one last smirk, and then everything happened so fast. I meant to move the party to a better venue, such as my bedroom, but he unfastened my jeans and yanked them down forcefully. He didn't take them off in a sensible way, either, but rolled them inside out, so the skinny cuffs were impossible to extract myself from. We got one foot out, but not the other, and then I was on my back, knees in the air. Off came the panties in the same manner as my jeans—in a pile around one ankle.

Huffing, I attempted to free my other foot, but Adrian grabbed my legs and dragged me five inches closer to him. My damp, sweaty butt squeaked against the floor, and I almost giggled, but then his face was between my legs and in my muff.

BA-WANG.

"Make me come," I moaned, feeling dirty again.

His tongue delved into my swollen cleft, and my body cried out a song of joy. Rivers of light and goodness flooded my body, and more was delivered as Adrian's fingers neared the docking point and entered, gliding easily on the slick wetness.

I arched my back, my head rolling back. Noises between grunts and moans came from my mouth without censor. I peered down to see Adrian on his stomach between my legs, his face hidden to me. His fingers were long and intimate, stroking and enhancing the force of his tongue on my nub. Further along his body, his butt muscles clenched and unclenched in rhythm with his hand, as though he was having sex with me. It was still his hand, and his fingers thrusting in and out with urgency, but soon I was coming.

I curled up, my sweating hands flat on the floor beside me, and I stared down at his gorgeous, long body before me as my body succumbed to an immensely satisfying orgasm.

When it was done, I pushed his face away.

"I can keep going," he said, and I believed it.

I quickly sat up, alarmed about the amount of water between my legs.

"Sometimes things get a little gushy," I explained.

"No need to explain." He sat up and shook out his arms, which he'd been propped up on.

"It's normal for some girls," I said.

He chuckled. "Really. There's no need to explain. I'm familiar."

I squinted at him suspiciously. Had he heard something from someone?

"The girlfriend who liked shopping," he quickly added.

I pushed myself back from the puddle and threaded my naked foot back through my underwear and jeans. Adrian took his cue and started to get dressed as well, even though he looked ready for the next round.

As we got back off the floor and surveyed the situation, I wondered what he was thinking. I got some towels and cleaned up the floor while he took the chicken out of the oven and apologized for using up most of the sauce "on some other *chick*."

Maybe he wasn't thinking about anything. I've heard that about guys—they can enjoy a blank computer screen inside their mind, whereas any woman will have the equivalent of a hundred windows open, everything going at once. I thought about all the tasks involved in moving the bookstore, the censored version of the evening I would tell Shayla, and about how many calories were in a blowjob when you accounted for the energy used in the blowing. My mind kept whirring. I thought about making some excuse and running out the door, and just running until I didn't have to think about anything anymore.

CHAPTER 8

After eating our dinner, we moved over to the couch in the living room. Adrian made himself at home, stretching his long legs out and across my lap.

"Don't be shy," I said, patting his shins through his clothes.

We'd mostly talked about store business all through dinner, and I was tired of thinking about work. My gaze darted over to the remote control. Watching TV was tempting, but didn't seem appropriate for a date. Then again, we'd done everything in reverse order, starting off with mind-blowing oral sex on the kitchen floor. How did you follow that?

"Swing your legs up here and I'll rub your feet," he said.

I lifted his legs with both hands and rotated my body so my legs were alongside his. Shayla and I sat this way sometimes, but she never offered to rub my feet.

He grabbed hold of my toes with his long, strong fingers. My eyes rolled up and I moaned, "Oh, Adrian, that feels so good."

He kept kneading my feet, which was surprisingly pleasant and nearly as intimate as what had happened on the kitchen floor.

"Is that a new tattoo?" he asked.

I cracked my eyelids open. My ink was covered by my clothes now, but he must have seen the new tattoo inside my hip bone when I was writhing around on his tongue.

"Doves Cry," he said.

"I was out with friends in LA one night, and pretty wasted. It could have been worse. I could have gotten *Adrian Forever* in a heart."

"That would be horrible." He grinned, his blue eyes sparkling with amusement.

67

"Oh, but it would be. I'd be too embarrassed to let you see, and we could only be naked together in absolute darkness."

"What does Doves Cry mean?"

I sighed. "That I shouldn't do shots." He kept rubbing my feet, gently pinching each of my toes as though counting them.

I explained, "It also means that everything is fine. I get knocked down, I cry, I get up again. Everything's going to be okay. Stuff happens to everybody."

Adrian pushed up the sleeve of his blue T-shirt. He'd ditched his black rock-band shirts that night for a tight-fitting V-neck. He flexed his meaty bicep and turned his arm out to reveal a small, hidden tattoo I hadn't noticed before.

"Cute!" I squealed, scrambling onto my knees to crawl along the couch toward him to get a better look. "Is that a star?"

He frowned, pretending to be deeply offended. "That's a compass."

"Of course! Very nice."

His voice husky and soft, he said, "Do you know why I got a compass?"

I shifted one leg so I could get comfortable, kneel-sitting on his lap, his long legs stretched out on the sofa behind me.

Our faces were so close, I could feel his hot breath on my cheek.

I licked my lips, then said, "Is the compass so you'll never get lost again?"

"We all get lost."

"Just like we all cry."

"And we keep going," he murmured. "We keep loving."

I froze, my breathing shallow.

"Even though we get lost in each other," he said. "We keep—"

I kissed him. The kiss turned from tender to desperate, both of us gasping, our hands tugging at clothes and pulling our bodies closer. I rocked my hips, feeling him thickening between my legs, and I was as desperate for him as ever.

He pulled away abruptly, his hands on my shoulders to keep me back. "Someone's at the door," he said.

I reached down between my legs and squeezed his shaft with my hand. "Tell me about it, big boy."

He snorted. "No, really. Someone's knocking on your front door."

A persistent rapping came from the front door.

I climbed off Adrian and went to answer, knowing with certainty from the knock alone that it was my neighbor Mr. Galloway, and he was in distress.

His face was ashen, his glasses crooked on his long, fine nose. He didn't seem as tall as usual, perhaps because I'd been hanging out with Adrian, or because whatever had him scared had made him hunch.

Mr. Galloway started talking, his words running together in a jumble. After a moment of confusion, I invited him in and got him sitting down on a chair in the living room. I ran to get him a glass of water, and when I came back, Adrian had taken control of the situation and was extracting the story.

In short, Mr. Galloway's battle with the rat who'd been terrorizing him in his house had reached its climax. Thanks to the cat, and some traps, the rat was cornered under the refrigerator. But victory had come with a cost. The rat was injured, and making horrible noises. My neighbor was beside himself, and tears ran down his cheeks. "I'm not a killer," he said.

Adrian stood, looking almost as pale as my elderly neighbor. "I'll take care of it," he said. "That's the house on this side?" He pointed in the right direction.

We both nodded silently.

Adrian disappeared into the kitchen for a moment, then walked by with a plastic bucket from under the sink. He went out the front door, and Mr. Galloway and I sat waiting in silence. The sun was setting outside, and the room was bathed in a golden light that seemed to cheerful for the occasion.

There was no noise, no screaming or banging from next door.

After eleven minutes and twenty seconds, Adrian returned, his expression solemn.

"Everything's taken care of," he said.

I helped Mr. Galloway to his feet and walked him back over to his house while Adrian stayed behind.

Mr. Galloway patted my arm when we reached his front door. "You're a true friend," he said.

His tears were gone, but his discomfort remained, hanging in the air between us. Mr. Galloway wasn't from a generation that was okay with men crying, not that things were incredibly different today.

"I'm sure we'll laugh about this tomorrow," I said. "But if you'd prefer, I won't ever mention it."

He looked down at his feet. "Thank your boyfriend for me," he said, and he quietly slipped inside his house and closed the door.

As I walked back over to my house and up the steps, I realized my body was trembling, even though the late summer sun was just setting now, the air warm and fragrant with the scent of the blossoms in Mr. Galloway's front yard.

Adrian met me on my porch, looking anxious. "I should get going," he said.

I wanted to say something to make everything right again, but the evening had taken a turn and there was no salvaging it.

"Okay." I stood on my tiptoes and stretched up to kiss him goodbye. I couldn't quite reach on my own, but after an awkward pause, he bent down and brushed his lips on mine.

"I'll call you," he said, and then he was gone.

I went back into the house, where I gingerly opened the cabinet doors under the sink. The plastic bucket wasn't there, thank goodness.

~

The rat was still on my mind Tuesday at work. I had so many positive things to think about, yet dark thoughts kept bubbling up the way they do on Tuesdays.

What's the deal with Tuesday, anyway?

It's always the slowest day of the week at the bookstore. Nobody can be bothered to work up a true hatred for the day, like they do Mondays, yet there's a bleakness to Tuesday, as though it's gradually dawning on everyone at once that the fresh, new week isn't going as well as planned.

The sound of cars driving by on the street shifted to that of wet tires on pavement. Rain came down half-heartedly.

A man came rushing into the empty store, his face down.

"Escaping the rain?" I said cheerfully.

"Always running from something, aren't I?" He swiped some raindrops from his brow with one sweep of his hand and turned his radiant smile on me.

Dalton Deangelo.

In my bookstore.

With his ridiculously hot chin dimple and dark eyebrows and all that sexy, alpha male attitude.

"The washroom is for customers only," I said.

Looking cute enough to take my breath away, he strode over to a display table. "I'm buying this." He picked up a book and brought it to the counter.

So far, we'd been recreating the day we met.

"Excellent choice," I said. " She won the Nobel prize for literature." I kept my eyes down on the book, avoiding Dalton's hypnotic green eyes.

"This is a great store," he said.

"How did that book about kegel exercises work out for you, by the way?"

"Not the way I expected."

I looked up into his eyes, too curious to avoid him any longer. His famous face looked the way I'd left it—perfect, from his defined jaw and cheekbones to those expressive, dark-lashed eyes. His black hair was damp and shiny from the rain. The planes of his face caught the store's light as though it had been set up exclusively for him.

"Why are you here?" I asked.

"I have to be somewhere, and I need a break from LA."

"I'm sorry to hear about… everything." I really was sorry that reporters had discovered his past, but even more sorry he'd been denied a normal childhood. One of the stories I'd read about him revealed that when he was four years old, he'd woken in the night and wandered out of his room to find a film crew and an orgy in his living room. The actress who spoke to the reporter said it used to happen all the time, and she felt sorry for the kid, but they had to shoot when and wherever they could. She'd hoped the money his parents were making would eventually build a better life for the kid, and everything would be worth it. But then he ran away from home as a teen, changed his name, and made his own life, without them.

71

"How are you?" I asked.

"Is that all?" Dalton replied.

"What else is there? Congratulations on buying the cabin. How's that going?"

"I thought you might actually apologize for what you did," he said.

My pulse started to hammer in my ears. The way he was looking at me—it wasn't his usual flirty expression.

"You're scaring me," I whispered, because he was.

"You promised you wouldn't tell anyone. You promised me."

I swallowed hard, but the lump in my throat wouldn't go down.

"I didn't tell anyone."

"Are you saying the video of the curvy blonde at the tattoo shop isn't you? Because it sure looks like you. I only watched it once, but the video's up to a couple million views."

My mouth dropped open.

Thunder rumbled outside, the rain picking up fury.

A lightning bolt punctuated my sudden realization.

The person who revealed Dalton Deangelo's secret past was me. I'd been worried about this. It must have happened during the night I couldn't remember clearly. My friend Mitchell wouldn't have betrayed me, so it must have been one of the model guys we were out with who'd recorded me on his phone. Then again, maybe Mitchell had betrayed me. People did that. After all, I had betrayed Dalton.

"I didn't know," I said, looking down at my shoes, away from his cold expression. "This is the first I've... oh, Dalton. I'm so sorry. I could literally die right here from how sorry I am. I never meant to hurt you."

"You haven't seen the video?"

"No! I didn't want to read all those terrible things people were saying about you. All those horrible people on the internet. I mean, I looked once, but just for a few minutes."

He sighed, and his tone softened a bit. "To be fair, you didn't say everything, but you dropped some huge hints, and that reporter, Brooke Summer, put the clues together and figured out where to look."

"This is all Brooke's fault." I still couldn't look up at him. *Please let him agree it's Brooke's fault.*

72

"Peaches, look at me."

"I can't. I'm too ashamed."

"Brooke Summers didn't sign a Non-Disclosure Agreement, but you did."

My mouth went dry. "You're going to sue me?" I glanced up, meeting his gaze. To my surprise, he looked amused, like he was making fun of me. My guilt morphed quickly into anger. "Good luck suing me, especially since I don't have anything. Not compared to you."

"You didn't read the NDA before you signed it, did you?"

"Why?" I crossed my arms.

Dalton pulled out his wallet, put some bills on the counter, and tucked the book under his arm. "I should get on my way. It's getting stormy out there."

He turned and walked toward the door, but slowly, like he wanted to be stopped.

I called out, "What do you want from me?"

He stopped at the door, his back to me. "Dinner on Wednesday?"

"I might have plans."

He grinned. "Bulldoodle."

I nearly cracked at the silly word, but I wasn't about to be thrown off by him so easily.

I said, "I might be able to see you Wednesday, but you're not the boss of me."

"I have a notarized document that says otherwise."

"WHAT?"

He opened the door to the rumbling storm. He transferred the book to the interior of his leather jacket. "Vern will pick you up at your house at seven."

"Wait, Dalton. Enough of your mysterious crap! I'm really sorry about what I said, but this is my town, and this is my bookstore. Stop coming into my life and messing everything up. I demand a copy of that stupid thing I signed!"

Bells jingled. The door closed behind him as he disappeared up the street in the rain. He probably hadn't heard a word after "wait."

After picking my jaw up off the floor, I phoned Shayla and told her everything.

"Plot twist," was her reply.

"That's all you've got? Never mind. Why am I talking to you? I'm pissed at you for not telling me I was the one who blabbed Dalton's secrets. You could have warned me."

"You made me promise to keep you from reading terrible things about you online. After that bombshell dropped, half your rabid fan base turned against you. It's like World War Three on the Team Peaches forums."

I hadn't considered how Dalton's bad press would spray back onto me. My heart sunk as I connected all the dots to a dark future where the underwear line with my name on it would lose so much money they would sue me rather than paying licensing royalties.

"Still there?" Shayla asked, her voice tiny. I'd dropped the phone away from my ear, as though a few inches would lessen the pain of the news.

"Just having a fuck-my-life moment."

"Why don't you see what Dalton has planned? Maybe you guys can salvage both of your reputations."

"You're good at this stuff, Shay. You're more sensible than me."

She sighed. "Fine. You beat it out of me. I'm boinking the dish washer."

"What?"

"I'm boinking the dish washer. With the parts that go boink."

"I don't understand. The dishwasher? You renamed your vibrator, or are you actually going after bigger appliances? Shayla, be honest. What exactly happened with our old refrigerator?"

"Not the dishwasher appliance. The person. From work."

"Wait. The funny high school kid?"

She giggled. "He just graduated, silly."

"Shay! Is that even legal?"

"He's eighteen and a bit."

"Are you guys dating, or what?"

"His parents are very strict. Please don't tell anyone, or they'll pull his college tuition. He's already working at the restaurant as punishment for getting caught with some pot."

"That seems ironic, considering the people you work with. No offense."

She giggled. "I think it's their way of teaching him a valuable life lesson. Showing him where people who party end up."

"The horrors." The door jingled as a customer came in with most of her body, shaking her umbrella outside the doorway. "Thanks for the chat," I said, wrapping it up.

"Wait, are you seeing Adrian tonight?"

"You tell me. What have you heard?" Curiosity took hold of me.

"Nothing much," Shayla said.

The woman approached the counter, her chin up in the manner of someone wanting to ask me a question. (It's funny how women will make that face, with the chin and eyebrows up, mouth slightly open, whereas men will hold their heads level and give you the stare, commanding you with their eyes, slightly amused that you'd be stupidly talking on your pink cell phone when they need you.)

I said goodbye to Shayla and got to work helping the woman. My job had to take precedent over my love life during retail hours, or else every aspect of my life would be a disaster.

Outside of the Christmas season, people don't require that much help with their shopping in a bookstore. I like to help, because it means talking about books, but sometimes I feel guilty about all the books I haven't read, especially when customers act shocked and say I "simply must" read some book that changed their life. Now, I have an open mind, but if I open a book and see a perfect rectangle of text with no paragraph breaks, that's not a book I'll be reading, no matter how life-changing.

Maybe if I was in prison.

Then I would read those heavy books.

I don't know about you, but I do daydream sometimes about being in prison and catching up on my reading. I'd also go to the gym a lot and get really ripped. Not that I want to go to prison...

Maybe one of those rehab places celebrities go? I'd love a fixed routine and dorm-style living, for a bit.

Obviously, instead of booze or drugs, I would check myself in for sex addiction.

Yep.

My addiction was sex with ultra hot guys.

All those chiseled abs and bulging biceps... the hot, urgent kisses... the licking and sucking, flesh against flesh... *the first step is admitting you have a problem.*

CHAPTER 9

As I locked the door Tuesday night, my throat tightened with a hint of nostalgia. The store's days at this location were numbered. I turned around and looked at Java Jones, across the street. After the move to the former Black Sheep Books location, I'd have to get my lunch from a new place, where the staff didn't know my usual order.

I crossed the street and went in to get a mocha—to get one while I still could!

Kirsten gave me a knowing look as she steamed the milk. Did she know that Golden and I were both dating Adrian Storm? And that Dalton was back in town? She sure looked like she was thinking about something. If the rumors were to be believed, she'd gone to sex rehab herself once. It hadn't cured her, though, which meant there was probably no hope for me and my inability to resist a bumpy man chest paired with a few compliments.

"What's new since lunchtime?" she asked.

"I don't know. What have you heard?"

"You'd better not forget about us, or I'll have hurt feelings."

"What?" I took the mocha, smiling at the perfect chocolate curls resting atop the foam.

"After you move the bookstore," she said. "I won't get to see your face twice a day. I don't know how long I'll last here without your funny stories."

My cheeks warmed as I fidgeted with the lid. How ridiculous was I to suspect everybody was so fascinated with my private love life?

"I promise I won't disappear," I said.

She came out from behind the counter and gave me a hug, squeezing me tight. "Get out of here before I get really emotional," she said.

As I walked back out with my mocha, my head felt like a helium-filled balloon, barely attached to my body. I'd always thought of Kirsten's friendliness toward me as professional courtesy, and nothing more. The idea I was more than a customer to her was humbling.

I hit the end of the block. Did I lock the door?

Once you ask yourself that question, you have to turn back and check.

The door was unlocked, which was a first. Even worse, someone was inside the bookstore. My heart started to pound.

The lights were off, but I could see movement.

I yanked open the door to find a familiar face.

"Adrian!" I yelled. "You scared me."

He was measuring the counter with a yellow measuring tape, and he wore black jeans and one of his old black band T-shirts, so he'd been nearly invisible with the interior lights out.

"The store's closed, ma'am. You'll have to try the library," he said, grinning.

"And get those disgusting library book cooties? With the grocery lists and curly hairs tucked between the pages?"

He chuckled. "I'm going to tell my aunt, the librarian, about your slanderous comments."

"It's not slander if it's true." I set my purse on the counter and peered down at the notes he was making with a carpenter's pencil. "How is your aunt?"

"Dating a hairdresser. He's a badass with tattoos, and a widower, too."

"Wow. Good for her." I looked around, noting that beyond the beaded curtains, the bathroom door was closed. Was Golden there with Adrian? Was that why he'd waited until we were closed and I was gone?

"I'm alone," he said, picking up on the unspoken question.

"Are you okay? You didn't tell me what happened with the rat."

"Peaches, I'd rather not talk about it, because I can't win. Either I'm a savage monster who murdered an innocent rat, or I'm a wimp who didn't have the nerve to take care of a problem. Either way, you'll never look at me the same again."

I stared at his face for clues, but he had his poker face on. "You're so weird sometimes, Adrian."

He finished measuring the countertop. Looking down at his notes, he said, "Want to catch a movie with me tomorrow night?"

"I've got other commitments."

He looked up, catching me with his blue eyes. "You're seeing... *him?*"

"That's okay, right?" I rubbed my arms, feeling a chill suddenly. "This is all so complicated. Maybe I'll just cancel."

"No, you should see him."

"You're just saying that because you're enjoying yourself, dating two cute girls at the same time."

He grinned. "Blondes, too."

I reached up, standing on my tiptoes, and ruffled his hair, which was even lighter than mine. He grabbed my hand and stuck my thumb in his mouth.

I groaned as my knees buckled, a thunderbolt of lust shooting down my back.

"What are you thinking about?" he asked around my thumb.

"Nothing." (Nothing but getting his jeans off.)

"What's that in the little paper cup?" He released my thumb and grabbed my drink.

"Mocha. And you're not licking it off my body. I don't share my mocha."

He took a sip without asking. "Sweet." He took a look at the label with the coffee house's logo. "How late is Java Jones open? I'm going to be here late, working out the moving plan."

Adrian was still working his weekend shifts at the bookstore, but he'd quit working at the pie shop. Gordon was paying him full-time hours to orchestrate the whole move and grand re-opening. I would have been stressed more over the move, but Adrian was so organized... and capable... and adorable.

I slipped my purse off my shoulder and set it on the counter between us, next to the coffee. "Then I'll be here late, too."

"You're off the clock."

"I don't mind."

"It's mostly going to be me staring straight ahead while the slow gears in my head grind away."

"That sounds fun! Where do we start?" I grabbed the bent metal tip of the measuring tape and started looking around.

"You should go home and rest up for tomorrow. People will be coming in looking for bargains because word's getting out about the move. Gordon wants to put all the greeting cards on sale."

"Those things are twenty years old! They're all thumbed through, and should go in the dumpster." I shifted back and forth, aware that my feet were sore from being there all day. "Adrian Storm, are you trying to get rid of me?"

"How much work do you think I'll get done if you're here?"

"You don't think we make a great team?"

"For some things, yes. You're really fun, but you're not exactly open to other people's ideas."

"That's not fair. You can't hold stuff against me from high school, and all those arguments over autograph pages. We're not kids anymore."

Smirking, he reached under the counter and pulled out a red binder. My handwriting was on the cover in black ink, and the book had initially been titled *Peachtree Books Do's and Don'ts*. That title had been crossed out, replaced with the more appropriate title, *Adrian, Study This or Death Will Befall You.*

"That's a joke," I said. "Wait, are you mad?"

"Not mad. I just have a lot to do tonight, and I won't be able to focus if I'm slobbering over your delicious peaches, now, will I?"

"Hmm." I pulled my purse back onto my shoulder. "You may have a point, for once."

"Does it ever get any easier with you?"

"Easy is boring."

I backed toward the door. "You have your keys?"

"That's how I got in."

"Adrian, a simple yes or no would suffice. Ever consider *you're the difficult one?*"

Before he could answer, I rushed out the door, jubilant in getting the last word. *Take that, Mr. Smarty Pants Adrian.*

~

I arrived home to discover we had company. Someone was giggling in the kitchen, so I went back to investigate.

When I reached the doorway, I heard a sound I should have recognized, but didn't. If I hadn't been thinking about my own sex life, I might have recognized the sound of a satisfied customer who'd successfully deployed The Assassin, or a regular human, for a job that needed doing.

I've heard Shayla's O-sound, but I'd never seen her O-face. Until that Tuesday night. Completely naked, she sat spread-legged on the peninsula of the kitchen counter, with a shaggy head of hair (thankfully) between me and Shayla's taco stand. The head was attached to a guy, fully clothed and taking his job very seriously.

Stopped in my tracks, I stood there, dumbfounded. You know how sometimes you're so full of different emotions and thoughts, your mind just overloads and takes a few seconds to reboot? No? Try walking in on your roommate having sex on your kitchen counter, and you'll see what I mean.

What probably had the biggest impact on me was the emotion on her face. I'd seen Shayla enjoy a four-cheese pizza, and I thought *that* was her O-face. But this was like pizza and Christmas morning and getting a raise, all at once. With her cheeks flushed and eyelashes fluttering, she was beautiful and real, a woman with curves and folds, and not a glossy magazine image. I'd never seen anything like it.

I was still standing there, probably with my mouth open and looking like a tourist in Las Vegas, when the guy between her legs turned around and said, "You must be Peaches."

"Oops," Shayla said, crossing one tanned leg over the other for modesty.

"I haven't been standing here for long," I said.

He stood and extended his hand to me. "I'm Troy, and I'm learning about the value of a college education."

Even though I had a pretty good idea about whose taco his hand had just been stuffing, I shook it anyway.

"I'm a college drop-out," I replied. "Consider me an example of what not to do."

He grinned, his smile making him seem more attractive. Troy had medium brown hair, brown eyes, and an average build—average for people, not actors and models. He actually looked like one of those young comedians who loses a few pounds and gets cast as a love interest opposite a hot blonde way out of his league.

Shayla had pulled a pack of cigarettes from somewhere and lit one, the tobacco sizzling in the otherwise quiet kitchen.

"Shay, not in the house!" I crossed over to the window and opened it all the way. She usually smoked on the porch. Actually, she usually snuck out under the pretense of taking out the garbage and puffed away over the Ninja Turtles ashtray, where she thought I couldn't see her.

"Can I mix you a drink?" Troy asked me, holding a fresh tumbler under the new refrigerator's ice dispenser.

"I could use a drink," I said, setting my purse on the wood table inside the small room. "Is that sushi?"

"Help yourself," he said, gesturing to the platter of rolls on the table.

Shayla kept smoking her cigarette and smiling, no sign of making any moves to put on clothes.

I popped one roll into my mouth, followed quickly by another. "I should go upstairs and leave you guys to your... oh, wow, these rolls are unbelievable."

I told myself I'd just have one more, then go up to my room. Or two more. I couldn't go up on an empty stomach.

Troy stood next to Shayla, whispering something in her ear.

"You ask her," she said. "Don't be shy."

He whispered something else.

She sighed. "Peaches, Troy would like to invite you to join us in my bedroom."

I turned to face them, still chewing a mouthful of sushi roll. "Ha ha."

"For real," she said.

I crossed the kitchen and slammed the open window shut.

"What would you want with me in there?" I asked.

Troy was blushing, his cheeks red. Without meeting my eyes, he said, "You wouldn't have to do anything you're not excited about."

"Can I sit in a chair eating sushi and offering commentary?"

Shayla rolled her eyes. "Peaches."

I reached for the drink Troy had made me and took a sip. "Troy, tell me the truth. Did you put something in my drink?"

Shayla gave me a mean look of warning.

"I'm very flattered," I said, giggling. "Listen, Troy, I'll have a threesome with you guys, but I don't think you can handle what I have in mind."

He looked up, a playful smirk on his face. "Keep talking."

I sloshed back the rest of the drink, then launched into describing a scenario, using words, hand gestures, and various items on the counter to demonstrate. The scenario became increasingly elaborate, and I dare say some of the positions surprised even me. I finished with, "And then I mount you from behind with my strap-on, Troy, and I will ride your ass until you don't know if you're coming or going, but you *will* cry, and you will call me by my stripper name, which is Luscious Hilda Mae Sparkles the Second."

In the silence that followed, an ashen-faced Troy reached for Shayla's cigarettes and lit one, hands trembling.

"Too far?" I asked Shayla.

She shrugged. "I'm turned on."

I blew her a kiss. "My pleasure, sexy lady."

She jumped off the counter, took Troy by the hand, and led him out of the kitchen and upstairs to her room.

I finished off the sushi and opened up one of the fortune cookies.

The slip of paper inside read: *The grandest lies are the ones we tell ourselves.*

I stared at the slip for several minutes. Was *grandest* even a word?*

*I looked. It is.

~

Wednesday morning, I opened the bookstore to find the lights on, the alarm off, and Adrian hunched over the computer. He was as still as a statue, his elbows on the counter on either side of the computer keyboard.

When he didn't greet me, I approached cautiously, walking around to the front of him. His eyes were closed, and he was either playing a joke on me, or fast asleep. He used to sleep sitting up in chemistry class, but this was remarkable.

I pulled out my phone and took some photos. He still didn't wake up. I looked around for something fun to do, settling on pulling my lipstick from my purse to give him a fun makeover. He woke up as soon as the lipstick touched his lips, and his sudden movement made me scream, which made him scream.

"Is this a dream?" he asked me, blinking and looking confused.

"Yes, this is all a dream."

"Good." His long arms snaked around me, pulling me into his embrace. His hands squeezed my buttocks as he buried his face against my neck, kissing me and groaning.

"And good morning to you, sir." I shivered as he pressed his lower body against me.

He pulled away and gazed down at me tenderly. "I was here so late, and I decided to stay up and have breakfast with you." He blinked a few times, then frowned. "But now I don't feel so great."

"You're probably dehydrated."

"Would you be offended if I went home?"

"No more offended than when you chased me out of here last night."

We stared at each other for a moment.

"Did you have a good night?" he asked.

"I had some sushi and watched a movie." I grabbed his arm and steered him toward the door. "Please go home. You're making me tired just looking at you."

He leaned down to give me a quick kiss. "You're the best. Do you still have those other plans for tonight?"

"I do." I dragged him to the door and sent him on his way. "Get some sleep!" I called down the street as he walked away.

I looked around to make sure nobody was looking my way. The scent of evil cupcakes wafted over from the bakery.

Shaking my fist at their fiendish vanilla-cinnamon smell, I ran back into the bookstore. The piece of cardboard I'd taped over the ceiling vent was still doing its job of keeping the scent from infiltrating.

The cardboard gave me a surprising blast of nostalgia. I'd been taping it in place when Dalton Deangelo had first crashed into my life, knocking me into his arms. What if he'd run into Java Jones that day instead? Kirsten wasn't as curvy as me, but she wasn't skinny, either. He could have dated her as "research" for his indie film, then claimed the research became genuine feelings.

Imagining him spouting all those cheesy lines to Kirsten made me cross my arms angrily. How dare he be so damn charming! And how dare he have me checking the time every ten minutes, nervously awaiting our date that night.

There were still no customers in the store, so I snuck back out, locked the door, and ran over to the door to the bakery. It was going to be a two-cupcake day.

MIMI STRONG

CHAPTER 10

Vern, Dalton's butler, driver, and personal assistant, knocked on the door of my house at 7:01. He apologized for being late.

"Looking good!" I said, admiring Vern as I stepped out onto the porch. He'd gotten a haircut and lopped off the weird ponytail.

"You're too kind. And you look very well yourself, Miss Monroe."

We both looked down at my gold, strapped sandals. "Is this footwear okay for what's in store tonight, or do I need hiking boots?"

He peered behind me as I pulled the door closed. "Where is your overnight bag?"

"You're scaring me, Vern. Am I leaving town? Do I need a passport?"

"Not tonight." He abruptly stopped talking and tried to cover by quickly adding, "Great shoes! The car is right this way, and of course I'll drive you back home this evening when you're ready."

He held open the back door of a dark car with tinted windows—the same vehicle from my first date with Dalton, but not the one Dalton had been driving himself in LA.

"How many cars does *the ol' Dalt-meister* have?" I asked as I settled into the back seat. The glass divider was only open a crack. "And please lower this. I'm not a fancy person."

The window lowered silently. "Mr. Deangelo has a few vehicles."

We began driving, the car's luxurious suspension making the pothole-filled street feel like a runway. Vern guided the vehicle north. I guessed we were heading to Dragonfly Lake, but I played it cool and didn't ask. Instead, I amused myself by probing the limits of Vern's confidentiality boundaries.

"How many turtlenecks does Dalton own?"

Vern chuckled. "Zero. He doesn't like how broad they make him look."

"Nobody looks good in a turtleneck."

"I'm sure you do, Miss Monroe."

"Does he have any food allergies?"

"Just an imaginary one to fresh-baked bread, but I'm sure you've heard all about that."

"Does he date many women?"

Vern stared straight ahead at the road, the edge of his face, from what I could see, not giving away any clues.

I added, "Just stay absolutely silent if it's a *lot* of women."

"Not many," he said quickly. "Between the series and now these films in the summer, Mr. Deangelo has a very busy schedule."

"He doesn't have time for a girlfriend."

"Not really." He turned and glanced back at me apologetically. "But he would make time for the right girl."

"And if he has to stay late on set, then what happens? Do you order pizza with the girl and watch a movie together?"

Vern laughed in response.

I continued, "But you do live in the house with him, right? If a woman moved in, you'd be a threesome. Just a cozy little family of three."

Still laughing, Vern reached for a button, and the glass divider between the seats began to rise.

I clicked my seatbelt undone. "Vern! Don't you dare! I will Indiana-Jones my way over that glass and into the front seat."

The barrier moved back down again.

We gave each other a hard time (mostly me bugging him) all the way to the woods. I pulled out my phone and was pleased to note my wireless connection actually worked. They must have put up the extra cell phone tower that had been in the works for a while.

Using GPS, I got a good look at where I was. We didn't have this technology back in my childhood, when Shayla and I were braving the tadpole-infested shoreline. I could see that the southeast edge of Dragonfly Lake had what looked like a miniature lake, extending out like a bubble. A clump of trees lay between the water and the Veiner cabin, which explained why I hadn't realized the cabin was lakeside, back when we visited on a school field trip.

"Everything okay, Miss Monroe? If your battery is low, I have several formats of chargers."

"I'm fine. Just a bit nervous about—oh, HELL, NO."

He parked the car on some grass and turned off the engine. "What's wrong?"

"That." I jabbed a finger through the air at the glinting UFO-shaped object. "Why did he buy a cabin if he's going to hang out in that little sardine can?"

Vern exited the car and circled around to hold my door, but I was already out.

A good look around answered my question. The serene setting was now a construction zone, with three bright green port-a-potties, various trailers with piles of lumber, and bright orange excavation and landscaping vehicles.

The Veiner cabin, constructed of local logs, appeared to be levitating, propped up on metal legs.

A dark-haired man appeared in the doorway of the cabin and carefully stepped down the muddy plywood ramp leading to the ground. Because of how he was dressed—steel-toed boots and a red-checked flannel jacket—I thought he was a construction worker, until he flashed me that million-dollar smile.

Banging and sawing noises continued from inside and around the cabin.

"We're running late," he shouted over the noise, striding toward me. "This noise will stop within the hour, and these guys will skedaddle out of here."

He waved to Vern, saying he had everything he needed, and the assistant/butler got back in the car and drove away.

"I'm glad you decided to stop by." He stood before me, swaying slightly, as if he wanted to hug me but needed a sign.

"Like I had a choice."

An alarming ringtone came from his pocket, and he hurriedly retrieved his phone. "I have to take this."

He turned his back to me, the phone held to his ear. "Yes, Jamie, I know." He kicked a rock from side to side between his boots. "These things take time, and I'm doing everything I can." His shoulder slumped. "Of course." He seemed to shrink down by an inch. "Hold off on the press release. She's here now, and she doesn't look happy. Gorgeous as always, but not happy. Blue dress that matches her eyes. Yes. I know, I know." He said goodbye and put the phone away.

I rubbed the goosebumps on my arms, regretting that I hadn't bought a jacket. The summer sun hadn't gone down yet, but the wooded lake area was always cooler than town.

"Should I even ask who was on the phone?"

"Probably not," he replied.

"You always keep me guessing, don't you?"

Dalton slipped off his flannel jacket and swept it around my shoulders without asking. He gazed at my mouth, looking like he might kiss me, but he didn't.

With a nod of his head, he turned and led me over to the barbecue set up near the round, silver Airstream trailer.

"We're just having burgers tonight, but they're excellent, and I got buns for you because... I want to show you I'm a thoughtful guy."

I rubbed my cheek against the collar of the flannel jacket, pretending I had an itch, but really just taking in the smell of Dalton's skin on the warm fabric.

Finally, I couldn't take the curiosity anymore.

"Dalton, who was on the phone and what the hell's going on?"

"An executive on the TV show. Most everyone thinks this whole porno scandal will blow over, but this one executive is like a dog with a bone. Jamie's the top dog, too, which is why I have a favor to ask you."

"Like my mother always says, *asking is free*. Ask away."

He dropped down on one knee.

"Peaches Monroe, will you marry me?"

CHAPTER 11

Dalton Deangelo had just asked me to marry him. He was on the ground in front of me, still on bended knee.

I could have said no, or asked if he was crazy.

Instead, I said, "Where's the ring?"

"Put your hand in the jacket pocket."

Slowly, without taking my eyes off Dalton, I patted the pocket area of the red flannel jacket he'd loaned me. Sure enough, there was a lump the size and shape of a ring box.

I kept staring down at Dalton's gorgeous face, his green eyes full of so many different emotions at once. I'd seen him like this before, proposing to one of his lovers, only he was offering to make her a vampire. My whole body felt like it disappeared, and I was nothing but eyes and a bit of face, floating in the air.

He got up and brushed the dirt off his knee. "Not ready to give me an answer? Okay, let's start with some easier questions. How do you like your burger? Medium? Well done?"

My voice came out like stinging nettles. "Burger."

He grinned, that chin dimple increasing the net value of his famous smile. "Burger? I'll take that as medium-well, the same as mine."

"You want us to get married for publicity?"

"Not exactly." He opened the hot grill and gently put the patties on with a sizzle. "I want to have a wedding for publicity, and I want to get married for love. Preferably to the same girl."

"Dalton Deangelo, you are one crazy son of a bitch, and it's extremely difficult to say no to you."

"About that. You'll find a copy of the Non-Disclosure Agreement inside the Airstream. I suggest you give it a read this time."

I stroked the square ring box through the thick flannel, curious about the contents, but my arms too limp to do much of anything.

He nodded toward the door of the silver trailer. "The table's all set up, and I'll bring the patties in shortly."

Oh. He wanted me to read the document now. Fine.

Mutely, I walked to the trailer and pulled open the aluminum-framed door. The stupid thing rocked and groaned as I walked up the steps and into the small interior. The only thing I really hated about the trailer was how I imagined it rocking around under my heavy footsteps, but I knew most of that was in my imagination and I shouldn't hold it against the trailer.

I stepped lightly over to the half-circle banquette seat at the nose of the trailer and sat down to read the multi-page document set out for me.

Without boring your pants off with all the legalese, the gist of it was that I had unwittingly agreed to do ANYTHING within my power to help mitigate any damages caused by my blabbing of Dalton's secrets, be it malicious or accidental or a weird drunken combination of both. (Which it was.)

ANYTHING.*

*That word, ANYTHING, was in all-caps throughout the document. I'm not sure how I hadn't noticed, back on that day in the bookstore when Dalton's lawyer made me sign the papers. Before you judge me too harshly, I'd like to ask if *you* read all those software license agreements you get on your computer. How about the fine print on your credit card applications? What's that? You do? Well, good for you. Have a cupcake, smarty pants.

The trailer shook as Dalton tromped up the steps in his steel-toed boots. He set the burgers on the nearby kitchenette's counter and bent over to pull off the boots.

Without looking at me, he said, "I wouldn't have had the nerve to ask you, but my life is in danger." He flashed his devilish green eyes my way. "Grave danger."

"Sure, it is."

"Drake Cheshire's life, to be more specific. My character could be murdered mid-season. Very dramatic."

"They'll cancel the show?"

"No. Not immediately. It could limp along for decades, because it's cheap to shoot in all those interiors and dark locations, and the fans will hang in through the thinnest, most ludicrous... well, you've seen the show." He took a seat next to me, his presence radiating into my space and touching me without touching me.

"And I love the show." I looked down at the table and shifted around my utensils. "You're a great actor, Dalton. Not just a good one, but a great one. You have this magic that nobody else can touch. When I'm watching you, the whole world disappears."

After a pause, he said, "Thanks."

I looked over and nearly drowned in his gorgeous green eyes. "I'm serious," I whispered. "There's no *One Vamp to Love* without Drake."

"They'll test some side characters and promote a fan-favorite to co-star with Connor."

"Ugh, he's the worst."

"My whole life would change. Instead of getting paid well and doing these great indie projects during the summer, I'd have to scramble and take what I could get."

"You could be a big movie star."

"Or I could drop to B-List and go on one of those dancing shows." He fanned his hand through the air between us, as though clearing away bad karma. "I'll be fine, Peaches. Whatever happens is going to happen. Why don't you and I get married just because it's fun?" He slid along the seat to be right next to me, his arm loosely around my back.

"Fun like trespassing on private property?"

He raised his dark eyebrows and pouted his lips for effect. "I'm not the one who slept on a sheik's pool lounger in Malibu."

I giggled at the memory. My life had gotten way more interesting since meeting Dalton.

He leaned in and kissed me on the forehead, right over the eyebrow.

I closed my eyes and savored his lips on my skin. When had we last kissed? Once, in LA, for the cameras, and before that, our last kiss was on the morning he left my bedroom. That had been before everything went sideways, and I got so angry... over a few mistakes that seemed so small now... especially with his hand on my leg.

He pulled away from the kiss and turned to look at the set table before us. "Burger?"

"I don't know if I can eat, but put one on my plate and we'll see what happens."

Grinning, he passed me some condiments. "Yes, let's put everything on your plate and see what happens."

The construction noises continuing outside seemed louder now.

"What exactly are you doing to that poor, little innocent cabin? Don't tell me you're putting those ridiculous airplane parts in as fans."

"No, but good idea." He took a bite and chewed slowly. "I'm just doing a full seismic upgrade and bringing the cabin into this century."

"Why buy a cabin here in Beaverdale?"

"It's a great cabin. And after the careful removal of just a few trees, it'll be waterfront."

"How many trees? Did you get permission?"

He insisted he did, and that he had permits, but I didn't know whether to believe him or call bullshit and walk out the door.

I stayed, though, and we talked about his renovation plans as we ate dinner. He asked about the bookstore, and I brought him up to speed on the move and expansion. I paused at one point, teetering on the edge of telling him about Adrian, but the right words wouldn't get in order and march out of my mouth. That always happens when I think about what I'm going to say. (In other words, infrequently.)

After dinner, we had strawberry cheesecake for dessert, and Earl Grey tea.

I stole a few glances across the small trailer toward the sleeping loft. The last time I'd been there, I'd given him something enjoyable, then snuck off when he fell asleep. Would that ploy work a second time? My inner thighs tingled at the imagined scenario.

We'd been quiet for a few minutes, sipping our tea with a gap of air between us on the banquette seat.

He cleared his throat and looked over at me, almost shyly. "When can I expect an answer to my proposal?"

CHAPTER 12

"I'm dating someone."

That was my response to Dalton's sudden proposal.

"But he's in Italy," Dalton said.

I grimaced, which was not my most dainty expression. "Not Keith. Someone else. Don't look at me like that. He's someone I've known for a long time. We had a thing back in high school." I grimaced again, embarrassed at the lie.

Dalton cracked the tiniest smile, and I wanted to kiss him so bad, to smother that smile under my lips and eat him up.

"What's his name?"

"Adrian."

"Do you think Adrian would mind if you married me?"

"Yes."

"Not if he's... disappeared."

I stood and grabbed my purse. "Is it late? It feels late. I don't hear any more construction going on out there. Should we go out and check?"

"Peaches, sit down. I'm just joking. I've made a few major purchases lately, and I wouldn't even have the funds available to make someone *disappear*."

"Not funny."

"You don't have to give me an answer right away, but I've tentatively scheduled an appearance together for this coming weekend. If things go well, and the tide of my PR problem turns, it could be the end of your obligation to me."

"Then what?"

"I don't know what happens next. Just because I have a plan doesn't mean I can see the future. All I know is how I feel." He held his hand over his heart. "I can feel you in my future."

"As more than an old friend?"

"Yes."

I stood with my back to the door, my fingertips grazing the cool, metal surface.

"Dalton do you know what I feel in my heart? Blood squishing back and forth, taking oxygen from my lungs and bringing it to my legs, which are going to walk out of here. Blood is still servicing my brain, which is in agreement."

"Don't get yourself lost in the forest." He pulled his phone from his pocket and made a call to Vern, telling him to come pick me up.

"I am sorry about blabbing your secret," I said. "Which is why I'll make an appearance with you this weekend. If you think it will help, it's the least I could do."

"What about the other thing?"

"Other thing? You mean the pr—" My throat closed off. I couldn't even say the word.

The proposal.

The ring.

A wedding.

Commitment.

Love.

Love?

It hit me in wave after dizzying wave, so I yanked open the door and took off down the steps. The sun had disappeared, and the woods were tall and foreboding in the dark. I started walking quickly in the direction of the lake.

A few minutes in the cool night air was exactly what I needed to clear my head.

I got to the lake's edge and thought about walking further, turning right or left, but that would mean making a decision, and my brain wasn't in a decision-making mood.

An owl hooted, breaking the static of anxiety playing on repeat in my head. The sound of the lake at night rose up around me in the moonlight.

I sat down on the gravel shore, unconcerned about getting my dress dirty.

The owl called to me, a three-hoot call. Another owl, closer to me, answered. Who-who-who.

PLUNK.

Something dropped in the water—something bigger than the first raindrop of a shower. The air was dewy, but the sky was dark and cloudless.

PLUNK.

I squinted at the shimmering surface of the lake. Was that sound made by frogs jumping into the water? Or by ducks submerging?

The owls were answered by other owls, further off in the distance, just barely audible to my human ears.

RIBBIT.

I jumped and held my hand over my heart, then laughed at myself for being scared by a frog.

Footfalls sounded behind me, and I took a deep breath of the lakeside air, trying to become one with the serenity.

Dalton sat down a few feet off to the side of me, where he began digging around, clinking pebbles. I knew even before he tossed the first one that he was searching for flat stones, perfect for skipping.

I felt around next to me, located a flat rock, and whipped it out onto the water. My rock made a satisfying smack as it hit the water with torque and then smacked a second time as it sunk.

Dalton tossed his rock, which smacked the water four times before disappearing.

I peeked over to see his teeth glinting in the moonlight, and him looking proud of his stone-skipping.

Searching more carefully this time, I found a bigger, flatter stone, and tossed it out. The stone skipped at least eight times before falling in, its final splashes soft and rapid, blending with the sound of the whatever else was out there, breaking the surface of the water just enough to make me curious.

Dalton tossed the next stone, and then another, not waiting for me to take a turn. He threw the stones harder and harder, grunting with effort, but he couldn't beat my record of eight.

A vehicle approached on the road behind us, tires crunching on the gravel road. The brief spotlight of the headlights as Vern turned the car around momentarily blinded me, taking my night vision. In the darkness, I got to my feet and started moving toward the waiting car.

Dalton got to his feet and carefully swiped the rocks and dirt from his pants. I could hear his hands swooshing on the fabric. Still, he hadn't said anything to me.

And what was there to say? *Marry me for good publicity? Because you stupidly signed a contract agreeing to do ANYTHING if you blurted out my secrets?*

I walked up to the car in silence. Dalton jogged up ahead of me and stood in front of the car door.

"You'll think about my offer?" he asked.

"Offer? You mean your demand?"

"Think about it."

"I don't have to think about anything. The agreement I signed says I'll do ANYTHING so that's what I'll do. Tell me what day to show up, and I'll be there."

"Are you sure?"

He was still blocking the door. I just wanted to get in the car and go home, away from Dalton and the hypnotic hold he had over me. I could pretend I thought the wedding was a nuisance, and that I didn't want it to be for real, but that wasn't entirely true.

I mean, really.

Marry the swoon-worthy Dalton Deangelo?

What girl wouldn't?

"Whatever." I waved my hand for him to move away from the car door.

"You'll marry me?"

"Should I wear my hair up, or down? I'm thinking up. When are you thinking we do this? Saturday? I've got the day off work."

He chuckled. "I'm glad you have Saturday off work. I'll send Vern to pick you up at your house as early as you can manage. How's six?"

"Sure, six." Like I was going to sleep at all the night before.

"You're the best." He leaned down to kiss me.

I held a hand up between us. "I have a boyfriend, remember?"

"Right. I guess I just got swept up in the moment."

"I'll kiss you when they do the kiss-the-bride thing."

"That's all I get?"

"Dalton, you'd better watch yourself. You only want me because I'm running away from you, but I'm not playing a game, so you'd better watch out."

"Watch out for what?"

"You chase me because I run, but one of these days I'm going to run right into your arms, and then you'll find out exactly what kind of man you are."

I grabbed the door's handle and used the door to shove him forcefully out of the way. I pulled the door shut quickly behind me and said to Vern, "Drive."

Vern did as instructed.

After a few minutes, Vern said through the opening, "I haven't been to that pie place. Chloe's, I think it's called?"

"Chloe's Pie Shack?"

"If you insist," he said chirpily. "Or I could take you straight home, if you'd like, but I'll admit I'd like to try their famous pie, and it's no fun to go alone."

"I usually go there with Shayla, and we get two flavors and split them so we get a bit of each."

"Shall we swing by the house and pick her up on the way?"

"No, Vern. We'll go, just the two of us. I wouldn't want to share you with her."

"Very well, then."

Smiling, I turned and looked back out the rear window of the car. We were miles from Dalton's cabin by now, but turning and looking back helped, somehow.

The things I'd said to him as I was leaving—about him only chasing me because I kept running away—I wondered if it was true. People say that about men, but they also say little boys in school pull your pigtails because they like you.

After a quiet drive, we pulled into the parking lot for Chloe's Pie Shack, which shares a building with Burt's Burger Barn (Burt is Chloe's father). The place was busy for a Wednesday night, but Vern and I got a nice table in the corner. A few people smiled our way, probably thinking I was out with my father. I scanned the restaurant for familiar faces, but didn't see anyone I knew by name. (Contrary to what some people think, not everyone in a small town knows everyone else.)

A redheaded boy around sixteen came by with our menus and two skyscraper-tall, thin glasses of ice water.

"You're one of Adrian's girlfriends," the boy said. "He's not working here anymore."

"I know," I said, giving him the stop-talking-now stare.

Vern and I looked over the menus and ordered the Mile-High Lemon Meringue, and the Choco-Ruby, the latter being a raspberry-rhubarb combination with chocolate lattice on top.

We mostly talked about the food and restaurant. Vern felt the sugar dispensers and chrome napkin holders were "perfect." I suggested we hold the wedding reception there. He barely twitched an eyebrow, but didn't say more.

The Pie Shack was warm with laughter and body heat. Part-way through the pie, I took off my jacket, which was the red-checked one Dalton had loaned me. I'd forgotten I was still wearing it, and I'd forgotten about the ring, which was still in the box, in the pocket. My finger twitched, as though my finger knew about the ring and craved gold and diamonds. Dalton was rich, so the ring would definitely be impressive.

Vern asked me what I studied in college, then I asked about his background. To my surprise, he'd been a commercial pilot for a couple of small airlines before he got into his current line of work. He'd enjoyed flying, but never got accustomed to the changes in air pressure from going up and down several times a day, day after day.

"Your digestive system shuts down up there," he said as he chased the last few crumbs around the plate. "And I enjoy digestion too much."

"Me, too."

The waiter came by, and Vern said to me, "What pie should we order to take home for your housemate?"

I glanced over at the specials board and ordered the Spooky Custard Berry for Shayla.

I hadn't thought about getting takeout for Shayla, but Vern really impressed me with his thoughtfulness. It made me wonder how much worse Dalton would be at dating if he didn't have some coaching from Vern.

We left the restaurant, and on the drive home, I asked Vern, "Did you pick out the engagement ring?"

Without pausing, he said, "No. He came up with that himself."

"I sense disapproval in your voice, Vern."

He chuckled and pushed the button to jokingly raise the glass between us by a few inches.

~

Vern dropped me off at home, and I ran into the house and up to my room.

Instead of looking at the ring, I folded the red jacket around the box and stuffed everything in a dresser drawer next to my bed. The red foil heart-shaped balloon my family gave me a week earlier had completely deflated, and the crinkled heart gently settled on top of the jacket.

When I woke up Thursday morning, I stared at the closed drawer for a long time.

I didn't look, though. I left the drawer closed and went to work early.

At the bookstore, I settled into my comfortable routine. Plenty of customers came in to check out the tables of deals on select books. Like most bookstores, we're able to send back unsold books. They get returned to the distributors. Overstock is not a problem in the book business, except for with a few smaller distributors, where Gordon pays for the books outright, but at a steeper discount to offset the risk. Customers really don't care about the business model of a retail store, though. If you're moving locations, they expect a sale, regardless of the economics.

After lunch, our delivery man, Carter, came in with three boxes on his wheeled cart.

"Those can't be for us," I said, shaking my head. "No new inventory until the move. I don't need more things to pack."

Carter stopped and pretended to have hurt feelings, both hands over his heart. "You're not happy to see me? I'm crushed."

The new ink on his arms had healed, and countless bright-hued fish swam up and down Carter's arm amidst fine, red-gold arm hairs.

"Of course I'm happy to see you." I smiled and stared up at Carter's friendly eyes, blue with an inner ring so pale it looked white. He and I had been friendly since he moved to Beaverdale to play guitar and enjoy the small-town life. We'd flirted a few times, but never dated. The topic had only come up once he'd found out I was with Dalton. As I stared up into Carter's eyes, fringed by pale gold eyelashes, I wondered if he was in my bookstore to further complicate my love life.

"These boxes aren't for you," he said.

"I'd celebrate being right, as usual, but people take it the wrong way. Maybe it's the song and dance I do."

He grinned. "Do you know I'm the other guy?"

"What other guy?"

"I'm dating Golden, who's seeing Adrian, who's—"

"I know the rest!" I put my hands on my hips and looked at Carter through the new filter of him dating Golden. They would make a cute couple.

"My other girl is my guitar, though. My dating life isn't as exciting as yours. I have thought about asking out Kirsten, from Java Jones, but I don't know."

"So, you're just here to let me know we're in the same dating chain?"

"And to say hello, because I've missed delivering to you."

His adoring gaze started to feel weird.

Some customers came in the door, putting an additional layer of awkwardness on the conversation.

Carter and I talked a little about the store's upcoming move, and then he left with the three boxes, which were actually for the music store a few blocks over.

After he was gone, I wondered if he'd come over to ask me on a date, turning our dating chain into a circle. Little did he know I was pretty booked up, what with the upcoming wedding.

~

Ten minutes before closing, Adrian came in, wearing shorts and running shoes with a sleeveless shirt that showed off his long, muscled arms.

"I hope you're hungry," he said.

I stared at his face, at the light glinting on the short beard growth on his face. He hadn't shaved that morning, and he had what always looked to me like brown sugar granules along his jaw.

"Of course I'm hungry," I said. "I'm totally hungry for our... date tonight?"

"You forgot all about me."

I was standing behind the store's counter, so I did what I always do and dumped out the pen holder for a good sorting.

"Remind me what we have planned," I said, smiling down at the pens as I arranged them by color.

"We're getting a quick bite to eat then hiking out to Phantom Bog."

"Hiking?" You'd think I'd remember agreeing to something so ominous. "Oh, right. Good thing I'm already wearing my most rugged sneakers. Do I need hiking boots? Because I don't own hiking boots, so we'll have to do something else, instead."

He leaned on the counter and peered over at my footwear. "Nice try, but those are fine." He paused, his face inches from mine. "Do I get a kiss hello?"

I kissed his cheek and he leaned back again, satisfied. "Want some help closing up shop? You count up the float while I get the sandwich board and lights."

"Yes, boss." I started punching the end-of-day codes into the credit card terminal.

As Adrian helped with the closing, I counted up the totals. I had to keep restarting my count because my mind wandered. *This is nice*, I kept thinking. Having Adrian help with closing and winding up the exterior awning for me... it was downright romantic.

What the hell was I doing messing around with Dalton Deangelo when I had the guy of my dreams within reach?

Eyes open, Peaches.

Over the past few whirlwind weeks, I'd forgotten about the promise I'd made to myself many years ago, to keep my damn eyes open. Life isn't about closing your eyes and making a wish. That way leads to denial, disappointment, danger, and a bunch of other D-words. Smart people keep their eyes open and make their own good fortune.

MIMI STRONG

CHAPTER 13

We got takeout from Burt's and drove west in Adrian's mother's car.

People in Beaverdale will argue over the name of Phantom Bog. Some people say it's named after the Phantom Orchid, which is native to Washington State. This rare orchid only blooms in conjunction with perfect soil conditions and a specific fungus it has a symbiotic relationship with. Local legend says this chlorophyll-devoid orchid will only blossom near the fecal droppings of Forest Folk.

These local supernaturals are not anything you'd want to encounter in the wilderness, unless you enjoy the company of human-sasquatch-hybrid cannibals. According to local parents, Forest Folk eat the toes of children who don't clean up their bedrooms, and they have Santa Claus on speed dial. (Unlike regular sasquatch or yeti, Forest Folk have telephones.)

If you happen upon a giant, hairy beast in the local forests, don't stop for photos. Run for your life. Not even lumberjacks would survive an encounter. Forest Folk regenerate body parts instantly, so even if you have an ax and chop off their terrifying arms, they'll grow new ones and use the old ones to beat you to death. Or so the local legends go.

What were we talking about again? Oh, right. Phantom Bog.

Some people say it's named after the ghosts that float up at dusk and go to their night jobs, making the floors of old houses squeak extra loud.

Speaking of scary things…

GRRRR.

A growl pierced the calm of the car as we drove through the woods. In the back seat was Cujo, the retired police dog who was living out his golden years with Adrian's family.

"I forgot he was back there," I said, fanning my face with both hands, which we all know is the best method for making your heart slow down to its normal resting speed.

"We can't go hiking without protection," Adrian said. "The Forest Folk will gobble our toes."

"They only eat your toes if you're naughty."

Adrian turned and raised his golden eyebrows, his cool blue eyes wordlessly reminding me of our session dry-humping at the skating rink, and then the oral showdown in my kitchen.

Were those things actually naughty, though? We were both consenting adults, being honest with each other, and any minute now I was going to casually let him know I might be dating another man soon—my husband.

Cujo growled again, and I hunched down guiltily in my seat. The dog was totally onto me, sensing my guilt.

Cujo and I had a "meet cute" story in which he thought I was a perp running through the forest, and I thought he was a mutant cannibal sasquatch, and he took me down like a bag of chips at a stoner party. We'd tried to make friends since that, but I could see in his big, brown eyes that if I so much as darted sideways quickly to avoid a bee, he'd gleefully make me eat dirt. Even there in the car, he was staring me down. I should have given him some of my burger, even though Adrian had a "no people food" rule.

Adrian pulled the car over to the side of the dirt road, and we rolled bumpily to a stop near the trees. To the left and right of us were some ruts in the ground, from other vehicles, but other than that, the spot didn't look any different from anywhere else along the road. If this was the condition of the parking lot, I had some concerns about the hiking trail.

Adrian turned off the ignition and let Cujo out of the car. The dog bounded off into the woods, wagging his tail like a puppy. When he wasn't biting the fleshy part of your ass, Cujo was a cute German Shepherd, and not nearly as terrifying as his namesake, the rabid St. Bernard in the Stephen King book and movie.

"Are you sure this is the right place?" I asked Adrian. "I don't see any signage."

Adrian propped his long running-shoe-clad foot up on a rock and leaned forward. "Stretch your calves and hammies. The bog is about a half hour's walk in there. The terrain's mostly flat, but a stretch now will help prevent injuries if you stumble."

"Hammies?" I stretched up and then leaned forward to stretch my hamstrings. "Do you really say hammies or is that just for my benefit?"

"I say hammies. This is the real me, Peaches. For better or for worse, I genuinely thought walking to a bog to see a rare orchid was a good date idea. I don't have a bunch of money to buy a cabin or a float plane, but I'll never lie to you, not even if it's to tell you what you want to hear."

"Back it up. Dalton bought a float plane? An actual airplane?"

"Yes, and he probably did it to impress you. Meanwhile, I take you to the woods to get eaten by mosquitos. Kind of a self-sabotage move now that I think about it."

"Forget about him, because I'm having fun doing this, and we're going to get some sweet orchid photos for our moms."

He let out a low chuckle. "Fair enough. I'll shut up about my insecurities."

"Dude, you're dating two of the hottest girls in town, plus you're sexy as hell. In LA, I had to pose in my underwear with this blond dude who was about your height, but not nearly as cute."

"You really think I'm cute?" He grinned at me, his gorgeous smile only making the question more ridiculous.

"Now you're just fishing for compliments."

I rested my foot on the rock next to Adrian's and stretched my calves, facing him. At least I'd worn stretchy jeans that day, which would be fine for the walk. An hour's walk sounded just fine to me. Walks are fun. When people say *hike*, I always imagine myself dangling from the side of a mountain, like a ripe plum about to plummet from a tree.

When we were done stretching, Adrian grabbed a backpack from the car. In the bag was bottled water, two extra jackets made of polar fleece, and some emergency supplies. I left my purse in the car, tucked under the front seat.

Adrian scooped my hand into his, and we started off into the woods, following some hand-lettered arrow signs nailed to trees. As we moved deeper into the woods, where the summer evening's sunshine didn't reach, the name Phantom Bog became more ominous.

Along the walk, we talked about the upcoming move for the bookstore, and all the things that needed to be done. Adrian had a neat idea to put a sliding door in between the new location and the coffee shop next door, so that some of their seating would spill over into the bookstore and bring a happy buzz to the space. We'd have to put up signs reminding people to purchase the magazines before taking them into the coffee area, but it would probably boost sales enough to be worth the annoyance of a few people treating the place like a community center.*

*Not that I have any issues with people coming in for a browse, but some folks seem genuinely clueless about how business works and think that the mere presence of breathing human bodies within a space generates revenue to pay the rent and electricity. No, sir, and no, ma'am. The first rule of retail is that the money goes into the register. I'd love to get revenue for the shop some other way, such as presence of bodies, so that our main objective could be creating happiness and promoting literacy, but until that funding comes through, they should just pay for their damn copy of Vanity Fair before they get biscotti crumbs between the pages.**

**Elderly ladies who copy the recipes out of cookbooks (Yes, this happens.) are still fine by me. I'm not a monster.

~

Still holding hands, Adrian and I stepped out into a clearing in the trees. Before us, some tattered orange ribbon stretched between posts in the ground, marking off an area the size of a high school track field.

We were at the bog already, the walk having passed quickly due to conversation and flirting.

Both of us looked up in response to a buzzing from the sky. I saw something uncommon for Beaverdale, because there's no airport nearby: an airplane flying overhead.

"Wow," I said. "He really did buy a plane, didn't he?"

Adrian frowned at the sky. "How did he learn to fly, though? It's not like pretending to be a vampire. You can't just *act* like you can fly. Actors can't fly."

"No, but butlers can, if they used to be pilots." The plane disappeared, so I turned back to Adrian, who had a sour expression. "Hey, don't be sad. You'll just have to build up another empire and get your own personal-assistant-slash-butler-slash-pilot."

Adrian snorted. "Don't think I won't."

"I'm sure you will. You've done all this stuff with the bookstore in a few weeks. You'll be running half the town in no time."

"You're only saying that to make me feel better."

"Duh. That's why people say nice things, or that everything's going to work out."

Adrian turned to frown at the empty sky, not even listening to me.

I continued, "Saying platitudes sure beats the hell out of saying everything's going to get worse and worse and then we all die." I grabbed his shoulders and tried to shake some sense into him. "Adrian, snap out of it! You never cared about planes before, did you?"

Weakly, he murmured, "I like planes, and boats, and cars."

"Snap out of it!" I shook him harder. "I don't care about that stuff, and neither does any girl worth being with."

He grumbled, "But the rich guy always gets the girl. When I was rich, I could get any girl I wanted."

I waved toward a fallen log. "Let's have a seat, crack open those granola bars, and you tell me all about the girls you got when you were rich. I want to hear about gold-digging sluts. In fact, that's why I came with you out to this amazing bog."

He shook his head, smiling sheepishly. "That was Greedy Adrian making a guest appearance."

Cujo trotted over and sat expectantly at our feet.

"Good dog," Adrian said, slipping off the backpack to retrieve the dog treats. The elderly German Shepherd accepted a big Milk Bone and settled down to crunch it with his remaining teeth.

The two of us humans walked over to the log and took a seat overlooking the view. The bog wasn't as muddy as I expected, and didn't look much different from the surrounding trees, except the ground was lower and no trees grew within the area. White and purple wildflowers dotted the sparse grass, and small birds hopped around feeding on seeds and looking at us sideways.

"Is Greedy Adrian a bad guy?" I asked.

The log was bumpy, and I wiggled around to where I didn't have a knot or branch trying to get to third base with me.

Adrian put his hand on my knee and rubbed his palm casually along my thigh. Under my jeans, my skin registered his touch with interest.

"Greedy Adrian is a hard worker," he said.

"Does he work through the night at bookstores?"

"He can be obsessive."

"Does he want to be the boy with all the toys?"

"How did you guess?"

"He's been staring at my bean bags since we sat down." I snapped my fingers in front of my chest. "Hello, Greedy Adrian. My eyes are up here."

"Grr," he replied. "Greedy Adrian wants what he sees."

I rolled my eyes. "First the bog and now the hot, sexy talk. I'm under your spell. Kiss me now."

Adrian took my sarcastic comment as a command and immediately planted his lips on mine.

I would have pushed him away, but his lips were so pleasant. And his tongue. And his hands, first on my back, and then slipping up the front of my shirt and greedily rubbing my breasts through my silky bra. All of these things were very pleasant, and the forest setting became very romantic. The dappled light was certainly better than the dark of the roller rink or the bright light of my kitchen.

My skin was practically steaming by the time he pulled my shirt off over my head. The cool air on my bare skin was a relief, cooling me momentarily before the burning-hot kisses that rained down from Adrian's gorgeous mouth.

I slipped my hands under his T-shirt, palming his chest and the ridges of his stomach muscles before tugging the shirt up and over his head.

We both turned on the log so we were facing each other, straddling our seat.

"You look like a goddess," he breathed as he admired me.

"Goddess of the bog?"

He reached around to my back and unlatched my bra, drinking me in with his eyes as he slipped off my bra and tossed it onto the pile of our clothes.

"You look like a sexy forest nymph. No, a forest nymphomaniac. Is that a real thing? Because maybe it should be."

I giggled, covering my mouth with one hand.

He cupped his palms around the bottoms of my breasts and tilted them up. His voice deep and husky, he said, "I'm feeling greedy again."

"You talk too much. Put my nips in your mouth."

He flashed his eyes at me and took a delicious mouthful of breast, giving it a hard suck to send tingles all around my seat.

He licked and sucked my breasts for what felt like hours, until I felt like a tea kettle about to whistle. I unbuttoned my jeans, guided his fingers down, and after a few more minutes of fingers swirling, I was whistling, indeed. All the way to completion.

With my moans of pleasure still fresh on my lips, I moved back on the log, leaned forward, and unbuttoned his hiking shorts. Adrian's wood came out to match the forest surrounding us, and I got to work making the most of the local natural resources.

This time, I didn't ask him to say any dirty things. The serenity of the forest was too beautiful, plus I already felt dirty enough, with all the little birds and creatures watching.

When we were finished exchanging pleasantries, we celebrated by sharing a ginger-ale and a couple of granola bars.

The timer alarm on Adrian's phone jarred us out of our reverie. Sundown was less than an hour away, and the walk back would take less than that, but only if we hurried.

I told Adrian to wait for me while I found somewhere semi-private to tinkle. I was embarrassed to be talking to him about bladder business, but wetting my pants on the walk or drive home would be worse.

"Go right here. I won't look." He shook his head at my modesty. "Fine, go wander off, but don't go far, and take Cujo to watch out for bears."

111

What I should have said was, "What bears?" Instead, however, I called the dog to come with me, and I stupidly blundered off into the bushes looking for somewhere semi-private.

I found a nice spot to wee, grumbling to myself about how much easier it is for boys, who don't have to locate an incline so as to avoid muddying their shoes. After I was done, I stood up to button my jeans, and Cujo growled.

Cujo wasn't growling at me, though, but at something behind me. Naturally, I assumed the shadowy shape was just Adrian, with his shirt pulled up over his head or something equally ridiculous.

"Oh, help," I squealed. "Please don't eat my toes, Mr. Scary Forest Folk Man!"

Cujo kept growling, his lips curled back in a snarl and his haunches up, his fur standing up.

I looked more carefully, and found a black bear less than forty feet away. The bear was still at first, then raised its snout up, sniffing the air. I could actually hear its breaths as it sniffed, then raised up slowly, standing on its back legs.

Cujo began barking, still holding his ground.

Adrian called out my name from nearby.

I didn't answer, because the bear seemed focused on the dog, and I didn't want to alarm it. I began slowly backing away.

Adrian seemed to be calling out my name, but I couldn't hear him over the dog barking and the pulse rushing in my ears.

I kept backing up, until something grabbed me. A hand clapped over my mouth, stifling my scream.

"You're okay," Adrian whispered in my ear. "I've got you and you're okay. We're going to quietly back up. We'll just back on out of here."

He pulled his hand from my mouth. Cujo stood halfway between us and the bear, still barking and growling. The bear was bobbing from side to side in a way that was both cute and mind-blowingly terrifying.

We backed up, putting more distance between us and the bear. Adrian finally called out softly, "Cujo, down. Come. Come here. Heel."

The dog turned to look our way, momentarily distracted, and the bear leapt forward, making its move.

I screamed. Adrian grabbed my arm tightly and commanded that we run.

CHAPTER 14

"No! Cujo!" I howled.

"He's fine," Adrian said through gritted teeth, and tugged my arm hard.

We ran through the woods, me with tears streaming down my face. We ran until I was out of breath and stumbling over branches.

Adrian stopped.

The woods were silent. No dog barks. Nothing.

Adrian whistled for Cujo.

No response.

He whistled again.

Nothing.

"I'm so sorry," I blubbered. "It's all my fault. I wasn't paying attention."

Adrian held his finger to his lips.

I held my breath.

A dog barked, just one little bark.

Adrian whistled again.

The bushes nearby rustled.

After several painful minutes of waiting, the German Shepherd came limping toward us from the shadows.

I've never been so happy to see a dog. I knelt down and hugged him, only to discover he was bleeding, pretty bad. The bear must have bitten or scratched him across the shoulder, and I could see that he needed stitches.

Adrian seemed to be in shock.

Something kicked in for me, and I felt utterly calm.

I looked for the backpack that had been on Adrian's shoulders, but it must have been left behind. We needed bandage, big enough to wrap around Cujo's shoulder to slow the bleeding.

I took off my shirt and ripped off the lower portion to create a wrap. While I tied a knot in the fabric to secure the makeshift bandage, Cujo licked my hand.

"You're going to be fine," I said gently. "You're a tough old bugger, and this is just a scratch."

I got everything tied up as tight as I could, and stood there trying to figure out the best way to carry the dog, who seemed to be getting weaker on his feet by the minute. His tail was drooping, and his eyes had lost their brightness.

"I don't know if I can carry him the whole way back," I said.

Adrian finally moved, kneeling down and scooping up the dog in his strong arms. "I got him," he murmured. "Can you get us back on the trail?"

"Of course," I said. "The trail is this way." I pointed to one of the trail markers, and we were off. I led the way, turning back periodically with encouragement for Cujo, who was still conscious, but just barely.

~

We called Golden from the car, and she was waiting at the veterinarian's clinic when we pulled into the parking lot. She'd called her boss, and the older woman who was the veterinarian arrived at the same time we did.

The two of them took a limp but breathing Cujo into the back and left us waiting in the front area.

Both of us stood so we didn't get blood on the upholstered seats.

I kept apologizing to Adrian, who insisted I hadn't done anything wrong, then started apologizing to me.

"I shouldn't have taken you all the way out there," he said, his face grim and eyes glistening.

"No, it's my fault. I wasn't paying attention. That's me. I get caught up in my head, and my eyes are open, but I don't see what's obvious. I'm so stupid. And now poor Cujo, that brave little man..."

Adrian put his arms around me and rested his chin on top of my head. "He'll be fine. They're still in there, and no news is good news.

And if he's not fine, everyone at the station will be so proud he was such a hero—" Adrian's voice pinched off with emotion.

I squeezed my arms tighter around his body.

The sun was gone, and nobody had turned on the lights in the waiting room, so we were in the dark. I could have looked around for a light switch, but the dark seemed soothing.

We stood holding each other, listening for sounds from the adjoining room. The veterinarian and Golden were speaking to each other with urgency, but not panic.

After an unbearable wait of one hour, the veterinarian came out smiling. "He's resting," she said. "We put him out so he wouldn't hurt himself while his body begins the repair."

"How many stitches?" Adrian asked.

"Not too many." Her voice pitched up high, the way it does when people lie.

Adrian started to wobble next to me, and as the veterinarian gave us a few more details, his responses were delayed and groggy. I steered him over to the one wooden chair in the room and forced him to sit down.

He wanted to take Cujo home, but they insisted he stay overnight so they could keep an eye on him. The vet lived nearby, and had cameras set up in the recovery cages for remote monitoring.

"We'll take great care of Mr. Cujo Fluffypants," Golden said chirpily. "And tomorrow you can take him home wearing the Cone of Shame, so he doesn't chew out those itchy stitches."

Adrian still looked stunned. "Cone of Shame?"

She explained about the plastic cone dogs and cats wear around their collar so they don't lick their stitches after surgery.

I ran out to the car to get my purse, which I'd left under the seat during our excursion. I caught a look at myself in the car window's reflection and gasped at the sight of my bare stomach. Half my shirt had been used as a makeshift bandage/sling, and I'd slipped back on the remaining half, which barely covered my bra. This was not my finest fashion moment, but at least everyone was still alive.

I came back into the clinic to find Golden standing next to Adrian, who was still on the wooden chair, having his hair stroked by the tiny blonde.

Conflicting emotions battled within me as I dug around in my purse for chocolate to give Adrian.

"Not hungry," he said as I thrust an unwrapped chunk his way.

"You're in shock. You need something to bring your blood sugar up."

Golden had stopped stroking his hair, and simply agreed with me, urging him to eat the chocolate.

The veterinarian came through, with her coat on and purse on her shoulder. She told Adrian they could deal with the paperwork tomorrow. She answered a few more questions, then apologized for rushing off, saying she had kids with homework waiting at home.

Golden took us back to see Cujo, who was stretched out on his side and looking comfortable, despite the plastic cone tapering out from his collar. Thankfully the wound was covered by bandages.

We gave him some pats through the bars of the cage—more for our benefit than his, since he was crashed out on drugs—and we left him there.

Golden gave us both a hug goodbye, and we went back out to the car. I felt lighter, like my whole body was filled with helium.

"It's weird to leave him here," Adrian said as he started the car. "I feel like I'm forgetting something."

"I'll pay for the vet bill."

He patted my leg, showing traces of his first smile since the accident. "Firstly, I wouldn't let you. Secondly, he has a fund set up for him that covers his care." He turned the car in the direction of my house.

We drove for a while without talking, the radio on at a low volume. The announcer came on and said something stupid about Hollywood stars taking over the town.

I wanted to say something to Adrian, but I couldn't think of what. Finally, he broke the silence.

"Peaches, I know things are really complicated right now, but no matter what happens, I've been blessed to get to know you better."

"Are you breaking up with me?"

"No. Do you want me to?"

I chewed the inside of my cheek for a moment. "I'm seeing Dalton this weekend, and I'm afraid you'll hate me next week. More than you already do."

"I will never hate you, and that's a promise. You're one of the most maddening and fascinating people I've ever known, and you have a good heart, as big as the sky. You have so much to give." He tapped the steering wheel, the smile on his face growing. "And you're a good kisser."

"I could say all those exact same things about you."

"Good."

We drove the rest of the way to my house in silence.

He got out and walked me to my door. "I'll buy you a new shirt," he said, looking down at the tattered, blood-spattered edge of my top.

I slapped the side of my stomach. "As nice as this one? Seriously, this is a great cut for showing off my hot model body."

"Do you want me to come in and tuck your hot model body into bed?"

He looked sleepy, like he would fall onto my bed and not leave until morning.

"I'll be fine." I gave him two kisses, a quick one followed by a longer one. "Call me first thing tomorrow and let me know how Cujo is doing."

He gave me another kiss, lingering and soft.

"Will do, hot model girl."

I opened the door and waved goodbye from the doorway.

MIMI STRONG

CHAPTER 15

Friday morning, I was back at Peachtree Books, in my regular routine, but feeling odd and unsettled, waiting for the next thing to run in the door and knock me off my feet.

Adrian called to let me know that Cujo had a good, long sleep, and was hungry and wagging his tail in the morning. The dog would be taking a load of antibiotics and going back to the vet for checkups, but he was heading home that afternoon.

I should have been relieved after the good news, but my body felt like a wound-up spring, tensely anticipating change.

The store would be moving next week, and there was no denying the massive upheaval that was coming. The books themselves were pouting, refusing to cooperate. Normally during the course of a day, I'd have one or two front-faced books topple off a shelf with the breeze of the door opening. That Friday, before I even took my lunch break, I'd had a total of four books swan-dive to the floor.

I got all the books back in place and ordered them to behave before I locked the door with the *Back in Five Minutes* sign in place.

Kirstin wasn't working at Java Jones that day, so I was served by a nice-looking man, around thirty, with a long, red beard and square glasses.

"Peaches Monroe!" he said as I approached the counter.

"You're the stand-up bass player," I said hesitantly.

"Correct! You win a prize." He drew a card from the front pocket of his black apron and handed it to me. "That's a free download of the hottest new single from the Bushy Beaver Tails, Beaverdale's almost-famous band."

I turned the card over to read the song title: *Shake Your Peaches.*

121

I didn't know what to make of that, but my face sure didn't care for it, and I found myself scowling.

"You inspired our best song yet," he said. "*Shake Your Peaches* is about love and confidence. We're all major fans of yours, and our drums player Lester constantly brags about being your cousin's cousin."

I shoved the card into my pocket, no longer scowling, but not feeling entirely comfortable. "I'm just a regular person."

"Sure, we all are. But you represent an idea that's long overdue—that everyone has a beauty, and not just cookie-cutter plastic pop stars. I swear there's a factory somewhere that grows them in vats, with their perfect hair and their cliched song lyrics. But we sure showed them, because we're all going to be in *Vanity Fair!*"

"That's right!" I'd almost forgotten about the photo shoot from several weeks ago—the promo for Dalton's indie movie. "I hope the pictures turn out."

The stand-up bass player grinned and pulled out his phone. "Some preview shots are online already, and they're hysterical."

He showed me a photo, and the shot was so stunning, I had to try hard to convince myself the gorgeously curvy blonde was me. I was dancing with Charlie (the guy who played Dalton's brother in the indie movie), while the seven-man band played amidst bales of hay. The second photo in the series showed three actors in teddy bear costumes attacking the set and terrorizing everyone.

In light of the previous night's horror, the fake bears didn't seem so amusing to me, personally, but the double-page shots were gorgeous.

"You should go on tour with us," the man said.

I laughed. "I can't sing."

"Neither can we, but we don't let it stop us."

"Don't lie! You guys are amazing."

His cheeks reddened and he chanted, "I *will* take compliments. I *will* take compliments."

We both laughed over the oddities of being in the public eye, and I eventually got my lunch order and rushed back to work.

I tried to lose myself in the routine, and pretend that the day was no different than any other Friday, but it was different.

On Saturday morning, I had a date lined up with Dalton Deangelo, and, as far as I knew, we'd be getting married for the benefit of the press.

Everything was happening so quickly, and I still hadn't told anyone. I hadn't even looked at the engagement ring. Part of me believed that if I ignored the issue, it would just go away. (I think we all know how well that worked out with my unplanned pregnancy.)

~

I got home after work to an empty house, because Shayla was working late. Usually, if I didn't have Friday night plans with friends, I'd have dinner with my family, but my mother had messaged that she was canning pickles from the garden, so the boys were going out for a boys' night. I thought about joining her to help with canning, but my mother can get a little intense about her brines.

Alone in the empty house, I downloaded and listened to *Shake Your Peaches* while I broke out the adult beverages. What goes best with shots of vodka? Beer. Also, Hot Pockets, Philly Cheese Steak flavor, with a side of sour cream.

"Happy bachelorette party!" I told myself as I prepared the plate.

Me and my party favors danced all the way up to my room, where I busted out the laptop and started shopping. There were so many great sales on! And free shipping! I got genuinely excited for Future Peaches, who was going to get so many amazing things delivered… if only I could click the checkout button.

"This has never happened before," I told my laptop, and it was the truth. My finger went limp when it was time to finish the business. I couldn't commit to a single internet order. Not even one pair of rainbow toe socks, half price.

My laptop was put to bed unsatisfied.

I had a few more shots of vodka, thinking that would help, but the booze only enhanced the feelings I was already having—feelings of fear and uncertainty.

I put my head down on my pillow to rest for a minute, since it was barely ten o'clock. Sleep quickly took me in its padded-walls embrace. Secure in sleep's straight jacket, I dreamed of dogs and bears at a picnic, laughing at me as I ran around catching ripe fruit, falling from the sky, in the folds of my skirt. I twirled, and the white skirt expanded all around me, turning the whole world into lace.

The clouds in the sky spelled out one word. Love.

The only thing that mattered was love.

~

Vern arrived to pick me up precisely at six in the morning, as arranged.

I'd been awake since five, and was showered and ready to go, my overnight bag packed. I had a slight hangover from the night before, but luckily I'd fallen asleep before I could do too much harm to myself or my credit card.

Vern stood on my porch, looking cheerful.

"Miss Monroe, I took the liberty of getting you a mocha from Java Jones. It's waiting in the car."

"Forget Dalton Deangelo, I want to marry you, Vern. Seriously. What will it take?"

"I don't mean to be gauche, ma'am, but you're not my type."

"I don't have the right equipment? Honey, I could get one of those harness things, and we could turn out all the lights and—oh, no! I'm sexually harassing you. Sorry. I'm so embarrassed, Vern."

He held the door of the car open for me. "I'm not feeling harassed, but apology accepted."

"That's good, because I'm already engaged to someone else, as you may know."

"Someone with smoldering green eyes?"

I began to giggle uncontrollably as I slipped into the back seat.

Vern gave me a knowing look and circled around to the driver's seat.

I sipped my mocha quietly on the drive out to the tip of Dragonfly Lake, where we drove past the cabin Dalton was renovating, to a dock with a float plane.

"Mr. Deangelo is meeting us there," Vern explained when he saw me looking around.

I approached the plane cautiously, the suitcase I'd borrowed from Shayla making loud noises on the wooden dock as it rolled.

"He's meeting us in LA?" I asked.

"No, San Francisco."

"Why not LA? Wouldn't that be a better location for all the press?"

"His favorite wedding gown designer is in San Francisco. The first fittings are today, and there are other plans for Sunday."

I stopped and looked up at the blue sky. "Vern, I can be dense sometimes, but are you saying the wedding isn't this weekend?"

He laughed. "This weekend? That would be preposterous. We haven't even discussed the dinner menu."

"Why did I think anything with Dalton Deangelo could be simple and quick?" I held up my hand. "Don't answer. That's a rhetorical question."

Vern swung open the door of the small plane and took my suitcase as I stepped up into the vessel. As he got my luggage stowed away and pointed out the safety features of the small, private plane, I tried to maintain a neutral expression.

We stood together in the center of the plane, which was even tinier than Dalton's Airstream trailer inside. What was it about that man and his little tin cans?

Vern pointed out the fire extinguisher and other things I hoped to never use.

I wondered what Shayla was doing back at the house. She was probably still in bed, the lucky girl. I'd popped my head into her room that morning to let her know I was heading out of town with Dalton. She sat up, stared straight at me, and asked me to bring back fancy cheese.

Fancy cheese.

It had seemed like such an odd request that I'd asked if she was sleep-talking and asked her to solve a simple math problem. She got the answer wrong, but I agreed to her request all the same.

When Vern was finished talking about "unlikely events," I pulled out my phone and asked if I could text while we were flying.

"Only if you want me to leave you up there," he said, pointing to the sky beyond the curved ceiling of the plane.

"You're bad, Vern."

"Just a little pilot humor."

"Why do you look so happy? I thought you quit being a commercial pilot because you didn't like it."

He glanced over his shoulder at the pilot's chair with fondness. "I love flying, but you can have too much of a good thing when you're doing multiple flights every day. This, however, is puddle hopping, and puddle hopping is fun! Now, pick a seat."

I chose a chair and buckled my seat belt as he watched. I wriggled in the seat, which was a little tight for my body, but not bad.

He continued, "I was in the air too much, but a few trips a week is wonderful. Do you know what I mean? With too much of something you love?"

"I may have reached that point myself, talking to customers about books."

"Are you tired of the books, or the customers?"

"Mostly the repetition."

He laughed. "So, you mean the customers, but you don't want to sound rude. It's okay, I understand."

"Oh, I love the customers, usually, but the novelty wears off when you're giving these little prepared speeches: *Yes, it's too bad there's no more Oprah's book club. Yes, it's a shame more people aren't reading these days, but you're here in a bookstore now, so why don't we have a look?* And so on, and so on." I put my hands up to my neck and pretended to strangle myself.

"You'll have to find something new to occupy your days in LA, when you move in with Mr. Deangelo."

"Move in…?"

Vern winked at me. "One step at a time, Miss Monroe."

He moved back toward the front again, asking if I was ready to fly. I gave him two thumbs up and a big grin.

Off we went.

Taking off from a lake was certainly interesting. The acceleration feels not unlike being on a regular runway, once you get going. Soaring up over lush trees was terrifying yet magical, over the roar of the engine. I was so struck by the beauty of the surrounding countryside, plus the miracle of flight, that a pair of fat, wet tears ran down my cheeks.

The plane had six passenger seats, and I'd picked the middle one on the right-hand side without any deliberation. Now that we were soaring, I realized it was my usual position when going on outings with my family. For a moment, I imagined my parents in the front row and Kyle beside me. They would love this. *What was I thinking?* I should have invited them along… except it would have meant explaining everything to them.

My father would make that judgmental face and say that a fake wedding was so like me, because I was "prone to whimsy." My mother would probably ask a million intrusive questions and try to pimp me to Dalton for more money and jewelry. Kyle would run around and try to press buttons.

I shuddered at the thought. Maybe it was for the best I made this first trip without them.

~

The flight was just under three hours, and we landed at a private air strip outside San Francisco. I'd snoozed for most of the trip and kicked myself for missing all the scenery.

Vern had spoken to me over the intercom to assure me that the plane had wheels that popped out of the floats, so we were safe to land on a regular runway.

"I knew that," I said. (I hadn't known that.)

The engine roared as we descended.

Vern set the plane down like a sleeping baby in a cradle. I kid you not, the man knew how to land a plane. Whatever Dalton was paying him, it wasn't enough.

We stepped out of the plane and our feet clanged on the way down the metal steps. As soon as we touched solid ground, I turned and hugged Vern, hard.

"You'll get used to the jet-setting lifestyle," he said, patting my back. "You're doing great. Sometimes I forget you're only twenty-two, because you seem so capable. It's perfectly acceptable to be scared sometimes."

We were standing at the edge of the airstrip, and the California sun wasn't nearly as warm as I'd expected. In fact, the weather outside San Francisco seemed cooler than when we'd left, which had been early in the morning and lakeside in Washington.

I reached down and unzipped my bag to retrieve a fleece hoodie. I didn't like the idea of covering up my best assets before seeing Dalton, but I didn't like freezing my nips off, either.

"Sorry I didn't prepare you for the weather," Vern said. "California is a big state, and San Francisco is much cooler than LA. I understand sweaters are the most popular items at the souvenir shops."

"This Washington girl knows how to layer, so don't you worry."

"You do seem very capable, but don't hesitate to let me know if you need anything. Anything at all."

I stared up at Vern's kind face.

"I feel like a bull in a china shop," I confessed. "The china shop is my life in this metaphor."

"Everyone gets emotional after a flight. We'll get some nice lunch in you and everything will be fine." He looked over my shoulder at an approaching vehicle—a boxy, black Range Rover. "Here comes Mr. Deangelo. He seems late, but he isn't. If you must know, I wore my lucky socks today, so we arrived ten minutes early."

"Your socks make you fly faster?"

"More pilot humor."

The vehicle pulled to a stop and the engine turned off. I didn't have much time before Dalton was with us.

I grabbed Vern's arm and stared up into his eyes. "Vern, level with me. Does Mr. Deangelo love me?"

"Yes," he said, without hesitation.

"Why doesn't he say it to me?"

"Why don't you say it to him?"

I grabbed a handful of my hair and twirled it with one hand. "Did he really tell you that he loves me?"

"Not in so many words."

"He needs to hire a screenwriter for his life."

"Miss Monroe, there's a reason greeting cards have words written inside them." He raised his eyebrows to stress the importance of what he was saying. "Actions are certainly more important than words."

Dalton approached, cutting our private conversation short.

CHAPTER 16

"How was the flight?" Dalton asked as he approached. "Did Vern do any fancy loop-de-loops?"

Vern grinned and pointed his thumb back toward the plane. "This plane isn't rated for loop-de-loops, sir. Maybe the next one."

Dalton came to a stop in front of me and took off his mirrored sunglasses, his green eyes brilliant as emeralds in the daylight. Sometimes, when he wasn't right in front of me, I thought of Dalton Deangelo as an abstract concept only. He was the smug TV actor who chewed up the scenery in a campy vampire soap opera. He was the whirlwind of fame and chaos that came into my life and made a mess of everything. He was a problem I had to deal with and think about.

But sometimes, like that moment on the chilly airstrip, he was just a man, squinting in the bright light and looking happy to see me.

He raised one dark eyebrow quizzically. "Well?"

"Well?" I replied.

Some people in orange safety vests came out of the nearby building and Vern went off to talk to them about maintenance and refueling the plane.

Dalton took the handle of my suitcase and started walking toward the vehicle.

"I'm not going to compliment you on how you look," he said.

"Fine."

"Even though that blue shirt under your jacket brings out your gorgeous eyes, and those tight jeans show off all your curves and make me want to peel them off in the back seat of this truck with the tinted windows."

"Do you ever look at me and not think about doing dirty, sexy things?"

He chuckled. "Nope."

We reached the truck, where he grabbed me and playfully pushed me up against the door, my butt against the hard metal. He leaned in over me, his arms stretched over my shoulders and his hands on the truck, and he smelled my hair, breathing in audibly.

I could hardly breathe, and all my nerves were tingling from being in such close proximity. He sniffed again, like a wolf.

"Tell me something," he murmured near my ear, his voice deep and husky. "When you put on those clothes this morning, did you think about me taking them off?"

"I don't know," I lied. "It was early, and I just threw on the nearest thing."

"You didn't think about me running my finger up and down the line of this V-neck?" Instead of touching my neck, he puckered his lips and blew a stream of air along my neckline.

I reached up between his legs and cupped his package through his jeans. "What about you, Mr. Deangelo? Are you wearing silk boxers under these tight jeans that show off your big package?"

"Careful," he groaned.

I lightly massaged the bulge. He was always trying to throw me off balance with his flirtations, and how did he like it when the tables were turned? From the feel of his manhood, he liked it very much.

"There's my pony," I said. "There's my Lionheart, and he's ready to ride. But he's a bad pony. He thinks he's going to buck and gallop and take me for a ride, but this naughty pony's about to get broken in."

Dalton let out a laugh I could only describe as *nervous sounding*.

"How was the flight?" he asked, his voice high. "Any turbulence?"

We were still alone over by the truck, so I grabbed hold of his waistband with my free hand and then plunged the other hand down into his jeans.

He gasped as I took hold of him by the gigglestick.

"The flight was long and smooth." I stroked his shaft, making up for the lack of wiggle room by squeezing harder. "We started off fast, splashing around, then we got higher and higher, and then after a few hours of heaven, I came."

"You came?" His breathing was ragged.

"I came here to go shopping, and we're going to shop so hard. I'm going to make your credit card beg for mercy."

"Oh, Peaches, I dare you to break me. I'm your wild pony. I'm your Lionheart. Promise you'll never stop trying to break me."

"Careful what you wish for." I released his swollen manhood and withdrew my hand slowly from his clothes.

"To be continued," he said.

"Why haven't you kissed me yet?" I asked.

"I'm afraid to."

"Because you know my lips are bad for you?"

He leaned down, his face moving closer and closer to mine. His breath was hot on my cheek when he stopped moving, lips inches from mine. "Your lips are the least of my worries. It's the rest of you that terrifies me."

"Then you'd better not kiss me, because I'm the whole package."

He pulled away another inch. If I stood on my tiptoes, I could have kissed him, but I didn't.

"If I kiss you, everything will get complicated," he said.

"Yes. If you kiss me, Dalton, I promise you nothing short of disaster."

"Then I guess you leave me no choice." He dropped his arms to his sides and stepped back, then opened the door of the truck. "Get in."

That was it?

I climbed into the back seat. He circled around to the back to load in my suitcase, then continued up to the front door and got in the front passenger side.

Kiss denied.

I zipped open my purse and got out my phone, pretending not to be bothered that he wasn't sitting in the back with me.

What game was he playing? I wished I had a copy of the Dalton Deangelo handbook.

I scrolled through my messages and opened the ones from Adrian, who was letting me know his dog was recuperating nicely.

"Oh, good," I said out loud.

Dalton turned around and looked back from the front seat. "Vern will be here in a few minutes."

"Okay, that's good, too. I just found out my boyfriend's dog is feeling better. We were all out hiking and we had a terrible run-in with a bear."

"You went hiking?" He had a mischievous look that annoyed me.

"With my boyfriend."

"He doesn't mind that you stick your hand down other guys' pants?"

My head started to bob side to side with its own attitude. "Of course he doesn't. We have a very modern arrangement. We're honest with each other, and it's great."

"I noticed something, back when we were outside the truck and you were grabbing my dick like it was the last organic turkey at the farmer's market on the day before Thanksgiving. You aren't wearing the ring I gave you."

"I need to get it sized for my finger."

"I know for a fact the ring will fit perfectly. You haven't even opened the box, have you?"

"Everything's in my suitcase, and, by the way, I brought back your sexy lumberjack coat."

He nodded, taking his green eyes off me for just a moment. When he looked down, he always looked so sad and thoughtful. For an instant, I felt bad about being so hard on him, and lying about the ring.

His thick, dark eyelashes fluttered, then he looked up again, sunny and smiling that million-dollar grin. "Have you been to San Francisco before?"

"Is that the one with all the hills? And the trolley cars?"

"Yes," he said, clearly amused by my description.

"No, I haven't been there, then. I think I'd remember something like that."

"I'll try my best to make this a memorable weekend for you."

"Hah! I'm scared to find out what you have planned."

He nodded slowly. "Trespassing is definitely on the table."

"No trespassing and no public nudity."

"Come on, sugarlips. You were spending too many days in a sleepy little bookstore, and then I came along and unlocked your repressed cravings for criminal activity."

I wagged my finger. "Oh, no, do not look so proud. I was a good girl, and you corrupted me. My mother's friend went on a cruise and she didn't even ask me to babysit her cat. People around town look at me funny, and they haven't even seen my peaches in their magazines yet."

"You're a star."

I took a pause to breathe. Was Dalton giving me a pep talk? I wished he was in the back seat with me, because I would have preferred a hug, or just his arm around me.

He continued, "When you become a star, you burn and burn. That fire touches everyone around you. Fame puts relationships on fast forward, and it shines a light so bright, there's no shadow for your secrets to hide."

"Especially when some stupid girl blabs your secrets, for which I am truly sorry."

"You did me a favor."

"Good! We don't have to get fake-married."

He grinned. "Nice try. You did *me* a favor, but you may have murdered my career."

I leaned forward and stuck my fingertip right into his chin dimple. "But what about this dimple? This gorgeous face is going to have an amazing career, no matter what."

"You were in LA for a few weeks. Didn't you notice something about every food server and coffee barista you ran across?"

I kept poking him in the dimple. "Shut up. You're Dalton Deangelo. Those sexy waiters and bus boys can't hold a candle to you."

He gazed into my eyes. "Marry me."

I giggled in response, because Dalton was basically a mutant superhero, and his power was projecting stupidity from his eyes, straight into my brain.

He pulled away from my dimple-poking finger and neighed like a horse, which just made me laugh harder.

In a silly voice, he said, "I'm Lionheart! Nee-hee-hee-hee! I'm your favorite horsie ride, Peaches, so you should marry me."

And that's when Vern opened the driver's side door to find Dalton holding his hands up like pretend hooves and me rolling side to side in the back seat laughing and trying not to pee my pants.

"You two," Vern said, shaking his head like an embarrassed dad.

"Peaches brings out my crazy side," Dalton explained.

Vern asked gruffly, "What are you doing up here in the front?"

"Well... there's no privacy glass between the seats in this truck, and if I'm back there with Peaches, she'll do something CRAZY like stick her hand down my pants—"

"Never!" I shouted.

Vern held his hand up to quiet both of us. "I've heard enough, Mr. Deangelo. Shall we proceed to the first location on the itinerary?"

"Yeah, hit the gas, man. Drive it like you stole it."

Vern started the engine and turned to face Dalton, a questioning look on his face.

"What? It's an expression," Dalton said. "I did not steal this truck, honest."

"Then why is there no tag on the keychain? No rental brand?"

"Because I rented from the cool place, for cool people."

"There's nothing *cool* about car rental agencies, sir."

"But we're in San Francisco, where everything is rainbows and unicorns and cool stuff."

"That would be an excellent slogan for the postcards, sir."

"Sarcasm!" Dalton turned and peered back at me, his eyes wide. "Vern, you're being so sassy today. Peaches has been a bad influence on you."

Vern steered the truck over to a security checkpoint, and then on to another road that looked like it would lead us to a freeway.

The two of them continued to argue lightheartedly about whether or not Vern was usually sarcastic, and how much I could be to blame for anyone's behavior. I got my phone out and sent some photos and a text report back to Shayla, who was just getting out of bed.

She didn't know about the engagement, and I felt bad not telling her.

Shayla: *Why San Francisco? Has he told you why?*

Me: *I'll let you know when I figure him out.*

Shayla: *He's a really good actor. I don't think you'll ever get anything out of him that he doesn't want you to know.*

Me: *I have my own methods and plans.*

Shayla: *Do tell!*

Me: *He's pretending we're just casual friends with benefits, but Vern told me he has real feelings for me, and I'm going to make him admit it.*

Shayla: *LOL! Good luck with that.*

Me: *We could have a moment. I just have to shut up and look pretty. Maybe by candlelight?*

Shayla: *He's never going to give you what you crave. You know I'm Team Adrian now. Unless Keith Raven comes back from Italy.*

Me: *Adrian is really great.*

Shayla: *I'm going for brunch with him and Golden. Doesn't that make you jealous? Don't you want to fly back here and claim that tall freak as your personal pleasure partner?*

Me: *If Dalton doesn't give me a little piece of his heart this weekend, maybe I will.*

Shayla: *Piece of his heart? Excuse me while I barf.*

Me: *Any advice?*

Shayla: *Got any unexplored holes to offer?*

Me: *You know I don't.*

Shayla: *UGH. I guess you'll have to talk to him or whatever.*

Me: *We could talk about our feelings. I can't believe I just wrote that.*

Shayla: *You could tell him about the you-know-what.*

(I knew she meant my pregnancy, and how I almost died when I went into labor at a very stupid fifteen.)

Me: *I want him to open up, not run away screaming.*

Shayla: *Honesty is a two-way street, sweetie.*

Me: *Stop making the I'm-right face. I can tell.*

Shayla: *I'm also doing your I'm-right dance.*

We exchanged a few more messages saying goodbye, and I put away the phone. Vern and Dalton were busy figuring out driving directions and the vehicle's navigation system.

The conversation with Shayla could have gone better. I didn't like the idea of her having brunch with Golden and Adrian, and I didn't care for her suggestion to tell Dalton my secret.

I pulled out my compact and freshened my makeup. One thing I felt good about was my new plan. No matter what it took, I would get Dalton to admit the engagement was about more than saving his career.

CHAPTER 17

Our first stop in San Francisco was at Pier 39, where we got to see the sea lions hanging out near the wharfs. They were actually a noisy group, grunting and barking at each other.

Dalton was feeling the chill in the air, so we went looking for a souvenir shop.

"No wonder you're cold," I said, poking at his shirt. "You've got holes all through here, and this fabric is crazy thin. Did you get this shirt off a hobo?"

"Maybe."

Vern, who'd been giving us some distance, saw me bugging Dalton about his shirt and said to me privately, "He's going through a fashion phase."

Dalton followed me into a souvenir shop. I bought him the most outrageously tacky zip-up jacket I could find, with an embroidered Golden Gate Bridge across the front.

"Perfect disguise!" he said as he zipped into the thick sweatshirt. "And feels like a hug."

He'd been getting stared at by a few people, but nobody had come up and asked him for his autograph or a photo yet.

The sweatshirt was a good disguise, and we looked just like all the other tourists milling around.

At the Pier 39 market, we walked by a table of leather goods that drew Dalton's eye. He selected a fanny pack—one of those bags that's built into a belt—which he paid for and quickly wrapped around his waist.

Grinning, he said, "Do I look like a tourist, or what?"

I pulled a pair of huge, pink-framed sunglasses from a nearby display and put them on. "These are so nobody recognizes me out shopping with some weirdo in a fanny pack."

He handed the vendor some money for my sunglasses. "My fiancée will take those glasses, and give us half a dozen of those pins."

Despite my protests, he proceeded to *flair up* my hoodie with an assortment of pins with goofy sayings on them, about leaving my heart in San Francisco, welcoming the zombie apocalypse, being a witty 1950s housewife, and loving frogs for no good reason.

Vern gave us an approving nod. "Excellent tourist disguise, but we've got eyes on us at six o'clock. Don't look, just turn around and keep moving."

I grabbed Dalton's hand and hurried with him into the crowd. As he had for the last few hours, Vern followed us, staying back about six feet and keeping his eyes open for potential trouble. He wasn't a tall man, or very imposing as a bodyguard, but Dalton assured me it was his keen eyes and instincts for avoiding trouble that made Vern invaluable.

(Instincts for avoiding trouble made Vern the exact opposite of Dalton, which was probably why they were such a good match.)

We had a quick lunch, then made our way back to the truck. From there, we started driving to our main destination, which was a bridal shop near Union Square. I'd never heard of Union Square before, but I'd picked up a tourist map and was poring over it in the back seat as we drove.

"San Francisco is pretty small," I said to Dalton, who was still keeping his distance from me by sitting in the front seat. "Seven miles by seven miles. You know, that's not much bigger than Beaverdale, space-wise, but there are so many people here, and they're all so colorful." I peered out the tinted windows to find street signs and place our location on the map. "Hey, can we go to the hippie area? And see those cool houses—the painted ladies? Oh, and I want to see Chinatown."

"Pace yourself," Dalton said, laughing. "You haven't even picked out your wedding dress yet."

I looked out the window. "Well, it's just a fake wedding, so it doesn't matter to me. I'll just pick the first one that doesn't make me look like the tooth fairy."

We drove for a few minutes in silence, then Vern pulled the vehicle over to the sidewalk and announced we were at the boutique.

"Great," I muttered under my breath as I stepped out. "Goody, goody, can't wait for this fresh hell," I grumbled.

My mother had told me all about her experiences shopping for a bridal gown, and nothing had changed in the last twenty-five years, based on what my cousin Marita had told family about shopping while curvy and pregnant.

The thing about wedding gowns is, you try on the styles, called samples, and then your dress is custom-made for you. That sounds great, but the samples come in three sizes at most, and they aren't big girl sizes. At best, the consultants will hold the back together while you admire yourself in the mirror. At worst, you stand there in your slip while they hold the dress up to the front of you.

Dalton took my hand and asked, "Are you mad that you have to do this with some stupid guy? I know it's traditional for the bride to try on dresses with her bridesmaids."

"Whatever." I shrugged.

Dalton asked me to wait a second as he talked to Vern and made arrangements for the rest of the day. From what I overheard, Vern was going to drop our things off at the hotel and take the rest of the day off. Apparently, he'd already had a long day, flying up to Washington from LA to pick me up.

I shook my head in amazement at the idea of having your own airplane, to fly wherever you wanted. I didn't even have a *car*.

~

The interior of the bridal gown store was white, white, white. The floors were an ashy, pickled wood, but everything else was white. Did I mention how white it was?

A woman clad in pale gray approached us, smiling and saying, "Welcome to San Francisco." She looked at my new funny buttons on my jacket. "My dear, those buttons are charming. We could add one to your gown for a little something blue." She laughed merrily at her joke.

I instantly liked the woman, and not just because she had a body shape similar to the curvy women of my family. Her gray suit hugged her body and showed off her shape, but the most stunning part of her was her snow-white hair, cut in a chin-length bob. She must have gone gray young, because her wrinkle-free face didn't look a day over forty.

She widened her eyes at Dalton. "D-man, you're wearing the *hell* out of that fanny pack."

His green eyes twinkled. "You recognized me right away, Nancy."

"Come here!" She didn't wait, though, but strode right up to him and grabbed his cheeks in her hands. "Wook at dat widdle face." As she fawned over him, she wiggled her butt like a happy pet greeting a favorite family friend.

"Good to see you, too," he said.

"Why won't you eat?" she exclaimed. "Have you heard of this wonderful thing? It's called pastry."

I have to admit, I liked Dalton even more now that this stylish woman was squeezing his cheeks and telling him to eat a cinnamon bun from time to time.

"Are you trying to set a trend?" she asked, pointing at his leather pouch.

"These are so practical," he said. "I should design my own line of man bags."

She snorted. "Man bags. Honey, think about what you're saying."

As he unzipped his fanny pack to brag about all the stuff he could carry, I looked around the storefront. The front was just a vestibule, and an arched door led, presumably, to the actual dresses. The adjoining hallway was also white and minimal, decorated with white objects, including a white vintage-looking telephone on the wall. If I wasn't mistaken, it was the exact same model as the yellow one at Peachtree Books.

"Where are my manners!" Nancy said, turning her excitement back to me. "Here's your beautiful fiancée. I can't wait to get her clothes off."

Dalton slung his arm around my shoulder protectively. "I know exactly how you feel."

Nancy tossed her head back and laughed. "Except I want to get her dressed in taffeta and lace, whereas you're a very naughty boy."

I interrupted to ask, "How exactly do you two know each other?"

"Nancy was our original costume designer on the show."

I gasped, realizing I was in the presence of greatness. "You did the zombie bride dresses?"

"And all the zombie bridesmaids," she said, smiling sweetly as her cheeks flushed with pride.

I started to gush, "You're amazing! My best friend and I both dressed up as zombie bridesmaids last year for Halloween. We used a hot glue gun to attach all the bones and jewelry to our corsets. We tried to imitate your beautiful designs. I had skeleton hands cupping my peaches, just like the slutty zombie bridesmaid."

She clapped her hands together. "Tell me you took photos. Show me, show me!"

I pulled out my phone and showed her the best pictures, while apologizing for modifying her beautiful, original designs. She told me to not be silly, and that she was beyond flattered.

Dalton interrupted us, saying, "I hate to be a downer, but I can't marry a zombie bride. Not again. Nancy, you promised you had some designs for the living?"

A tall, slim woman in a gray dress appeared in the doorway. "Everything's ready," she said to Nancy.

"No skeletons," Dalton said.

Nancy rolled her eyes at Dalton's comments. "D-man, don't you wrinkle your forehead like that or you'll need Botox before you're thirty, unless you already are, ha ha. I've got something much better in mind for your fiancée, based on the notes you gave me."

She waved us through to the next room, which was mostly white, but with some relief in the form of a gray carpet and gray furniture. Dalton took a seat on the chaise lounge and unzipped his Golden Gate Bridge sweatshirt. He held his hand out to accept a tall flute of champagne from one of the three gray-clad assistants in the room.

Nancy herded me over to a curtained changing area, moving like a border collie herding a reluctant lamb. One of the other ladies handed her a gown, which she handed to me.

"This is the mermaid gown," she said. "If you look closely, you'll see it's not white, but hues of iridescent blue and green."

The dress looked like it had floated out of my dreams, shimmering and beaded with everything from crystals to tiny starfish. Nancy wasn't a less-is-more designer; she was more of a heck-yeah-let's-add-more-beads designer, and she made it work.

After a few moans of wordless appreciation, I finally said, "That is so gorgeous, I could eat it. Sorry to be weird, but you're a genius. Get me a fork and I will eat this dress."

Nancy laughed and called over her shoulder, "You're right D-man, I do love her already!"

"That's why I'm locking it down," he replied.

Nancy rolled her eyes again. "Locking it down?" she whispered. "Please tell me the proposal didn't include that particular phrase."

"Hard to say. The whole thing happened so fast." That wasn't entirely a lie.

She backed away, still smiling. "This is where I leave you, my dear. Gwendolyn and the others will see to your needs, and as far as I'll ever know, you love everything. But you must be honest with the girls about what you like or don't like, and don't worry about my feelings. This is your dress, for your special day."

Nancy disappeared, and the tall woman took her place and officially introduced herself as Gwendolyn. At her beckoning, I took off my clothes, down to my underwear. She lightly patted my face with a tissue to ensure my makeup didn't transfer to the dress, then she was joined by another girl and they lifted the gown up, over my head.

To my relief, this dress wasn't a tiny-sized sample. It was actually *too big*, and they used plastic clamps to take up some space at the back.

The dress was so breathtaking, I could barely look at myself in the mirror, for fear of bursting into tears and flooding the whole corset.

"Show your fella," said Gwendolyn.

I walked out of the changing room slowly, trying to pretend this wasn't a big deal. The staff assured me that it wasn't that unusual these days to have the groom be part of the dress-selection process. *Bulldoodle.* They were humoring me, but they were so nice about it.

142

Dalton looked me up and down, and he didn't say anything at all for several minutes. I started to worry, and sweat, and worry about sweating, then worry-sweat some more. Was he getting cold feet?

Finally, he shared his thoughts, his voice husky and cracking. "The mermaid of my dreams is real."

"He likes the dress," Gwendolyn said, translating helpfully.

"Me, too," I whispered, wrapped up in Dalton's adoring gaze—his cool, green eyes the water for my mermaid dress.

Gwendolyn said, "Not so fast. We're not going to take it easy on you just because we like you. Now get back in that change room because you have at least ten more different dresses to try on."

"Like hell! Not until I get a glass of champagne."

Laughing, she agreed to this, and they brought me a glass in the changing room. I got back down to my underwear to cool off, tossed the champagne back and said, "Gown me up!"

~

After a dozen gorgeous wedding gowns and almost as many glasses of champagne, I walked out of the boutique feeling like royalty.

"Did you pick the mermaid dress?" Dalton asked. "Or the one with the pink ribbon thing?"

"Not telling."

"You seem really into your dress, for someone who keeps using the word *fake* to describe our wedding."

In response, I zipped open the fanny pack he wore right under his belt buckle and started rifling around in the contents. "Got any gum? You should keep gum in here."

"Keep looking."

"You don't have any gum, you pervert."

He made a silly face, sticking his tongue out to the side. "No need to stop looking."

After a few moments of furtive digging and face-making, I noticed people were staring, so I stopped. I zipped the little bag closed and linked my arm with his, resting my head on his shoulder as we meandered down the sidewalk.

For the rest of the afternoon, we wandered in and out of stores, including an enormous Bloomingdale's.

Every time I looked at something for more than a second, Dalton tried to buy it for me. It took a while to convince him that sometimes I was looking just because I was curious, and I didn't actually *want* a diamond-encrusted gold and pewter egg.

I did, however, find a watch that was so pretty, it made me want to wear a watch. Dalton had his credit card out before I'd even finished dropping my first hint.

I wore the watch out of the store, admiring it in the bright sun.

"That watch will go perfectly with your ring," he said.

"You're right."

"You haven't even looked at the ring."

"You don't know everything, D-man."

He shook his head, smiling. "Only Nancy calls me that."

"How about David?"

His smile disappeared at the mention of his original name, and he started walking faster. I had to trot to keep up, as we headed up a hill. San Francisco really is as hilly as it looks in movies.

I caught up and linked my fingers with his. "Dalton, I want to know who you are, and I want to know who David Blake is, especially if I'll be marrying him."

"My name's been legally changed."

"So, I'll be Mrs. Deangelo?"

"I don't know. Will you?"

"I have to. I signed the agreement that I'd do ANYTHING."

"If you change your last name, you'll be Peaches Deangelo. Hmm."

"I could hyphenate. How long is your publicist planning for us to be married?"

"How do you know I have a publicist?"

"*Someone* was posting pictures of an egg white omelette on your social media accounts while *you* were drinking champagne in the bridal boutique. Plus you told me, back when we first met."

"I can't get anything by you." He stopped and peered at the menu posted outside a restaurant with a sprawling sidewalk patio. "Dinner here?"

"Sure. And then what?"

"After dinner, I'll take you back to my hotel room and make sure you know your wifely duties."

My jaw dropped and I held my hand over my mouth. "Excuse me, but I told you I *have* a boyfriend."

"Yes, but you're both seeing other people, so don't act like you're not going to spend tonight in my bed. He's with that little blonde right now, probably. I know things too, Peaches. I have my little birdies who tell me stories."

"Who told you?"

"I took your little friend out for a milkshake. Not the tall one. The short blonde. She's cute as a button."

I staggered back two steps. It's hard to explain exactly how Dalton talking about Golden made me feel, but I kinda wanted to projectile vomit all over his face.

I stammered, "Why would you do that? Talk to my friends, about my life?"

He tilted his head to the side. "Is talking to your friends really so different from you asking my butler about me?"

"Very different. Vern is smart, and he wouldn't tell me anything you didn't want me to know, I'm sure. Golden, on the other hand, is... excitable."

"She sure is." He grinned his Drake Cheshire, devious vampire grin.

"If you so much as touched one of her perfect little curls, so help me, I will never look at you again." I started looking around for something to beat him with.

He kept grinning, enjoying my jealousy.

The nearest thing was a plastic bucket full of water, put out for people's dogs. I picked it up and tossed the water on Dalton. "Stop smirking!" I yelled.

I doused him.

If we hadn't already attracted the attention of some people sitting on the nearby sidewalk patio with the yelling, my throwing dog water on Dalton had certainly done the trick.

CHAPTER 18

Dalton slowly wiped the water from one eye then the other.

Calmly, he said, "I wasn't smirking for any particular reason. This is just how my face looks sometimes." He slowed down his speech for emphasis, sounding like a Jack Nicholson impersonator. "And you should *know* about my *resting smirk face* by now if you watch a *certain* popular TV series."

People were taking photos and video of us with their phones now.

"What did you *do* with Golden?" I demanded.

He wiped more dog water off his face with the sleeve of his sweatshirt. People were definitely staring, and recognizing him. He nodded for us to get walking again, draping his arm behind my back.

I shrugged his arm away, not wanting him to touch me.

"Don't even tell me what you did with her," I said with disgust.

"Vern and I were getting milkshakes at the ice cream shop, and she was there. She asked to take her photo with me, and we got to talking."

I covered my ears with both hands. "Shut up!"

He leaned over and spoke loudly enough for me to hear him clearly through my hands. "I bought her a milkshake and we talked for a bit, then I left with Vern. You can ask him yourself, since you don't trust me."

I slowly lowered my hands, feeling like a jealous idiot. What had come over me? Temporary insanity? Could I blame the plane trip, the bridal shop, the champagne, or all of the above?

We were walking downhill now, and moving pretty fast. I didn't think anyone around was watching anymore, but my rage had given me this weird tunnel vision, where I could barely see in front of me.

147

"You surprise me," Dalton said.

"I'm sorry about the dog water, but maybe I shouldn't be. I think you were trying to provoke me."

"Oh, the dog water didn't surprise me. I saw the bucket, and I knew what you were going to do before you did. No, I'm surprised how jealous you are. Honestly, it's kind of sweet."

I held one hand up to the side of my face to prevent him from making eye contact with me. "Please don't say I'm sweet. I'm a horrible person. I went to LA to stay with you, and went right to another man's apartment. Then as soon as I found out you were coming to town, I latched onto the nearest guy, just to throw him between us."

"You're free to kiss who you want. I don't own you, despite what the agreement says."

"If you want to date Golden, you have my permission. She's a really nice girl, and you could do much worse."

He chuckled. "Thanks for the offer, but I'm starting filming for the show next week, plus I have to get married to another blonde. She's a real cutie."

"You'd better be talking about me, or I will find another bucket of water."

Dalton made a gagging expression. "Some actual water would be refreshing. I think that last one was mostly dog slobber." He rubbed his face with his dry sleeve. "Is water supposed to be stringy?"

I pointed to the door of a casual-looking burritos restaurant. "Let's go in there and get you cleaned up."

He agreed, and I stood near the counter studying the menu board while he washed off the dog slobber. When he came back out, he looked up at the menu board and said, "What are we having?"

"You want to eat here?"

He breathed in deeply through his nose. "Why not? The food smells good."

I pointed to the cash register. "We need to order up there and pay now, then they'll call our number, or maybe they'll just bring it out."

He looked down at me, smiling and shaking his head, as if I was the dumbest but cutest person he'd ever met.

"Peaches, I've eaten at a cafe before. I'm practically a regular person."

"Right. A regular person who has an airplane."

"Just a little airplane."

"And a butler."

"Just a medium-sized butler." He nudged me toward the cash register playfully. "Order something, cutie. I'm hungry."

He was right about the restaurant smelling good. It seemed to be a family-run business, with three little kids running around behind the counter. After I ordered, I talked to the curly-haired woman, asking if she was the owner. She joked that she owned the kids, but the bank owned the restaurant. We talked for a few minutes, with me asking the ages of all the children, who were five, eight, and eight, the latter being fraternal twins.

Dalton and I took our drinks to our table and sat near a window. We'd come down a hill to get here, but there was still a nice view of the city in one direction.

"You want kids?" he asked.

I took a sip of my iced tea.

This moment could have been a good time to open up to Dalton, but there were people around. It would be bad enough to hear Dalton incredulously say I *must have known* I was pregnant, without looking over into strangers' open mouths, full of half-chewed burritos.

I countered with, "Do you really think your PR problem is so bad you need to have a PR baby?"

He slipped off his sweatshirt and stretched back like a sleepy lion before raising his arms in the air. His thin shirt stretched even tighter across his pectoral muscles, and he flashed me one bump's worth of his abs. There were many reasons the man inspired legions of fangirls to flock to any convention he was scheduled to attend, and two of those reasons were his pecks. Another two were his arms—those gorgeous arms lazily stretching and flexing before me.

"I had fun with your little brother, at your cousin's wedding," he said.

My skin started to tingle. The way he was looking at me while talking about kids and my brother—did he know something?

"What exactly did you and Golden talk about?"

I was pretty sure Golden didn't know Kyle was my son, because I sure as hell hadn't told her, but you just never know in a small town.

He said, "Why are we back to talking about your friend? Am I going to get a drink or two thrown in my face?"

"Only if you waggle your slutty vampire eyebrows when you talk about her."

He chortled, leaning forward across the table on his elbows. I tore myself away from his hypnotic green eyes. The wood table had a hand-made checkerboard marked with wood stain. I traced the edges with my fingernail.

"You and I would make beautiful babies," he said.

I fanned my face with my hand, then removed my hoodie jacket. "We'd have chubby little babies, and everyone in the media would make fun of them."

He sat back quickly, a look of shock on his face. "I'll sue every last one of them." He looked left and right, flexing and releasing his fists. "Damn it, you've got me all worked up about these fictional babies. I'll do anything to protect them. Anything."

I smiled, remembering how cute he had been, ferrying Kyle around on his shoulders at my cousin Marita's wedding, then getting all the kids dogpiling on him.

"Don't get all crazy," I said. "Our kids would be fine. Kids are resilient and brave. They're fearless, you know? They have to learn caution."

Right on cue, the owner's three children came running to our table with our food on trays. All three wore proud grins on their faces. The five-year-old set out our napkins, smoothing them down with her chubby hands and taking her job very seriously.

"We'll hire actors to play our children," Dalton said, smiling now. "These waiters seem talented."

The twins putting our food on the table got big eyes.

"Do you have an agent?" Dalton asked the twins.

When they were suitably freaked out, he said, "It's okay, I'm just kidding. Thank you for the food."

They both giggled and scurried away with their little sister.

"You're good with kids," I said.

He unwrapped the foil around his burrito and studied it seriously. "No rush," he said. "We'll try marriage first."

I reached for my ring finger, as though I could feel the engagement ring even when it wasn't on.

~

After dinner, we walked around the city until the sun disappeared and some of the more interesting city residents became aggressive in their panhandling.

We took a taxi to the hotel, then an elevator up to our room on the top floor.

Dalton opened the curtains so we could enjoy the view of the harbor through the floor-to-ceiling windows.

As I stood there admiring the twinkling lights and the shimmering water beyond the city, he stepped in close behind me. He took both of my arms and placed my palms against the glass. "Don't you dare move," he growled near my ear.

Standing behind me, he pressed his hot body against my back while he lifted my hair and kissed the back of my neck. My palms squeaked against the glass, and it took effort for me to push them back into place and hold still as his hands explored my front and unzipped my jacket.

My heart reacted, speeding up and rushing energy flow everywhere, especially between my legs. My lower body was thrumming with pressure as he pressed his body against my buttocks while unfastening the button of my jeans. He slid my jeans down and helped me kick them off.

He bit my earlobe, his breath hot on my neck. "I'm going to pull your hands off the window for a minute to get your shirt off, but don't turn around."

I murmured in agreement, and he gently removed my layers, stopping at my bra. "Such a pretty bra," he said softly as he kissed the strap on my shoulder. "Would you prefer to wear your pretty bra while I take you in front of the whole city?"

"Yes," I said, fully aware of what I was agreeing to.

"I've had some things delivered to the room," he said.

"Like what?"

151

He ran his finger from the nape of my neck down to the top of my panties, lighting up my whole spine with his touch. "You'll see. Don't turn around."

The suspense was killing me. Standing in front of an enormous window in my underwear was killing me. Was the window even tinted for privacy? The room behind me wasn't bright, but had a warm glow from a few lamps. Oh, hell. I didn't care. The cars on the street below looked like toys, anyway.

Dalton left me for a moment, and returned with a large shoebox. Still standing with my hands on the glass, I peeked under my armpit at him as he knelt and took a pair of insanely-stacked platform heels out of the box. In a flash, I remembered standing on the books in my bedroom. Dalton was taller than me, as most guys were, so we needed adjustments for certain positions.

He slipped one crazy platform-heeled shoe onto one foot, and then the other. They fit perfectly.

He stayed kneeling by my heels, shirtless now, but still wearing his jeans. He kissed the backs of my calves while complimenting the curvy new shape they took on thanks to the heels. My alignment was different, with my hips tilted and my back more curved, my round buttocks thrust up and beckoning.

I moaned as his lips rained down on the backs of my calves, then behind my knees, then up my thighs. I'd waited so long for him to kiss me, which only made it better. Had I ever been kissed so thoroughly? I couldn't remember, couldn't think... could scarcely breathe.

My palms squeaked on the glass, reminding me to push them back up.

Dalton and I hadn't been together since that night in my bedroom, before the LA trip and all those fights.

I'd been so scared we'd never touch each other again, and scared we would. I glanced over at the door to the room. How fast could I run in these crazy shoes? Not fast at all! Maybe that was why he chose them.

With one smooth movement, he reached up and yanked my panties down and off. With the next movement, his finger was between my swollen lips, gliding against my slick skin and probing that hot, swollen spot that made me whimper.

He stayed kneeling, kissing my lower back and the sides of my hips and legs, his hand clutching at me rhythmically, fingers delving inside.

He continued doing this until I was about to burst, then eased off. After a gentle bite on my lower back, he said, "You're the most beautiful sight in all of San Francisco."

"You make me feel like the luckiest girl in the world."

He got to his feet, and a second later, his jeans hit the ground.

"You're about to get very lucky," he breathed, his voice husky and sexy.

"Break me." I took a small step sideways with one foot and leaned forward, my hands inching up on the glass and my forehead touching the cool surface. I was burning up, my skin hot and wet all over.

A wrapper crinkled.

"Say it again," he murmured.

I licked my lips and arched my back some more. "Break me, Dalton Deangelo. Shake me. Take me. Break me."

He slid between my legs, then smoothly between my legs, lengthwise. He moved in close, the front of him pressing against my back as I straightened up my torso for more contact.

He slid back and forth, gliding between my folds, the head nudging my nub as it appeared and disappeared between my legs. I looked down at his bare feet, on the floor between mine. His toes flexed up and down as he adjusted his position. He kept teasing me with it, slowing and pressing against my opening, nudging in briefly before slipping away and gliding past.

"Break me," I said.

He grabbed my breasts through my bra and cupped them firmly. Still he teased, his long, thickness sliding forward and back lengthwise, the condom fully slippery by now.

"Take me," I said.

His breath caught in his throat. He pulled back and slipped in with one firm thrust.

I cried out so loud, it was practically a scream.

His hands were everywhere, and he plunged in and out of me in desperation. He slipped one hand down my front, where he spread me apart and rubbed me in rhythm as he pounded me from behind. My hands were slipping all over the glass, and the movement pushed me forward, until my breasts were also mashing against the glass. I could barely catch my breath, let alone find something to hold onto.

I felt his pressure build, but I was too excited, too nervous. "Go ahead," I said.

With a grunt, he did, pounding harder and faster into me until he lost his rhythm and jerked against me, helpless in the rushing stream of his own pleasure. When he was finished, he gently bit my shoulder and rested against me. By now, I felt like the lunch meat in a Dalton-window sandwich, which is a little awkward, but not in a bad way.

I stared down at the tiny cars on the street below and wondered if any of the tiny people were looking up at me. They might wonder why a naked girl was panting and sliding around on a window.

Dalton pulled out and away, excusing to the washroom.

A moment later, he popped open the door and called out, "Get in here! You need to see this tub."

"Do I need to wear the shoes?" I took two tentative steps to turn myself around and found myself teetering and grabbing for the nearby curtains to keep myself from wiping out. *Real sexy, Peaches.*

"You don't need those shoes in the tub!" he replied.

"Not anywhere," I muttered as I carefully stepped out of them and down to solid ground.

CHAPTER 19

I pulled the cord to shut the curtains, then slipped off my bra and walked over to the bathroom.

He met me at the door, a towel slung around his waist.

Kissing my neck, he said, "Don't think I've forgotten about you. I want to make you come tonight. Many times."

"It's been a long day." I looked over at the tub, which was the size of a multi-person jacuzzi. Dalton had turned the water on and it was filling via multiple spouts. "Let's pace ourselves," I said.

As the tub filled, I carefully removed my beautiful new watch and set it on the counter.

I climbed into the hot, welcoming bath, and soon we were bobbing around in sudsy, fragrant hot water. (Okay, one of us was "bobbing" a little more than the other, and I *do mean* my peaches.)

I'd never been in such a fancy hotel room before, and I wouldn't have been surprised to learn Presidents had stayed in that suite. The bathroom alone was bigger than should be legally allowed, on account of spoiling people forever. After a night there, how could I ever go back to my own hovel of a bathroom? With the sink and the tub and the toilet all sharing the same room? (This fancy bathroom had a separate enclosed space for the potty, in case you're wondering, and, yes, there was a bidet, too.)

We took our time soaking in the tub, playing footsies and making eyes at each other from opposite sides of the tub.

"Does this hot tub remind you of anything?" Dalton asked.

"Do you mean the time we almost got shot by some crazy guy with a shotgun?"

"That was a good day." He took a breath and disappeared down into the water. His hands pulled my knees apart, and he dove at me with such speed, I practically screamed, but it turned into a sigh when he just gave me a gentle, underwater lick.

He surfaced in front of me, wiped the water from his eyes, and kissed me.

It had been too long since I'd felt his lips on mine, but now that we were kissing, the time and distance disappeared.

After a moment, he pulled away.

"That was a great kiss," he said.

"You're welcome."

He smiled, looking almost shy. "Earlier today, at the airstrip, you made me a promise."

I gazed into his beautiful green eyes, made brighter by the hot water of the tub. "I did? That doesn't sound like me, because I make threats, not promises."

He grinned wider. "I said that if I kissed you, everything would get complicated. You agreed with me, and promised me *nothing short of disaster.*"

That did seem familiar. "How do you have such a good memory? Oh, duh. From memorizing scripts. Wow, I'm going to have to be careful what I say around you."

He kissed me again, then settled onto his knees before me in the enormous tub. "I do remember things. You and Shayla rented an apartment, sight-unseen, when you went away for college. You said the landlord must have taken the photos from a ladder, outside the windows, to make the place look bigger."

I splashed some water his way jokingly. "Showoff. Let me think about this. Your first apartment had rats and a toilet in the kitchen."

He laughed. "A tub, but close enough."

"And look at us now, in this fancy-schmancy hotel bathroom. It's a good thing one of us has talent and good looks, and the other is great at playing a vampire."

His eyes flew open in mock anger. "Someone's going to pay for that horrible joke."

I was running through a few comebacks in my head when I noticed his attention drifting down to my breasts, looking like pale,

156

flesh-colored islands in a sea of bubbles. I ran one hand down the middle of my breasts seductively, then cupped both of them and pinched my nipples to firmness.

His eyes didn't stray from the waterline. I continued to stroke my fingertips around my breasts, enjoying the look of concentration on his face.

He swept the surface bubbles aside so he could see all of my body.

"That's new," he said, looking down at my new tattoo, on the inner edge of my hip bone.

"Oh, that. I had a lapse of judgement in LA."

He traced the tattoo with his finger. "You had more than one lapse of judgement in LA."

"But it's cute, right? My tattoo?"

"*Doves Cry*. Of course it is. Everything's cute on you."

I smiled, and then relaxed in the warm water as he ran his hands along my thighs.

"Touch yourself," he said, and I knew he meant further down than my breasts.

He waved more bubbles aside, so the water was clear. I settled down into the tub further, and I parted my legs so he could see everything. I slid my hand down my front and theatrically ran my index finger up and down over my sensitive area. Damn, but that felt good, especially with him watching.

I could feel my cheeks flushing, but I couldn't tell if it was from embarrassment, or arousal, or both.

His voice deep and thick, he said, "Keep going."

I opened my mouth to say something lippy about me doing his job for him, but the expression on his face was so serious. I slid down further, curving my spine to a comfortable shape. Self-conscious of how much I was hunching, I rolled my shoulders back and adjusted my position so my arm wasn't squashing my right breast in half, but angled underneath. That small change, however, put my hand in an awkward position.

Dalton must have sensed this, because he said, "Don't worry about a performance. I don't want porn. I want to see the truth. Do you trust me enough to show me your true beauty?"

"I don't know. Can you kiss me some more?"

"Yes," he breathed, and he moved in close again, licking and sucking my lips, then kissing me as we shared one breath, back and forth.

As the heat built, I slipped my hand down and started again, with my hand down between us, the back of my wrist bumping his body rhythmically. We kept kissing until I was gasping, close to coming. He pulled back just enough to get a glimpse down between us.

I rubbed up and down, then in a circle, desperate for release, then angry with myself for my desperation, because that's exactly how you chase an orgasm away.

"Grr," I said, then I pushed him away so I could cross my legs. "Stage fright."

"Don't be frustrated. I saw exactly what I wanted to see. Thank you for showing yourself to me."

I snorted. "Now it's your turn."

"Men are disgusting. Nobody wants to see that. We're like those horny little monkeys in a nature documentary." He reached for the bottles of hair product near the tub. "How about I lather you up and give you a scalp massage?"

"Are you serious?"

He raised his eyebrows as he took the cap off a bottle and poured the fragrant cream into his palm. "Try me."

I dipped my head back to fully re-wet my hair, and then I let Dalton Deangelo, TV's sexiest vampire, play hair stylist on me.

After he washed and conditioned my hair, I did his. I told him he had gray hairs (he didn't) and we had a few tense moments until I admitted I was joking. He told me he'd had people fired from the set for less, and I got the sense he wasn't entirely joking. I could relate, though. During my brief stint in LA as an underwear model, I'd encountered a couple of people I would have gladly had fired.

We finally climbed out of the tub when we both developed prune fingers plus an insatiable curiosity to see what kind of goodies were in the mini-bar.

Each clad in our white hotel robe, we sprawled out on the king-sized bed and dug through the packages of candy and nuts like two kids with their Halloween treasure.

"I'm not surprised you're hungry already," I said as Dalton tore into a foil-wrapped bag of nuts.

"I have a fast metabolism."

"Maybe. But I noticed when we were at the restaurant, you only ate the middle of your burrito. You peeled away most of the burrito wrapper, which is the best part."

"I'm just not willing to do carbs," he said with a shrug. "Do you think you can sustain a fake marriage to a guy who doesn't eat carbs?"

"About the fake marriage... will it be an actor who does the ceremony? Or will we legally be married? Because if so, I should probably make you sign a pre-nup, to protect my assets."

He laughed. "You think I'll go after half your country furniture and your used book collection?"

"Yes. You're probably broke now, after buying a cabin and an airplane, plus no sane person eats the things from the mini-bar. That tiny can of Diet Coke you treated me to probably cost you seven dollars."

"Nothing but the best for my fiancée."

"In that case, let's order room service."

He rolled over to the side of the bed and grabbed the phone. "Name your pleasure."

"I meant for breakfast, silly."

He put the phone down and grabbed his crotch suggestively through the thick, white robe. "I've got your breakfast right here."

I chucked a bag of peanuts at him. "Gross."

He lay back on the bed and unfastened the terry-cloth belt. Without saying a word, he began calling me over to him with just his green eyes, set in that devilishly handsome face.

And me, I was powerless to resist. I crawled over to him—awkwardly, due to the fluffy robe. I snuggled up alongside him, aware of the heat and tension building between my legs. He curled up to look around us at the mess of wrappers on the bed, then he kicked everything off with his feet.

"You're messy," I said.

"You make my life very messy."

"Nothing short of a disaster."

"Get on top of me," he said.

"Don't tell me you have a crushing fetish? Or you want me to smother you?"

"I want to feel every ounce of your beautiful body, on top of me. Rest your legs on mine and your arms on mine. I want to feel you."

"Is this a fetish?"

"What does that even mean? You like my body, don't you? I see you admire my lean, cut muscles."

I rolled away, onto my shoulder, facing away from him. "That's different."

The room was so quiet, I could hear him lick his lips.

I tightened the tie on my robe as an internal argument raged in my mind. I wanted a guy who appreciated my curves, but not *too* much... but why? Because a fetish objectified me and made me less of a person? Or was it because I couldn't accept his adoration? Could it be true that despite all my attitude and pride in my curves, deep down I didn't truly believe fat was fabulous? Breasts are mostly fat, and everybody loves them, so why not celebrate a round, full ass, whether you're into spanking or not?

"You saw the photos in my wine cellar," Dalton said.

"Yes." I had seen the vintage framed Polaroids of his LA home's former owner. The woman wasn't your average housewife. From the pictures, she was always naked at parties, and had an appetite for everything good in life, from cake to multiple lovers. Dalton had hung her pictures in his basement wine cellar, in a display that was somewhere between a shrine and a joke.

"I like those photos," he said plainly.

"You don't bring people down there to laugh at her?"

"Well, you do have to laugh at the clothes and the hairstyles. The giant beehives? Come on."

Still on my side, I pulled my feet up into the robe and tugged the sleeves down over my hands.

"You're a chubby chaser," I said, my voice flat.

"We never talked about my childhood best friend, did we? Yours was Shayla. You two went swimming in the lake when it was full of tadpoles, and you were inseparable. If you met a girl tomorrow who reminded you of Shayla, you'd instantly feel something, wouldn't you?"

"There's *nobody* like Shayla. She's one of a kind."

"But you know what I mean, right?"

I stared up at the ceiling. In the dim light, with just a few lamps on, it was hard to tell if the ceiling was white, or painted a color. Trying to figure out the color of the ceiling was a good distraction from having to think about what Dalton was saying.

"My neighbor's name was Chelsea," he said. "She was a year older than me, and I followed her around like an adoring puppy. Her parents must have felt sorry for me, the kid whose parents were always having grown-ups-only parties and kicking me out of the house. I spent so much time at Chelsea's house, I had my own spot at the table and chores written in a list on the fridge."

"They sound like nice people," I said.

"They were," he said, and he went on to describe the dinners they made, the mother chopping onions with a cigarette hanging out of her mouth because she claimed the smoke prevented the onion gas from causing tears. When she fried chicken with another cigarette in her mouth, she claimed the smoke infused the meat with a barbecue flavor that was a gourmet thing.

Dalton described the family so well, I could see the striped wallpaper in the dining room, and see the father as he pushed the dinner plates aside and taught the kids how to play poker, all of them placing bets with stacks of Ritz crackers instead of money.

"Chelsea was like a sister to you," I said. "Was she a plump girl?"

"There was no shortage of food and love in her house."

"Oh."

He chuckled. "She was not always sisterly, though. We would play these crazy games that she designed."

"Doctor games? Shayla and I grew up with a ton of boy cousins, but none of us got the memo about doctor games. We didn't do body examinations at all. Mostly we would mix together a bunch of gross things, like toothpaste and Kool-Aid, and we'd make each other drink the medicine."

"We did that, too. Not the mixing, but we loved to play with those Alka Seltzer tablets and mix them with other fizzy things to try to make bombs."

"That's not how you make bombs."

"Which is a good thing!" He shuffled around, changing his position so he was curled up facing my back, spooning me. "She and her family moved away just when things were getting interesting. Most of her new games involved her lying on top of me. My favorite was with her piling all the couch cushions and blankets on top of me, then she climbed on top of everything, and I had to escape the avalanche."

I giggled. "That sounds fun."

"I got my first major boners trying to squirm out from under that avalanche."

"Oh my."

"When Chelsea saw the bulge in my jeans, she would…" He trailed off.

"You're killing me with suspense! What? What did she do?"

"She'd punch me in the stomach and chest. Not really hard, to hurt me, but it did distract me enough sometimes to make the erection disappear."

I'd started giggling, and now I laughed even harder. "Chelsea sounds awesome," I said.

"She's probably working as a dominatrix or something. Her parents moved to Colorado, and we were just kids, so we didn't stay in touch."

"And she was a chubby blonde?"

"Actually, she had brown hair."

I let this new information wash over me. *There was no shortage of love or food at Chelsea's house.* Dalton had all these pleasant memories of having a big girl on top of him, so who was I to deny him this pleasure as an adult?

After a minute, I said, "Do you want me to pile all the cushions from the hotel room on top of you?"

He threw his arm over me and clinched me tightly to him, his hand squeezing one breast through the robe. "I'm big, but not big enough to get you through all those cushions."

"Who said anything about sex? I was planning to punch you repeatedly in the chest and stomach."

He nuzzled the back of my neck. "Mmm. Dirty talk."

"Is that a boner I feel?"

He thrust against my buttocks, the padding of our robes making whatever he was doing feel less like foreplay and more like a general mashing. He nuzzled my neck some more, his breath hot near my ear. "The offer for you to climb on top is still open."

"I bet."

He nuzzled my neck some more, then rolled onto his back, the thick robe still covering his turgid member.

Climb on? Oh, what the hell.

With the encouragement from his eyes, I slowly climbed onto him and stretched out completely, my legs atop his, and our hands palm to palm. He had to bend his elbows for my hands to interlock with his.

"You feel as good as you look," he said.

"Guess my weight and you win a prize."

He smirked. "Yeah, right! The prize is you punching me in the nuts, no matter what I say."

"You know me so well."

"You're not a number, and neither am I."

I whispered my weight, in pounds, watching his face for a reaction. He whispered back, "What a coincidence. That's what my dick weighs."

Then he quickly reached down between us, adjusting his allegedly-heavy dick and parting both of our robes, so that it rose up between my legs.

I punched him gently on the shoulder, then lowered my face to his. Our smiling mouths met, and we had one of those giggle-kisses, where your lips don't quite seal together because you're laughing through the kiss.

He rocked his hips, and the length of him filled the space between my legs, stroking lengthwise against me. We kissed deeper, our mouths connecting completely, and I started rocking my hips, grinding against him.

We still had our robes on, and for a moment, I felt like we were two teddy bears, mashing each other through our plushy stuffing.

The orgasm that had been so elusive for me was now sharp in my veins, the urgency and desperation cutting me like a knife.

I shifted up and we hesitated for all of a second before I eased down, the tip of his bare manhood inside me. I started to shudder, electric all over and desperate for just one more inch. Just a few seconds more, just one more inch. I gasped as he nudged into me, and it felt as if all of my skin was coming together at one point.

At last I snapped, and I was coming, sweet relief flooding my system.

I cried out and hunched forward, rounding my back and burying my face against his shoulder. My muscles clenched and unfurled as wave after wave of ecstasy released.

I slowed, still riding the last waves.

"Oops," I said, shifting up quickly and pulling his half-inserted part from me, agonizing though it was.

"I didn't come," he said.

I did the math in my head. My period was due any day. Take it from me: the rhythm method is definitely how people get babies, but this particular oops couldn't have happened at a better time of the month.

"I'm sure we're fine," I said, still somewhat breathless. "My cycle is regular, and I should have Aunt Flo on Monday. That's probably why I'm so frisky right now. Hormones and whatnot."

He grinned up at me. "I thought I was the one who made you feel this way."

"You are." I rolled to the side so I could open both of our robes fully. I rested back down with my body touching his from chest to toe. I rocked my hips, pressing against his hardness, nestled between our bodies. "I want some more."

He said, "Grab a condom, you insatiable mermaid."

"I will this time, but we need more convenient birth control soon."

He blinked up at me. "I've been tested for everything, in preparation for marriage."

"Me, too, a while back. And I usually play safe, this evening the surprising exception."

He slipped his hands around to my buttocks and squeezed the flesh. "How am I still so hard, despite this unsexy conversation?"

"You're my stud-pony, my Lionheart."

I scrambled off him and started hunting around for the condoms he'd mentioned. "You're getting colder," he said as I hunted around the pile of clothes on the floor. "Warmer," he said as I stepped back.

We played the hotter-colder kids' game until I found the pack. I tossed off my robe and climbed up onto the bed, where I pretended to not know where his you-know-what was. "I roll the condom on here?" I asked as I grabbed first one of his big toes and then the other. We played the hotter-colder game for a while, and I finally found the right appendage, but only after sucking on various body parts.

With the appropriate preparations in place, I climbed on top, straddling him on my knees with my hands on his chest, and we went at it until I came again, and he did, too.

When we were finished, we cuddled together on the bed and bickered over which one of us was going to get out of bed, cross the room, and turn off the standing lamp.

The last thing I remembered before I fell asleep was him combing his fingers through my hair and saying it was the most beautiful hair in the world. "You should wear it twirled up in a twisty thing for the wedding," he said.

"A bun? A chignon?"

"Twisty thing," he repeated sleepily, and he rubbed his fingertips against my scalp. "Such pretty, pretty hair."

MIMI STRONG

CHAPTER 20

I woke up to the sound of Dalton talking to another man in the adjoining room.

The fancy hotel suite was similar to an apartment, with the bed in its own room with double doors, and the hallway door opening to a living space with sofas and tables. The double doors were only open a crack, but once I was awake, I could hear them clearly.

The man thanked Dalton, then the suite's door opened and closed. Dishes clinked. The double doors to the bedroom opened and a rolling tray entered. I could smell both bacon and coffee, though everything was covered in gleaming, metal domes.

Dalton wore a pair of blue jeans, and no shirt. His usually-bare chest had the stubble of some hairs I hadn't noticed before. Sometimes you have to see someone a bunch of times before you see everything.

"I got your mocha," he said. "They didn't have Pop Tarts, though, so will blueberry pancakes be nearly as good?"

I sat up, holding the sheet across my breasts for modesty in the bright morning light. He'd opened the curtains and the room was gleaming with the promise of a mostly sunny day, with just a touch of the famous San Francisco fog over the harbor.

"How did you know about my Pop Tarts?"

"The first night you were staying at my house in LA, you gave me heck for not having Normal People Food."

"Right." I climbed out of bed just long enough to grab a T-shirt and panties from my suitcase and slip them on before climbing back into bed. "Your house is really great, by the way. I was impressed.

Especially when I came over to get my computer, and you turned on those crazy fans. You were acting so weird."

"Me?" He lifted the domes off the food. "You were dating my look-alike. How was that not supposed to make me crazy? And you even brought Carter Crow into my house."

"Keith Raven."

Scowling, he stood near the foot of the bed, picking at the fruit tray. "That guy wasn't right for you."

My stomach pitched uneasily, and I regretted bringing up Keith, especially mentioning his name.

"He's out of my life now," I said.

"Was it just physical?"

I held my hands out. "Duh."

He got a smug look I didn't like at all, with a twisted grin. "Fair's fair."

"What do you mean? Did you hook up with someone, too?"

"Would you have a problem if I did?"

"No, but *you* might."

He raised his eyebrow at me, but kept on eating strawberries, standing near the foot of the bed and looking like the devil himself.

I took a deep breath and let out an audible sigh. "I'm a hypocrite. Whatever or whomever you did, so long as it's in the past and nobody I know, it's fine."

He didn't say anything.

My insides started to hurt. I narrowed my eyes at him, squinting like I had a superpower for reading his mind, and *maybe I did*, because I knew, without a doubt, that he'd slept with someone we both knew.

"Who?" I asked.

"It was just physical," he said.

I grabbed a pillow from beside me and hugged it to my chest. "Who? Just tell me and get it over with. Alexis?"

He stuck his tongue out in disgust. "Ew, no. She's like a sister to me."

"Golden?" As I asked, I imagined the two of them doing it in the back of his car after getting milkshakes, and I was filled with murderous rage.

"Of course not. She's dating your other boyfriend, remember?"

"Yeah."

"Plus she's not my type."

"I know!" I exclaimed, feeling better instantly. "Brooke Summer, that copper-haired reporter skank. You totally boned her. Hah! I hope you broke her heart."

"Brooke? No, not exactly. By which I mean not at all." He waggled a finger at me. "Interesting reaction on your part, though."

He began to pace the room, still shirtless. As I looked at his body and face in motion, I felt a buzz of excitement from Miss Kitty. I didn't care so much about where he'd been, but about where he was going to be… in the next five minutes.

Maybe he hadn't slept with anyone I knew, and this was just one of his games.

"Stop teasing and get in this bed," I said.

He paused, then walked over and sat down next to me.

I grabbed the button of his jeans and started unfastening it.

"I took Justine out for drinks a few times," he said.

"Who?"

"She was your stand-in for the TV commercial. Pretty girl. Curvy. Blonde."

I finished unbuttoning his jeans and pulled my hands away.

Whispering, I said, "You screwed her to get back at me."

"And I broke her heart."

"Are you going to break mine?"

"Probably," he said.

Without thinking, I reached up and slapped his face.

He rubbed his cheek, but didn't take his eyes off me as he reached down and removed his jeans and underwear.

"Is that what a real woman does?" he asked. "Slap a guy when he tells her the truth?"

I hauled off and slapped the other cheek.

"Get on your knees," he said.

"You vampire sociopath."

He kept staring at me, his green eyes intense. My lower body was buzzing like an angry hornet's nest.

"Roll over," he said slowly. "Get on your knees and yank your panties down."

Trembling and buzzing, I did as he ordered. I got on my hands and knees on the bed, and I tugged my panties down.

He moved in behind me and plunged two fingers into my aching core, wetting them quickly. Next, I felt the head between my cheeks, up high, the door above the one where babies get made. He rubbed his fingers along me, in and out, then drew the slickness onto his hiimself.

I gasped as he plunged in, filling me. I was hot and clinching as he slid in and out of me, tight around his hardness. His hands gripped and held on tight to my hips as I moaned in pleasure and angled to receive him deeper and deeper.

I bucked against him, urging him on, harder and faster. His body slapped against my flesh, and he pounded my ass like the man of my dreams, made real.

My hand was damp with sweat, and so was his as I guided his arm around and down to my sweet spot. He scarcely grazed the nub, and I started to come, getting banged from front and back, moaning like crazy.

With a few more thrusts, I exploded in a wet, gushing orgasm, running down my leg. He grunted a few swear words, then pulled out and spurted, hot across my back.

I slowly reached for a pillow and held it to my chest as I eased back down to the bed, lying on my stomach. He couldn't see my face, but I mouthed a word: WOW.

He cleared his throat, but didn't say anything.

And what do you say, exactly, after something like that?

He got off the bed and grabbed a handful of tissues, then cleaned up my back.

"There's some in your hair," he said softly.

"I guess I'll take a shower."

He cleared his throat again. "I'll go run the water."

He left for the bathroom, and I grabbed some more tissues to get the fluid from between my legs. By now, my little gush had happened enough that it wasn't such a shock anymore. Sex is messy, and what's wrong with a little extra juice? Dalton didn't seem to have noticed.

I walked into the bathroom and joined him in the spacious shower. "Our breakfast is getting cold," I said.

He nodded and stepped aside so I could have a turn under the largest sprayer in the multi-spray shower.

"We'll have a bite, then flower shopping," he said.

"Flower shopping? So, we're not going to talk about the nasty things we said to each other a few minutes ago?"

"I think we both got a lot off our chests." At the mention of *chests*, his gaze went to my breasts, and he began to lather them up with the soap in his hands.

"Did you pull that little trick with Justine? Telling her to get on her knees and yank down her panties?"

"Why don't you tell me what you did with Keith? Did you suck his thing and tell him he was so big, he was choking you?"

"Please. Too big for this mouth?"

He backed me up against the marble wall of the shower and kissed me hard, our teeth clinking. He was already getting hard again, pressing against my stomach.

"That mouth of yours," he murmured. "I want it wrapped around my dick."

"Stop saying dick, and it might happen."

"Dick," he repeated, thrusting it against my body.

"Shut up." I wrapped my hands around his neck and pulled him down to kiss me.

We kissed for a few minutes, his desire growing more demanding and hard.

I got down on my knees under the warm water, and I gazed up at him, from his muscular abs and chest to his gorgeous, famous face.

What was going on with us? The night before, I had encouraged him to *break me*, and now, it seemed to be happening. There's something so scary about getting exactly what you ask for.

I grabbed hold of him, and I didn't just do what he requested. I *worshipped* him.

~

After the shower, we steered the food trolley over to the round dining table in the front room, and quietly ate the now-cool breakfast. Dalton offered to order up more food, or take me out, but cold food was better than waiting.

171

My mocha tasted like a regular coffee, then I found all the syrup at the bottom, in one surprising slurp. (Ah, the unmixed beverage. The bane of the mocha drinker.)

Dalton did a funny thing before he got dressed. He took five pairs of pants out of his suitcase (why he'd brought five pairs for a weekend stay was anyone's guess) and he smoothed them all out flat on the bed. He took out five shirts and did the same with them, pairing them up with the jeans, then mixing and matching.

I stepped out onto the balcony for a minute in my robe to check the weather. It was sunnier than the previous day—short-sleeves weather, but not too hot—a perfect day for sightseeing.

I came back into the bedroom to find him with his fist held to his lower lip, still studying the mix-and-match outfits.

"Are we still trying to look like tourists today?" I asked.

"Right!" He grabbed the fanny pack from the previous day and started trying it on top of the flat clothes.

I left him to his big decision of the day and got myself dressed in the spacious bathroom. I chose a short denim skirt, with a pair of pale gray footless leggings underneath. The weather was warm enough for bare legs, but my inner thighs chafe like crazy if my skin gets damp, and I had a feeling Dalton would be saying and doing things to make my temperature rise.

I put on ankle socks and lace-up sneakers, and wore a loose blue tunic on top with a green belt. The green belt had a carved wooden closure, but it also had a tendency to suddenly spring open without provocation, so I had to use a hair elastic to keep it fastened. The things we do for fashion!

Dalton was putting on his shirt when I walked back into the bedroom. He'd chosen dark gray pants and a black T-shirt with a graffiti print, sun-bleach lines, and a dozen tiny holes in it—the kind of shirt a charity shop would just garbage directly from the donation bin.

"Dalton, tell me the truth. Did you get that shirt from a designer shop, or off the back of a hobo?"

"I'll never tell."

I struck a pose at the doorway. My blond hair was swept back in two pigtails, like a little girl.

"What do you think of my outfit? Do I look like Chelsea?" I asked.

"Who?" He blinked a few times.

"Chelsea. The girl who lived next door."

"Right. Ha ha. No, you look like an adult, which is a good thing."

Something felt off, so I decided against the pigtails and quickly pulled out the elastic bands.

We gathered our things from the room and headed out to the elevator. I wore my brand-new watch and kept admiring it every time it caught my eye.

"Wow, it's noon already," Dalton said. "We completely missed our cake appointment. I'll tell them it's all your fault." He gave me a devilish grin.

My mind wasn't on what he was saying, because I was still thinking about the pigtails, and Chelsea.

We got down to the lobby, where I found out he'd rented a scooter for the day, and Vern wouldn't be joining us until later.

A scooter? I wasn't thrilled, but decided to politely give it a chance.

Even as we donned our helmets and climbed onto the scooter, I kept troubling my mind over what he'd told me about Chelsea.

Could I ever trust anything that came out of the smooth-talking actor's mouth? Or his motivations?

The big fight that broke us up initially was over his indie movie—specifically, the fact he'd started dating me as *acting research* into dating a bigger girl.

This new story of his, about having his first love be a chubby neighbor... well, it seemed awfully convenient. Why hadn't he mentioned her earlier?

Also, his story about the family next door had been rather detailed, as though constructed. My heart sunk. *He'd probably made the whole thing up to win me over.* Why else would he have not known who I was talking about when I said Chelsea's name? It's not *that* common of a name.

And let's not forget about the wardrobe. Was it normal for a man to spend so much time on his appearance?

Sitting on the back of the scooter, trying not to feel self-conscious about the view of my roundness ballooning out the sides, I wrapped my arms tighter around Dalton's lean torso. I could hold on to him as tight as I could, but he was liable to slip away in the light, like San Francisco's fog.

I had to ask myself those questions—the ones so many women in LA must ask themselves daily.

Can you ever truly *know* an actor? Can you ever trust him?

~

We did miss our appointment with the bakery, but we got to the florist right on time.

This visit was different from the dress shop. The people knew who Dalton was and fawned over him, but they weren't friends.

I was annoyed by how uptight everyone at the florist seemed—as if it was their duty to educate me about why certain flowers I liked the look of weren't appropriate. They wanted to do orchids, no doubt because they would be more expensive.

"Absolutely not," I said after they pushed the third orchid package on me. "My mother would be appalled. She's a member of the Beaverdale Orchid and Dandelion Wine Society." I suppressed a smirk, amused at myself for haughtily name-dropping a club nobody outside of Beaverdale would have heard of.

"Then of course she would love orchids," the man said.

"Do you like puppies?" I asked.

He nodded.

I explained, "If you went to a wedding and they had the chopped-off heads of puppies, would you be happy?"

The man gasped.

Dalton, who'd been smirking, stood abruptly and grabbed my arm to help me up.

"Thank you so much for everything," Dalton said to the agitated florists. "My fiancée has been under too much pressure from me to get everything arranged on such short notice. I must apologize. It's my fault that I can't wait to marry this gorgeous woman, and enjoy her marvelous sense of humor forever." He grinned at me, his eyes flashing additional messages. "Very funny joke about the puppies," he said.

"Yes, it was a joke," I said slowly.

"We'll come back after my fiancée has had a rest," he said.

I frowned at him, sending a wordless message into his brain: *Not here! I hate these people.*

His eyes widened: *Of course not here. Let's get out without making a scene, because I am a famous actor, and I do not need more bad publicity thanks to you.*

Me: *I want to throw something at someone.*

Him: *Calm down.*

(At least that's what I thought he meant by the eye flashes and tense expression.)

Squeezing my hand firmly, he led me out of the florist amidst a flurry of apologizing and ass-kissing by the staff.

I stepped out of the door. People jumped at us. I shrieked while what seemed like a hit squad of people surrounded us, cameras flashing.

MIMI STRONG

CHAPTER 21

Someone at the florist shop must have tipped off the media, and here were this city's paparazzi. They weren't as insane as the ones in LA, but they did shout their demands:

"Show us the ring!"

"Peaches, are you going to wear white?"

"Nice watch, but where's the ring!"

"Kiss for us! Come on, just one kiss! You look so beautiful together."

"Kiss for your fans who love you both!"

Dalton grabbed my shoulder and steered me around to face him.

"Shall we make it official?" he asked.

"Kissing for the paparazzi makes our engagement official?"

"Do I really need to answer that?" He dialed up his grin to full-vampire-smirk.

I tilted up my chin in response. The flash frequency increased, and he leaned down to kiss me in full view of everyone. This kiss was different from his usual ones. Our lips barely touched. It was a very cinematic kiss, and not the good face-mashing kind, which probably wouldn't photograph as well.

After the kiss, we posed for a couple more shots with his arm around me.

The photographers kept asking about the engagement ring. I held up my hand and apologized. "Getting sized," I said. "I have fat fingers."

They seemed to accept this response, and, after a few more pictures, they ambled away, dispersing in all directions.

177

Dalton kept his arm around me and steered me down the street. "You probably shouldn't have said *fat fingers*."

"Are you worried they'll make fun of my fat fingers? They've said much worse."

"Some of them were taking video. I should get you an appointment with a media advisor. It's fine to say self-deprecating things, but never insult yourself."

"Fat is an adjective, not an insult."

He was quiet for a moment, then said, "You're right. I'm sorry. But the world doesn't see it that way."

"Who gives a damn what the world thinks?" We crossed the street with the light.

Still with his arm around me, but not looking me in the eyes, Dalton said, "People in the public eye care what the world thinks. They have to."

"Oh, right." I chewed on my lip and thought everything through as we walked up a hill, back to where the scooter was parked. "I may not give a damn what the world thinks about my fat fingers, but I should make an effort to present myself in a positive way, right? Like, even if I feel down, I should keep smiling so other chubby girls can dream of marrying a handsome, famous actor."

"Famous actors who are former porn stars."

"Come on, baby. You weren't a porn *star*. You were a porn *nobody*."

He stopped walking abruptly and turned to me, his green eyes bright and darting around warily before focusing on me.

"You truly have a gift for speaking the truth, whether you know it or not. You're right. I was a porn nobody. I was a total nobody until I was invited to read for Drake Cheshire. I don't even know how they got a hold of my number."

"Fate, I guess. Like when you ran into my bookstore that day."

He winced and pretended to be interested in the hand-carved wooden toys in the shop window behind me.

"Confession time," he said. "I knew you worked there. I saw you admiring the flowers outside another store the day before, and I asked the guy working there about you."

"I don't understand. You ran in that day because Brooke Summer and her camera crew were chasing you."

"Brooke only spotted me because I'd walked up and down that street three times, trying to get up the nerve to go in."

I shook my head. "I don't believe you. Stop messing around with my reality. I want to trust you, I do, but you're setting off my bullshit detector."

"You don't believe me that I saw you and fell in love at first sight?"

I pressed my lips together to stop the "no" from flying out.

His chest rose with a deep breath, and he gazed off into the distance. "Peaches, if you don't believe it, the press never will."

"What the hell?" I pushed him back, my palms striking his chest hard.

"What? You can say whatever you want, but I can't? You're supposed to be helping my cause, not making a scene over orchids, like some spoiled bitch on a *Real Housewives* show."

"I think I liked you better when you were spouting all the corny lines from your scripts. The things you actually come up with yourself betray your stupidity."

His eyebrow quirked up to match the corner of his smirking mouth. "I liked you better when you were on your knees."

I narrowed my eyes at him. "Where's Vern? I want to go home."

"Let's take the scooter back to the hotel."

"Forget the scooter!"

"I *knew* you didn't like the scooter. Why didn't you just say so back at the hotel instead of being all tight-lipped and saying the scooter was *fine?*"

"I didn't want to be difficult!" I yelled.

"This truly is a spectacular effort you're making to not be difficult!"

"It's not easy being this easygoing!"

He started waving his hands excitedly, still yelling, "Thanks a lot for your valiant efforts to be easygoing!"

"Your shirt is stupid and full of holes! Why do you take so long to get dressed only to pick a stupid shirt with holes?"

"This shirt cost two hundred dollars! And I'm not stupid!"

I turned, looking around for something to throw. Another bucket of dog water sat a few steps away.

Just as I was reaching for the white bucket, Dalton shoulder-checked me. "Oh, no you don't," he said, grabbing for the bucket first.

I tried to take the bucket from him, and succeeded only in dousing myself with the water, soaking my skirt.

The empty bucket clattered to the sidewalk.

Dalton slowly backed away. "You did that to yourself," he said.

I tried my best to shoot exploding laser beams from my eyes at him, but found myself lacking in superpowers.

"You take the stupid scooter back," I spat out. "Call Vern and get him to pick me up here." I pointed to the coffee shop on the corner.

Dalton put his hands in his pockets, calmer now and hunching his shoulders. He didn't say he was sorry, but he did *look* sorry.

"You're sure?" he asked. "We've still got a couple hours to sightsee."

"I'm sure." I turned around and started walking to the coffee shop, grumbling about how I wasn't sure, not about Vern picking me up, not about marrying Dalton, and not about anything.

I walked to the cafe without looking back.

My jean skirt had taken the brunt of the aqua assault, so I visited the restroom inside the cafe and slipped it off and into my purse. I removed my belt and smoothed out my blue tunic to cover my butt. Clad in the thin gray leggings, I was showing a little more thigh than usual, but shedding a layer felt liberating.

I walked out of the bathroom unsure what had happened and what I was going to do next.

The coffee smelled good.

I ordered a mocha at the counter, and when I turned around, I realized getting my drink in a mug was a mistake, because every table was taken.

A dark haired, older man waved to me, catching my eye. He beckoned for me to join him at his table, so I did. He explained, in broken English, that he found the residents of San Francisco so friendly and welcoming.

"I'm just visiting," I said. "I'm a tourist myself, from Washington State. That's north of here."

He looked confused, his white-flecked dark eyebrows knitting together. "But you look so... what is word... comforting."

"Comfortable." I nodded, smiling. "I've been traveling more lately."

Another man with dark hair, much younger—maybe nineteen—joined us.

"I'm Arturo," the handsome young man said, reaching out to shake my hand.

"Chelsea," I replied, blushing over my lie.

Arturo turned to the older man. "Dad, I leave you alone for five minutes, and you've got the prettiest girl in all of San Francisco to come sit at our table."

I fanned my face, trying to be modest, but eating up the compliments.

Arturo didn't have a thick accent like his father, but he certainly was Italian. The compliments didn't stop, and neither did his eyes, scouring my face, my eyes, my jaw, my hair, my collarbone, my breasts, and my hands as I self-consciously reached for my mug.

The two were investigating a business opportunity for their family business back in Italy. As they told me a little about their home, and life in the Italian countryside, I wondered if my friend and former lover Keith Raven was meeting strangers at that very moment and discussing the same. For a moment, talking to these visitors, I felt a connection with Keith, and a warmth.

Keith had described our time together in such positive terms. When I left for the airport, he said he could feel me sparkling in his heart, like a diamond.

As Arturo and his father playfully competed for my attention, I felt what Keith had described. A brightness.

Time passed quickly, and soon a familiar-looking man was hovering near the table.

"This is my friend Vern!" I announced, and introduced him to the Italian men.

Vern nodded to the door. "We'll be chasing the light," he said politely.

I went to shake the Italian guys' hands goodbye, but they both stood as I stood, and insisted on kissing me on the cheeks.

As I exited the cafe with Vern, the cool air and quiet outside made me realize how noisy the cafe had been. A singer with a guitar had started playing on a small stage about thirty minutes earlier, and everyone had carried on at a louder volume.

The convivial meeting in the cafe was exactly the kind of experience you want to have when you're traveling, yet not the kind of thing you can ever plan or seek. Isn't it so beautiful that the best moments in life are this way?

Not that I didn't have a good time with Dalton... mixed with some bad times, and let's not forget the weird.

"Thanks for coming to get me," I said to Vern. "We were shopping for flowers, and then—"

"No explanation needed. I understand how Mr. Deangelo can be."

"This disaster might be on me." I let out a big sigh that morphed into a self-aware laugh. "The funny thing is, when we got here, I was making dire predictions about a disaster, and then it happened."

"We reap what we sow." He held open the back door of the large truck.

Dalton was not inside the vehicle.

"Are we picking him up at the hotel?" I asked as I got settled into my seat.

"No." Vern closed the door and left me hanging as he walked around to the passenger side.

I asked, "Is he meeting us at the airport?"

Vern adjusted the rear view mirror to make eye contact with me. His eyes looked sad, viewed apart from the rest of his face.

"He's catching a commercial flight back to LA."

"But we didn't say goodbye."

"He asked me to give you this." Vern handed back an envelope. "I packed your luggage for you and everything's in the back. We'll be going straight to the airport from here, and I'll have you back home in time for a late dinner, unless you'd like to pick something up quickly here?"

I mumbled that the original plan sounded good, and we started driving.

I tore open the envelope and pulled out a commercial greeting card with a frog on the front. The frog wore a tie, so clearly it was a boy frog.

The caption under the boy frog said: *I've got something to say!*

Inside was a giant *RIBBIT* in puffy letters.

Underneath that was a smaller line in red text: *In other words, I'm sorry. Can you forgive me?*

The card was hand-signed *Dalton, a.k.a. D-Man.*

Dalton's signature was the only thing that hadn't been pre-printed on the card.

"This is terrible," I said.

Vern heard me mumble and asked if I need anything or had any questions.

"I'm fine," I said.

I stared down at the card with the frog, in all of its terribleness. It was exactly like something my father would give my mother—that's how bad it was.

But the dumb card was better than nothing.

As we drove, I started to get doubts.

Did I actually *deserve* an apology, regardless of how terrible the apology was? The cause of our recent fight didn't seem obvious, in retrospect. First, I'd insulted his moth-eaten shirt. But he'd sprung some new information on me about stalking me. And I'd called him a liar, which was possibly true, but unsubstantiated. Then he'd tossed dog water on me before I could toss it on him. He did have a point that I should have said something sooner about the scooter, but I honestly had been trying to be easygoing.

And now I had a *RIBBIT* card.

I didn't know whether to tear the card in half and toss it out the window, or put both card and torn envelope carefully in my purse with my wet jean skirt, to take home and start a scrapbook with.

MIMI STRONG

CHAPTER 22

I brought the RIBBIT card with me to work on Monday morning.

A few times during the day, I'd pull out the card just to look at it. Holding the card in my hands made me feel like a kid at the end of a fantasy movie—the kind of movie where everyone says the events were just a dream, yet the girl unfurls her hand to find a shimmering, magical feather.

The RIBBIT card was my magical feather, and Dalton was real. The engagement was both fake and real at the same time. Thinking about that made my whole body ache.

At twelve-fifteen, things were going fine at the store when I got hit with a Lunch Break Returner.

I wiggled my toes inside my shoes to keep from screaming.

Lunch Break Returners are all about Getting All The Things Done, especially on Mondays.

If you open a retail business yourself some day, take my advice and find a way to not be there between twelve and one o'clock on Mondays. Put a scarecrow behind the counter, leave the door unlocked while you go for coffee, and put a help-yourself bucket of cash next to the cash register—like the honor-system candy buckets some people put out at Halloween.

Let them serve themselves.

The woman said, dramatically, "I was shocked and horrified by some of the *words* in this book."

"Yes, I understand." (She'd already stated the reason for the return, unprompted, several times.)

Like most Lunch Break Returners, she wore business casual dress and pumps that were a size too small, judging by the way she shifted back and forth on her feet. She probably wore the pumps into the office and kicked them off under her desk for most of the day. As I pondered all of this, I frowned inwardly that my keen insights into the habits of Beaverdale bookstore customers had very little value in the non-bookstore job market.

I asked, "Would you like the refund on your credit card, or store credit?"

She huffed, "Store credit, of course. It's not YOUR fault these publishers allow *words* like this in books these days."

I could tell she really wanted me to ask her about the specific words, but I wasn't playing the game that day.

Slipping my hand into my purse, under the counter, I felt the raised lines of the word RIBBIT inside my card. It wasn't a dream! I really was engaged to a famous actor, with a fabulous non-retail life ahead of me. Unless *this* was the dream, and Dalton was the dream within the dream.

"Will this store credit even be valid at the new location?" the woman asked, her voice sharp with suspicion.

"Nope. And we're starting the move tomorrow, so you'll have to use it before six o'clock today."

Her eyes widened and her jaw dropped. (You should never joke around in retail, especially not where the customer's money is concerned.)

"Kidding!" I added quickly. "Of course the credit is good at our fabulous new location, and I hope you'll come and shop often. We're putting in a section of audiobooks."

She said huffily, "Good. Your new location is more convenient for me, because my hairdresser is on that block. I don't know why this store is all the way over here. There's never any parking."

I glanced out the window reflexively, then held my lips tightly together as I looked at the unobstructed view of a street with over half the parking spots wide open.

Honestly, one of the biggest obstacles I've had to overcome to be a decent retail employee is to resist the overwhelming urge to state the obvious to people. For example, they'll walk in as I'm sweating and dusty from organizing shelves and unloading boxes, and they'll comment on how nice it must be to *sit and read books all day.*

Your job as a retail employee is not to tell the truth during small talk.

Your job is to be friendly and put the money in the register, while only speaking the truth about your fine products, which you stand behind one hundred percent. If you happen to sell crap you don't believe in… good luck with that.

I gave the woman one of our new postcards with the new location's address. She left with a smile on her face, which made me feel good. I hadn't been completely ruined by fame! I still had the retail touch.

The rest of the day passed quickly.

Adrian came in at quarter to six and brought the sandwich board inside with him.

"Let's close up shop," he said.

"But it's not six yet." I trotted quickly to the area behind the counter, putting the furniture between us. I'd been meaning to talk to him about my engagement to another man, but hadn't found the right time, or gotten drunk enough.

He replied, "Have it your way. I'll hang out here and we can count down the final minutes, like they do on New Year's Eve."

"Don't say that. You're going to make me all nostalgic and weepy."

He rested his elbows on the counter and leaned across to kiss me hello. I reached under the counter and quickly tucked my frog card away and zipped up my purse, then pretended to get distracted by the special orders shelf needing adjustment.

"Did you forget about our date tonight?" he asked.

"Of course not," I lied.

He kept staring at me, his blue eyes darting from my eyes to my lips, as though he might be able to read my weekend activities on my face.

I crossed my arms and tried to put on a poker face.

"How's Cujo?" I asked. "Still wearing the Cone of Shame?"

Adrian laughed, his smile relaxing his face and making me relax, too.

"Except for meal time," he said. "We left the cone on for his first dinner at home, and he scooped all the soft dog food into the cone by accident. Then he could *smell* the food, but couldn't reach it with his mouth, so he was like this, trying to get it with his tongue lolling out." Adrian tilted his head and lolled his own tongue out while whimpering.

I had to laugh. "Poor little man. I need to see him soon so I can thank him for being my hero."

"Hey! He's your hero? What about me?"

"The guy who led me right into the bear's territory in the first place?"

"And then dragged you right back out again. Like a hero."

"Thank you for that. I guess I owe you. Dinner at DeNirro's? Unless we made plans for something else?"

"I could go for some Italian. Can we close up the store yet?"

I looked down at my brand-new watch. "Seven more minutes."

Adrian reached across the counter for my hand, then drew it near him as he studied the fancy watch. "This is new."

I cleared my throat. "A gift, from this weekend."

He let my hand go and turned his head to the side. "I don't want to hear about him, or the expensive gifts he buys you."

I leaned on the counter between us, reached up with one hand, and stroked the side of his face with my fingertips. "Adrian."

It hurt me to hurt him.

"Seven minutes." He pulled away from my hand, looking down as he withdrew his phone from his pocket. "I'll step outside and call DeNirro's to see if we need a reservation. What do you think? Monday night? Shouldn't be too busy, unless they ran a coupon in the Beaver Daily."

"I'll start counting the float."

"I'll flip the sign." He walked to the door, where he stopped and looked back at me. "You know, this is the end."

"The end?" My heart leapt up, my pulse banging in my throat.

"Say goodbye and make it a good one."

Adrian knew I was breaking up with him? I stood there in stunned silence. I had to tell him everything that was happening, yet I didn't want our new relationship to be over. He wasn't just some guy. He was *Adrian*, and we'd known each other for years. *We had history.* When I was with him, I felt like we had a future.

He patted the wall next to the door. "Goodbye old bookstore! I hope you like wine!" To me, he winked and said, "Say goodbye to the store. Something like that."

"Five minutes!"

He paused, seemingly frowning at my watch, then retreated out the door to phone DeNirro's about reservations.

I ran the reports on the credit card machine and double-checked that there were no customers in the store. I'd been pretty sure nobody was there at the time Adrian had arrived, but sometimes a person will be reading quietly on the other side of the shelf and make me scream when they reappear. Not this time, though.

I walked around turning off the lights and saying goodbye to the store. The whole thing seemed silly and premature, since we were coming back the next day to oversee the movers, but I did it anyway, running my hand along the bead curtain leading back to the bathroom, and letting the clinking chimes ring through the space.

"I'll miss you," I said to the space in general.

"I won't miss you, evil jerkface," I said to the cupcake vent as I passed underneath on my way out.

Adrian was leaning up against the building's exterior with one foot resting on the wall. With his blond hair and high cheekbones, plus wearing his tight jeans, sneakers, and black T-shirt, he looked like a troubled youth in an indie Euro movie—like he was waiting in some Swedish city's alley for a drug dealer.

"Hey, sexy," I called out.

He moved languidly away from the wall, stretching his arms theatrically over his head. His sleeve rose up enough to reveal his compass tattoo.

"Hey, yourself," he replied. "You're a beautiful stranger I've never met. What are you doing in this dangerous part of town? Are you looking for a good time with a hot stud?"

"I sure am. Do you know one?"

He gave me a supermodel stare, sucking in his cheeks and running his hands up and down his long torso. "I'm not rich, but I know how to work. Hard."

"I'm the kind of girl who appreciates a man who works. Hard." (Ack! What was I doing, flirting with the guy I was supposed to be breaking up with? What was I doing besides, obviously, getting way too hot under my clothes, thanks to the dirty talk.)

He said, "Then I suggest we load up on carbohydrates, and get down to our *hard* work." He jumped up and down in two jumping jacks, then crouched. "Race to you DeNirro's."

"Excuse me, Mr. Monster Legs! As if I could ever win a footrace with you."

"I'll give you a head start. Run!"

With that command, I did. I ran down to the corner, looked both ways, and darted across the street, then off in the direction of the restaurant. As I raced up to the door of DeNirro's, I could hear Adrian's footfalls behind me, and I moved faster, giddy with adrenaline. He grabbed me, swooping his long arms around my body. I squealed and trembled, panting heavily.

Adrian pressed me to the restaurant building, my back to the wall, and kissed me. Both of us were breathless, and I wrapped my arms up around his neck, yearning for more of his lips on mine.

He pulled away silently and gave me an eyebrow waggle before leading me into the restaurant.

For a few minutes, I forgot about the things I needed to say. I was just a small-town girl on a date with her boyfriend.

We ordered the sampler plate for two, which was a new special they were offering, with a bit of everything.

As we crunched on bread sticks and waited for the meal, Adrian started drawing parallels between the sampler platter and our lives.

He said, "A little taste of one thing contrasts with everything else and makes you appreciate each thing more."

"We can't appreciate one delicious thing on its own? Like a bowl of one flavor of ice cream? Maybe rum raisin?"

"Isn't two scoops of different flavors better, though?"

"But you always like one flavor more than the other," I said. "It's inevitable. You always get the one you *really* like on the bottom, so you can finish with it."

He smiled, his big teeth bright in the candle light. Adrian had worn braces for a while, then went straight to the lip piercing, always distracting from his perfect smile.

He continued, in a grave tone, "The key to happiness is the right blend of novelty and routine."

The way he was smiling, I knew he meant his dating life, and not store business.

I asked, "Who's the novelty and who's the routine for you? Golden is the routine, I bet. How can I *not be* the novelty?"

"I have a confession to make."

My body got tense, the hard chair I was sitting on suddenly uncomfortable.

He was breaking up with me.

My skin got clammy. No! Yes! No!

Adrian swirled his water and ice cubes, looking down at the red-checked tablecloth, his fair eyelashes hiding his eyes. If he was breaking up with me, that was a good thing, probably. Then I wouldn't have to do the same to him.

I couldn't keep dating him while I was getting fake-married to Dalton Deangelo, could I?

No, *really?*

I was asking myself for permission to have it all.

Was that so crazy? Any crazier than me being an underwear model, or any of the other insane things that had happened to me lately?

"I tricked you," he said. "We didn't have a date for tonight, but I pretended we did, and you're so sweet and easygoing, you went along with it."

I chortled with relief. He wasn't going to break up with me at DeNirro's after all.

"Adrian, did you just say I'm *easygoing?*"

"You're pretty cool."

"Thank you." I wished I could have gotten that recorded, to send to a certain you-know-who to prove I was easygoing.

Adrian swirled his drink again. "In fact, you're so cool, that you agreed to a date with me tonight, even though you're somebody else's fiancée." He glanced up, catching me with his cool, metallic-blue eyes. "What's the deal with that?"

BUSTED.

CHAPTER 23

My heart nearly stopped.

Oh, Adrian totally knew. But of course he did. How could I have been so stupid? Beaverdale wasn't in a remote mountain village with no internet.

"It's not what you think," I said.

"Really? I figured it was a publicity stunt you two cooked up."

I took a second to process this information.

"Okay… so it is exactly what you think. You're a smart guy, Adrian."

"I'm no valedictorian."

I reached for the basket of bread, feeling more confused and mixed up than ever.

"What happens now?" I asked.

"Are you really marrying that guy, or just doing the appearances? You should probably start wearing an engagement ring, because I've been reading some of the gossip sites. I'm not the only one who suspects your timely engagement is a stunt."

I dropped the bread and covered my face with my hands. "Oh, Adrian. I'm the worst."

"We promised to be honest with each other."

"I know. Things have been crazy."

"I can imagine."

"I just want to climb into my bed with a book and make the whole world go away."

"I feel the same way sometimes, but everything falls apart if you close your eyes and ignore your problems for too long."

With my hands still over my face, and my eyes closed, I asked Adrian if anyone was close enough to the table to hear what I was about to say.

"Just me," he replied.

"Please don't ever tell anyone. Your parents don't even know, because my mom didn't even tell your mom." I kept my eyes closed and my hands over my face. "When I was fifteen, I had a baby. That's Kyle, who my parents took as their own."

"And you only missed school for a week."

My hands dropped and my eyes flew open. "You knew?"

"Don't worry. I never told anyone. My mother doesn't know. My parents bought the cover story that your mother never told anyone, and hid her baby bump because it was a high-risk pregnancy."

He kept talking, saying that he'd noticed my body changing shape, and my weight loss when I returned to school from being sick. He'd come to his own conclusion after seeing my mother with the baby, but respected and cared for me enough to never ask, despite his curiosity.

His words became foreign, like a language I couldn't understand. How could I have been so stupid? I was still the same dumb kid, oblivious to what was right in front of me. Would I ever use my brains, or was my father right about me being prone to whimsy?

Oh, no. Everything was such a mess.

I tried to fight the tears, but they came. The waitress arrived with more food, and I turned away, blowing my nose on a napkin.

A hand landed on my shoulder and I opened my eyes to find Adrian kneeling on the floor in front of me.

"I'm here," he said. "Tell me what to do. Should we leave here? Can I get you something?"

"I'm sorry," I sputtered.

He stayed right there, one hand grounding me on my shoulder and the other hand on my knee, completing a circuit of touch.

He said, "We'll just take a minute here. Nobody's paying any attention to us. I can drive you home if you want."

I shook my head. "I don't want to be alone right now."

He squeezed my shoulder. "I understand."

"I'm scared."

"Life is scary, but you've got people who care about you."

I sniffed. There was a break in the tears, like the sun coming through the fog. I wiped the wet napkin across one cheek then the other.

My voice gravelly, I said, "I'm okay now." I licked my dry lips. "Wow, that sampler plate smells good."

Adrian gave me the most heartbreakingly sympathetic look, and I nearly started leaking from the face again, but swallowed it down.

"We should try to eat a little of that food," I said.

He squeezed my shoulder and knee again before slowly removing his hands.

I took a deep breath, filling my lungs with fire and my nose with aromatic herbs. The sounds of the music and people chattering around us came back to me.

"I've never seen you like this," Adrian said.

"A red-eyed nightmare?"

"Soft and vulnerable."

I shook my head. "Oh, no. Do not call me soft. Do not make me double-punch you in the asshole."

Chuckling, he got to his feet and made his way back around the table to his chair. I gave my nose one final swipe, then pulled my chair in to better survey the feast before us.

"Oh, yeah," I said as I used the large serving fork to transfer some deep-fried tortellini to my plate. Everything looked so good. I even took a bit of green salad, though it looked suspiciously like kale.

"Fried pasta, yeah," Adrian said in agreement, doing the same.

For the rest of our dinner, we talked about the bookstore, and the big move that would be starting the next morning. Gordon had sprung for professional movers, agreeing that the expense would be worthwhile, because we'd have less downtime.

Adrian and I joked about the town-wide panic that would begin Tuesday, when all of Beaverdale went from having two bookstores to having zero. By the time we re-opened a week later, there'd be so much built-up demand.

Giggling, I said, "We might sell fourteen books by lunch time."

"We'll be run off our feet," he said.

"What's that called when two people want to pay for stuff at the same time?"

He grinned. "A lineup. We'll probably have one of those happening all the time."

"Let's not get ahead of ourselves."

He laughed. "So I should cancel the order on that deli-style, take-a-number system?"

"No, keep that. We can use it to keep track of who we're dating."

He blinked for a minute, then started laughing so hard he had to hit his hand on the table.

Our waitress came running over, worried he was choking, and the confusion that ensued made me laugh so hard, I must have looked like I was choking.

We finally finished eating, working together like a team to finish every item on the platter.

The owner, Mr. Russell DeNirro himself, came over to our table just as we were finishing, to ask us what we thought. I got nervous, because he's basically a celebrity chef in the town, plus I've had a crush on him probably since I was twelve. I'd always wanted him to flirt with me the way he did with my mother, and not refer to me as "kidlet" when he brought out my birthday cake with sparklers and candles on top.

"How is your beautiful sister?" Mr. DeNirro asked me. He meant my mother, whom he'd been jokingly referring to as my sister for the last decade, since she couldn't *possibly* be the mother of such a mature-acting kidlet.

"Still married to that guy," I said, playing along.

Mr. DeNirro shook his head. "That guy! A man should be so lucky." He turned to Adrian. "And you're Stormy's son, aren't you."

"Guilty," Adrian said. His father's cop name around town was Stormy, which is a pretty cool nickname, albeit not as cool as Peaches.

As he backed away from the table, Mr. DeNirro pointed a finger at me. "We'll see you soon for your birthday, won't we?"

"Of course!" Even as I said it, though, I got a bad feeling. My birthday was coming up in October, and given the way my summer had gone, I couldn't imagine where I might be when I turned twenty-three.

Coming to DeNirro's for my birthday, and getting my photo taken at one of the red-checkered tables—that was my tradition. My routine.

If Adrian was right about happiness being the perfect blend of novelty and routine, I was out of balance. With the store moving, and the fake wedding coming up, nothing at all felt routine or safe.

"You're not even listening," Adrian said.

I jerked my head up to look at him. "Beg pardon?"

He smiled, his blue eyes focused on me. "We've got a killer day ahead of us tomorrow, and a killer week. Would you like to walk down to the movie theater and watch a movie?"

"Do you know what's playing?"

"Does it matter? I'll put my arm around you and we can cuddle in the back row for two hours, just me and you."

There's only one screen in our town's movie theater, so I didn't have any idea what I was committing to, but I agreed. Sitting in the dark for two hours with Adrian's arm around me sounded perfect.

~

The movie was one of those romantic comedies where the hard-working business executive woman hires a smokin' hot man she thinks is gay to be her escort for a fancy dinner, then gets drunk and gives him a lap dance, only to discover that's not a roll of candies in his pocket, and he's not so gay after all.

The movie was good, and I liked it almost as much as the one about the workaholic business lady who pays a male art model to pretend to be her boyfriend at a family picnic, only to get drunk and make out with him, and find out he isn't so gay after all.

Come to think of it, if high-powered executive ladies would just *ask* their gigolos if they're gay or not, a lot of comedy hijinx would never happen. But then, uptight business ladies would never find out that deep down, they don't want to be president of the company as much as they crave the animal touch of a younger man, plus all his hot baby gravy. I'd be offended if it wasn't so damn enjoyable to watch. Especially the makeover scenes. Sigh.

Adrian and I walked out of the theater with smiles on our faces.

"Sorry it wasn't an action flick," I said. "There's a new Tom Cruise movie next week, and I'll take you to that."

"I didn't mind this one. I like a story about two people overcoming one simple and incredibly stupid misunderstanding to find lasting happiness together."

I laughed, and Adrian looped his arm around my shoulders as we walked up the street. "My car is this way," he said.

"You mean your mom's car."

His eyes went to my gold watch.

My words hung in the air, and I instantly realized I'd said the wrong thing.

He was quiet, looking down as we walked under the glow of a streetlamp, our shadow becoming squat, then stretching out.

"I was just kidding," I said. "I don't care that you borrow your mom's car, or live with your parents. I just say dumb things, all the time. It's kind of my thing."

"You know, I won't be poor forever. I'm taking a break right now to get some perspective. When I get out there again, I'll have experience, as well as the wisdom from losing everything once."

"Out there? Do you mean you won't stay in Beaverdale?"

He snorted. "Why would I stay?"

"Hmm." I didn't explain further, but just let his idiot question hang in the air until it came to him.

After a moment, he said, "Of course you'd go with me."

"And knock around in some giant, empty house while you work yourself into the ground?"

"Wow, Peaches. Since you have a crystal ball and everything, would you mind grabbing us some winning lottery numbers while you're at it?"

We got to the car, and he held the passenger door open for me.

I looked up at the starry sky. "Maybe I'd rather walk home."

"It's past eleven. Just get in the car, and please don't be mad at me for not including you in my imaginary future." He grabbed me in a hug and nuzzled my neck as he tickled my sides. "I want you in my future. You know I want you. I tell you every time I see you, how crazy you make me."

I giggled as he kept nuzzling my neck.

"Ooh, I want you, I want you," he growled.

"Okay, okay!" I pushed him away and got in the car.

He got in and started driving us back to my house.

We didn't talk much on the short drive, and when he walked me up to the porch, I couldn't tell if he expected an invitation inside, or just hoped for one.

He stopped on the second-to-last step for the porch, so we were nearly eye to eye. He brushed my hair aside and dove for my neck.

"You can't sleep over," I said as he kissed my neck under my ear, where his lips felt so good.

"We won't sleep," he growled.

I bit my lower lip, trying to think of the proper thing to say. I'd never dated anyone seriously enough to have to tell them to take a hike because I had my period. (Yes, it had come earlier that day, phew!)

"I've got cramps," I said, even though the ones from earlier that day had subsided.

He looked confused. "From the pasta?" His eyes moved back and forth, the old hamsters turning the wheels of Girl Translation in his brain. "Oh!" he said, finally. "We could just cuddle."

I clasped him on both sides of his face and looked him directly in the eyes, enjoying this rare moment of us being equal heights. "Adrian, you are the sweetest part-time, shared boyfriend a girl could have."

He moved in closer, and instead of kissing me, he rubbed the tip of his nose on mine.

"See you tomorrow," he said, and he left.

The house door behind me swung open so suddenly, I jumped in surprise.

Shayla stood in the door, looking furious. "Young lady, get in this house immediately."

"Oops." I hung my head and marched right in. My first guess was Adrian wasn't the only one who'd read about my engagement on the internet.

"Engaged?" she said as soon as we were inside the house.

I was right! Unfortunately, I was also in trouble.

"Ugh. Famous people can't get away with anything, can they? Ha ha. It's funny because I'm pretending I'm famous. But I'm not."

"Does Adrian know?" she asked.

"Strangely enough, yes."

She uncrossed her arms, her whole demeanor relaxing. "Oh. Then I guess I'm not that pissed after all." She sat on the couch and patted the seat next to her. "Tell me everything."

I told her to hang on while I ran upstairs for a pee, then I came back down, sat on the couch, and told her everything. And by everything, I mean that I sorta fibbed and told her some of the details, but not all of them.

She was confused, not quite understanding why Dalton and I were getting married, but I was still seeing Adrian. Part of the NDA was that I couldn't talk about the terms of the NDA with anyone. I made it seem like I was engaged to Dalton because we were friendly, and I wanted to help. It was true, even if it wasn't the whole truth.

When I looked over at the clock on the TV equipment, it was nearly one in the morning.

Shayla blinked at me, her expression incredulous.

Speaking slowly, she said, "So, this fluid just comes shooting out of you?"

"Seriously, that is the particular detail of my story that you're focusing on?"

"Your pussy has superpowers." She tilted her head to the side, her eyes lighting up. "Maybe it's a Monroe family trait! Maybe I can shoot stuff out of mine."

"My pussy isn't Spider-Man."

She pulled out her phone. "I gotta look this up. Hmm. Squirting. Is that female ejaculation? Ew. I don't like that word at all."

I swatted the phone out of her hand and stuffed it between the couch cushions. "Focus, Shayla. What should I do? Keep dating Adrian, or try to have a normal relationship with Dalton?"

She laughed. "Normal? Not with porno boy."

"Don't call him that."

"I don't know." She looked up at the ceiling, her brow wrinkled. "If you do this thing with Dalton, you'll be in LA a lot, and you won't be able to spend as much time with me. Do you think I've been anti-Dalton just because I love you so much and don't want to lose you?"

I swallowed hard. Damn my period hormones for making me feel like I was on the verge of tears all day.

She continued, "Or, deep down, am I envious of all the good things happening for you, because even though I love you, I am still a petty monster at times? I mean… how can I possibly think I'm a good judge of character? I was sleeping with my no-good cheating boss for how many months? It's not like I'm the queen of great decisions. Wow, I can't believe how self-aware I'm sounding right now. There you have it, though. I'm a disaster, so any advice I might have about your love life should come with one of those warnings. You know, like they run on those advertisements for the phone numbers you call to get a psychic to tell your fortune. Entertainment purposes only. That's me. Entertainment purposes only."

And with that, she withdrew a box of cigarettes from somewhere and started for the front door.

I followed her out to the porch and sat beside her on the bench as she smoked. We stayed there for twenty minutes, with nothing but the sound of the moths overhead, banging themselves into the porch light, mistaking it for the moon.

~

Eventually, Shayla and I got chilly enough and went back into the house.

Upstairs in the bathroom, as we were brushing our teeth for bed, I asked, "How are things going with… um…"

"Troy?" Shayla's golden brown eyes burned like the embers in a fire.

We were both framed in the mirror over the sink, two cousins with similar body and face shapes, except she wears a size or two smaller than me on the bottom, and bigger on the top. She got the bigger chest and I got the junk for the trunk, but together we're the perfect woman, part blonde and part brunette.

"You tell me how things are going with Troy," she said, her eyebrow quirking up dramatically. "He gave me seven orgasms on Saturday."

"Beats the hell out of chocolates or flowers."

"And now he's going." She spat her toothpaste in the sink and rinsed her mouth. "His mommy and daddy rented a house off campus, for him and a friend. A nice house. He said I could visit, but

I knew he didn't mean it. He'll be knee deep in college girls before Thanksgiving."

"So, now what?"

"Living vicariously through you, plus maybe a new set of batteries for the Assassin."

"I thought the Assassin came with a charger?"

"New batteries is just an expression."

I rolled out some dental floss and started on my back molars. After a moment, I asked, "Do you think anything weird would happen if you didn't orgasm for, like, a long time? Do you think all that energy would go into other things?"

"Yes. The energy goes into eating Bugles from the box and cackling like a witch as you stick them on your fingertips like pointy little claws. That's what I was doing before you got home tonight."

"You ate all the Bugles?"

"I put them on the grocery list."

"We should eat more kale."

She stared at me in the mirror until we both cracked up laughing.

When she finished laughing, Shayla said, "But seriously, what are you going to do about this Adrian-Dalton love triangle thing?"

"Ignore the problem and hope it goes away?"

"You're not going to like my advice. In fact, you're going to hate it."

"Break up with Dalton?"

She pointed her finger at me, via the mirror, then turned to face me and point directly at me.

"I totally got you," she squealed. "I was bluffing. I said you'd hate my advice, then you revealed that the guy you *really* want is Dalton. Reverse psychology, boo-yah! I knew those college psych courses would pay off some day."

"Or maybe I was just guessing what you'd say, given you're Team Adrian. Reverse-reversed, boo-yah yourself."

"My work here is done." She clapped her hands together in a dusting-off motion and left the bathroom for bed.

My phone buzzed with an incoming message, but I don't ever take my phone out inside the bathroom, because of my irrational fear* that if I check messages while sitting on the toilet, the camera feature will suddenly switch on and send a video feed to everyone on my contacts list.

*This irrational fear is unusual, but no more weird than my mother's. She won't store the milk directly under the light bulb inside the fridge, because she worries the light bulb will come on while the door's closed, and the heat will spoil the milk.

I finished getting ready for the night and climbed into my bed.

I had an incoming text message from Adrian: *Are you still up?*

Me: *I'm in bed, but I'm awake, obviously.*

Adrian: *I can't sleep.*

CHAPTER 24

Me: *Have you tried counting sheep?*

Adrian: *Not yet.*

Me: *Hey, have you ever noticed that people don't suggest masturbating as a cure for insomnia? Unless you think that's what people mean by counting sheep?*

Adrian: *Hmm.*

Me: *Do you actually have insomnia, or are you looking for an excuse to get a photo of my other nipple, so you have a matching set?*

Adrian: *I'm going to start "counting sheep" right now.*

Me: *Oh! Oh, baby. You're so hard. Look how big and hard you are.*

Adrian: *More.*

Me: *My mouth is all wet and I'm licking my lips. I want to put your long, hard sexy thing in my mouth.*

Adrian: *And?*

Me: *You're in my mouth right now, and I'm sucking your thunderstick so hard it's turning purple.*

Adrian: *Ow.*

Me: *Now I'm being gentle. So soft and gentle, like a feather. I'm just tickling around the head with the tip of my tongue. Around and around with soft, gentle licks. Then I'm sucking hard again, but not too hard this time.*

Adrian: *Ah.*

Me: *Now I'm sliding you in and out of my hot, juicy mouth. I'm so hot for you. Where do you want to come? Do you want to come in my mouth?*

Adrian: *Tits.*

Me: *You dirty boy! I'm still sucking on you, and I'm also unlacing myself out of this really tight corset. It's such a pretty corset, covered in lace and pearls, but I need to get it off because you're going to give me the real pearls. A pearl necklace.*

Adrian: *Yes.*

Me: *Now I'm sucking on you, and I'm also rubbing my breasts with my hands. I'm squeezing my big, gorgeous breasts, and I feel like I'm going to burst. Are you ready?*

Adrian: *Yes.*

Me: *I can't wait anymore! You're going to burst. I'm taking it out of my mouth, and it's all glistening and wet. Now I'm lying on my back, my big breasts ready to receive your present. I'm stroking you with my hand to make you come.*

Adrian: *Now.*

Me: *And now it's coming out like a big jetstream of beautiful pearls, all over my breasts! Oh, oh, I'm coming, too! I'm writhing around on the bed, and your pearls are on my chest and my neck and my face. Some went in my mouth and they taste so good and they're making me come. Seven times!*

Adrian: *Wow.*

Me: *Are we still going?*

I didn't get a message for about a minute.

Adrian: *Okay. I have counted sheep.*

Me: *Do you feel sleepy now?*

Adrian: *I wish you were here with me.*

Me: *Get some rest. Tomorrow's a big day.*

He replied with a cartoon kiss picture.

I did the same and said goodnight.

Then I tucked my phone away carefully inside my purse, slipped my hand under the blankets, and rubbed one out in about two seconds flat.

~

Tuesday morning, I met Adrian at the store, where he was friendly, but all business. No mention was made of pearl necklaces or thundersticks.

We began the big move of Peachtree Books, and, even though I'm more than capable of lugging around heavy boxes and dismantling bookshelves, I played the Girl Card and let the big, burly movers do most of the lifting. Gordon Oliver Junior was there with his clipboard, and Adrian had his tool belt on, so I jotted down coffee and muffin orders, then went back and forth between Peachtree and Java Jones.

We managed to get everything loaded into the trucks by six o'clock. Instead of working a double shift, the movers drove the trucks back to where they usually parked overnight, and would return in the morning, to the new location, where we'd unload.

Three things about the move surprised me.

1. Given all the people we had on site, I thought we would have been done by lunch time, but everything took so long. I bet if the movers had been paid a flat rate instead of hourly, they wouldn't have spent so long messing around with things needlessly. (Here's a hint, guys: I'm no rocket scientist, but I know not to spend twenty minutes re-arranging a dozen huge boxes to save three cubic feet of space for a two-mile move.)

2. You'd swear, by the assortment of stuff found under the shelves (dice, bookmarks, dog treats, candies, elastic bands, and two rubber balls), that we hadn't cleaned the store. Ever.

3. The store didn't look bigger without the stuff. It didn't look like an enormous lofty space for roller skating. It just looked like a very sad retail store that specialized in dust.

Gordon didn't even seem excited at the end of the day, now that he could see what he was getting for the wine store.

"I guess I'll deal with this eventually," he said, and started papering up the windows with brown paper.

Gordon explained the paper was to create an aura of mystery and excitement about the renovation. Personally, I think it was to protect the old gal's modesty, so people wouldn't see the store nearly naked, looking worn out and forlorn with her scratched-up floors.

I'd said goodbye the day before, but I *felt it* that day when I walked out, leaving behind nothing but memories.

"I need a new body," Adrian groaned as he rubbed his lower back.

We stood outside the bookstore, watching more brown paper go up in the windows, until there was nothing left to see.

"You could come to my house for a hot bath," I offered. "We boil the kettle a few times to get it full and hot, but the tub's got a good shape, and I have lots of girlie lotions."

"Will you get in with me?"

"Hah! The tub's not as big as…" Not as big as the one in the fancy hotel—the one I shared with Dalton in San Francisco three days ago.

Adrian gave me a loose hug and kissed the top of my head. "Thanks, but I've gotta go shower."

"You could shower at my house."

He looked down at me, his blue eyes looking sad—sad that I was so stupid, and couldn't figure out he had a date with Golden that night.

"Another time," I said, speaking before he could elaborate on exactly why he wasn't coming over. "I've got some things to do on my own, anyway."

"Say hi to Shayla for me," he said.

I got another kiss on my forehead, plus a brief one on my lips, then he was off, rubbing his lower back.

A second later, I heard something that sent a chill down my spine.

My mother.

Yelling: "Petra Grace Luanne Clever Monroe!"

I turned around to find a middle-aged woman with freshly-streaked hair marching in my direction. (Yes, I have three middle names. Long story.)

"Mom, your hair looks great! Did you get a trim?"

She shook her phone at me. "Thissss!" She pointed to the phone as she got closer. "Thissssssssss."

"Mom, you sound like Golem, with his Preciousssss."

She stopped in front of me and shook her phone at my face. When the phone finally held still for more than a second, I was able to make out a photo of me and Dalton, posing together in San Francisco. Judging from that clue, as well as the fact her expression matched the one she gets when talking about my father's ugly recliner or his methods for watering the hedges, it was safe to say she knew about the engagement.

"Surprise!" I said.

"My hairdresser." She shook her head, to upset for complete sentences. "I said of course not." She shook the phone some more. "Your own mother!" She made a choking sound, then some more garbled words.

"I was going to tell you, Mom. I've just been so busy, with the—"

"San Francisco!"

"You can come with me on the next trip. The plane seats six, plus the butler. I mean, the pilot. The pilot-butler."

She started crying. "My baby's getting married!" she wailed.

"Actually—"

"In two weeks!" She threw her arms around me, gripping me in one of the tightest hugs I'd ever experienced in my twenty-two years on the planet.

She gushed, "We don't have long, and I need to find the perfect Mother of the Bride dress, and it's short notice for the family back east, but I'm sure a few will come, and there's so much to arrange, and—" Her words choked off in a happy sob.

"Two weeks?" That was funny, since I didn't remember setting a date for my PR wedding.

I really needed to get Shayla working for me on a regular basis. I needed someone to google me and filter out all the mean gossip while keeping me up to speed on my wedding dates and whatnot.

My mother asked, "Will Kyle be the ring bearer? I'll have to get him a tuxedo. What are the colors?"

I couldn't see her face, because she kept squeezing me, twirling us in a circle in her excitement.

"Mom, you're making me dizzy." I pushed her away and held her at a distance, my hands on her shoulders. "You're not mad at me?"

"Of course I am. Furious. Can't you tell?" Her flushed cheeks rose like apples on either side of a huge smile, and her eyes held happy tears.

"I'm getting married in two weeks." Saying the words out loud didn't make the situation any less surreal.

"We haven't even met Dalton's family yet, and your father and I barely met him that once. Why such a rush? Is there something else I should know about?"

She gave my midsection an accusatory look.

"Mom, I'm not pregnant, I swear."

"You can understand why I wouldn't take you for your word."

"I'll pee on a stick if you want." I leaned in and whispered. "Aunt Flo is in town at the moment, so I'm pretty sure."

"You probably didn't tell us about the wedding because you thought I'd disapprove, but you couldn't be more wrong. Now, you know I love your father—love him to pieces—but plenty of days I find myself wondering what might have happened if I'd married that famous actor, instead of just getting rogered by him."

I looked around the street, feeling self-conscious about people overhearing us. "Mom, do you want to go somewhere a little less sidewalk-y to discuss getting rogered?"

"Good idea. My car's back at the hairdresser's."

We walked up to her car and got in. She started driving, and told me there'd been more to the story of her affair with a famous art restoration client than she'd originally let on. The man hadn't just rogered her at the art studio. He'd also flown her to Europe, and rogered her in the Swiss Alps, and in a small, very hot Venice apartment above a glass-blowing studio. Name a major city in Europe, and he'd rogered my mother there.

We pulled into a parking spot at the Barking Dog, an English-style pub near the edge of town. I begged her to stop talking about the specifics of her European tour.

"Mom, all this time, I thought you saw those museums and art galleries on a backpacking tour with your girlfriends."

"That's what your father thinks, too, so let's not tell him. You know men. They get so jealous and possessive."

"Be honest with me. Dad is still my father, isn't he?"

"Sweetheart, you've got his brains. Isn't that evidence enough? Besides, everything ended with (the movie star; name redacted to protect my mother from Scientologists) long before I even met your father. He's the one who healed my heart, you know." She popped open the car door. "Kyle's with your father. Let's get dinner here. I'd love to eat a meal I don't have to cook or wash up after." She gasped. "Lucky you, marrying rich. You won't have to scrub anyone's dirty gonchies. The maid will do that for you."

We walked into the pub, me shaking my head as my mother listed all the things other people would take care of for me.

Once we were seated, I said, "Money isn't everything. Aren't you worried that we don't know Dalton very well?"

"My first impressions are rarely wrong," she said, sounding confident. "He seemed lovely at your cousin Marita's wedding, and he was nice to Kyle, and he loves my beautiful daughter—though who wouldn't—so I'm not worried."

"What about Dad?"

"No boy will ever be good enough for his daughter, but he got over his fury about you parading around in your underpants, so he'll come around."

"He was upset about me modeling?"

"Livid. I had to give him a Time Out."

"Wow." A Time Out was something relatively new to the Monroe household, invented to calm down Kyle when he went through a tantrum phase. When you get a Time Out, you have to sit quietly with a blanket covering your entire body. You can wail and cry and rant as much as you want, but you can't come out of the blanket until you've settled down.

I'm certainly no parenting expert, but speaking as the *subject* of a few Time Outs when I was a teenager, I must say there's something very soothing about wailing and blubbering about the unfairness of life while under a fluffy blanket. You eventually get bored of your garbage and move your mouth to the edge of the blanket for more oxygen. Once you inhale that sweet, fresh air, you realize that's what sanity tastes like, and you want sanity.*

*And you also want to eat your dinner, and not inside a blanket that smells like your breath.

"Your father eventually came around," my mother said.

"I had no idea. He acted so calm when he was working on the contract."

"Men guard their emotions. Their kind have many advantages in this world, from height and strength to writing their names in the snow, but they hide their feelings. Maybe it's another advantage they have over us. I don't know."

The waitress came by to drop off our Diet Cokes and take our food order. We both asked for the beef dip with a side of horse radish. I never order the beef dip, unless I'm out with my mother. It had been too long since we'd gone out, just the two of us.

Once we were alone again, I asked my mother, "How do you get a guy to open up to you?"

"You have to listen. And what I mean by *listen* is you have to shut up on occasion." She started to laugh. "I'm still working on that, but Aunt Gracie told me that trick on my wedding day, and she's a wise lady."

"You have to shut up?" I joined in with her laughter. "Sounds like more effort than it's worth. I mean, how many feelings could they possibly have?"

She began laughing harder, tears at her eyes. "Men have plenty of feelings. There's Sleepy and Grouchy and... wait, no, those are the seven dwarves."

"Same difference."

She howled with laughter. "Being sexist is so much fun."

"Did I ever tell you about the he-man gorilla showdown, where Dalton cranked up the crazy airplane fans in his house?"

She wiped at her eyes with a napkin. "Maybe you shouldn't. He's going to be my son-in-law."

"You should know what you're getting into," I said, then I relayed the entire story, including the bit where Dalton whispered something in Keith's ear as we were leaving.

"Well?" Her eyes were big. "What did he say?"

"I don't know."

She sat back, crossing her arms. "That's not much of a story, without the best part."

"I'll find out, Mom. I'll tell you, unless it's something gross."

She made a face. "Now, about my dress," she said, and we moved quickly into talking about wedding preparations.

The food came, and I was surprised by my hunger. The day of moving had been long, but sitting in the warm pub with my mother, as people came and went around us, pool balls clinking on the nearby pool table, everything in my life seemed to be working out for the best.

Basking in the warmth of my mother's happy glow, I completely forgot the wedding was fake, and that I'd still be spending the rest of the week lugging around boxes of books with the other guy I was dating.

After the plates were cleared, my mother got out her phone to check for messages, and I did the same.

I had a new message from Dalton: *Hey.*

"Speak of the devil," I said out loud.

"Is that your *fiancé?*" She put an extra-strong emphasis on the word fiancé.

"Yup, just my fiancé. Checking in."

"Tell your fiancé I said hello."

"I will tell my fiancé that!"

We went on for a bit, and the waitress who refilled our Diet Cokes must have thought we were crazy.

My hands were sweating as I wrote back: *Your apology card was very sweet. I liked the frog.*

Dalton: *I took your advice about getting someone to help with my heartfelt speeches, but the card was the best I could do on short notice.*

Me: *I'm sorry I got so worked up in San Francisco.*

Dalton: *I need to ask you something.*

Me: *Ask me. Don't ask me if you can ask me. You're killing me with the suspense.*

Dalton: *Would you bring your family this weekend to a winery I have booked for us? I want your people to meet my people.*

Me: *Do you mean meet your family?*

Dalton: *Yes.*

I must have started breathing funny and making a face, because my mother asked what was going on.

I explained, "Dalton wants to have you and Dad go on a trip this weekend, to a winery. We'll meet his family. I don't know what that means. His mother... well, she died a while back. And I didn't think he was speaking to his father, but I guess they've sorted things out."

She nodded. "A wedding, like babies, can bring people together. Weddings are as much for the extended family as for the young couple. If it wasn't for weddings, we'd only see each other at funerals."

"Dark, Mom. Really dark."

"His father was in a lot of those adult movies. Do you think he's proud that his son has done so well at acting? It can be difficult for a parent, when their child does *too* well. We all hope for the best for our kids, but... we don't want them to be ashamed of us."

"Please, Mom. Tell me you haven't watched any of his father's porno movies. Or his mother's." I made a gagging face.

She rolled her eyes and feigned innocence. "I wouldn't even know where to look for such a thing."

"When you meet him, don't ask about porno stuff."

213

"What if the wrong words slip out of my mouth? Like I try to compliment him on his *pants*, and instead, I say he has a nice *penis*."

I smirked. "You know what, Mom? Maybe just pull him aside immediately and get all that out of the way. Tell him how much you enjoy getting rogered."

She nodded along, oblivious to my sarcasm. "Perhaps he could give your father some tips."

"Yes, Mom. Definitely ask my future father-in-law for porno sex tips on behalf of Dad."

"Oh, I don't know. I wouldn't want him to think I was weird."

I swirled my straw in my drink and took another sip, patiently waiting for her to move on to other topics.

CHAPTER 25

Wednesday through Friday, I could hardly work up the effort to worry about the weekend, due to all the work setting up the bookstore's new location.

We weren't going to be open to the public until Saturday, and three days had seemed like plenty of time to get set up when we were planning, but reality is nothing like a spreadsheet.

Adrian and I worked non-stop, more worried about getting things ready on time than about unpaid overtime.

On Wednesday, while we were setting up shelves and trying to come up with categories and organization that would make sense to the customers, he started telling me the silliest, corniest jokes. They weren't funny.

We stayed until midnight, and I knew I had to get home to rest when the jokes started to be funny.

Thursday, he brought me in an extra one of his Led Zeppelin shirts from high school. I thought he was making a joke, but he insisted I wear the shirt, because he was wearing one, and it was Led Zeppelin Day. I checked that the brown paper was covering the windows, then pulled off my shirt and squeezed into the black Led Zeppelin T-shirt, my peaches distorting the logo. Adrian nodded his approval, then clicked the button for the stereo. Led Zeppelin blasted from the speakers, and we got to work.

When the playlist circled around to *Whole Lotta Love*, we stopped what we were doing and sang along, playing air guitar and drums, screaming the lyrics as loud as we could. (Have you listened to the lyrics? That is a sex song if I've ever heard one. And the drum solo alone is awesome.)

~

On Friday morning when I arrived, the store seemed almost ready. It looked like it was one hour of hard work away from being ready to open. Curse my optimism! We were still troubleshooting the computer system late that night, at ten o'clock.

"Get going, you still have to pack," Adrian said.

"I'm only gone for the weekend. Just one night."

"Don't get married this weekend, okay? I still want at least one more date with you before it turns into adultery."

"Ugh."

He said, "If you don't have the stomach for adultery, I understand. We had a good run."

I turned my head to give him a sidelong look. "Are you breaking up with me?"

"Am I?" He rubbed his facial hair, looking tired but still sexy. He hadn't shaved since the weekend, and had the golden-brown beginning of a beard. "My body hurts and I can't think straight." He rubbed his stomach. "When was our last decent meal?"

I checked my watch. "We had candy necklaces at six, which was four hours ago."

He frowned. "Candy necklaces are not a meal."

"I'll stick around and order us some pizza."

"No, you should go. Pack your bag and fly off in your private jet to meet porn stars."

The contempt in his voice irritated me. Especially him calling the tiny plane a private jet.

"I'll go. Have a nice weekend with your other girlfriend."

He pushed aside the computer keyboard in irritation. "Have a nice weekend with Mr. Porn Dick."

"Oh, I will. And I'm going to tag team him and his dad."

As soon as I said the words, I regretted it.

We stared at each other for an eternity, then Adrian cracked up.

"You are just all kinds of wrong, Peaches Monroe. That must be why I love ya so much."

In the silence that followed, I swear I could hear the sound of his eyelids clapping as he blinked.

"You love me?"

"Who wouldn't love a girl who nails the drum solo for *Whole Lotta Love?*"

"Do you mean you love me as a friend?"

He looked irritated. "I'm not asking you to marry me, am I?"

I picked up my purse and started for the door.

He ran out from behind the counter and caught me in his arms.

"What I feel for you is real," he said. "You're my friend. You're the smartest, coolest chick I know. And I love everything about you."

I turned slowly to face him, looking up into those eyes so cool and blue they made me shiver.

"Adrian…"

"Go have a great weekend. Don't give me another thought. Get me all the way out of your head, and if I make it back in there, into your head, let me know."

"Kiss me. I won't go until you kiss me."

He bent down and kissed me, his beard scratching my upper lip and chin. The kiss traveled through my body with a buzzing ball of energy.

He pulled away, opened the door, and shoved me out.

I knocked on the door, leaning over to peer through the tiniest crack in the brown paper on the window.

He didn't answer the door, so I knocked again and yelled at the glass, "I dropped my purse on the floor!"

A few seconds later, the door opened. Adrian had my purse in his hand.

We stared at each other for a moment, then he stepped outside the store, dropped my purse on the sidewalk and grabbed me in his arms. He turned me and roughly pushed me up against the storefront, mashing his lips into mine as he clutched my buttocks, lifting me up so my feet weren't even touching the ground, pinning me to the wall.

Except… that last bit didn't actually happen.

I'm sorry for lying, but Adrian didn't step out of the store.

If something like that had happened, things over the next few days would have been much different.

What actually happened was I stepped outside the door and it locked behind me.

Finding myself in the dark, as well as in a different part of town from where my bookstore usually was, I felt like I was forgetting something. It must have been the surroundings, though, because my purse was right on my shoulder, where I'd put it.

I hadn't dropped my purse when he'd kissed me.

I spotted a bus off in the distance and smiled at my good timing. I hustled across the street and got out my change for the short ride to my neighborhood.

As soon as I got home, I took off the Led Zeppelin shirt, hung it at the back of my walk-in closet, and put Adrian out of my mind while I packed for the next morning's plane ride.

~

We hadn't even boarded the airplane, and I was already regretting inviting my parents.

They didn't bring Kyle, because he was congested with a summer cold. The doctor had warned against flying, because of Kyle's history of ear infections, so he was staying behind at a friend's. Also, and more importantly, Kyle was a seven-year-old kid, and (I suspected) my mother thought he might get in the way of all her wine drinking and vacation enjoying, plus the *many* porn-star questions she had in mind for Dalton's father.

My father had a lot of questions about the plane, which Vern was happy to answer, but only to a point. I suppose that because of my father's line of work—selling model helicopters—he felt he was an expert in all things aviation. He didn't ask Vern questions just to hear the answers, but to show off his knowledge of aviation terms.

We stood on the dock next to the plane, and my father said, "What would you say is the absolute ceiling on this old girl?"

Then, I kid you not, he kicked the metal leg connecting the floats to the plane.

"Dad, don't kick the tires," I admonished.

Vern dodged the question with aplomb. "Don't you worry about the maximum altitude we can reach under normal operating conditions. You just keep your eyes on the fluffy white clouds, and I'll get you to wine country."

"Are you wearing your magical socks?" I asked Vern.

"Of course I am." Vern winked at me and ushered the three of us into the little plane.

Dad sat in the front on the left, as I'd expected, and my mother took the right. The first thing she did was pull out the paper airsickness bag and say, "Good thing we had a light breakfast. These barf bags are tiny."

"Add that to your review," my father said.

"You know I only formally review the showers," she said.

"You'll like the resort," I promised them. Under my breath, I muttered, "It's everything else I'm not so sure about."

Vern did his safety spiel, asking my father to hold his questions until the end, and we were off.

During the flight, my mother read wedding magazines, occasionally handing me back torn pages of things she thought would be perfect for the wedding.

"I already have a dress," I said for the tenth time as she handed me another gown.

"That style would also look good on Shayla. I'm worried about that girl. Her mother says she's taken up smoking again."

"That's not the only filthy habit she's got."

My mother unbuckled her seatbelt and switched to the seat beside me. "What do you mean?"

I would have asked her to promise not to tell, but I don't like making my mother lie to my face. Without getting into any specifics, like names, I told her Shayla had a history of dating inaccessible men, and she was seeing someone younger who was leaving for college.

"She must be so heartbroken," my mother said. "I'm so glad my days of dating are behind me. I do enjoy looking back on the more pleasant memories, but there was also a lot of pain."

I glanced up at my father, who seemed to be engrossed in his thriller novel, turning a page as I watched.

"Mom, this marriage to Dalton might not work out. Don't get your hopes up."

"Don't get married if you're not sure. And be honest. Why the rush? Is there a baby?"

I patted my stomach. "I'm only pregnant with a cinnamon bun or two. Actually, I went to the doctor yesterday and got myself hooked up with birth control."

"You're on it now?"

"My uterus is closed for baby business. Sorry to disappoint, but you won't have anyone calling you grandma for a while."

"I'm too young to be a grandma, never mind what that yummy mommy at Kyle's summer camp thinks. Silly woman in her yoga pants and her high-heeled sandals." She patted her cheeks. "Look at this face. No soap. Just warm water."

"Yes, Mom. By the way, Mr. DeNirro asked about *my sister*, as usual."

She gave me a knowing look. "That man is always undressing me with his eyes, which is why I'm careful to wear my best underwear whenever we go out to dinner."

My father closed his book and turned around to give us a stern look. "I'm right here," he said.

My mother leaned forward and patted his shoulder. "Don't you worry, Mr. Monroe. We've got a king-sized bed, and they're putting us in the honeymoon suite. You won't have *anything* to complain about this weekend."

I opened my own paperback and tried to climb into the pages, rather than imagining my parents in the honeymoon suite.

The rest of the flight was smooth and beautiful. We nudged down into the fluffy clouds and began our descent to the winery.

Vern spoke over the intercom rather than turning around in his seat to address us: "If you spot a lake down there, let me know, because there's no runway at the resort. Heh heh. Just a little pilot humor. Don't you folks worry, I know where the lake is. It's that blue thing, right? Hey, what does this red Ejection Seat button do? You folks have your parachutes on, right? Heh heh."

Despite Vern's terrible comedy routine, we landed on the water and emerged safely on the dock.

A young man in a white shirt and red vest drove up in a golf cart to transport us up the hill to the resort.

Vern sent us on ahead, saying he would make the next trip with all the luggage, so we wouldn't have to crowd into the cart.

My father took the front seat, next to the resort employee, and immediately asked him what kind of gas mileage the cart got. It turned out the vehicle was electric, so my father had a dozen more questions about where it plugged in and how long the battery took to charge.

My mother grabbed my hand and squeezed it. "Are you nervous?"

The golf cart putt-putted up the trail. Technically, it whirred, not *putted*, but the speed was putt-putt speed, if you know what I mean. Like, we could have gotten out and walked faster.

"I wasn't nervous until you asked." Indeed my palms were beginning to sweat in the dry heat, with the eleven o'clock sun high overhead. The golf cart had a canopy, but the sun on my one exposed arm was sizzling through my light application of sunscreen.

We crested the hill, and the driver stopped the cart for a moment as we took in the view. "Welcome to the winery," he said.

The rolling hills and grape fields looked surprisingly Italian, for American soil. The square fields were bordered by fences of green trees with impossibly round, perfect silhouettes.

"Stunning," said my mother.

"I'm all turned around," said my father. "Which way is north?"

My mother answered, "Your phone has that compass thing."

"I'm sure this young man knows where north is. Sometimes it's nice to talk to a human being rather than pointing your nose at your phone all the time."

My mother shot me a look, then mimed the motion of zipping her lips shut. The resort employee didn't know which way was north, but eventually the two of them figured it out.

We pulled up to the resort, which had a grand entryway with tall wood pillars on either side of glass doors. The building itself looked like a golf club in *Architectural Digest*, with rich honey wood mixed with modern steel and glass. Inside, it smelled like wine—so much like wine, that I wondered if they brewed and stored the stuff right in the same building.

"Smells like wine in here," my mother said to the woman checking us in at the front desk. "Do they make the wine right inside this building?"

The woman smiled politely. "This is a fully-functioning winery! You'll notice when you turn on the taps in your room, that red and white comes out of the spigot." She looked down at the computer. "Oh, there's a note on here that you'd prefer hot and cold water, so I'll just flip the switch."

My father and mother turned slowly toward me, both of them with confused/amused smiles.

"Interesting place," my father said.

The woman continued with some more joking information about the resort, including a bit about the frames of the beds being made from cork, in case of grape juice floods.

The resort wasn't at all as formal as I'd expected.

As we walked toward our rooms, through beautiful hallways dotted with portholes in the floor that revealed glimpses of the working winery below, I silently awarded Dalton Deangelo ten points. Say what you will about the guy, he picked a great location for our families to meet.

My parents went into their suite, saying they needed two hours to "freshen up" before we were to meet for lunch in the dining room.

How they needed two hours to "freshen up" after a flight that was barely that long would have been anyone's guess… if not for my mother's giggles and not-so-subtle whispers to my father.

They went off to do old-married-people things, and I checked into my room, looking forward to having a nap.

As I opened the door, two things surprised me:

1. Vern was a genius butler and had somehow gotten my bag into my room ahead of me.

2. There was a shocking blood trail leading to the bed.

WAIT! No, it wasn't a blood trail at all, but dark red flower petals. And I was not alone in the room.

CHAPTER 26

"Don't be scared," said the man reclining on the large bed. "It's just me. Your soon-to-be husband. I wore your favorite shirt."

He stuck his finger out through one of the holes of his gray T-shirt with the graffiti-style print.

"You look weird. Are you wearing eyeliner?"

He laughed and rubbed his eyelids. "It's pronounced *guyliner*. Don't you read *In Style*?"

I stood awkwardly next to my luggage, fiddling with the handle. Damn it, but just seeing Dalton Deangelo's lean, sexy body sprawled out on the bed was causing a panic in my panties.

"Why are you over there?" he asked. "Don't you want to see where the rose petals lead?"

The line of red petals ran from the door, around the bed. Unlike the fancy suite in San Francisco, this was a modest single room, with the bed in the middle of the room and a small sitting area over in the corner. I kicked off my shoes and walked along the plush carpet, over to the other side of the bed, where I found a red pile of stuff: more petals, and some fabric. I bent over and picked up the fabric, shaking it out.

"Boxers?"

"Yes," he replied, his voice low and growly.

"I don't get it."

"You will." He grabbed me and pulled me onto the bed with him.

Howling with laughter, I said, "Honestly, I don't get it."

He wrestled with me and pushed me onto my back. He grabbed the hem of my T-shirt and paused to look me in the eyes for one

223

second, flashing a warning with his emerald green eyes, then he ripped the fabric, exposing my front.

"No, you didn't!" I gasped.

He was smirking, still playing, but I didn't find his ripping of my nice shirt nearly as amusing. He straddled me, resting his butt comfortably on the area about my hipbones.

I stuck my thumb and finger into the holes of his designer shirt, and gave him a little dose of his own medicine.

"Hotter," he said.

I clawed at the neckline of his shirt and tried to rip there, but the fabric was too tough.

"Colder," he said.

We were playing the hotter-colder game again? I had a pretty good idea now where the rose petals led.

I reached down and unfastened the button of his jeans. A damp clump of red rose petals fell out, revealing his bare skin and the smattering of hair that led down from his navel.

"You're not wearing any underwear," I said. That meant the boxers on the floor were his, and the rest of the rose petals were... falling out as I unzipped his jeans and loosened everything.

He was already quite hard from the squirming, and the touch of my fingertips quickly brought him to full attention.

"I bought you a dozen roses," he whispered.

"And then, apparently, you had sex with them."

He grinned, that devious vampire smirk making its first appearance of the day. The panic in my panties turned into a full-scale fire drill.

"That's right," he said. "I sexed up all your pretty roses, and now I'm going to do the same to you."

I thumbed over the tip, slick under my touch.

"You'll have to settle for a hand job," I said. "My parents are down the hall."

"I've been up all night, working overtime on set. That's why I still have a bit of eyeliner on. I took something to keep me awake, and now I can't settle down until I get what I want."

I wrapped my hand around his shaft and stroked up and down. "You can't always get what you want."

He grabbed my wrist and pulled my hand away, then climbed off me to remove his jeans and what remained of his tattered shirt.

"Get your clothes off," he commanded.

"No." The panic in my panties had turned into a party, and I wanted him to take me. I wanted him with every nerve ending and every inch of skin, especially the inches that wrapped inside me, but... the word *no* kept coming out of my mouth. I liked how that word made him scowl.

He said, "What will it take to make you say yes?"

"A little conversation might be nice. You could ask how my flight was."

He finished kicking off his own clothes and arranged himself on the bed, lying on his side next to me.

With one gorgeous, dark eyebrow raised, he growled, "How was your flight, my darling?"

"Not bad. A girl could get used to flying." I pulled off my torn shirt and cast it aside.

He nodded, catching on to the rules of the game.

"Did the staff here tell you about the wine that comes out of the taps?"

"Yes, they did." I unbuttoned my lightweight travel chinos and slipped them off, so I was down to my bra and panties. "I'm on birth control now, by the way. Speaking of things spurting out of taps."

He put his hand on my leg, but I swatted him away.

"But are you still with that other guy? Austin?"

"Adrian? For the record, I've never actually had full intercourse with him, but I might."

He glowered at me, but didn't say anything until I unfastened my bra and slipped it off.

"Nice watch," he said.

"My fiancé bought it for me."

"On second thought, that watch won't go with your ring."

I blinked, trying not to let on I'd completely forgotten about the ring, during my hectic week of moving the store.

"I'm a stylish girl. I can pull off anything," I said.

"Pull off those panties." He sniffed the air. "I want to bury my face in there."

Sighing, I said, "If only someone would ask me one more question."

"Would you like me to do you two times before we have lunch with our families, or just once?"

I ran my fingertip under the waistband of my panties. "You can do better."

"Fine." He looked up at the ceiling, as though searching for clues.

We were both lying on our sides now, inches of space between our bodies. I reached over and walked my fingers up along his side, feeling his firm muscles and his ribs.

He asked, "When you were a kid, who did you want to be when you grew up?"

I batted my eyelashes. "I wanted to be a kindergarten teacher, until I spent some time with a real four-year-old. Then I wanted to work in finance, or marketing, because it sounded glamorous."

"Who do you want to be now?"

"I don't know."

"Wrong answer." He reached over and yanked my panties down himself.

A few seconds later, my legs were apart and he was chin-deep in me, setting off all the fire alarms.

I gasped as he drove his tongue deep, then long.

Between ragged gasps, I asked, "What was the right answer?"

He growled, and continued to torment me with his lips and tongue.

I grabbed hold of his hair with one hand, my breast with the other, and writhed atop the bed.

"I'm going to come," I moaned.

He pulled his head up and wiped his chin with the back of his hand. Moving like a jungle cat, he crawled up along me, his torso over mine.

He blew across my nipple, then gave it a lick.

"Who do you want to be?" he asked again.

"I don't know."

He latched onto my nipple, sucking hard.

I shook with pleasure.

"I don't know," I repeated, moaning.

He pulled away, then blew on my wet nipple.

"The correct answer is... Mrs. Dalton Deangelo."

With a thrust of his hips, he slid the full length into me at once.

My eyes rolled up and my back arched, then I went limp with pleasure as he thrust into me, again and again.

I moaned some religious things, and then some even more profane things, and then I started to come, my legs wrapped tightly around his hips to keep him close as I shook with pleasure.

My inner tremblings set him off, and he thrust deeper than ever, jetting inside me, hot and creamy.

After climax, we continued moving together, rocking slowly, coaxing more pleasure from each other's bodies.

We stopped moving, and by the look of his heavy eyelids, Dalton was threatening to fall into a post-coitus slumber, right on top of me.

"Oh, no, you don't," I said, and I pushed him off me.

He staggered off to the shower.

I gave him a few minutes' head start, then I tried to figure out how to get in there to join him without making an absolute disaster of the sheets. Finally—and I'm so glad there were no witnesses—I squirmed off the bed with my hand cupped between my legs, and walked into the bathroom that way. I'd not had a guy come inside me in many years—the unplanned pregnancy being one of the last times. The doctor had assured me this new birth control was effective immediately, but I still felt weird, and tried to squeeze it all out into the toilet.

"Everything okay?" Dalton called out from the other side of the shower curtain.

"I'm not pooping!" I clapped both of my hands to my face. Damn it, that's exactly what I'd say if I *was* pooping.

Why am I such an idiot?

And why am I talking about this?

Let's just pretend I didn't mention the toilet, at all.

In summary, Dalton and I had the hot sex, we came together, and then, magically we were in the shower, just like sexy people in sexy TV shows.

Inside the steamy shower, Dalton poured some shampoo into his palms and offered to wash my hair.

And then, just like sexy people in sexy TV shows, we had a very sexy shower together, rubbing bubbles on each other's sexy bodies and not doing anything awkward or embarrassing.

~

After the shower, I blow-dried my hair while Dalton started getting ready for lunch.

When I came out of the bathroom, I discovered he had opened my suitcase and taken out my clothes. My first instinct was to punch him for touching my stuff, but then I realized he'd set my clothes out in outfits, the way he'd arranged his clothes in San Francisco. And it was so cute.

He adjusted the boxer shorts he wore on his otherwise gorgeous and naked body. He pointed to his green shirt and my green shirt. "These? Or are the colors too similar? Like we're on some sports team?"

"You mean the Room Twelve sport-sex champions?"

He frowned. "Your gray shirt is nice, but somebody ripped up my favorite gray shirt."

Was he stalling for time, or really that worried about our clothes?

I wondered if he was nervous about me meeting his father, so I said, in a way I thought might be reassuring, "For the record, neither I nor anyone in my family has watched videos of your father. My mother swore she hasn't. But she may have *questions*."

He hunched forward. "Is it hot in here?"

"Not really."

He leaned over, his breathing labored. "Can you open the window?"

"I can turn up the air conditioning."

He began gasping. "Window."

I ran for the window and opened the sheer curtains and then fumbled for the handle, praying nobody outside could see me in my underwear.

When I turned around, I found Dalton sitting on the carpet, his spine curved and his head between his knees.

What was this new side of him all about? He'd gone so quickly from joking about the roses to being a nervous wreck. I thought being overwhelmed with emotion was my job.

"Dalton?"

He just kept rocking.

I sat behind him and rubbed his back. His skin felt feverishly warm. "You're having a panic attack. I used to get these at college. You're okay. Just keep breathing."

Between gasps, he said, "I can't breathe."

I put my arm around him, the way other people had comforted me when I got upset. "I'm right here, and we're not going to move or do anything until you feel ready. Want me to cancel lunch?"

He rocked forward and back, emitting no words, just a low groan.

"Can I get you some water?" I asked.

He shrugged away my hand, flinching from my touch.

I stood up, not sure what to do next. My mother was just down the hall. What would she do? It was almost one o'clock already, and I could sense my mother getting ready to knock on our door for lunch.

Dalton kept rocking, lost in his own world.

I grabbed the bedspread and tossed the clothes off, then carefully draped the bedspread, fuzzy side down, over Dalton.

"You're getting a Time Out," I said gently. "For as long as you need, and nobody's going to bug you."

I stood with my hands on my hips, wondering if I was doing the right thing. Should I be calling for medical assistance? Or trying to find Vern?

From deep within the blanket, came a feeble, "Thank you."

"Are you good in there? In your blanket?"

"Yup."

"It's almost one o'clock. Do you want me to go down to the lunch without you, or do you want me to stay here?"

Brightly, he said, "You go."

"Okay. I'll be wearing the green shirt, FYI. With a purple skirt, because I'm crazy like that. Woo! Green and purple. With silver sandals."

I got dressed, one eye on the rocking blanket.

"You look pretty," he said.

"You're under a blanket and you can't see me."

"You're always pretty."

I looked around the room and did a last-minute mirror check on my hair and makeup. "Dalton? Do you want me to stay here with you?"

The blanket answered, "No, you can go. I might have a nap."

"Don't fall asleep under the blanket and suffocate."

Sounding very calm now, he said, "I'll get into the bed and tuck myself in."

Pretending this wasn't the weirdest thing ever, I went to the door and said, "Okay, I'm off to lunch with my parents and your father, whom I've never met before. We're just going to…"

The blanket didn't move. "Have fun!"

I opened the door and stepped out into the hallway, muttering, "We're just going to have the world's most awkward lunch, ever."

My parents emerged from their room down and across the hall, wearing entirely new outfits.

My mother asked where my fiancé was. I explained that he was in the room, exhausted from work, and having a nap. She seemed more than a little disappointed, and I had to push her down the hall, away from the door.

Once we were a few doors away, I explained, "He's having a panic attack about seeing everyone, so I gave him a Time Out."

She nodded and said I did the right thing, as if leaving your fiancé in a room with a blanket over his head was a completely normal thing. My father just kept on walking, more interested by the portholes in the floor than anything else. In light of the recent revelations, about him hiding his true feelings about my underwear modeling contract, his nonchalance did seem suspicious to me.

We walked into the resort's dining room, ready to meet Dalton's father, the porn star.

CHAPTER 27

We got to the resort's dining room, where we had little challenge spotting Dalton's father.

Was he the round-faced, bald man reading the same thriller novel my father had brought on the plane? Was he the silver-haired man walking through and leaning shakily on a cane? Or was he the man with the jet-black hair and his first three shirt buttons undone, a gold medallion worn proudly against his tanned skin, flirting with not one, but two waitresses at the same time?

My father, bless his heart, started to move toward the round-faced man with the novel. Giggling, my mother grabbed his arm and directed him toward the flirty man with the black hair. I had no doubt he was Dalton's father. The man seemed to be commanding the whole room from his seat in the middle.

The two blushing waitresses pulled out chairs for us before walking away.

I don't know how he did it, but Dalton's father managed to stare at both of their butts as the girls walked away.

He stood and reached his big tanned hand toward my mother. "The luscious Peaches," he said.

She tittered predictably, then introduced herself, my father, and me.

"Where is my son, the handsome and legitimate actor?" the man asked loudly.

His breath carried a sample of the amber liquid also in his tumbler on the table.

I took my seat, smoothing down my purple skirt in an identical motion to my mother smoothing her own skirt, sitting next to me. My father chose the end seat of the table set for six, facing us from the head position and leaving an empty seat between himself and Dalton's father.

"Dalton's not feeling well," I said. "He was exhausted from working on set all week—"

"Don't I know what that's like!" the man shouted proudly. And then, for several seconds, I'm sure all four of us imagined the forty-something man bouncing around on big boobs and whatnot, plunging in and out of...

I tried to shake the images from my mind, but they were persistent. The next wave of horror was worse, when I noticed he had the same ears as Dalton, and the same nose and lips. I thought male porn stars were always average-looking, except for the gay stuff. Did he do gay porn? Not that there's anything wrong with that, but now a whole bunch of very different round, bouncy things sprang to mind.

I rearranged the silverware in front of me and rolled the cloth napkin out onto my lap—as though an extra layer would make me feel less exposed.

"Dalton," the man said, snorting around the name. "If you ask me, *David* is a fine name for a young man. Dalton isn't a name, it's just good *branding*. My son always had a keen mind for getting inside people's heads, though, so I suppose I shouldn't be surprised." He grinned, as if to prove that he wasn't being incredibly rude.

"He's sleeping in the room, and I'm sure he'll be rested by dinner," I mumbled to my lap.

"How should I address you?" my mother asked sweetly.

He gave my mother a scandalous look. "You can call me Daddy."

My father cleared his throat and pushed his chair back.

The man quickly waved his hand for everyone to calm down. "Sorry, sorry," he said. "I'm used to the convention circuit, and it's just my natural instinct to be friendly toward the ladies. My fans, they see me on screen, and they feel like they know me already, so I try to match their expectations. I apologize that I come across as too... friendly."

"We're going to be family," my mother said.

My father cleared his throat, as if to say that last point was debatable.

"Call me Jake," he said. "My real name is Richard, but I don't care for people calling me Dick, unless the word Big's in front."

At this point, I couldn't take it anymore, and I started laughing. Big Dick. Can you imagine? And my mother. And my father, his lips practically white from being pressed together so hard.

"Big Dick," I said, between gasps for breath. In a moment, tears were streaming down my cheeks.

To my father, I said, "Dad, just ask him what kind of car he drives, would you? Someone, please. Be normal."

My father took a breath, then asked, "Did you drive up here, Jake? We arrived in a plane, but I didn't see another one back there at the dock. Just a few boats."

"I'd love to have a boat," Jake replied. "Everyone needs a hole to pour money down, especially in between wives."

My father blinked and looked over at my mother.

"I'll allow it," she said, letting him know he could enjoy the joke without being taken to task for a smile later.

"Drove up in my Audi," Jake said, moving on quickly to talk about his car.

By the time the waitress came to bring Jake a refill—"Make it a double, princess, and keep 'em coming, because there's nothing worse than the taste of melted ice."—the two men were discussing gas mileage, and the cabin Jake had purchased from an environmentalist couple going through a divorce. Apparently, the cabin had solar panels and a wind turbine, and generated eighty percent of its own energy.

My mother, who I never would have pegged as someone interested in living off the grid, seemed fascinated by all of this. Or maybe she was just dazzled by his eyes, which were a darker hue of Dalton's green emeralds.

We ordered our lunch and began eating. Jake ordered the full English breakfast for lunch, and he poked his fork into a big sausage, then held it up for us to admire. "The adult entertainment industry has changed a lot in the last decade or so," he said, still waving the sausage.

My father, in all seriousness, said, "Of course. The whole distribution system has changed, with high-bandwidth internet."

"Plus Viagra." Jake winked at my mother. "If you ask me, I'd say that little blue pill was invented by women. Not that I ever touch the stuff. Don't need to."

"That's enough," I said, reaching across the table and taking the fork out of his hand. I shook the fat, greasy sausage off the fork's tines. "Jake, I'm starting to see why Dalton has been avoiding you all these years. You can't behave yourself for ten minutes, can you?"

"Peaches," my mother hissed at me.

Jake swirled the amber liquid in his tumbler and brought it to his lips, his dark green eyes fixed on me.

"From what I've heard," he drawled slowly, "you're no stranger to bad behavior yourself."

I grabbed a knife from my place setting and reached across the table toward Jake's plate. "I'm no angel, but I don't go waving phallic-looking greasy sausages at other people's mothers!" I proceeded to dice his sausage into coin-shaped slices.

"You've raised a hell of a good woman," Jake said to my parents, his face smooth with honesty. "I wish the boy's mother was still around, because nothing would make her happier than to see the fine people he's surrounded himself with. You Monroes, you're *good*, but you know that. You're not like me. Your daughter isn't ashamed of you, hiding up in her room."

My mother replied, "We are all just so sorry for your loss. Petra told us your wife passed away recently?"

"She passed unexpectedly. That's what the papers said, because that's their code for suicide. Cause of death was an overdose, but I don't believe it was an accident."

"Very sorry for your loss," said my father, who had been quiet since the topic moved away from solar panels.

"I don't touch drugs now," Jake said, swirling his drink once more. "Booze, on the other hand, is perfectly fine in moderation." He winked at my mother, smiling again. "Unlike women and love, for which there should never be moderation."

My father looked up and caught my eye from his end of the table. His expression wasn't angry, or upset. Just confused. As if he couldn't understand why. Why did I keep doing these whimsical things that affected the whole family?

My mother responded by reaching over and grabbing my father's hand. "I agree," she said. "No moderation on love."

Jake got a big grin on his face. His teeth weren't nearly as perfect as Dalton's, but he had a similar chin dimple, and some of my good feelings for his son were making me like him, even though he was crude and eye-sexing my mother way too much.

"No moderation on love," he repeated. "I should write that down for the speech at the wedding."

I pushed my chair back and stood. "Oh, HELL, no."

He gave me a devilish look. "I promise the speech will be very tasteful."

My mother grabbed my wrist and gently sat me back down. "You two threw everyone into a tizzy with your whirlwind wedding, so now you're going to have to deal with it." She asked Jake, "He's your only child, is that right?"

"Yup. I got the old snip-snip right after the boy was born. Doctor had to go in two times, because my swimmers kept finding a way."

My father's chair squeaked as he turned and looked wistfully at the quiet, bald man with the paperback.

"Does Dalton have any cousins?" my mother asked. "Peaches is very fond of all her cousins. She didn't have a sibling her own age, but we were blessed, weren't we?"

"I'm blessed," I said, nodding in agreement and watching Jake closely. I was intrigued by the idea of my fiancé having cousins. Perhaps one of them was single and cute, ready to be set up with Shayla at the wedding.

"Funny you should mention that," Jake said, leaning in and glancing around as though making sure nobody would overhear a big secret. "I've got a bit of a surprise for the boy, and I can't wait to see the look on his face."

In unison, my mother and I leaned forward and said, "What's the surprise?"

He tilted his head, his dark green eyes flitting from me to my mother and back again. "Wouldn't be much of a surprise for him if I told ya, now, would it?"

"Good surprise or bad surprise?" I asked.

"Do I look like the kind of father who'd spring a *bad* surprise on his son a week before he married such a pretty girl… who smells like a pretty little alpine wildflower?" He sniffed the air. "Did you just shower?"

"I'm sure your surprise isn't that great." I returned to eating my lunch, which had gotten cold.

My mother said, "I certainly look forward to meeting more of your family, especially since soon they'll be our family."

Jake chuckled and waved for the waitress to refill his drink. My father waved his hand as well, and asked for the same as what Jake was having.

My mother shot him a look that said you're-seriously-drinking-before-dinnertime?

He shot back the can't-beat-em-join-em look.

The waitress arrived and my mother ordered a glass of one of the winery's reds, then changed her order to a bottle.

~

Thanks to the wine, we got through our first family meal without too much horror.

My mother did inform Jake that while she couldn't say she'd seen one of his films, she couldn't say she hadn't, because she had watched the *occasional* adult film, "mostly for ideas."

My father finished his second double scotch and had the pleasant expression of an old man who has turned off his hearing aid and is nodding along deafly while he ponders the meaning of life, or about circuit breakers, or that touchdown he scored in high school.

After lunch, I ran over to the room to check on Dalton. He'd moved onto the bed and didn't even stir when I came into the room, or when I whisper-yelled, "HEY, ARE YOU SLEEPING?" a couple of times.

I fixed my hair and makeup in the bathroom, then came out to watch him sleep. "I shouldn't have given you all that hot sex," I said.

The sex had relaxed him too much, but at least sleeping was better than having a panic attack.

We had an itinerary for the day, so I left him to sleep some more.

I met my parents and Dalton's father in the lobby, and we joined the other resort guests for a tour. I was the only sober person there, which was fine. Everyone was happy.

The resort staff were all universally charming, and the tour was excellent, but once you've seen one vat of mushed grapes, you've seen enough. The tasting part was more interesting, especially when Jake made his move on a couple of single ladies in their thirties.

From the way the three of them were carrying on and tasting wine from each other's glasses, I had a pretty good idea Jake would be bedding one or both that night. And good for them! They were all consenting adults, after all, and none of them was my mother.

After the tour of the facility, all the guests went on a horseback tour of the area.

The horses were all big and sturdy, or "tourist sized" as my mother noted. I would have preferred to walk on my own feet, but I saddled up without complaint, because everyone else seemed so excited, even my father.

~

Rosy-cheeked from our horse ride, we shared another meal together around six. This time everyone sat at a communal table with all the guests present. Everyone else was unconnected to our group, but there was another set of parents meeting each other before their offspring got married in a few months.

My father was happy he got to sit next to the man who'd been reading the same novel. The round-faced man was an engineer and high school science teacher, and the two of them got along like a barn on fire. My mother made fast friends with the man's wife, and so I didn't feel guilty at all sneaking away right after dinner.

After fumbling with the silly key-card lock, I pushed open the door to the room. The curtains were mostly closed, and the room was dim. The air conditioner wasn't running, and the air was warm, but not hot. The window that I'd opened was open just a crack now.

The lump on the bed made a groggy, growling sound.

I whispered, "Do you want to get up now for a bit, or sleep right through to morning?"

As I asked him the question, I felt rather... *wifely*. Is that a word? I approached the bed and placed my hand on Dalton's forehead to check his temperature. He was warmer than I expected, but not feverish.*

*I have no medical training, yet I believe that if someone had a fever, I could probably tell just from my hand on their forehead. This might be a woman thing. Men have men things, too. For example, they think they can strap furniture to the roof of a car, and if they also reach out the window to hold on with their hand, that'll keep everything nice and secure.

Dalton stirred, pulling my hand so my arm disappeared under his covers. I thought for sure he was going to put my hand somewhere sexual, but he stopped with my palm over his heart.

He licked his lips, the smacking sound audible in the quiet room. "Am I alive?" he asked.

I closed my eyes and felt his heart beating under my hand, strong and steady.

"For now you are, but if you make me share another meal alone with your father, you might not be alive for long."

He wiggled his body back on the bed and lifted the blanket in invitation for me to join him. I kicked off my shoes and slid in, my back facing him in spooning position. He gripped me tightly, like a favorite teddy bear.

"How is dear old Dad?"

"Oh, he makes quite the first impression. I can't believe I was worried about my mother being the embarrassing one."

"You know, they weren't that bad at parenting. They were absent mostly, and left me to fend for myself, but all that made me who I am."

I wrapped my arm over Dalton's, warming quickly in his embrace. It was hot under the covers with no air conditioning on.

"Did your father always drink a lot?"

Dalton chuckled. "Yes, but he was always a fun drunk, you know?" He laughed some more. "You never hear about that in the celebrity biopics. 'His father was a fun drunk, and never even beat young Dalton, even when he probably deserved it.' Nope, that wouldn't make the cut. Not sensational enough."

"What was your mother like?"

Dalton paused for so long, I thought I'd sent him into another panic attack with the worst question.

"She was the most beautiful woman I'd ever seen," he said. "She was my mother, and she was perfect."

I bit my lower lip. My heart broke for Dalton, because I knew his money had destroyed his mother—or at least that's how he viewed it.

"I'm sorry I won't get to meet her," I said.

"We have some nice family photos. Picnics and stuff. I'll show you all the albums some time."

"I'd like that." I brought his hand to my lips and kissed his knuckles tenderly.

"I guess it's pretty obvious why I want to hold onto you," he said.

"What? Do you mean like this?" I squirmed up against him, still being held in the front-spoon position.

"My mother's gone. And before that, the only other woman I loved, Kiki. She died. So, it doesn't take a three-hundred-dollar-an-hour shrink to connect those dots, does it?"

"I don't understand. Are you worried I'm going to die?"

His voice tiny, he said, "Maybe."

I shifted away and rolled over to face him, our noses touching at the tips.

"The doctor said I'm in great shape. She said I could probably cut back on the Pop Tarts, but I'm not going to die. Well, not for a long time."

"Me neither."

I reached up and stroked his cheek, which was stubbled with dark hair.

He closed his eyes and smiled, so I kept touching his face, exploring every plane and texture. His eyelashes felt thicker than mine—no surprise there, because his dark, thick eyelashes were stunning. His eyebrows were softer than they looked, as was his hair at his temples. It grew in thick, but the individual hairs were fine and soft like satin. His skin was perfect and smooth, neither oily nor dry, and his jaw seemed to have more stubble than the last time I'd seen him, just a few hours earlier.

"Dalton, does your beard grow extra-fast when you're asleep?"

"This is my panic beard. It grows when I have a panic attack."

239

I gasped.

His eyelids flicked open, and his face went into full-smirk mode.

"You fibber," I squealed. "I actually believed you for a few minutes."

"Never trust an actor."

I laughed, but uneasily. Dalton Deangelo was so cute, and charming, and I wanted to open my heart to him completely, but how can you trust a guy who tells you not to?

He stretched his arms overhead briefly, then rolled away and jumped out of the bed. He already had boxer shorts on, and grabbed the nearest shirt and jeans and got dressed in record time.

"Everyone's probably still in the dining room if you want to go down and join them," I said.

He disappeared into the bathroom. "Is that what you want to do right now?" He popped his head out of the door, toothbrush in his mouth.

I propped my head up on my hand, my elbow on the soft, warm bed. I'd gotten a few ideas while cuddling, but didn't want to let on my bad-girl horniness and act desperate.

"We could go for a walk to catch the sunset," I offered.

"You're the boss," he said, then disappeared to finish getting ready. "Want me to shave?" he called out.

"Your panic beard is sexy. Leave it on."

"I might give you whisker burn!"

"I'm willing to take that risk."

I sent my mother a short text message letting her know I was going for a walk with Dalton, and would see them for breakfast as planned.

Mom: *Come to the lounge for a drink! I want to see my future son-in-law!*

Me: *Don't get too attached, Mom. You know Hollywood marriages.*

Mom: *Don't toy with my heart.*

Me: *Is Jake still hitting on those two chicks? Do you want to make a bet he brings them both to breakfast?*

Mom: *Ha ha I'm laughing out loud.*

(My mother hadn't caught on to texting abbreviations.)

Mom: *He gave us a hint about the surprise. Dalton is meeting his cousin tomorrow. Don't tell him.*

Me: *Sounds like an ambush. I should probably warn him.*

Mom: *Up to you. Your father is telling me to put away my phone. Hugs and kisses. Love, Mom.*

I smiled down at my phone. It never failed to amuse me when she formally signed off her text messages.

CHAPTER 28

Holding hands, Dalton and I walked away from the resort and down toward the lake.

"Are you nervous about the wedding?" he asked.

"Where is the wedding, by the way?" I laughed at the absurdity of the bride-to-be inquiring about the wedding's location, a week before the date.

"I can't tell you, because if people know, we'll be swarmed with paparazzi."

He wouldn't tell me?

I kicked at some loose stones on the dirt path. I'd changed from my dressy sandals into a pair of blue running shoes. The combination of sneakers with my purple skirt and green top had seemed cute in the room, but I probably looked like an overgrown toddler. I felt like one, too. I wanted to kick Dalton in the shin and shove him down the hill.

Why did he have to say all the right things, and then ruin my mood with just a few words? Keith Raven would never do that to me. He always put himself in my shoes, and thought about how I would feel. I glanced around at the vineyard countryside, imagining myself in Italy. I could have gone there with him, accepted his invitation. If I'd chosen Keith, I would have avoided all of this mess with Dalton, and all these feelings.

"The cabin," Dalton said.

"What?" I'd been so consumed with thoughts of pushing him down a hill, I'd forgotten what I was upset about.

"Vern is working out all the arrangements. We'll have tents, of course. The cabin and the Airstream will be used for washroom facilities, and by the caterers."

243

"The wedding is in Beaverdale?" I kicked at some more pebbles. "But what about the publicity? I thought the whole point of our fake wedding was to have people see us get married?"

"Do you remember the photographer from our *Vanity Fair* shoot? She's got the exclusive. The pictures are already sold to *People*. Seven pages, I believe."

I stopped walking and hunched over. My mouth filled with watery saliva. I moaned, "This is happening."

He rubbed my back. "Just breathe."

"I'm getting married in seven days."

"Aren't you excited about your pretty dress? We'll have to schedule a fitting for Shayla for her bridesmaid dress. You did ask her, I assume?"

With my hands on my knees, I continued to stare at my blue sneakers in the dirt. "I don't think I asked her. I'm a terrible person. I was only thinking about me."

He kept rubbing my back, his hand a soothing presence.

"I knew you didn't have a handle on all this," he said, chuckling. "That's why I've got someone coming into Beaverdale next week to help you."

"You hired me an assistant?"

"Something like that."

I cleared my throat and straightened up. The nausea had passed, and now I felt eerily calm. The sky around us glowed pink and orange, the sun nearing the horizon, and a beautiful blue lake lay ahead of us on the path.

I looked right into Dalton's mischievous green eyes, and he stared back at me as if I was the most fascinating person he'd ever met.

How did he do that?

How did he turn any moment—even one with me threatening to vomit—into something beautiful and romantic? It wasn't just his beautiful eyes and perfect face, scruffy with dark stubble. It was something else.

An acting term popped into my head: *commitment*. With everything Dalton did, he *committed*, utterly and completely. Why couldn't I do that? Why was I always running away?

He swept some loose hair from my face and behind my ear, bringing me into his stillness, his calm. "Aren't you curious about your assistant?"

I saw something in his eyes—the way they looked bemused.

"Mitchell," I said.

His eyebrows rose with surprise, and he was speechless for a few seconds.

"So much for me keeping secrets from you," he said, grinning.

"Lucky guess." I smiled back, and then my smile travelled all through my body, getting more powerful, until I was jumping up and down giddily. "Mitchell is coming! I get to see Mitchell!"

"He's booked at the Nut Hill Motel. I figured he can still bunk on the couch at your house if you want, but this way you still have some space, and Shayla won't feel like she's getting pushed out."

I squealed. "Mitchell and Shayla are going to meet!"

Dalton frowned. "You didn't get this excited to see me today."

"I was trying to figure out why and how you screwed a dozen red roses."

He chuckled. "What? That wasn't romantic? With the petals on the floor?"

"Was it supposed to be romantic?"

He took my hand and tugged for me to keep walking down the trail toward the lake.

He said, "The roses were very romantic. I know a thing or two about romance. And now we're going to the lake, for a paddle around in the canoe."

"Oh, hell, no. Canoe? Have you not noticed how top heavy I am? Not to mention how bottom heavy?"

"C'mon, it'll be fun."

I laughed. "*C'mon, It'll be fun?* That's exactly what someone says right before absolute disaster."

He stopped walking and kissed me, his chin prickly against my chin. I melted in his arms. Man, he was a good kisser. It was a shame he was so amazing at sex, because we didn't spend enough time on kissing, just like this.

He pulled away, and I actually swooned, wavering back and forth like I might fall down and tumble the rest of the way to the lake. The sky around us was electric pink.

"Something happens every time I kiss you," he said.

"Absolute disaster?"

"I fall deeper."

I blinked, holding my breath. Deeper? Deeper in love? *C'mon, say it.*

He kissed my lips, the tip of my nose, and then my forehead, lingering. "Let's find that canoe before the sun disappears completely."

"We can't go boating in the dark. We'll get lost."

He pulled me down the hill. "At least we'll be lost together."

I trotted to catch my feet up to my body.

This canoe expedition seemed like a spectacularly bad idea, even before it began. But Dalton wanted to go, and I didn't want to say no. As you may have noticed by now, I had a difficult time saying no to the man.

We located the canoe in a wooden shed, not far from the dock. The resort had posted a number of rules for guests using the boats, including a rule about signing in at the front desk and getting the key to unlock the padlock chaining the canoe to the wooden shelf.

Dalton didn't like the idea of asking permission—no, sir, not one bit. He grabbed a hammer from the nearby tool wall and whacked the padlock three times.

"You're such a delinquent," I said.

The padlock hadn't released yet. He shot me a devious grin, looking like his vampire alter ego in the dim shed. "You get so wet for me when I'm bad."

"No," I lied.

"I'd stick my fingers in your panties right now, but I don't have time to prove a point. Grab your end of that canoe and let's get out on the lake."

Grumbling, I grabbed the end of the canoe, which was shockingly light. How was this puny boat supposed to hold two people?

"As for your wet little panties," he said, "I'll check those once we're out on the water."

"No way." We started walking the canoe down to the water, and I had to laugh at Dalton, because he'd obviously never canoed before. I explained to him the portage technique, with the canoe held upside down over our heads.

We clumsily got the canoe and the oars down to the water's edge, and he was still obsessing over my panties.

He said, "You're already in a skirt. Take your panties off and bunch them up in my pocket to make things easier."

"Maybe I should go back to the resort and let you go for a canoe paddle by yourself. You can paddle your canoe all by your lonesome. Paddle away, my friend."

He laughed.

I continued, "In this metaphor, the canoe is your penis."

He waved me ahead of him. "Ride my penis. I mean my canoe."

"It is rather phallic," I said, climbing in carelessly—so carelessly, in fact, that one might guess I was trying to capsize the canoe immediately, on the shore, so we didn't have to go out onto the lake. If a person guessed that, they would be correct.

To my disappointment, the canoe was more stable than it looked, and did not tip me out.

Dalton kicked off his shoes and socks, rolled his jeans up, and waded out to join me in the canoe. He hopped in easily and used one paddle to push us away from the shore.

My stomach lurched as we began to move out into the water. The motion was smooth enough, like a car ride, but unsettling—like how an elevator ride can sometimes make you feel discombobulated.

"You've really outdone yourself now," I said once we were away from the shore.

He continued to paddle, the muscles of his forearms flexing and drawing my eyes to his body and its beauty. The sky was still pink, and the sun seemed to be holding still for us, stopping time as we moved out onto the placid lake.

"Outdone myself?"

I explained, "First the Airstream trailer, which was small. Then the float plane, smaller yet. Now a canoe. Dalton Deangelo, the next place I expect you to take me is the inside of a coffin. Maybe that one Drake Cheshire sleeps in on your show."

"Cozy," he growled.

"You'll make me your vampire bride."

He stopped paddling and pulled the oars into the boat.

"Is that what you want?" he asked.

I laughed. "Yes, make me your vampire bride."

"You know how that starts."

I wrapped my hands around the wooden bench I was seated on, leaned back, and let my knees fall apart.

He moved quickly—not as quickly as an actual TV vampire, but fast enough to make me regret not donning the lifejacket currently lying on the canoe's bottom, behind me.

The canoe rocked, but it was made for some movement. I eyed the water line along the edges.

Dalton knelt before me, reaching his hands up under my skirt to pull off my panties. He held the silky bundle to his nose and breathed in deeply.

"My vampire bride-to-be," he growled.

There was no one around to hear us, out in the middle of a lake at sunset, but still I whispered, "The first bite is on the thigh."

He grabbed my knees and roughly spread my legs.

"The *inner* thigh," he said, his voice almost terrifying, combined with the lusty expression on his face.

As he lowered his face between my legs, I considered the countless times I'd watched him do this on my TV screen, and how much I'd wished those inner thighs could be mine. Now the gorgeous man of my dreams was with me, on a canoe, and licking my inner leg.

I gasped as something sharp pinched my soft flesh. He was nibbling me, pressing into my skin with his sharp eye teeth—not hard enough to break the skin, but enough pressure to get my pulse racing and my palms sweating.

My skirt stretched loosely over his head, and I didn't dare pull the fabric up to look, for fear of causing him to stop. He applied suction to my inner thigh, and it was absolutely the greatest thing that had ever happened to my inner thigh. I thought I couldn't get more excited, and then he moved to the other side, breathing his steamy breath on me along the way. As he sunk his teeth into the other thigh, then sucked at my flesh, my whole body started to hum, my skin electric.

He released my skin and nudged his way back to the center, the stubble of his chin poking, but not painful. He didn't lick me just yet. He held very still, breathing in and out of his mouth, nearly touching, but not touching.

I pulled up my skirt, worried for a second that he didn't have enough oxygen. He raised an eyebrow in my direction, then opened his mouth wide and dove at me, as though consuming a peach whole. Lips and tongue and pleasure. I rolled my head back and gazed up at the pink sky, and at the highest point—midnight blue with stars.

His tongue moved tirelessly, sweeping pleasure over and over my bundled nerve endings.

He brought me to the edge of coming, then moved back to my thighs, biting and sucking.

The horizon around us turned red.

He pulled his face away and I looked down into his eyes.

His beautiful eyes were dark now, almost black in the light.

He straightened up, on his knees. With a quick turn of his hands, his jeans were unfastened and dropped. He rose up stiffly from his dark curls and sinewy muscles.

Before I could reach for him, he plunged inside me half-way. My skirt bunched up in the frenzy and the hem tried to follow him inside me. He pulled the skirt away and plunged deeper, his powerful thrusts sliding me back on my wooden bench seat.

He noticed my shifting body and growled something about me not getting away so easily. He grabbed me around my lower back and slid me toward him, burying his sword to the hilt.

His hands moved to the back of my neck, and he pulled me in for a powerful kiss, his tongue and manhood trying to touch tips inside me.

As he thrust rhythmically, getting even harder and pulsing in warning, I started to climax. The canoe rocked, the water splashing around us. I gasped and looked around for the life jackets, making mental note of their locations.

He thrust deeper and deeper, rocking every inch of me with desire.

The pressure increased, the desire to come, and there was no stopping now. I held on tight to the edge of the seat as he drove himself into me, harder and harder, faster and faster.

I tried to hold my breath, in anticipation of being dunked in the water, but the shortage of oxygen only made me come harder, letting out an animal groan to match his as he unleashed inside me.

The stars were so bright, but they paled next to the fireworks. I blinked in disbelief as my body shook with pleasure, my skin sizzling with steam. The fireworks were noiseless, and they disappeared. *Just a hallucination.* Bright lights flaring to the beat of our hearts.

He kissed me roughly, drove into me a final time, and stayed.

We held each other tightly as the canoe stopped rocking and settled once more, everything still on the glass-smooth lake. Frogs and crickets hummed with activity on the nearby shore. A breeze ruffled the left-hand side of my hair, and then came around to the right, like magic.

Dalton slowly withdrew, gasping with sensitivity when my muscles clutched at him on the way out.

He nodded down and quietly did up his jeans. The sun had set, and locating my underwear was difficult in the thin blue light, but he finally found them bunched in his back pocket.

"Careful," he said as I wriggled around to put my panties back on.

My jaw dropped in mock disgust. "You're telling *me* to be careful? Me? Um, excuse me. You're the one out here in the middle of a lake, drilling me like you're a greedy mining corporation and I'm a mountain full of diamonds."

"Yes, but I was moving front to back. You can rock a canoe safely from stern to, um, the other part."

"You mean starboard?"

"No, this is starboard." He jerked his body to rock the canoe to one side. The midnight blue water around us splashed a warning.

I raised a finger. "Don't."

He rocked the boat again. "Starboard."

This time, the canoe rocked far enough to the side that a wave of lake water splashed over the edge to pool at our feet.

I gasped and lifted my feet.

CHAPTER 29

I'll never know why I was so concerned about getting my blue sneakers wet. They weren't suede, after all.

Something about water splashing into the vessel—the vessel that was supposed to keep the water on the outside—made me freak out.

I lifted my feet and leaned back, forgetting that I wasn't sitting on a chair, but on a bench, with no back. Once I'd tipped the point of no return, I was going down. I landed on my back in the hull of the boat.

I wasn't hurt so much as I was shocked, and the wind knocked out of me. Wheezing, I struggled to get over the shock and catch my breath.

Dalton chose this moment to be heroic, which, in this instance, involved standing up. He was, unfortunately, well to the starboard side of the boat, and I think you can figure out the rest.

Everything flipped, and keeping my blue sneakers dry was no longer a concern.

Into the cold water we plunged.

I surfaced in the dark, gasping for air and flailing around for something to hold me up. The bright yellow life jacket bobbed up right beside me. I grabbed the jacket and clutched it tightly to my chest as I got my bearings.

"Dalton?"

Only frogs answered.

I told myself not to panic, but you can imagine how well that worked.

"Dalton!" I yelled.

From the darkness came his reply. "On a scale of one to ten, how upset are you?"

"I don't know." I kicked my feet and twirled myself around in the water until I spotted him, treading water with one hand on the overturned canoe. "This water is warmer than I expected."

"It's a nice night for a swim."

"Dalton... I don't mean to alarm you, but where the HELL IS THE DOCK?!"

"Right behind you," he said calmly.

"Oh." I looked, and saw lights on by the dock.

He explained, "I turned the lights on at the shed, remember. I've had my eye on it the whole time. You don't think I'd take you out on a lake at sunset with no exit strategy, do you?"

I splashed a wave of water his way. "You're a disaster."

Even in the dark, I could tell he was smirking as he replied, "No, *you're* the disaster. My life wasn't like this before I met you, Peaches Monroe."

Grumbling a few choice words, I joined him at the canoe and helped him right the thing.

If you've been on a canoe a time or two, you'll know that getting back in after you've been capsized is not the easiest operation. In fact, if it ever happens to you, I recommend getting in a time machine, going back in time, and warning yourself against renting a canoe.

After no small amount of humiliation getting my body back into the canoe, Dalton shot himself in like a trained dolphin at Sea World, and we were paddling back to shore.

We got the canoe and everything put away, then walked back up the hill, which was much steeper and longer than when we walked down or came up in the golf cart.

Back at the resort, Dalton stopped by the front desk and notified the woman working there that we'd *accidentally* broken the canoe's padlock, but to charge the repair to his room.

The woman looked at me, sopping wet and doing the Dripping Walk of Shame, then over at Dalton, equally waterlogged. Without a doubt, she knew exactly what had happened, more or less.

"The hot tub is open until midnight," she said cheerily. "Please note that there is no lifeguard on duty."

He gave her a wink, then strode over to me and wrapped his soggy arm across my soggy shoulders.

"What do you say, dear? A little hot tub party?"

"Sure! But if you don't mind, I'll just pop by the room to get my swimsuit this time."

We proceeded to our room, my wet shoes making those squippy-squippy noises that only wet shoes can.

~

Lucky for us, we'd left our phones and wallets back in the hotel room, so nothing was drenched in the lake except my pride and last shreds of dignity.

I checked my messages while I got into my bathing suit and a robe. I had the usual assortment of messages from Shayla, not about anything in particular, plus one from Mitchell. He was pretending to be just saying hi, but betraying his excitement about his upcoming visit to Washington State.

Mitchell: *What's up, Peach-a-bootylicious? We have to hang out soon! I should plan a road trip.*

Me: *Dalton told me about the surprise! I know you're coming up to help with the wedding!*

Mitchell: *What wedding?*

Me: *Don't make me beg!*

Mitchell: *The secret's out? What do you know?*

Me: *That you're coming up!*

Mitchell: *EEEEEEEEEEEEEEE!!!! I'm so excited! Can you tell?*

Me: *Dalton is trying to get my phone from me. We went for a canoe paddle and he tipped me over. He's a disaster!*

Mitchell: *You love him!*

Me: *Maybe.*

Mitchell: *I'm going to cry like a hooker at your wedding.*

Me: *Like a hooker?*

Mitchell: *Like a hooker in church on Christmas morning.*

Me:...

I couldn't respond, because Dalton tried again to take my phone from me again.

"Who the hell is making you giggle like that?" he demanded.

"Calm down, it's just Mitchell. Jealous much?"

His chest puffed up. "I don't get jealous."

Right, I thought. So, I just *imagined* all those times he got jealous about me being with other guys.

I opened my mouth to respond, but then decided I would let him believe what he wanted to believe. He'd had a rough day, but we were enjoying a romantic evening. I don't allow other people to shush me, but, from time to time, I'm capable of shushing myself.

We grabbed some towels from the bathroom to take to the steam room and hot tub, and ventured out of our room for more excitement.

CHAPTER 30

Sunday morning.

How had the window gotten on the wrong side of the room? Who was that snoring? Why was I in bed wearing my one-piece swimsuit and a flip-flop on one foot?

It dawned on me that I wasn't at home in my own bed.

I opened my eyes and took in the unfamiliar but not unpleasant surroundings of the winery resort's second-best room. My parents were down the hall in the luxury suite. Sleeping next to me was TV's Drake Cheshire.

Hmm.

No, this wasn't my usual Sunday morning.

My bladder had a mission for me, though, so I bravely swung my legs out from under the covers. My bare foot landed on something warm and soft. I recoiled and huddled back on the bed.

There on the carpet, spread-eagle on his back, was Dalton's father, Jake "Big Dick" Blake. I covered my mouth to keep from screaming.

Jake wasn't naked, exactly. He was technically in a pair of boxers, but not *all of him* was in his boxers.

The boxers were the kind with a loose split down the front. A very loose split.

That's right.

The porn star's one-eyed trouser snake was wide awake and catching a little morning sun.

Keeping my eyes carefully averted, I shimmied over to the foot of the bed and slowly climbed off. I slipped off the one flip-flop, which I didn't recognize as my own, and went into the bathroom.

255

I locked the door, turned on the shower and fan for privacy, and sat down with my face in my hands as flashes of the previous evening came back to me.

Putting the pieces together took some time.

I got into the shower in a daze.

As I finished my shower and got dried off, I had most of the events sorted out.

We'd gone to the hot tub the night before, where we had the steamy room to ourselves. We'd been sitting in the hot tub for about five minutes' worth of kissing when Dalton's father came into the room. He had a woman on either arm and a bottle of liquor in one hand.

Although I knew better than to drink in a hot tub, I figured a few shots* wouldn't kill me, but would help with the tension in the steamy, cedar-paneled room.

Dalton and his father had barely seen each other over the past eight years, but they both seemed to want to mend their relationship.

The two men made uneasy small talk, trying to out-grin each other. The two women climbed into the hot tub with me, and started chatting like my new best friends.

*Public service announcement: hot tubs make you sweat, and booze makes you stupid. The result is extreme dehydration, heart failure, and worse. By worse, I mean when you're drinking with a bunch of dudes and realize there's one guy who doesn't bother getting out to empty his bladder. End of PSA.

Jake climbed into the hot tub and started passing around the bottle. Pretty soon, the five of us were all singing *We Are Family* by Sister Sledge. Acapella.

Long story short, after the staff kicked us out at midnight to lock up, Jake walked us back to our room to make sure we got in safely. He sampled some items from the mini-bar, then passed out on the floor, wearing the same boxer shorts he'd been using as his swimming trunks* at the hot tub.

*The boxer shorts were in violation of posted hotel policies, which also included strict rules against drinking in the hot tub.

Refreshed from my shower and several glasses of water, I came out of the bathroom with a fluffy robe wrapped tightly around me.

The guys were both awake now, and Jake appeared to be wearing a pair of Dalton's jeans, which fit perfectly. They both sat shirtless at the small table, laughing over the events of the previous night.

"Why aren't you in your room with your new girlfriends?" Dalton asked his father.

"I called the room and told them to get started without me. Sharon's going to motorboat Karen for a while."

"What's the motorboat again?"

"Just my general term for everything you can do without a dick."

Did they not see me, standing right there? Apparently not.

They both laughed about motorboating, and for an instant, I wanted to return to a more innocent time, when the idea of seeing his father caused Dalton to have panic attacks.

Jake launched into a graphic description of giving oral sex to two women at once. "The trick is stacking them right," he said. "Front to front. Never back to back, or you've got too far to go, unless you like back-munching, which is—"

I didn't hear the rest, because I'd grabbed some nearby clothes and snuck out of the room.

Now I was in the hallway wearing nothing but a robe, my clothes in one hand.

You know that expression, about how when one door closes, another opens? The door directly in front of me swung open, as though someone else had been expecting me.

A man stepped through the doorway and startled when he saw me.

MIMI STRONG

CHAPTER 31

"Connor!" I said.

Standing in front of me was the other sexy actor from *One Vamp to Love*. For those of you who aren't fans, Connor is the angsty, brooding, do-gooder vampire brother to Drake Cheshire. While Drake goes around bedding hotties and biting them on the inner thighs, Connor is always finding new potions and elixirs to lessen their vampire powers, because he feels they are abominations of nature and blah-blah self-loathing boring crap.

"It's really you, Connor."

"Nice to meet you," Connor said, extending his hand. "I'm Connor Adair, the actor, not Connor Cheshire, the vampire. I won't bite."

"And what brings you to this winery? Are you here on some mission to give your brother an elixir to slow him down? I'm afraid you're a bit late for that." I let a nervous laugh escape my dry mouth. I'd gotten used to staring at Drake/Dalton's face, but seeing Connor in the flesh was a whole new level of surreal. Was I still drunk from the previous night?

"He's my cousin," Connor said. "In real life, by real human blood. Didn't my uncle Jake tell you?"

"Derr." (Yes, I actually said that, as I looked down at my toes.)

My toes didn't have any answers, so I looked up to see Connor nodding, a troubled expression on his handsome face. He did have similar features to Dalton, which I'd always assumed was good casting. His dark hair was cut shorter than Dalton's, and his nose was thinner and longer, giving him a look I associated with sophistication.

His eyes weren't green, but a bright blue, also rimmed with thick, dark lashes.

"You really are his cousin," I said, astonished that I hadn't known sooner.

"If you didn't know that, I'm guessing he doesn't, either. I only found out on Friday, when my mother told me. She hadn't told Dalton yet, because she wanted to speak to his father first."

"Jake? I'm so confused. Why didn't he tell Dalton?"

"He didn't know. My mother works under her married name, and it was a long time ago that her family, meaning my family, disowned Aunt Lyra."

I just couldn't stop staring at Connor's face, noticing the similarities. "Wow. You're cousins."

"I just hope he can forgive his aunt for not telling him."

I waved to the door behind me. "Get in there and join the reunion. I'll warn you, though. It's a shirts-optional family gathering, and you can only talk about sex."

Connor wrinkled his nose with distaste, which was a common expression of his character on the show. Shayla and I called it the who-tooted face.

"I'd rather meet them at breakfast, as planned. Maybe you'd like to put some of those clothes on and come down with me to the dining room?"

I agreed to the plan, and he let me into his room to get dressed while he waited out in the hall. I'd managed to grab a not-bad outfit in my haste: a plum-colored dress with a paisley tie belt, and pink ballet flat shoes. I left the robe in Connor's room and joined him to walk to the dining room.

We sat in the breakfast lounge, which was by an east-facing window looking out over the vineyard. The morning sun was bright, but made bearable by roll-down screens that reduced the light without blocking the view.

I ordered my mocha, and Connor got a matcha latte, saying he was addicted to the strong green tea ever since his first trip to Japan. He explained that it's normally served as a ceremonial tea, and not in a giant mug with foamed milk.

"Jake is your uncle? How does Dalton not know about this?" I asked.

"We're related through our mothers. They're twin sisters. I mean, they *were* twin sisters."

"Identical?" My mind raced off, jumping to conclusions. If you have an identical twin who starts making adult films, and showing all of herself... doing things... that would mean...

"No," Connor said, shutting it down. "They're not identical."

"Okay. I guess if they'd been identical, Dalton might have noticed your mom looked just like his. Wow, that would be a good twist on your show. But why didn't he know that you're his cousin?"

"My family disowned Dalton's mother," Connor explained. "I knew my mother had been born with a sister, but the way they all talked about her, I assumed she'd died."

"And what does your mother do? Is she also in acting?"

"She's Jamie Adair. The executive producer of the show."

Hmm.

Connor Adair.

Jamie Adair.

I had seen her name in the credits, but I wasn't the show's number one fan or anything.

So, they didn't know Dalton, their relative, yet he ended up on the same show.

I narrowed my eyes at Connor. Sure, it was early in the morning and I was hung over, but the whole story had a wrongness to it.

I said, "It seems like an awfully big coincidence that your estranged cousin ended up on the same TV show as you." I swirled my mocha, looking into the foamed milk for answers. "Then again, you guys look so similar. And you were both raised mostly in LA, so becoming an actor isn't that crazy, but..."

"It wasn't a coincidence," he said. "My mother kept tabs on her nephew all those years. She secretly created *One Vamp to Love* for both of us, only she never told anyone. I had to audition, just like everyone else, and she put out an open call for the part of Drake." He chuckled. "You know, when a man runs a hardware store and hires his son to take over one day, nobody bats an eye. But when you give a prime acting role to your son, you get in a lot of flack for Hollywood nepotism. Let alone casting both your son and nephew."

"You never knew?"

"I've always felt close to Dalton. We fight like brothers, but… I love the guy." He grinned down at his pale green drink. "Even though he gets twice the fan mail as I do, you gotta love Dalton. He's like a force of nature." He looked up at me, his blue eyes as calm and clear as the sky behind him. "But why am I telling you? You're getting married to the guy."

"Apparently."

"What's the deal with the wedding, anyway? Is it for publicity, or is it for real?"

I glanced around the still-empty dining room. Could I trust Connor? He didn't seem to know about the arrangement, but wouldn't it be just like his annoying character to do something to mess up Drake's plans? *I mean Dalton's plans.* Damn. This whole thing was so confusing.

He continued, "You guys are a really cute couple."

"We're very much in love," I said, smiling sweetly. "I can't wait to get married to that man of mine, and be his wife."

Connor winked. "He's a lucky guy."

"Everything's moving so quickly, but when you're as deeply in love as we are, why wait?"

"True. So, are you two going to commute back and forth between LA and that crazy cabin he's renovating? What's your schedule going to be like?"

I had to admit to Connor that I had no idea.

He didn't find this unusual at all, saying that most actors live with a suitcase packed at all times, their lives arranged around intense shooting schedules and appearances. Since I was marrying into that lifestyle, it was good that I seemed ready for anything.

The next hour passed quickly, with Connor telling me about their production schedule for the show and some of the plans he had on the back burner.

My life seemed rather small and simple in comparison, but he insisted he was interested in hearing about all my family members who were part of town history, as well as my current job at the bookstore.

We were so engrossed in conversation, I didn't notice my parents had arrived until my mother tapped me on the shoulder. They were both frowning at Connor, looking worried.

My mother leaned down and whispered in my ear, "He looks different from what I remembered."

They hadn't seen Dalton since my cousin Marita's wedding, and were understandably confused by me dining with this other man, who looked so similar.

I quickly explained that Connor was the other main actor on Dalton's show. My parents took the news in stride and joined us at the table.

We were just looking at menus when Dalton and his father joined us, both wearing shirts this time.

Dalton spotted Connor and greeted him with a complicated handshake, then introduced him to his father before asking why he was at the resort.

Connor said, "Funny story. I'll tell you in private."

Dalton circled around the table to my side and gave my mother a big hug. "So good to see you, Mr. and Mrs. Monroe." He shook my father's hand and sheepishly muttered an apology for not doing the "traditional thing" and formally asking for permission to wed their daughter.

Dalton took a seat next to me, and the six of us looked back and forth at each other, the majority of us waiting for Jake to say something scandalous.

Jake, who was at the head of the table, opposite my father, took a long look at Connor, then at Dalton.

Jake was the one who'd invited Connor there, so he knew the connection, but wasn't letting on.

Slowly, he said, "Look at you two. That's some good casting. If I didn't know better, I'd say you two were brothers. What do you say, there, Connor? Remind me again what your mother looks like. Is she a pretty lady who enjoyed some Big Dick before he got the ol' snip-snip? What I'm asking is, do you look like your daddy who raised ya?"

My mother laughed uncomfortably, then everyone grew silent and leaned in.

Connor's jaw moved up and down, but no words came out. I couldn't handle the suspense, or everyone thinking what they were thinking.

They knew there was a surprise family member coming, and I could just FEEL them jumping to the wrong conclusions.

Unable to handle the misunderstanding any longer, I blurted out, "Connor and Dalton are cousins! Connor's mother was sisters to Dalton's mother!"

As soon as I said the words, I realized that revelation didn't rule out the other possibility that had been raised. I turned to Jake, aghast. Were the guys cousins as well as half-brothers?

"Hmm," Jake said, narrowing his eyes at Connor.

Connor burst out laughing. "Jake Blake, you may be a genuine motherfucker, but I'm pretty sure you didn't fuck my mother."

The waitress who had come to our table said, "I'll come back in a minute," and disappeared.

"We're cousins?" Dalton asked, staring with wide eyes at Connor. "No kidding. So that means Jamie is…"

"Aunt Jamie."

Dalton nodded his head forward and held the back of his hand to his mouth, as if he might throw up. After a moment, everyone at the table's eyes on him, Dalton looked up and said, "I was invited to audition, and it seemed odd at the time."

Next to me, my mother murmured, "The family connection."

Dalton shook his head, his cheeks colorless and face smooth. He'd shaved, and looked so young in that moment. Softly, he said, "I have a family."

I reached over and squeezed his hand.

He turned to me, eyes wide with surprise, as if he'd forgotten I was there.

He continued, saying directly to me, "And now you'll be my family." He looked over to my mother and father. "And both of you, too. All of us."

"I know, man," said Connor. "It's crazy. I love you, man."

"I love you too," Dalton said to his cousin.

We were quiet for a minute, everyone staring at Dalton.

My mother began to cry. "This is so beautiful," she sniffed.

Jake waved for the waitress, then turned back to Connor with a grin. "I remember now, I did meet your mother a few times, back before things got real bad with your family. I'm fairly certain I didn't bang her. Not my type, really."

My father cleared his throat. "And what rare kind of woman, pray tell, is not your type?"

Jake seemed surprised by the question. "Same as any man. The type who don't laugh at my jokes." He looked at Connor pointedly. "And redheads, of course. I'll never touch a redhead unless I'm being paid."

"My mother's a redhead," Connor explained to the rest of us.

Everyone at the table nodded and visibly relaxed, as if confirmation of her being a redhead was as good as a DNA test, and, based on the rant about redheads Jake launched into next, it was.

The waitress returned, and we all ordered breakfast.

Thankfully, it wasn't long before the food came to our table and Jake's attention turned to eating.

As we ate, my mother leaned over to me and said, "How did you sleep? Our room is over the hot tub room, and some drunken idiots were in there singing all night."

I whispered back, "How awful. Considering how nice this resort is, I'm surprised they let in so much riff-raff."

My mother giggled. "Like me and your father? I hope you're not ashamed of us."

"No, Mom." I glanced over at Jake, who was regaling everyone with a story about the most notorious redhead in the adult film industry. "You'd have to try hard to outdo Dalton's family."

"The cousin seems nice," she whispered. "Is he single? You should introduce him to Shayla."

"I'm sure he has plenty of women throwing themselves at him."

"Sure," she snorted. "Skinny Hollywood types who don't eat. These actor types, they need a real woman to anchor them." She blinked and waved her hands. "No offense meant by the word *anchor*, but I've been reading up on some of these Hollywood marriages, and the ones that last are the ones you don't see splashed all over the magazines. Like that lady who married the cameraman. They're still married, right?"

"Julia?"

My mother gasped. "Look at you, calling her by her first name. I'd love to meet her someday. You know we share a birthday, right?"

Someone's phone started ringing, and everyone reached for their pockets.

"Mine," called my mother. "Stand down, everyone."

Dalton's end of the table went back to their conversation, and my mother checked her phone.

"That doesn't sound good," she said.

"Something wrong with Kyle?" A wave of panic washed over me. Here we all were, having a great time at a resort, and he was back home without us, feeling sick.

She frowned and showed the phone to my father. He put down his utensils, and the two of them whispered back and forth.

Dalton held his hand up to quiet his father momentarily, and asked us what was wrong.

"I'm sure he's fine," my mother said. "Our son, Kyle, has a fever," she explained to Connor. "He's seven."

"I had no idea," Dalton said, looking shaken.

"He's probably fine," my mother said, her voice betraying her concern with a tremble.

Dalton pushed back from the table. "I'll call Vern to prepare the plane. You can fly out within the hour."

She said, "But I don't want to ruin the rest of the weekend, and everything you have planned."

"Mom," he said.

My heart clinched at him calling her that.

He said, "Go and be with your son. We've got plenty of time. So much time."

They argued back and forth for a few minutes, until my father stood and started toward the doorway to the rooms.

I stood as well.

Dalton looked up at me with surprise. "Vern can make two trips. It's a short flight."

How could I explain to Dalton that I carried a mother's guilt with me?

His father and cousin were staring at me with interest.

How could I say that I'd already let Kyle down once by not acknowledging him and getting prenatal care, and that I'd die if I ever let him down again? How could I explain I was as drawn to him because of the fever as my mother was?

I couldn't explain without telling him the truth—the terrible thing I'd been able to tell the other men I'd been dating, but not Dalton.

Without words, my eyes somehow conveyed enough of an explanation.

He stood as well, and said, "I'll help you get packed and on your way."

"I can get my bags packed, I don't need a butler," I snapped.

"It's up to you," he said.

"Peaches, you can stay," my mother said.

"You know I can't," I replied, and started walking away from the table. I tried not to think about the wounded expression I'd seen on Dalton's face.

MIMI STRONG

CHAPTER 32

Kyle's fever had already broken by the time we landed on Dragonfly Lake Sunday afternoon.

The three of us picked him up from his friend's house, apologized for probably infecting the other little boy with whatever he had. Kyle was feeling well enough to request ice cream, so we stopped at Moody's Milk and News for frozen treats.

Kyle and I sat in the back seat of the car, eating our Fudgsicle and Creamsicle, respectively.

He wasn't content to just eat, though, and kept poking me in the leg to get a reaction.

I said to him, "Kyle, I know Mom already said you could be the ring bearer at my wedding next weekend, but I think I might get someone else."

He stared me down, his eyes squinting. "Who?"

"Oh, anyone would do. I just need a little girl, so her dress matches mine."

"No. Carrying the ring is my job. Mom said."

"Fine, I guess you'll have to wear the pretty dress I bought."

His eyes widened.

"The skirt is so pretty," I said. "With ruffles, and flowers."

"Mo-o-o-o-m!" he wailed.

She sighed. "Peaches, don't antagonize your brother."

"Gimme a bite of your Fudgsicle," I said, even though I don't care for the burnt taste of chocolate ice cream. "One bite, and I'll let you wear the boy's suit Mom got you."

He gave me the sweetest, most innocent expression, and held the drippy Fudgsicle toward me. "Okay."

"You're going to smack me in the nose when I try to take a bite, aren't you?"

"No. I love you."

"Kyle, why do you love me?"

"Because I do."

"I love you, too, but I don't want your Fudgsicle, because your germs are on it, and I don't want to get sick before the wedding."

"Okay." He stuck it back in his mouth.

After he'd eaten it right down to the stick, he asked me, "Are you really getting married? Because some people said that you can't, because you're fat."

My mother turned around in her seat, her face livid before she toned her reaction down in front of Kyle. Through clenched teeth, she asked him, "Sweetie, are the kids that you play with talking about Peaches?"

He turned to the window. "Sometimes."

I stared at my mother, feeling sick to my stomach. Through all of the craziness of the summer, I barely considered how my actions would affect him. If I married Dalton, the gossip would only get worse, especially when Kyle returned to school in September.

My mother turned to my father and said, "Hey, we're married, aren't we?"

"Yes, I believe we are," he said calmly, turning on the turn signal to get onto the road home.

"And were there any problems due to me being fat?"

He smiled. "Are you fat? I hadn't noticed."

"Most days I don't notice, either," she said. "Except for sometimes, when I meet really, really, really stupid people. Mostly I just feel sorry for them for being so stupid."

Kyle laughed. "The girl who said it. She is stupid."

I remembered what my mother had said two weeks earlier, about Kyle acting out recently. If kids were teasing him about his sister, that would certainly explain him being upset. I made a mental note to spend more one-on-one time with him, so I could talk to him about any problems he was having.

Kyle started telling us more about this girl who was mean. She was eight years old, and her mother already had her on a diet.

My mother gave me a knowing look. "I believe I know exactly who this girl's mother is, and I look forward to having a little chat with her."

My father said, "Maybe I should be there with you when that happens. Just in case."

"As backup for the beatdown," I said, nodding. "Go, Dad."

"Something like that," he said.

My mother rolled her eyes and turned back around in her seat.

In a low voice, I said to Kyle, "Hey, if you ever need me to take care of someone, just say the word."

He gave me one those cute I'm-so-confused-by-you faces.

"I've got your back," I said, nodding gravely.

"You're weird."

"You eat boogers."

"Your whole head is made of boogers. And your butt."

We traded insults until we got to the house.

Mom thawed out a meatloaf from the freezer, and we sat together and enjoyed our family dinner. I wondered how Dalton and his father and cousin were doing back at the resort, but mostly I relaxed and savored the comfort of being with my people.

MIMI STRONG

CHAPTER 33

Monday morning, I arrived late to Peachtree Books, now open at the new location. I was shocked to discover the store was already open.

A brunette woman, about fifty, swept the front sidewalk clear of dirt and debris.

"Hi, boss! I'm Laura," she said. "I would have waited for you, but I still had my key, so I hope you don't mind. I called Adrian and got the alarm code. He said to say hello if you showed up." She swept a little more, stirring the dust mostly into the air. "Adrian said to go get you a mocha if you didn't already have one in your hand, so I'll just go do that."

"Interesting."

She handed me the broom, then disappeared up the street.

I walked into the store, surprised to find three—no, four—customers browsing the books. They seemed to be shopping independently, which meant either our new location was going to be much better for business, or I was about to get flash-mobbed.

I darted back out the door and looked around for people acting suspiciously. Was there a flash mob waiting in the wings? The mailman waved, but that was it. Everything seemed normal enough.

I went back in and stood in the middle of the new store for a minute, feeling awkward. Everything looked perfect and organized, the way it had been on Friday.

Except for a few balloons tied to the tops of bookshelves, nobody would ever guess the store had only been open since Saturday.

Good job, Adrian.

The customers were browsing fine on their own, so I made my way to my spot behind the counter and dumped out the pens from the tin, to give them a good sorting.

Ten minutes later, Laura returned with two takeout cups, including a mocha for me. And a gingersnap cookie.

"Laura, I love you already," I said.

Yes, things were going well.

Adrian thought he'd pull one over on me by hiring some woman without my permission, but I wasn't going to freak out.

Laura and I talked some more throughout the day, and I learned she'd been an employee of Black Sheep Books until about a year ago, when she couldn't stand the owners anymore. She did, however, love the books and the customers, and had brought her resume in on Saturday to give to Adrian. He hired her on the spot. On Sunday, she came in and trained to learn the point-of-sale software, and now she was mine. All mine.

Having a full-time weekday employee made me giddy... until the end of the day, when I closed up the cash register.

The sales for the day were up twenty-two percent from a typical Monday that time of year. That was good, but not amazing. We seemed to be busier at the new location, but not enough to justify two weekday employees. Sure, the sample size was small, but the writing was on the wall.

I didn't say anything about my worries to our new employee, who looked so happy, and had been friendly and helpful with customers all day.

Either Laura or I would have to go.

I was getting married to a wealthy actor, whereas Laura was a single mom with two teenage boys.

She needed the job more than I did. She *wanted* the job, whereas I simply *had* the job and kept showing up.

Thinking about my future, I felt like I was up in a plane again, and everything below me seemed small in the distance.

We locked up for the day, and I told Laura I'd see her Tuesday.

Then I started the long walk home. I could have taken the bus and saved myself a couple of miles, but I had a lot of thinking to do, and I always think better when I'm walking.

I was a third of the way home when my senses tingled that I was being followed by a car. I whipped around to see a German Shepherd, wearing a cone around his neck, hanging out of a car window. He had the dog equivalent of a giant grin on his face.

"Penny for your thoughts," Adrian called out from the driver's seat.

I kept walking, because I still had a lot of thinking to do.

"You hate me that much?" he called out. "I hoped you'd be happy that I hired Laura to help out for a few weeks, so you could do all the wedding stuff."

"You told her it was only a few weeks? By the way she was talking, she must think the job's hers permanently."

"I wouldn't do that to you." He waved for the car behind him to go around, and continued to roll along slowly next to the sidewalk while I kept walking. "Is this it? You hate me now? Because if you hated me, things could get less complicated."

"Maybe I should hate you. You're a billion times better than me at running the bookstore. It took you less than a month to improve the business more than I did over the years I've been there."

"I've got a brain for spreadsheets and a body for sin. Hop in. I'll take you home, or anywhere you want to go."

I looked back at Cujo, hanging out of the back seat's window, his tongue lolling out happily.

"Hey, hero dog," I cooed at him. "I'm sorry you have to wear that plastic thing, buddy. Think of it more as a Cone of Pride."

"If you want to thank Cujo, get in and we can take him to the park with the pond, where he can terrorize the ducks."

I stopped walking, and the car stopped. Adrian leaned over and nudged open the passenger door.

The truth is, I didn't want to talk to Adrian.

I wanted to get a big eraser and scrub away everything that had happened in the last few weeks between us, so we could go back to just being friends. My adolescent crush on him was cute, in retrospect. Messing up each other's lives and feelings wasn't cute. Having innocent people (and dogs) get hurt in the process that wasn't so cute, either. I wished I could take everything back.

MIMI STRONG

CHAPTER 34

Instead of saying those things I felt and being honest, I climbed into the car and said, "Laura's a great hire. You did the right thing." I fidgeted with the seat belt. The damn thing was made for the skinny Storm family and cut into my belly and my feelings. "Stupid seatbelt," I muttered. "Stupid world. Stupid small chairs and small clothes and stupid inadequate seat belts."

I tossed it aside, the buckle banging the leather interior and leaving a scar before the belt retracted.

Rubbing the scratch with my fingertip, I apologized to Adrian, the car, and Adrian's mother.

Cujo began to howl miserably in the back seat.

I turned to Adrian. "What's wrong with your dog?"

"He howls when people are in distress. He's very sensitive to emotions."

"Awesome," I said flatly. "Now I'm causing emotional distress to your dog, on top of nearly getting him killed."

"Are you having a bad day?"

"I don't know. I'm all mixed up."

"Mondays."

I took a breath and looked around. We were heading away from the town center, in a direction I didn't usually travel.

"Yeah, Mondays," I said. "You didn't text me back today. How did the soft opening go? I had a look at the sales numbers, and they were good. We can afford to have two people working on the weekends, at least. Were you run off your feet?"

"Keeping busy was good. I didn't have to think about you, off doing *things* with Dalton Deangelo."

The memory of sex in the canoe and then getting dumped into the lake brought a smile to my lips. Yes, I had done *things*.

"How is Golden?" I asked.

"Never you mind."

"Did you sleep with her? Because it's okay if you did."

"And I suppose that answers my unspoken question about what *you* got up to over the weekend."

"You know, Dalton and I *are* getting married on Saturday."

"Am I invited?"

"Would you come?"

"If you wanted me to."

"Adrian, stop being so perfect. You're too good. You deserve better, and I've done nothing but jerk you around and hurt you."

Cujo began to howl again.

"And I hurt Cujo," I added. "When I think about what happened in the woods…"

"Stop being so hard on yourself."

"Why? What makes me so great? I'm a college dropout with a dead-end job, or maybe no job. If you haven't noticed, I go around shooting my big mouth off at people without a second thought to their feelings. I already act like one of those people with a reality TV show, so can you imagine what a monster fame will make me?"

"You're scared."

"Duh. Two points for Adrian."

Cujo barked twice.

"Three points," I said.

Cujo barked three times.

"Adrian, your dog can count!"

Adrian started to laugh, still facing ahead at the road as he drove into the parking lot for the park with the duck pond. He laughed harder once we parked, squeezing the top of his nose between his eyes with his fingertips.

Was he messing with my head?

"Cujo," I said. "Count to three points."

WOOF WOOF WOOF!

Adrian wiped his eyes. "I forgot about that trick. He can only count to three. He's not a genius, but he is a very smart dog."

"Cujo, two points."

WOOF WOOF.

Tail wagging, he tried to come up into the front seat, but the cone around his neck got caught on the headrest and he got stuck, which only made us laugh harder.

We opened our doors and I let him out of the back seat.

He sat patiently, his gaze darting back and forth between me and Adrian for permission, the white spots above his eyes looking like reverse-eyebrows.

"Go get the ducks," Adrian said, nodding toward the pond.

Cujo bounded off, a beast made of nothing but fur and pure joy.

If only human lives could be as simple as dog lives.

Adrian reached for my hand. "Let's walk. We'll do one circuit around the pond, then get some dinner."

I pulled back my hand and slipped it in my pocket.

He nodded, his knowing expression breaking my heart.

Just a gesture, and two hearts shear.

He knew this was the end for us.

After a moment, he said, "Let's at least have our walk around the pond. We're already here."

"Sure." I started walking, my hands still in my pockets. We brushed elbows as he joined at my side.

Twenty minutes later, we were at the one-third marker when Adrian spoke.

"I'll work at the store through the Christmas season, then I'll probably be on my way in the new year. I'll head off to a new city and get a fresh start. Have you ever been to Chicago?"

"Is that the Windy City? No, I've never been there. I've hardly been anywhere."

"I'm sure you'll go to lots of places."

"All the places I read about in books. Not Narnia, though, obviously. Or Hogwarts."

Adrian kicked a pebble off the path. "I feel like I've been to the moon. In my head, I know I haven't, but my heart tells me otherwise. When I see those photos from space, I always think, *I've been there*."

"Because you've been alone, and you've been lonely."

"I know you don't believe me, but I'm quite sure I've actually been there. I've walked on the moon."

"You'll find someone," I said.

"She won't be like you."

"I hope not. That would be a disaster. You'd fight over every little thing."

"Couples argue because they're afraid of losing control. When I fall in love again, I'm going to surrender."

The corner of my lip twitched. Surrender? So many great jokes came to mind, involving whips and chains and leather accessories.

I didn't say a word, though, and soon the only sounds were our feet on the path and the ducks quacking at Cujo, who'd tired of the chase and lay on the shore, content with watching.

CHAPTER 35

Tuesday.

Four more sleeps until my wedding.

I tried to get to work at the bookstore early, but Laura got there even earlier.*

*Actually, I was late again.

We finished stocking shelves throughout the morning, and I covered the store while she went for lunch.

I looked around for more things to keep us busy, but everything was done. All we had to do was help customers.

When Laura returned from lunch, I disappeared into the new office we had at the bigger location. I closed the door, and called Gordon Oliver Junior.

And then I resigned.

He was disappointed to hear I was leaving, but offered to write me a letter of recommendation.

"I feel bad," I said. "I've been so distracted lately, I probably haven't been a good employee at all."

"Peaches, on your worst day, you're more fun to be around than most people on their best day."

I laughed. "Fun?"

"At the end of the day, we all want to be with someone who's fun. The customers love you because you care, and you're honest. The store has an excellent reputation in town, and it's because of you."

"Gordon, don't make me cry."

"You don't have to stay for the full two weeks of your notice," he said. "That's more of a professional courtesy for when nobody's been hired yet. We do have Laura and Adrian, plus Amy wants to come back and work a few shifts after school and weekends."

"I guess everything will carry on just fine without me," I said, my voice thin and betraying my hurt feelings—silly as they were.

"You always have a job to return to," he said. "Either at the bookstore, or here at the wine shop."

"The wine shop," I said brightly. "That sounds fun. I bet all you do is sit around and taste wine all day."

"Har har," he said.

"Gordon, are you available Saturday to come to my wedding? You can bring your girlfriend. There's just one catch. I can't tell you where it is, so you have to meet with everyone at the bus stop, where you'll get transported to the location."

"Of course I'll go! I already got the invite, anyway. You know I wouldn't miss your wedding for all the Bordeaux in Bordeaux."

"So... Laura seems to have a handle on everything here."

He hiccuped. "What time have you got there? One o'clock? I'll mark your timesheet. You're done selling books, Peaches. Right now. Walk out that door and live your life."

"Are you drinking?"

"It's Taste Test Tuesday here. Now get going. I forbid you from working another minute."

I thanked him, said goodbye, and put my purse on my shoulder. On the way out, I stopped to let Laura know her position had been made permanent, and I was happy for her.

She squealed and hugged me.

I was almost at the front door when I remembered something. I ran back to the counter, shook the pens out of the cup-holder tin Kyle had decorated, and tucked it into my purse. "Someone I love made this for me," I said.

Laura grinned. "I understand completely. Good luck with your wedding. Let me know if I can help."

"You could start a rumor that the location is Duck Pond Park."

"I could totally do that," she said. "People have been pumping me for information ever since Sunday. Typical small town nosiness."

I winked at Laura and walked out the door, my thoughts alternating between the positive and the negative:

Yay, I'm free! No more talking about book clubs while I'm hopping around on one foot desperate to pee!

Oh, crap. I'm unemployed. I'll have to sell my designer dress on EBay for rent money.

I can go home and have a nap!

What if Dalton doesn't love me and he crushes my heart on our wedding night? What if he's sleeping with that Justine chick on the side? What if his whole story about the chubby neighbor was a lie, and this is just a phase, and soon he'll be back to skinny actresses?

Yay, I get to wear a pretty dress on Saturday!

I settled on the happy thought about my dress.

Then I caught the bus home, made and ate a batch of Rice Krispie squares, and napped the rest of the day.

Unemployed life is amazing!

CHAPTER 36

Wednesday.

Three more sleeps until my wedding.

Wednesday was the date Mitchell was scheduled to arrive in town to help me get ready for the wedding—not that I needed much help, since Vern was busy coordinating most of the preparations, with help* from my mother.

* By *help*, I mean my mother provided equal parts help and hindrance, netting out to neutral. Whatever. At least they got the flowers sorted out between the two of them, and no orchids were beheaded.

I'd been text-messaging with Mitchell for days, but he was deliberately vague about how he was arriving in town. Vern was still in Washington State, with the plane, so I imagined Mitchell was driving up from California.

And he was driving up, as it turned out.

In a sexy red car.

The car pulled up in front of the house around two o'clock Wednesday afternoon, and Shayla and I ran out to greet Mitchell.

"You upgraded," I said, referring to his blue two-door Miada.

With an impish smile on his adorable face, Mitchell tossed the car keys to me. "You're the one who upgraded," he said.

The keys landed in the grass before me.

A minute later, I picked up the keys, along with my jaw, off the grassy front lawn.

I mumbled, "Shayla, Mitchell, introductions, go."

As they said hello, I shuffled like a zombie toward the pretty red car in my tunnel vision.

The car was gorgeous—sporty and expensive-looking, but with four doors, so it wasn't all that impractical, though the gas mileage would probably make my father cringe.

I'd never owned a car before, much less gotten one as a gift. I climbed in the driver's side and found an oversized bow wrapped around the headrest of the passenger side, along with a card.

My hands shook as I opened the envelope.

The card read:

I couldn't decide between blue or red, since you look so beautiful in both colors, so I let Mitchell pick which one to drive up. - Dalton

P.S. It's really yours. And so is the matching one that's parked in front of our house in LA.

I held my hands over my mouth and screamed with happiness. Two cars? Was I still napping and dreaming?

The leather on the seats felt buttery, and there were so many buttons to adjust everything—buttons I didn't know cars had.

Shayla and Mitchell had to forcibly drag me from the car. I apologized and hugged Mitchell, picking him up off his feet without even thinking.

"I'm not a toy," he howled, laughing and struggling for me to put him down.

Shayla stared at Mitchell, with his curly gold hair and light blue eyes, then turned to me. "You're right. He's fun-sized, just like Golden."

Mitchell pointed to me. "Golden? That's the blonde veterinary assistant who's dating your former high school crush who you fooled around with this summer but never slept with, and broke up with on Monday, by the duck pond? He talked about the moon and made you sad?"

Shayla elbowed me. "If Mitchell already knows everything, how are he and I supposed to bond with each other? We were supposed to gossip about you at the fitting today."

Mitchell did a fun hand swoosh. "I'm sure there's something. Peaches can't go five hours without doing something shocking, unless she's asleep."

"That's my girl," Shayla said proudly.

Mitchell followed Shayla up into the house, both of them chattering away without waiting for the other one to respond to a question.

Mr. Galloway waved from his porch, catching my eye.

"I didn't mean to eavesdrop, but congratulations on the new car, and on the wedding, of course."

"You are coming, right?"

He beamed. "Yes, and I have a date. Do you know Dottie Simpkins? Pink hair. Very interesting lady."

"Wow. You're ready to start dating again, and you're diving in at the deep end. Watch out she doesn't make you husband number seven."

He chuckled, looking like a man smitten. He was definitely under Dottie's spell, and that made me almost as happy as getting my new car. *Almost.*

"Where is this wedding?" he asked.

"Secret location. Show up at the bus depot and they'll take you there."

He looked around for anyone who might be in hearing range, then held up his hand alongside his mouth and whisper-shouted, "I hear they're setting up tents at Duck Pond Park."

I held one finger to my lips. "Shh."

He winked and nodded. "The secret's safe with me."

I made Mr. Galloway promise to come to the bus depot anyway, and then I went into the house to join the Shayla-Mitchell gossip session in progress.

MIMI STRONG

CHAPTER 37

The drinking started innocently enough.

We were showing off our booze collection to Mitchell, and he suggested we sample the vodka he'd brought up with him.

The vodka was tasty.

We became too inebriated to go anywhere, but then Shayla called our friend Chantalle Hart and asked for a favor. She got Chantalle to agree to driving us around for a spur-of-the-moment bachelorette party.

With a sober person as our chaperone and driver, the three of us in the wedding party were free to get into as much trouble as we wanted.

And we had no problem finding trouble.

From the house, we proceeded to Cougar Town, where we consumed chicken wings, nachos, and as many drinks as they'd serve us.

That place was pretty dull, even for a Wednesday night, so we left in search of our own fun.

After a dire warning about what I'd do to people if they threw up in my new car, we got back into my sweet ride and started driving up and down Leonardo Street while passing around the vodka bottle.

I can't say for sure whose idea it was to break into Dalton's cabin, but we all agreed the idea was excellent.

Chantalle made a few wrong turns, but eventually we found the heritage site for the cabin, at the edge of Dragonfly Lake.

"This is the wedding site?" Shayla asked as we pulled up to the cabin.

"That's a secret!" I yelled at her.

Chantalle turned back to me. "It's okay. I won't tell anyone. I'm just glad I'm invited."

"Peaches, honey, I don't think the wedding is going to be here," Mitchell said. "I think Dalton lied to you, to throw us off. That man is as cunning as he is gorgeous."

I groaned. "He's such a liar!"

"This place is a total construction site," Chantalle said. "There's no way you can have a wedding here. Are the guests going to sit in those dirt-digger things and have tractor wars?"

"That would be awesome!" Shayla said brightly. "Who cares. We're still breaking in. I gotta pee."

We parked the car and all jumped out.

We ran up to the cabin first, but found the door locked tight and all the windows boarded up for the construction.

"I could climb down the chimney," Mitchell offered.

Shayla and I thought that was a marvelous idea, because after as much vodka as we'd had, we were pretty sure anything was possible.

Luckily for Mitchell, Chantalle ran over to the Airstream, found it unlocked, and called us over.

Giggling, we all climbed up the steps into the trailer.

It was even smaller with four people inside.

We all squeezed into the kitchenette and were absolutely silent. I was trying to figure out where the wedding was going to be, and Mitchell was fascinated by the trailer's compact interior.

"Hurry up!" I yelled at Shayla, who was in the bathroom.

"These walls are paper thin!" she howled. "You guys have to talk or something. I can't go if people are listening!"

We all covered our mouths to keep from laughing.

None of us started talking. It was more fun to torture Shayla.

I don't know why drinking makes you kinda mean toward your friends, but I like to think you only abuse the ones you love.

While we were huddled there in the kitchenette, one of the cabinets began emitting an odd noise.

"The trailer is haunted!" I squealed.

Mitchell and Chantalle screamed, and we all pushed and shoved each other to get out the door. We ran down the steps and to the ground outside.

"Totally haunted," Mitchell said in agreement.

"I'm never going in there again," I said.

A few minutes later, Shayla came out with some papers in her hand. "That noise was a fax machine, you dummies."

"It must be a time-traveling Airstream," Mitchell said, his eyes wide. "How else would you explain having a fax machine?"

"Probably architectural drawings or whatever for the cabin," I said.

Shayla gasped and ran to the car with the papers, where she sat on the passenger side. She left the door open and the interior light on.

Chantalle slid into the driver's side and grabbed the papers from Shayla. "What's the big deal? Looks like these are different wording options for a screenplay. This fax is from the office of some writer dude. That makes sense, since Dalton is an actor. Except..."

Mitchell shot me a grave look then asked, "Is the content anything Peaches should be concerned about?"

Chantalle laughed. "That's a funny coincidence. It's actually wedding vows for something. Hmm. That's odd. It says Peaches Monroe in this script."

Mitchell ran around to the driver's side of the car, grabbed the papers, and ran back to the Airstream yelling, "No good can come of this! We were never here. This did not happen!"

I slid into the back seat of the car and pried the vodka from Shayla's hands. The booze had smelled of vanilla and other herbs when we started, but now it went down as easy as water.

It crushed me to learn that Dalton had someone writing his vows. If he actually loved me, why would he hire someone else to say it?

Chantalle was confused and upset. "I don't understand what's happening, you guys. What is up with everyone this summer? Golden is dating Adrian and Carter, and Carter is dating Golden and Tiny-Shirt Trisha, and I can't keep track of who else Trisha is dating, but I think Lester's in there, and Kirsten. Has everyone lost their minds? And why is everyone acting like I ate a box of kittens? What's the deal with the script?"

Mitchell slid into the back seat next to me and wrestled the bottle from my hands. "The fax has been returned," he said. "We'll just pretend we were never here."

Chantalle turned around and asked again, "What's happening?"

291

"Peaches has trust issues," Shayla explained to Chantalle. "Back when they first met, Dalton used a bunch of scripted lines to get into her panties."

I snorted. "And he also used his eyebrows. His sexy vampire eyebrows." I grabbed back the bottle. "But mostly I'm upset because you can't ever trust an actor. He's always acting!"

Mitchell gave me the saddest look. "Oh, Peaches. He might be corny, but he does love you."

"Does he? Then why hasn't he said it?"

The two girls in the front seats turned around so fast, they bumped heads with a crack.

Rubbing her head, Chantalle said, "What on earth is going on? Why would you marry a guy who hasn't said he loves you?"

Shayla gasped. "You're pregnant again? Gimme that. You can't drink."

I gave her my steeliest shut-up look. "I'm not pregnant, nor have I ever been, Shayla. You should know, as my best friend."

Still rubbing her head, and looking like she really regretted agreeing to be our driver, Chantalle asked me again, "Why are you getting married? For money?"

I began to laugh, rolling back in the seat and slapping my hands on my knees. "Got ya! I totally pranked ya!"

"You're joking?" Chantalle asked.

Mitchell gave me a skeptical look.

"Totally joking," I said. "I know all about the scriptwriter thing. Dalton's really into me. He totally loves me. He just isn't so great with his own words."

"That makes sense," Chantalle said, nodding in agreement.

"I don't feel so good." Shayla let out a burp that sounded and smelled anything but good.

"We'll continue the party at our house," I said, still pretending to be having a great time. "Or back to Cougar Town!"

I expected Mitchell to agree with me, but he'd already passed out and was sleeping like a golden-curled baby, a sweet smile on his cherubic face.

Chantalle started the car and made a five-star turn in the mucky front yard.

"Hey guys, Mitchell's asleep," I said.

Shayla unzipped her purse. "He'd look cute in my red lipstick."

"Do you have blush with you?"

"You know it, girl."

Chantalle tsk-tsked us. "You guys are mean drunks."

"We're fun drunks," I said.

"We're totally fun drunks," Shayla said.

Chantalle muttered, "Remind me not to pass out around you two."

MIMI STRONG

CHAPTER 38

For the second time in less than a week, I woke up in an unfamiliar place.

If I wasn't mistaken, and that bright thing searing my eyes was indeed the sun, that meant it was…

Thursday.

Two sleeps until my wedding.

Squeezing my eyes shut, I felt around myself timidly. I still had clothes on, and I was on top of something soft and non-human. All good so far.

Someone stirred next to me. I rolled to my side and opened my eyes, finding myself face to face with beautiful golden-brown eyes.

"Shayla, where are we?"

She wrinkled her nose. "By the smell, a dumpster. Wait, is that your breath?" She puffed on her palm. "Nope, it's mine. Sorry."

We were on a bed, in a hotel room. If I knew those hideous linens, we were in the Nut Hill Motel. There was another bed next to ours, empty.

A door clicked open and Mitchell came out of the bathroom with a towel slung around his waist. "Rise and shine, dummies!" he sang. "I'd like to especially thank whoever applied lipstick to my junk. *Very funny.* I guess I was supposed to wake up and think I'd enjoyed the pleasures of a woman last night?"

Shayla smirked.

Mitchell continued, "Unfortunately for your little prank, you left the lipstick tube in my shorts where you dropped it. You do get points for originality, of course."

Shayla kept a straight face. "I don't know what you're talking about, Mitchell. We went back to Cougar Town last night, and you disappeared for about twenty minutes with an older lady in a leopard print dress. Did you say it was red lipstick?" She turned to me. "Peaches, *that woman* at the bar last night was wearing red lipstick."

"She was!" I snickered. "Before that, she kept calling him apple dumpling and slow-dance-grinding to Bon Jovi ballads." I blinked innocently at Mitchell. "We would have stopped her, but you seemed into it."

Mitchell threw his hands in the air. "I'm cured! I'm totally straight now! I like vagina!"

Shayla and I both clapped and cheered.

He grabbed the garbage pail and swept the empty mini-bottles from the top of the dresser into the plastic bin.

"Those were all open when we got here," I said. "Right, Shayla?"

She nodded solemnly.

The funny thing about the lipstick on Mitchell's penis was that he actually did it to himself. He woke up and caught me putting lipstick on his mouth, and confiscated it.

We went back to Cougar Town, where he did actually dance with an older woman. Actually, he danced with several, and they adored him.

Chantalle drove us back to the hotel room, then left us to continue the party. Mitchell drank most of the mini-bottles, then told us he was going to play a joke on Mitchell. (Yes, he referred to himself by name.)

The fact he'd done it to himself only made the lipstick prank funnier.

"He's crazy," Shayla whispered to me. "Can we keep him?"

"Yes, let's keep him."

Mitchell set his suitcase on the dresser and unzipped it to reveal very orderly contents.

"You're taking me for breakfast at that chocolate fountain place," he said. "Then we all go to our dress and suit fitting appointment."

Shayla and I agreed to the plan and did our best to get up and make ourselves presentable while wearing the previous night's clothes. We pinkie-swore to never drink again.

~

The three of us went to brunch at Pancake International, which gave me a moment of *déjà vu*. Shayla and I had gone there with Golden just a few weeks earlier, and sat at the same table with the mismatched wooden chairs. Mitchell is a similar height to Golden, and has curly blond hair as well, so it was funny, but the good kind of funny.

The waitress even said, "You three again!"

This visit, however, Adrian wouldn't be flirting with me by text message. Our whole fling had started and ended since the last time I had the Elvis in Paris (crepes with peanut butter and bacon.)

I pulled out my phone and looked over the last messages from Adrian. We hadn't spoken since our walk around the pond on Monday. I composed a dozen messages, but couldn't hit the send button.

Shayla grabbed my phone from my hands and tossed in in my purse. "Busted," she said.

"Fine, I'll cover the tip," I said.

Mitchell raised his eyebrows appreciatively. "I get it! That's a good trick. I should use that on my friends. They're always texting when we hang out." He chuckled. "They should be punished."

Shayla waggled her eyebrows. "You always hurt the ones you love."

"Aw, I miss you guys already," Mitchell said. "I'll have to catch a lift up in Dalton's plane next time he comes to Washington."

Shayla leaned over and kissed him on the side of the cheek. "I always want what I can't have. Mitchell, are you sure you don't have a straight side? We could get married."

"Double wedding?" I offered. "We've got plenty of food."

Mitchell laughed, his cheeks flushing with embarrassment, or maybe happiness.

~

We finished breakfast, and stepped out into the sunshine.

The sun glinted off an approaching convertible, cherry red, with the top down. At the wheel was Dottie Simpkins, a scarf wrapped around her pale pink hair. Sitting next to her was my neighbor, Mr.

Galloway, waving to me. A rust-colored labradoodle sat in the back seat.

"Hello, Dottie! Hello, Mr. Galloway!" I called out, waving back.

Mitchell snorted with laughter. "I love this town."

"We don't all know each other," Shayla said. "But sometimes it *does* feel like we're the charming extras and backdrop to someone else's movie."

"That's why Dalton was here filming," Mitchell said.

Shayla got a grumpy look as we started walking down the street toward the seamstress.

After a few minutes of silence, Shayla said, "I'm trying to be a good sport about Dalton swooping in here and taking away the best thing about this town."

"I can't be your roommate forever," I said.

She muttered something I couldn't hear.

"Listen, I'm nervous, too," I said. "I've never had a real relationship with a guy. Dalton is the first guy I've even slept with more than ten times."

Mitchell snorted, then said, "Wait, sorry. You're serious? You've never been in love before?"

I stopped walking and rubbed my stomach. We were still a few blocks from the seamstress. "I feel weird. Too much bacon. Everything's jumping around inside me."

Mitchell fixed me with a serious stare. "Peaches. That fluttering is love, not bacon."

"Are you sure? It feels like bacon. Does love feel like bacon?"

Shayla nodded in agreement with Mitchell. "You usually eat all your bacon and some of mine, but you hardly touched your breakfast. The fluttering must be love."

"I wish Dalton was better at expressing his feelings," I said. "Then I could be sure."

She grabbed my hand and shook it in the air between us. "Maybe if you wore your engagement ring, you'd be more sure. Stop being such a weirdo and let yourself fall. If I can let you go with a smile on my face, you'd better smile, too."

"Oh, Shayla." I stared into her golden brown eyes, glowing like embers. "Oh, no! I forgot to buy you fancy cheese! When I was in San Francisco. I'm a terrible friend. I'm going to be a terrible wife."

"I don't care about cheese," she said. "I care about you, because you're not a terrible friend. You're a *great* friend."

"I'll still be a terrible wife."

"Probably," she said, smirking. "But neither of us was the best at friends before we started hanging out. I remember calling you names because you wouldn't go in the lake when it was full of tadpoles."

"You were kind of a dick about it," I said. "And when you were fourteen and hormonal, I thought it was over. I was pretty sure one of us might kill the other, but I hung in there."

"We learned to be friends, together," she said.

"I guess."

"You'll be a good wife. You'll screw up plenty, but you'll get the hang of it, eventually."

Mitchell gave me a sweet smile of encouragement. "I think you'll be amazing, right from day one, but I'm a better friend than Shayla."

She laughed and pretended to push him over.

"Thanks for the pep talk, guys."

Mitchell started jogging down the street. "Enough mush! We need to get fitted."

Shayla grabbed my hand and tugged me toward our destination.

~

The dress designer, Nancy, had sent one of her own seamstresses up to do the final fitting and adjustments of the gown I chose. The woman was tall, thin, and familiar-looking. It turned out she was the sister of Gwendolyn, one of the assistants I'd met in LA. Her name was Ginnifer with a G.

"We're ahead of schedule," Ginnifer said. "Even if you've changed three sizes, we'll be able to make the alterations, but by the look of you, you're as perfect as the day you were first measured up." She laughed. "Less than two weeks ago."

Shayla and Mitchell went off with the other assistants, and I followed Ginnifer to the back room, so nobody else would see the dress ahead of time.

Everything appeared to be falling into place.

Standing next to me at the altar on Saturday would be Shayla, of course, and Mitchell. We'd already chosen a pale gray as our bridal party color, and Mitchell would look dashing in his gray suit with a pink tie. Shayla's gray dress had a pink highlight across the bust. If I didn't love my custom gown so much, I would have wanted to wear Shayla's dress.

According to Vern, Dalton had expanded his side to include his cousin, Connor. His other attendant was his friend, Alexis. I hadn't been a big fan of Alexis since she sold photos of me in my underwear to the tabloids, but she was like a sister to Dalton, so I would just try to get over bad first impressions. I had sprayed her with a garden hose on my front lawn, so we'd both done regrettable things.

"I love your curves," Ginnifer said as I wriggled into the slip I'd be wearing under the dress.

I laughed. "Oh, please. You're tall and slim, and you could probably model these gowns."

She smiled and unzipped the bag for my dress. "I didn't mean I envied you or don't accept myself. Just that I admire every bride, in her beautiful pre-wedding glow. Bridal gowns are infused with magic, don't you know? They allow us to see what's always been there."

"Oh." I stared at my gown, flat from the bag.

"Do you see something?" she asked. "What do you think?"

"It looks flat," I said. "Like it's just waiting for some curves to fill it out."

She beamed. "Exactly. Arms up. We'll do the formal side first, the party side second."

I raised my arms in the air and waited.

She took her time, moving slowly and deliberately, and then she gently swooshed the crinkling fabric over my head and smoothed it out.

With my eyes clenched shut, I waited as she fastened all the buttons at the back.

"May I?" She wiggled the clip holding my hair up in a messy bun.

"Sure." I waited as she let down my hair and fixed it loosely around my bare shoulders.

"You can open your eyes now," she said.

I hesitated.

If I opened my eyes and saw myself in the gown, I knew I would feel something. I didn't know what that *something* would be, but it scared me. I was a cup about to overflow.

She whispered gentle encouragement, saying, "Open your eyes and see what your future husband will see."

I opened my eyes.

The woman in front of me looked beautiful and confident. Her blue eyes sparkled. She still had plenty of fight, but she also looked ready to surrender.

No more holding back.

No more running away.

Just surrender.

~

After the fittings, Vern met with us to go over some things with the caterers. Everyone kept asking me how I felt about every little thing.

Did I want coconut flakes on the fruit skewers?

Yes, I thought I did, but when I agreed to the coconut flakes, I was informed that the chicken dish had coconut milk, so if a guest had allergies, that was two things they couldn't eat, and *was I okay with that?*

When I said to leave the coconut flakes off the fruit skewers, I got a ten-minute demonstration of banana chunks turning various colors based on adjoining fruits.

I thought the whole point of hiring caterers was to have them take care of things for you. Was this their way of making me feel I was getting Dalton's money worth?

I would have to report all this to him when he arrived in town the next day.

As I moved down the list of catering choices and other tasks, I made another list in my head, of things I needed to say to Dalton before the wedding.

After much soul-searching, and fighting back tears when I saw myself in my beautiful gown, I'd figured out a few things.

I'd always admired how Dalton was able to commit completely to a role. Even though he had won my heart at first by saying lines someone else had written, I could feel how much he meant the words.

Love doesn't always translate into perfect little speeches. What matters most is what you do. Even though I'd run away from Dalton so many times, he never gave up on us.

Now things were going to change.

After always telling myself to keep my eyes open, I was ready to close them and take a leap of faith.

Dalton needed to know that I wasn't going to run anymore. He didn't need to chase me, because I was his.

I loved him.

He'd captured my heart, and I didn't even care that our wedding had been rushed for publicity, or that he had someone else writing his vows, as long as he meant every word.

As soon as he arrived in town Friday, I would make good on my threat. I would run right into his arms, and we'd both find out what kind of man he was.

CHAPTER 39

Friday.

One more sleep.

Assuming I'd even be able to sleep.

Friday afternoon, I was hanging out with my best friends at home, anxiously awaiting Dalton's arrival.

I was practicing throwing the bouquet to Shayla when I got a phone call from Vern.

Shayla and Mitchell sat quietly, picking up on my nervousness.

Vern asked me a series of questions about the catering, and whether my mother had gotten her shoes dyed to match, but I could tell he was leading up to something.

"Vern, just tell me the bad news already," I said.

"Mr. Deangelo has been delayed on set and won't be flying in tonight," he said.

"Dalton's not flying in tonight," I told my friends.

Shayla seemed concerned, but Mitchell looked devastated. He adored Dalton to the point of babbling incoherently in his presence, and now he seemed even more upset than I was.

That made me feel even more uneasy.

Vern had a few more details, and said Dalton would have phoned me himself, but he was on location where they had bad cell phone reception.

"Don't they have some sort of schedule?" I asked. "They've been doing this show for years. You'd think they'd be more organized."

Vern chuckled on the other end of the call. "I guess you've got a few things to learn about the life of an actor's wife. Don't worry about the rest of the wedding party. Connor and Alexis are on their way now in a rental car."

"That wet blanket Connor got to leave on time? But Dalton's the star of the show. Why does he have to work late?"

"We'll fly in first thing in the morning. Don't worry."

"When people tell me not to worry, it only makes me worry harder."

He chuckled again, which made it difficult for me to take out my anger on Vern.

"Which dress did you choose?" he asked.

"It's a surprise."

"The one with the cupcakes on the bosom?"

I snorted. "Not likely. Dalton's afraid of carbohydrates. I wouldn't want him to run away screaming."

"Hmm."

I wanted to ask what Vern meant by that non-verbal response, but he said goodbye, excusing himself to drive back to the set in case Dalton needed anything.

I tucked the phone away with a pitiful sigh.

The three of us had been hanging out in the living room of the house, resting up for the big day and eating cut vegetables with dip in a last-minute attempt to be healthy before the big day and all the photos.

Shayla was comforting Mitchell, assuring him Dalton would be coming, and wouldn't let us down.

Us.

Hah!

I shook my head at how crazy my life had become.

And then the front door of the house opened without warning, and Jake "Big Dick" Blake walked in, his cowboy boots thunking loudly on the floor.

"There's my girl," he said.

I jumped to my feet and introduced Dalton's father to my friends, who invited him to join us.

Jake sunk into the sofa, cozily nestled between Shayla and Mitchell. I took a seat on the chair across from them and braced myself for extreme inappropriateness.

Mr. Blake smelled of booze and cologne, but he looked sober enough, and downright presentable, with most of his shirt buttons fastened.

He withdrew a small box from his pocket and held it out to me. "Sorry to crash your party, but I had to bring you something."

Speechless, I took the simple brown gift box and lifted off the lid. Inside was a flower made of blue and gold sparkling cabochons.

"It's just costume jewelry," he said.

I took the broach out gently. "This belonged to Dalton's mother?"

"Yes. From his great-grandmother. I don't know if he'll recognize the piece, but his mother and grandmother wore it on their wedding days." He cleared his throat and stuffed his hands in his pockets. "If it doesn't go with your dress, I understand."

I blinked back my tears and assured him that of course the beautiful blue and gold flower would go with my dress.

The four of us looked back and forth at each other, savoring this special moment.

Then Jake turned to Shayla and said, "So, what's your deal, pretty lady?"

~

I left the three of them to entertain each other and excused myself up to my room.

There was another piece of jewelry I hadn't dealt with yet.

Still in its box, in the pocket of the rolled-up red and black flannel jacket Dalton had loaned me, was the ring he used for his proposal.

I hadn't dared open the box, and every day I waited, the psychological barrier became greater. Everyone had been pestering me to see the ring, especially Kyle, since he was going to be the ring bearer, after all.

Loud laughter floated up from downstairs. This wedding was such a joyous occasion for everyone else, and I guess that's why the ring scared me. What if, when I slipped it on my finger, I felt nothing? What if that moment gave me absolute clarity? What if it didn't?

With shaking hands, I unrolled the jacket that had traveled with me to San Francisco and the winery resort. I pulled the square box from the pocket, and, bracing myself for the worst, opened the lid.

I yanked open the box for my engagement ring from Dalton.

Inside, nestled in navy-blue velvet, was a bright green ring. Made of plastic.

WHAT?!

I yanked the ring from the indentation.

My eyes weren't playing tricks on me. It really was made of green plastic.

Attached to the back by a cheap-looking string was a note the size of a fortune from a fortune cookie.

The note read: *IOU one gold ring with a BFD.*

I stared at the green, plastic ring and tried to figure out who knew about the box I'd kept hidden in the jacket. Had Shayla organized a pre-wedding prank to pay me back for all those times I put the milk carton back in the fridge empty?

No, this was too strange, even for her.

This was all Dalton. He'd been so sure that I hadn't opened the box, and this was why.

I pulled out my phone and called his number, ready to leave him the Voicemail of Doom.

"Peaches?" he answered.

"Dalton? I thought you didn't have phone reception."

"I don't. My phone just suddenly rang. I guess it's the height. I'm up on the crane for a special shot we're doing. I'm falling through the sky, into the forest."

"But it's daytime."

"Connor gave me a potion."

"Oh. Of course." As I imagined him strapped into a harness, filming, I felt silly about ripping into him over a joke ring.

He said, "Are you still there? The reception's not very good. I'm gonna lose you." He laughed. "Peaches, hang in there! I'm not gonna lose you!"

"Stop joking around. This is serious. Why did you give me a plastic ring and what the hell does BFD mean?"

"BFD? Big Fucking Diamond."

"Oh."

"I'm so disappointed," he said, sounding down. "I thought you'd understand everything as soon as you saw the ring."

I pulled out the ring and slipped it on my finger. In a flash, the memory came back to me.

Dalton had just rescued me and Mitchell, while we were running from a crazy security guard. Dalton drove us to a park, where we stopped the car for Mitchell to be sick.

Mitchell got out of the car and barfed up booze and pool water, plus the green plastic ring, which had come from the vending machine, the night before. Mitchell had used the ring to propose to me, before swallowing it.

I stared at the ring on my finger.

"This ring was in Mitchell's stomach," I said.

Dalton laughed. "I gave it a good cleaning."

"You are SO weird! Why? Why would you propose to me with this ring?"

"Because you'd already said yes once. I thought it was good luck. Mitchell thought it was a great idea. If you're not happy, take it up with him."

Dalton said something else I couldn't make out, probably to someone there with him on the crane.

Damn it! Why couldn't he have just finished work on time and been where he was supposed to be?

"Dalton, I need to tell you some things." I held the phone to my ear with my shoulder as I fidgeted with the green ring on my finger. It actually did fit perfectly.

He said, "Hurry up, because we've got to take this shot soon. Everyone's waiting."

"Dalton, let them wait. I need to tell you that I love you."

He didn't say anything.

"Are you still there? Don't tell me I lost reception."

"I'm here," he said.

My heart crushed with each second he wasn't saying it back to me, but I wasn't giving up yet.

"Dalton, I felt bad leaving you at the resort last weekend, but there's something you don't know about me. That cute little boy you met, Kyle, he's not my brother. He's my son, and you don't have to be his dad or anything, because he has the world's greatest dad already. But you need to know that if he's ever sick or needs me, I have to run to his side. I want to love you as much as I love him, but I can't guarantee that you'll ever take the number one spot. I do love you, though."

"Peaches…"

"So this is me, running into your arms. You've caught me. I'm wearing your green, plastic ring on my finger, and I know you can't see me, but I really am. I'm crying and smiling at the same time, because my heart is breaking, but I think it's breaking right open to let you in."

He didn't answer.

I pulled the phone away from my ear slowly.

The icon was red, showing the call had ended. He was gone.

"And there we have it," I said to my empty room, like a crazy person.

CHAPTER 40

Nobody answered. My phone remained silent, the screen turned black.

"Peaches has laid her heart out," I said in my announcer voice. "Will Dalton return her love? Or will he continue to play mind games with her until the end of time? Does Peaches regret not going to Italy to be with Keith Raven? Yes, she kinda does."

Someone knocked on my bedroom door. "Are you on the phone?" Shayla asked.

"Nope. Just talking to myself. Come on in."

Shayla came in, an exaggerated smile on her face. "Peaches," she breathed. "What do you think about me being in… movies? Jake says he wants to make me a star."

I shrugged. "Whatever you want to do, I'll support you completely."

She frowned. "I was hoping to get a rise out of you. Are you okay? Feeling nervous about the big day?"

I looked at the watch on my wrist—the beautiful watch Dalton bought me in San Francisco. Had it only been two weeks ago? I was so mixed up, I couldn't even figure out the time from the watch face. I had to look over at my digital alarm clock to figure out it was half past two.

"It's two-thirty," I said. "I'm planning to hold off a few hours before I start freaking out."

"This time tomorrow you will be drinking mimosas with me. And then, another six hours later, you'll be married," Shayla said.

"We'll see about that."

She grabbed my hand. "What happened to your ring? It's all green."

I'd been sitting on my bed, and now I let myself fall back onto it. "Long story," I said.

She climbed onto the bed next to me. "Mitchell already told me about the ring. Wow, it doesn't look like it was in someone's stomach. Are you sure it's the exact same one?"

"Does it matter?" I groaned.

My phone began to ring, but it wasn't the ringtone I'd programmed in for Dalton, so I didn't move to answer it.

"Do you want me to answer that?" Shayla asked.

"Tell them I died."

She answered the phone, then handed it to me. "It's your uncle, the mayor," she said.

I sat up and begrudgingly took the phone.

"Don't hide up here all day," she said.

"I'll be down in ten minutes," I said to Shayla.

"I kinda like Dalton's father. You'd better not leave me alone with him," she joked.

I waved her out of the room so I could talk to the mayor.

"Uncle Steve," I said brightly.

"Excited about the big day?"

"Of course I am," I said cheerily.

"Everything's falling into place," he said.

I told him I was glad.

He gave me an update on some of the arrangements he'd been making—super secret, hilarious arrangements.

Talking to him about our evil, nefarious plans made me smile, and lightened the weight on my shoulders.

Maybe, if I just hung in there, everything was going to work out just fine.

If not, at least that Saturday would be a memorable one, for the entire town.

CHAPTER 41

Saturday.

Wedding day.

Everyone around me was moving fast, talking fast, thinking fast. I looked at the face of the watch on my wrist. The hands seemed to be swirling around.

Suddenly it was three o'clock, and I had a mimosa in my hand.

We were still at the house. Shayla and Mitchell practiced a choreographed dance they were putting together for later that night. I watched from the couch in my pajamas, my wedding gown hanging up in my bedroom like the ghost of my future.

Suddenly it was four o'clock.

Nobody had heard from Dalton, or Vern. If they were going to arrive on time for the wedding, they would have to be in the air by now.

My mother arrived and forcibly dragged me off the couch. I insisted I had plenty of time, and that if I didn't, I'd just wear my flannel pajamas and everyone could suck it up. I was the damn bride. It was my special day.

"She's been like this all day," Shayla said, then they demonstrated their dance for my mother.

Everyone was moving so fast. I twirled the green ring on my finger, then pulled it off to give to my mother. "Here's the ring for Kyle," I said.

She demanded to know where the real ring was.

I blinked up at her.

My attendants flew into action, explaining the whole thing to her, including a dramatic re-enactment, with Mitchell pretending to throw up the ring.

My mother didn't seem impressed. She turned to me. "You got a tattoo? Peaches, those are permanent." She shook her head. "Now go get yourself into the shower this minute. You smell like a thrift store sofa."

Head nodded down, I obediently plodded upstairs and climbed into the tub.

~

We drove up to the site of the wedding in my new car, with Mitchell driving, and Shayla holding my hand in the back seat.

The photographer who was covering the wedding for the exclusive magazine photos sat in the front seat, taking photos.

She'd arrived in town with little fanfare, by helicopter, but without her entourage of assistants. She insisted we all call her by her first name, Ruby, and treat her exactly the way we would a regular wedding photographer.

"This is how I got my start," she'd said. "Taking photos of beautiful brides like you, on their special day. Of course that was fifteen years ago, and all the technology has only made it easier."

Ruby kept clicking photos, swapping out digital memory cards as needed. Eventually, I did get used to her being there, but not so comfortable that I let down my guard and showed my true emotions. There's nothing sadder than a sad bride, and sad brides don't sell magazines.

We arrived at the cabin, and my mouth opened in shock.

The wedding would be here, after all.

There were still a few signs of construction in progress, but the location had been transformed by the tents and decorations. The trees surrounding the area were strung with so many lanterns, streamers, and bundles of flowers, it looked like something from a fantasy movie about elves.

My wedding helpers had hired a local florist, Gabriella's, to do the flowers. Looking at their arrangements, I finally understood why that florist has such an amazing reputation in town.

The ceremony itself would happen down at the edge of the water, where guest chairs decorated with pale pink flowers sat waiting for the arrival of the guests in their buses.

My parents pulled in behind us and parked at the edge of the property, next to my car. Kyle came flying out of the back seat and raced straight for the biggest tent and the ice sculpture.

Shayla and Mitchell worked in tandem like a team, and got me into the cabin, where I would be hidden away until the band played my marching music—assuming the groom showed up.

Time passed.

My uncle, the mayor, called to brag about how well the diversion was going, across town. At least that part of the plan was working.

I checked and re-checked the clasp of the broach Dalton's father had given me.

I stared at the watch on my wrist and watched helplessly as the hands spun around, time slipping away.

Why wasn't Dalton there yet? Why hadn't someone called?

I checked my phone for the millionth time. I had a bunch of messages from people I hadn't talked to in years, congratulating me.

There was also a text message from someone else, from my recent past.

Keith Raven: *Hey, I wanted to wish you luck and send you blessings on your special day!*

Me: *Thanks. I thought you hated Dalton?*

To my surprise, I got a response back immediately.

Keith: *Life's too beautiful to hate people. You know me. Besides, I knew you two would end up together.*

Me: *Yeah, right. He's late for the wedding. We're not married yet.*

Keith: *He'll be there.*

Me: *How would you know?*

Keith: *That day I first met him, at his house, he told me so.*

Me: *What did he tell you, exactly?*

Keith: *He said to take special care of his future wife.*

Me: *We'll see about that, if he ever shows up. I'm about ready to rip off this dress and run out of here.*

Keith: *No, you won't run away this time.*

I said goodbye and wished him the best in Italy.

Then I went back to feeling anxious again.

The buses full of wedding guests arrived at the cabin site, their big engines groaning to announce their arrival, even though I couldn't see anything from the near-empty room at the back of the cabin. I sat in my chair, staring straight ahead with a pretty smile as I got my makeup touched up. Ruby took more photos, and I practiced smiling.

Mitchell darted in and out, getting more and more agitated as the scheduled time for the ceremony came and went.

I started mentally preparing the speech I would give, thanking everyone for coming, and joking about how Dalton was already married to his TV show, but we'd try again next weekend... or something like that.

My father kept pacing and pacing, until I begged my mother to take him somewhere else. I tried to get everyone out of the room, but Shayla wouldn't budge from my side.

I looked down at my dress and tried to lose myself in its beauty. I hadn't chosen the mermaid gown, or the cupcake gown, or any of the elaborate dresses I'd tried on. They were all so beautiful and ornate, but not for me. The assistants finally slipped on the designer's simplest white dress, and something happened. When I looked in the mirror, I didn't see the dress. Just myself. With a look of wonder on my face.

Of course, because it was one of Nancy's designs, it wasn't completely plain. The dress had a secret.

The outside was minimal, but the lining of the dress was a bright fabric, with crazy, asymmetrical stripes in all shades of pink. When I saw the lining, I had commented that it was a shame to hide it away on the inside. That's when I learned that with a quick flip, the dress fully reversed. I would wear a matching slip on the inside, so neither side would get sweaty, but I would have two dresses for my special day.

I know what you're thinking.

Why go through the effort of making it reversible when you could just have two dresses? The answer is I don't know. I don't know why we girls love half the things we do.

"Stripes are pretty," I said.

Shayla set down her mimosa and stared at me blankly.

"Maybe I'll go out in the striped side," I said to Shayla.

She seemed surprised to hear words coming from my mouth. "But that's for the party, later."

"He's not coming. I suggest we save this disaster now and flip into party mode. Forget the wedding, it was just a publicity stunt anyway. If people don't want to stay, they can get on the bus and join the picnic at Duck Pond Park. Uncle Steve says half the town is there, and the Bushy Beaver Tails are going onto the bandstand at sundown."

"Everyone fell for it?"

"Hook, line and sinker." I was too sad to elaborate, but my uncle had told me that twice as many people had already shown up as had come to the previous year's town-wide picnic.

By pretending it was a secret, we'd created the biggest party in town history. Everyone had tried to crash the wedding to sneak a peek, only to find mayor Steve Monroe and the whole town council welcoming them to join the festivities. Even a bunch of rednecks from Wolfspit had shown up, dressed in their finest jeans and flannel jackets.

The entire Beaverdale mall had closed early so everyone could go to the event of the year. That annoying gossip reporter, Brooke Summer, was there with her film crew and looking despondent that it wasn't the wedding site.

That last part made me smile briefly, before the sadness returned.

"Let's give Dalton ten more minutes," Shayla said.

We did.

"Five more," she said.

I stood, shaky on my feet, and opened the door of the room. The caterers were bustling around the cabin, using the new kitchen to finish preparing the dinner for our guests.

I opened the front door of the cabin and paused. Something was buzzing.

With Shayla right behind me, I stepped out of the cabin. Everyone was looking up at the sky and pointing. A small airplane appeared in the sky. The plane got closer and closer, but didn't drop down for a landing. It soared overhead, then kept going, disappearing into the clouds with my last bit of hope.

CHAPTER 42

I turned to go back into the cabin, my hopes dashed. It was over. I was taking off the dress and setting it on fire in the cabin's wood stove. Someone else could inform the guests.

Shayla screamed and tugged my hand. I followed her pointed finger, up to a dot in the sky.

A sash of orange unfurled above the dot, slowing its descent.

As the parachute got closer, I could make out words on the chute: *Dalton Loves Peaches.*

Shayla squeezed my hand. "I think he found a way to tell you how he feels."

I shook my head. "This is really over-the-top dramatic, even for Dalton."

My father jogged up to my side, his cheeks flushed.

"That's our cue," he said.

"You knew?"

"Not the specifics, but I was told there'd be a cue, and I'm fairly certain this is it. I'm sure they'll start the music any minute."

Shayla quickly flipped the veil down over my face, then ran off to the lakeside, where she joined the rest of the wedding party at the altar.

The man in the parachute touched down on dry land nearby, and Connor rushed over to help him out of the harness. From where I stood, I could tell it was either Dalton or a very convincing stand-in.

Meanwhile, the plane, presumably piloted by Vern, came in for a less dramatic landing.

Once the plane's engine turned off, the lakeside location seemed more tranquil than ever in the ensuing hush.

The entire forest seemed to be watching, holding its breath, waiting.

Dalton took his place at the edge of the water, with the others.

Something brushed my bare arm. I looked down in wonder as my father linked his arm with mine, and tugged me toward the carpet laid out down the aisle. The music was already playing. The bridal march.

I forgot how to walk, stumbling forward only to keep from falling down. My feet found their places, one in front of the other.

Everything moved around me in streaks of color.

I took my place next to Dalton, avoiding eye contact while the officiant began the ceremony.

I nodded along, then repeated my parts after the officiant. My vows were simple, the boilerplate standard stuff about loving, honoring, and cherishing.

Something I said set off Dalton's smirk, which was impossible to miss, even out of the corner of my eye.

I expected him to have more elaborate vows than mine, but he repeated the standard stuff, with no sign of the stuff I'd seen on his fax.

Kyle marched up perfectly and presented the green ring on a pillow, which Dalton slipped onto my finger.

The officiant announced that we were now wed, and gave Dalton permission to kiss me.

He flipped up my veil as I turned to face him. His smirking expression said that he planned to do a whole lot more than kiss me, but there was something else there, too. Love?

"Peaches," he said.

"Yes?"

Out of the edge of my vision, I noticed the entire assembly of guests lean forward on their rented chairs, straining to listen.

"Did you happen to see my parachute?" he asked.

"Did you happen to get an invitation with the starting time on it?"

A chorus of laughter rippled across our audience.

He grinned. "Sorry I kept you waiting."

"I don't mind waiting, but if you can't send me a text message, I have to assume your fingers are broken, or soon will be."

He got down on one knee in front of me. Everyone buzzed with confusion. "Attention, everyone!" he called out. "I know I'm doing things backwards, but you should know I screwed up my proposal, and don't you think Peaches deserves a beautiful proposal, even if it's at the wedding altar?"

Everyone cheered.

MIMI STRONG

CHAPTER 43

Dalton turned back to me, gazing up with those gorgeous eyes of his—gorgeous not because of the particular shade of green, but because of the adoring, amused way he looked at me.

The sun was setting now, and the trees and lake were cast in a warm glow, almost unreal against the darkening sky.

"Peaches, I'm not good with words. Not unless someone else writes them out for me."

"Oh, Dalton. Words don't matter. Only actions."

He reached into his jacket pocket and pulled out something tiny, which he clutched in his fist.

"Miss Monroe, you've opened your heart to me, and, like a fool, I fell right in. When I'm with you, I can hardly catch my breath, much less my balance. I'm always falling, every time you look at me, every time you touch me. And now I'm utterly, helplessly in love." He held out his fist and unfurled his fingers. "Will you do me the honor of accepting this BFD, and being my wife? I love you so much, and I plan to love you more and more, every day."

Off in the distance, one frog called out to his friends.

"Well?" Dalton asked.

Tears welled up in my eyes. I could scarcely breathe.

Fanning my face with one hand, I said, "Yes, of course I will marry you. I already did, but if you want me to, I'll keep marrying you every day."

"Nothing would make me happier."

He took my left hand, slid off the green, plastic ring, and replaced it with the new one, plus a slim band that fit alongside it. My Big

Fucking Diamond gleamed in the golden light, but it was nothing compared to the fire I felt in my heart.

Dalton got to his feet. Amidst cheers from everyone, he wrapped his arm around my back and pulled me in for a tender, gentle kiss.

The photographer darted closer, snapping pictures of our kiss.

I started to pull away, content that we'd gotten the shots, but Dalton seized me and spun me around so I was hidden from the camera by his body.

"This one's not for show." He grabbed me tightly, his hands down on my hips, and he kissed me ferociously, just the way I wanted.

~

The rest of the wedding was as perfect as any girl could wish for.

My mother insisted she hadn't cried during the ceremony, but her mascara told another story. My father said he couldn't have been more proud, and that seeing how happy Dalton made me was all the proof he needed. Then he hugged me and wandered off to go show Kyle the airplane by the dock.

All the family who'd been at Marita's wedding was there, and half of them were insisting that they'd "known it wouldn't be long," just from seeing Dalton dancing with me at that wedding.

After the sun went down, Vern got the projection screen unfurled between two of the bigger trees, and images of both me and Dalton as children ran as a slideshow. Sometimes the image was just one of us, filling the screen, and other times it was a split screen with a theme, such as both of us dressed as pumpkins for Halloween.

One photo in particular, though, made me smile.

Dalton was lying on someone's living room floor, covered in a mountain of pillows and cushions. A round-cheeked, round-bodied, happy-looking girl with brunette pigtails sat atop the mountain.

His story about the neighbor, Chelsea, was real. He hadn't made her up after all. I wished I'd known sooner, but then again, all those little doubts were beautiful in their own way, because they made me look deeper into my heart.

Dinner was served under the biggest tent, and from where I sat at the head table, I couldn't hear what Dalton's father was saying to all my aunts and uncles. By the looks on their faces, they certainly weren't bored. Not one bit.

Marita and her new husband made a very special toast, congratulating us, and then announcing the upcoming arrival of their first child. People clapped and cheered and generally pretended to be surprised. (My family is nothing if not supportive.)

Throughout everything, Dalton didn't leave my side. He was either holding my hand, staring adoringly at me, or both. When nobody was looking, he'd drag me off behind a van or a tree and try to get his hands up under my skirt. I swatted him away every time, telling him to wait just a little longer. He threatened to take me out on the lake in a canoe, but I called his bluff. He hadn't acquired a canoe... yet.

I tore myself away from Dalton just long enough to freshen up and reverse my dress to the colorful side, carefully transferring the blue broach to the bodice again.

By then, the music had started and the party was in full swing.

The band was a folk rock duo from out of town, but they took requests and played great cover songs, which made everyone happy, and isn't that exactly what weddings are all about?

I danced with my father, who mentioned he might take flying lessons.

"Do you still think I'm too young to get married?" I asked him as he twirled me around.

"Not if it makes you happy," he said. "You are happy, right?"

"Of course I am." The song ended and I kissed his cheek.

He went looking for my mother, who he was afraid to let out of his sight with Jake around.

Dalton took my hand. "May I have this dance, wife?"

"Of course, husband."

The band started the next song, and we danced under the twinkling lights strung between the trees, under the moon, and the starry sky.

~

After the last song had been played, and the caterers and tent rental people finished packing everything up, Dalton and I walked down to the edge of the water alone.

He'd offered me a dozen options for where we could sleep that night, and I chose the Airstream trailer. I didn't care if we rocked it off its foundations, because choosing the trailer felt right.

Dalton and I had crashed into each other in a tiny bookstore, then shared intimate moments in the backs of limousines, and who could forget the canoe excitement?

"Mrs. Deangelo," he said, gazing down at me as we stood in the loose pebbles near the water's edge. "You married me on this spot, today. Any regrets?"

I picked up a flat stone and tossed it out onto the water, where it skipped seven times.

"No regrets. Everything that happened, good or bad, was a pebble that formed the path that brought us here."

He looked down at the broach on my dress. "My father must have given you that. He surprises me sometimes."

"He surprises a lot of people. Every time he opens his mouth. He's kind of a loose cannon."

"Well, it takes one to know one," he teased.

"Don't laugh. You're the one who married me!"

"How about for our first anniversary, we throw a big party here, and we *both* jump out of the plane and parachute down?"

"Sure, baby. Anything you want."

"This is going to be fun," he said, looking solemn. "I'm going to share my life with you, forever and ever, happily ever after."

He leaned down and sealed his promise with a kiss.

I gazed up at his loving face.

"I love you, too, baby. Let's go get that trailer rocking."

He grabbed my hand and whinnied like a horse. "Your Lionheart is ready for everything you've got."

Giggling, we rushed up the path and into the trailer.

He whinnied once more, and then we stopped talking.

Slowly, gently, we undressed each other. We lay our nice clothes carefully across the little round table at the front of the trailer, and then he led me down the short distance to the elevated sleeping nook. I slipped off his shorts, and he removed my slip, bra, and panties, dropping them to the floor.

He climbed up into the nook first, then helped me in.

We lay on our sides, face to face, and kissed slowly as we stroked each other's bodies, hands caressing every inch of skin.

The touching and kissing moved seamlessly to making love. We moved together, first one gazing down at the other, and then rolling again to switch places. He moved deep inside me, and neither of us dared look away from the other.

I came first with him on top, and then again after a roll. After the third orgasm, I was delirious with ecstasy, and lost count. He shifted my leg and drove deeper, trembling with his desire. I gazed up at him through my eyelashes, and I saw his face change before he climaxed. I saw him surrender to love, for the second time that day.

CHAPTER 44

One year later.

What happens next, after you marry the perfect man?

First of all, you float around in a cloud of happiness, and the things that usually bother you don't seem so bad. I feel like the weather has gotten better since I married Dalton, but it could be all the time we spend in sunny LA.

We've been married a year now, and so many wonderful things have happened in the last twelve months.

I've got an incredible new career. I'll tell you about it in a minute, but first let me catch you up on what everyone's doing.

My new bestie, Mitchell, convinced my original bestie, Shayla, to move in with him after his roommate took a job in an off-Broadway play in New York. Shayla gave notice at her job and moved to LA two weeks later.

If you think I spend a lot of time over at their apartment, you'd be right! I've added several pieces of inspirational art to their art wall.

Shayla is still working in the restaurant business, only now she's a manager, and working her way up the corporate ladder. She has vowed to stop dating unattainable, inappropriate men. That's what she says. What she actually does is another story. It's a lot like how Mitchell swears off dating models, only to dive right into a relationship with the next one, swearing it's "different this time."

Speaking of male models, Keith Raven is doing well. I thought he'd get back together with his ex, Tabitha, but he fell for an Italian girl. I don't know too many details, because we haven't kept in close contact. Our brief relationship was so intimate that I don't feel right talking to him now that I'm happily married.

As for my other ex, Adrian Storm, he kept to his word and worked at the bookstore through Christmas. After that, he hired and trained a replacement, and left for Chicago. We haven't stayed in touch, but whenever I see his parents over at my parents' house, they tell me he sends his best.

Adrian and Golden became an official, monogamous couple at the first annual Beaverdale Duck Pond Park Picnic, which happened the same day as my wedding. I felt sorry for Golden for a while, because she seemed to have been his second choice, though who could say, really? They had this whole funny drama between them that seemed straight out of a romantic comedy movie. He wanted her to come to Chicago with him in January, but she wasn't sure she could give up her job, then he proposed, and she freaked out and said he was only worried about being alone, and didn't actually love her. He packed his bags and took a bus to the airport to leave a day early, so when she came to her senses, he had already left town, and… you can guess where this is going, right? Yes, she raced against time to get to the airport, where they declared their love for each other in front of everyone getting frisked and scanned for security.

Good for them, I say!

My parents just celebrated their twenty-seventh anniversary in March of this year, and added a twenty-seventh decorative pillow to their bed. They may have to get an extra bed soon, just for the pillows.

My mother told me that every time they see Dalton's father at a family event, my father is *extra attentive* to her needs for several weeks after. They seem as happy as ever, though my father still has the recliner up in the attic for when he needs to annoy her about something.

Kyle is eight now, and he surprises me by how great he is at sports. The kid is way more coordinated than I was at his age, and he'd be on every sports team in town if my mother let him. I really notice the changes in his maturity. He's more guarded with his emotions now, mostly because he wants to spare my feelings. It's not always easy for him, having a big sister who gets talked about on the gossip sites, but I try to make time for us, one on one, whenever I visit. I think he's going to grow up to be a remarkable man one day, and I'm going to cry at every single graduation and milestone. When he's old enough, we'll tell him the truth about how he came into this world, and I think he'll understand.

I've been in touch with Kyle's father, Toby. He's living in Idaho these days, where he got married to an older woman with two children from a previous marriage. They're expecting another baby any day now, and he called me last month, almost too emotional to speak. He wanted to apologize to me for not being more supportive after Kyle was born. I think he was nervous as hell about being a father, and dealing with some pretty colossal guilt. I told him the same thing I'd been telling myself for years. We were just dumb kids, trying to do the best we could, and everything worked out, so there was no point punishing ourselves. We certainly weren't going to do it again!

After that phone call, I went a little baby crazy. I poured a glass of wine and got the laptop out, my excuse being that I was looking for a gift for Toby. His little baby girl would be a part of our big family one day when she was old enough to meet her half-brother.

I'm telling you, I started looking at changing blankets with little ducks and kitties, not to mention the frilly dresses, and a fever took hold of me. For an hour, I wanted nothing more than a little girl to dress up in adorable baby clothes.

Then I got another phone call, this one from Dalton, inviting me last-minute to a film opening. I dashed around my fabulous LA house, running between my two giant walk-in closets to find the right shoes and handbag to wear with one of my red carpet dresses. As I touched up my makeup in the back seat, while Vern drove me to the TV set to pick up my husband, I knew that my baby fever could wait a while—at least until the novelty of this fabulous new life wore off.

We have the best of both worlds, with our LA life, full of glamorous parties and Dalton working way too hard, plus our quiet getaways to the cabin in Washington State.

In October, I was able to celebrate my twenty-third birthday at my usual place, DeNirro's. My whole family joined us. I had the deep-fried tortellini, and Dalton went crazy and ate an entire basket of bread all by himself. (Don't worry, fans, his personal trainer made him sweat it all off.)

We get up to the cabin at least twice a month, which makes it all the more shameful that we haven't gotten around to hanging up our wedding photos or any of the other artwork we collect on trips. I guess there's no rush, since we have our whole lives ahead of us to get everything perfect.

Perfect.

That word has taken on a funny meaning for me. Whenever I do an interview, people ask me what it's like to be married to the *perfect* man.

I don't dare tell them the truth—that he does about a million things that drive me crazy. For example, he takes twice as long as I do to get dressed. He's got to lay out the clothes and carefully ponder what designer-hole-filled T-shirt to wear that day. Perhaps the most maddening thing he does, though, is tease me with little tidbits from his scripts for the show. He'll tell me enough to get me excited, but not the whole storyline. All through the season that just ran, I kept threatening to quit watching entirely. It was bad enough having to see him put his lips and teeth on beautiful actresses, let alone being subjected to the same brutal cliffhangers as regular people who weren't married to the star. For crying out loud!

At least I get some perks from being Mrs. Deangelo, and I don't just mean the nice house, beautiful pool, and staff to take care of me. Dalton makes even married-people sex feel deliciously naughty. I've had those crazy high-heeled platform shoes on so many times, I'm starting to be able to walk quite gracefully in them.

Of course these are all things I can't tell reporters and magazine editors, so when they ask me what it's like, I just smile and say, "Perfect."

I've been doing more press lately, so I can build up publicity contacts for when my movie comes out.

Hold on now, don't get too excited! Nothing is for sure, and I certainly won't be the one on screen, so you won't see me up there.

The big news is that not long after leaving the bookstore, I found my new career—the one thing I'd always dreamed of doing but hadn't dared tell anyone.

The whole time I worked at Peachtree Books, I was doing research for this dream job, and I didn't even know it. I brought home so many books, and whenever I ran across one that would make a perfect movie, I'd imagine how to adapt it to the screen. I'd figure out what scenes to cut, which ones I might change around a bit, and I'd even cast the roles with my favorite actors and actresses.

I didn't realize it at the time, but when I met Dalton's aunt, I also met my fairy godmother. Her name is Jamie Adair, and she's a powerful TV executive. She doesn't just run the vampire show, but a half dozen others, as well. The woman is tall and thin, with bright red hair and even redder lips. When you first meet her, you think she's "hell on heels" (to borrow Dalton's father's term of endearment), but she's actually very kind, and very family oriented.

I've learned that she and her sister, Dalton's mother, were as different in personality as in looks. Jamie was a skinny child with red hair, and Lyra was the beautiful brunette who charmed everyone she met. Unfortunately for Lyra, she fell in with a party crowd as a teenager and never met a drug she didn't like. She was clean through her pregnancy with Dalton, and on and off for many years after that, but eventually her demons caught up to her.

I know in my heart that it wasn't the money Dalton sent to his parents that killed her. Poor people die of drug overdose all the time. What was probably the hardest on her was being rejected by her son, and losing contact with him. I can imagine what that would feel like, yet I can't blame Dalton for wanting a different life for himself.

We all dream of being someone, after all.

Jamie wanted to be a Hollywood big shot, and she didn't stop working until she got there.

And now she wants to be my fairy godmother, and help me out the way her mentor helped her.

In between my underwear modeling gigs (I've done two more campaigns since my first one), I've secured the rights to one of my favorite books, and I'm adapting it into a movie screenplay.

The story has a little bit of horror, plus some romance, and a big mystery. I think it's going to be amazing, but the agonizing thing is I won't know for years.

Seriously, these movie things take forever. For example, I've seen an early cut of the indie film Dalton shot in Beaverdale, but we don't even have a date for when it will be in theaters. They're going to do the film festivals, and then hopefully get wider distribution after that.

This constant waiting means we Hollywood types have to always be working on multiple projects. That's why I'm also working on writing an original comedy series about a charming girl who works at a bookstore and just happens to be curvier than your typical actress. If that one goes ahead, we may need to fly in some actresses from outside LA for the auditions.

Well, that about sums up my life up until now. If you'll excuse me, I'm about to jump out of a perfectly good airplane with my husband. He says it's the best way to sneak onto the Weston Estate and enjoy their natural hot spring without setting off the security system they have set up along the road.

I don't know why I let him talk me into these things.

I guess it's because I love him so much.

The end.

MIMI STRONG
www.mimistrong.com